JERUSALEM'S HEART

Other Books by Bodie and Brock Thoene

Jerusalem Vigil
Thunder from Jerusalem
Shiloh Autumn
The Twilight of Courage
The Zion Covenant Series
The Zion Chronicles Series
The Shiloh Legacy Series
The Saga of the Sierras
The Galway Chronicles
The Wayward Wind Series

BODIE AND BROCK THOENE

JERUSALEM'S HEART

THE ZION LEGACY

Book III

VIKING

VIKING
Published by the Penguin Group
Penguin Putnam Inc., 375 Hudson Street,
New York, New York 10014, U.S.A.
Penguin Books Ltd, 27 Wrights Lane, London W8 5TZ, England
Penguin Books Australia Ltd, Ringwood, Victoria, Australia
Penguin Books Canada Ltd, 10 Alcorn Avenue,
Toronto, Ontario, Canada M4V 3B2
Penguin Books (N.Z.) Ltd, 182–190 Wairau Road,
Auckland 10, New Zealand

Penguin Books Ltd, Registered Offices:
Harmondsworth, Middlesex, England

First published in 2001 by Viking Penguin,
a member of Penguin Putnam Inc.

1   3   5   7   9   10   8   6   4   2

Map illustration by James Sinclair

Grateful acknowledgment is made for permission to reprint "The Panther" and
an excerpt from "Exposed Cliffs of the Heart" from *The Selected Poetry of Rainer
Maria Rilke,* edited and translated by Stephen Mitchell. Copyright © 1982 by
Stephen Mitchell. Reprinted by permission of Random House, Inc.

PUBLISHER'S NOTE
This is a work of fiction. Names, characters, places, and incidents either are the
product of the author's imagination or are used fictitiously, and any resemblance
to actual persons, living or dead, business establishments, events, or locales is entirely coincidental.

LIBRARY OF CONGRESS CATALOGING-IN-PUBLICATION DATA
Thoene, Bodie, 1951–
Jerusalem's heart / Bodie and Brock Thoene.
p.   cm.—(The Zion legacy ; bk. 3)
ISBN 0-670-89487-7
1. Jews—History—20th century—Fiction.   2. Israel—History—1948–1967—
Fiction.   3. Israel–Arab War, 1948–1949—Fiction.   4. Jerusalem—Fiction.
I. Thoene, Brock, 1952–   II. Title.
PS3570.H46 J495 2001
813'.54—dc21   00-043758

This book is printed on acid-free paper. ∞

Printed in the United States of America
Set in Minion

For Ramona Cramer Tucker
who knows our hearts

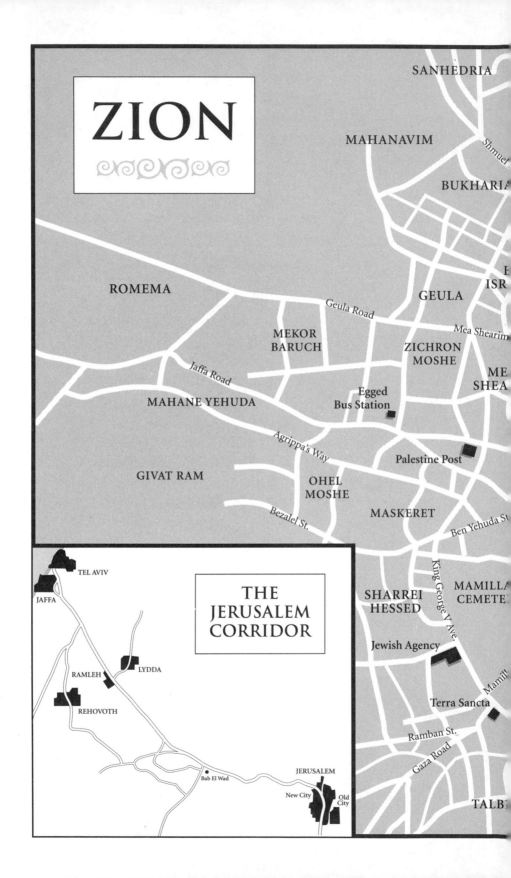

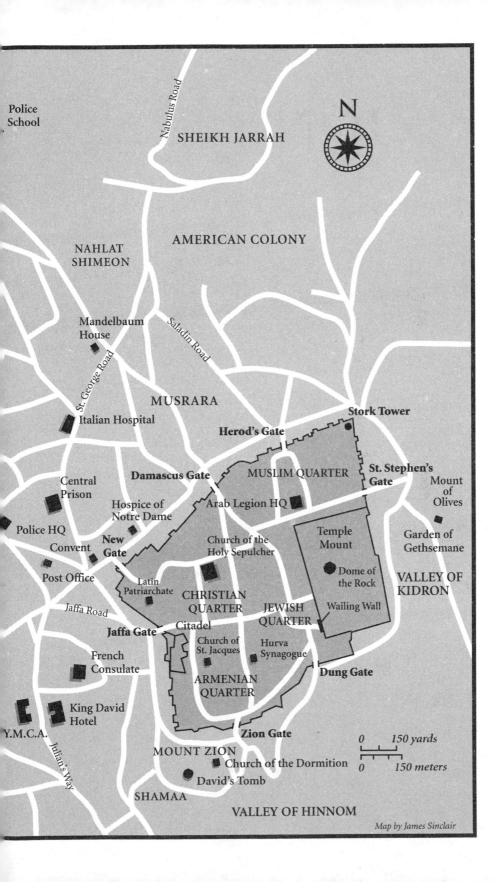

Police
School

Nabulus Road

SHEIKH JARRAH

N

AMERICAN COLONY

NAHLAT
SHIMEON

Mandelbaum
House

Saladin Road

St. George Road

MUSRARA

Stork Tower

Italian Hospital

Herod's Gate

Damascus Gate   MUSLIM QUARTER   **St. Stephen's
Gate**

Mount
of
Olives

Central
Prison

Hospice of
Notre Dame

Arab Legion HQ

Temple
Mount

Garden of
Gethsemane

Police HQ

**New
Gate**

Church of the
Holy Sepulcher

Dome of
the Rock

**VALLEY OF
KIDRON**

Convent

Post Office

Latin
Patriarchate

CHRISTIAN
QUARTER

JEWISH
QUARTER

Wailing Wall

Jaffa Road

Jaffa Gate   Citadel

Church of
St. Jacques

Hurva
Synagogue

Dung Gate

French
Consulate

ARMENIAN
QUARTER

King David
Hotel

Y.M.C.A.

Julian's Way

Zion Gate

MOUNT ZION   Church of the Dormition

David's Tomb

SHAMAA

0   150 yards

0   150 meters

VALLEY OF HINNOM

Map by James Sinclair

SUNDAY

May 23, 1948

"I will make you into a great nation
and I will bless you;
I will make your name great,
and you will be a blessing.
I will bless those who bless you,
and whoever curses you will I curse;
and all peoples on earth
will be blessed through you . . ."

Genesis 12:2–3

"Blessed are you when people insult you, persecute you and falsely say all kinds of evil against you because of me. Rejoice and be glad, for great is your reward in heaven, for in the same way they persecuted the prophets who were before you."

Matthew 5:11–12

CHAPTER 1

The hot desert wind rose in the east with the sun.

Known as the *Khamseen,* the breeze moaned over the besieged Old City, piling misery onto misery. There was no refuge from it, no shelter or shade from its incessant presence. The air above the pavement buckled and quavered in its heat. Breathing was labored. Living creatures became weak and motionless; even walls and stones shimmered and trembled as the Khamseen passed. Dust swirled into the atmosphere chalking every surface with gray film. By noon the sky congealed into a pale canopy of blue-white haze.

Today the Khamseen carried the reminder that Jerusalem perched on the rim of stark and brooding wasteland. Immense nothingness, bleak and sterile, stretched out beyond the border. And from these sterile wastelands men of Jordan, Syria, Iraq, and Egypt came with the Khamseen to encircle Jerusalem, to blow the hope of Israel to dry dust. Gnawing hunger and thirst were their allies against the Jewish population of the Holy City. Water rations were reduced to four cups a day per person. Food allotments dropped to seven hundred calories a day—two hundred less than had been possible in the Warsaw Ghetto.

Lori Kalner, her dust-caked face streaked with tears, knelt with Alfie Halder and Rachel Sachar beside the roses of Gal'ed. Here the dead of the Jewish Old City had been planted.

Three-year-old Abe Kurtzman leaned against Lori and whispered the names of his brother and sisters.

The child asked Alfie, "But when will they wake up?"

Alfie responded, slow and childlike in his reply, "When the true King comes back to walk in the garden. He will wake them up."

"And Mama?"

"Mama, too," Alfie said gently. The body of Abe's mother was still beneath the rubble of their home. Perhaps it would never be reburied in the patch of earth on Gal'ed Road.

"I would like to be here when they wake up." Abe looked toward the plume of smoke that rose into the sky like a banner beyond the walls of the Old City. Then he put his small hand on Lori's cheek. "Why are you crying, Lori?"

"Because I am glad . . . glad you are awake. We were waiting for you to wake up." Thoughts tumbled through her mind. Long days had passed since the child had eaten, willingly sipped water, or spoken. Now at the moment of a Jewish victory against the Arab advance into the New City, the little boy had returned from the brink of death.

It seemed like a miracle to Lori. Was it also some portent of salvation for the desperate Old City populace?

Perhaps now the Haganah and the Palmach would once again break through to relieve the Jewish Quarter!

"We should go back to the Hurva." Rachel touched Lori's arm in warning and scanned the sky as if expecting a renewed shelling from the Arab Legion. "Moshe and Dov are on their way back through the tunnel." Rachel's voice was hopeful. Moshe and Dov, like the Hebrew spies in hostile Canaan, were still behind enemy lines and trying to get home.

"Go ahead," Lori encouraged, understanding Rachel's urgency to know if her husband would truly make it back to safety. "You should be there. We'll be along."

Rachel gave Abe a brief squeeze and hurried away toward the towering stronghold of the Great Hurva Synagogue.

"I don't want to go." Abe followed Rachel with his gaze, then shook his head adamantly. "The soldiers will make us go away."

"Aren't you hungry, Abe?" Lori urged. Then she gave Alfie a pleading look. Could Alfie convince him?

The big man cleared his throat. "Hey, Abe. It don't matter if they make us leave the Old City, see. The true King will still come sometime soon. And the bad soldiers will have to leave, but we will come back."

What was Alfie rambling about? Surely resupply was within reach!

Go? After Moshe and Dov had blown up the Arab cannon on the wall? After the Arab Legion's advance into the New City was stopped? Was Alfie imagining things? Was it the heat? The wind? The ache in his empty stomach?

"But who will water the roses?" Abe asked as the Khamseen and the sun beat against their backs. "If we go away. Who?"

"We'll be safer in the synagogue," Lori consoled the child.

"They will make us go forever," Abe protested loudly. "I don't want to!"

Lori said softly, "It will be all right. I promise."

Alfie looked at Lori with a pained expression on his broad face. "Don't make no promises. You should stay here with Abe long as you can. While it's quiet, see?" he muttered. Then, a warning. "They will promise, you know. Promise bread. Things to eat. Promise everybody can come back."

"Who, Alfie? Who will promise?"

Alfie continued as though her question did not require an answer. "And he will do what he wants here for a while. Take what he wants. Burn what he finds. He done it before. He thinks this is the end of God's promise, see?" Alfie squinted his eyes as if he heard a voice on the Khamseen. "See? On the top of that." He gestured toward the dome of the Mosque of Omar.

Lori looked, expecting to see a sniper perhaps, but there was no one. "I don't see anything, Alfie."

Alfie shrugged. He was sure of what he saw. "He's there. Drinking blood. Don't matter to him whose blood. Muslim. Jew. Don't matter to him. And he talks and talks and talks about Jerusalem, and everybody wants to believe. But he's a liar."

Lori shuddered at Alfie's vision of evil.

Was Alfie saying Jewish hopes for the Holy City were in vain?

"I got to go back now, Abe," Alfie said. "I got to carry things, you know?"

The roses on the graves of Gal'ed bloomed blood red beneath the blistering heat.

■ ■ ■ ■

The Khamseen's breath parched the Holy City, as it had for long ages before.

It was on such a day as this that Christ faced the hot wind of the Khamseen in the wilderness. *If you are truly the Son of God, turn these stones into bread. . . .*

In the same way the United Nations mocked the starving Jewish populace of besieged Jerusalem: *If you are truly God's Chosen, turn Jerusalem's stones into bread and Jewish blood into water . . . Save yourselves!*

Jerusalem!

The restored nation of Israel was a mere nine days old. May 23, 1948, was only one day in three millennia of bloody history. What had changed? Once again a handful of Jews stood against the winds that desired to possess Jerusalem above all other cities of the world.

Two thousand years earlier the Khamseen wailed from the pinnacle of the great temple: *All this I will give you if you will bow down and worship me!*

Before that hour, and since, the kings of the world coveted Mount Zion from distant lands. They heard the voice of the Khamseen. They believed the lie and bowed down, trembling, to worship the winds of desolation.

Again and again the ramparts of Jerusalem had fallen and been rebuilt. From Assyria, Babylon, and Rome, armies encircled the walls and followed the wind.

All this I will give you if you will bow down and worship me. . . .

From Europe Christian knights came to slaughter the innocent and profane the name of the One they claimed to serve.

Bow down and worship me! Jerusalem will be your kingdom!

The hordes of Islam burned the sacred parchments and baptized the land with Christian and Jewish blood in the name of Allah and his Prophet.

Bow down!

For seven hundred years the Turks joined in the butchery.

Worship me . . . !

Kaiser Wilhelm of Germany rode through the ancient gates on a white charger.

All this I will give you!

Time passed.

The Khamseen, oracle of death and desolation, blew across the sacred mountain of Zion, turning kings and soldiers, priests and paupers, to dust.

Jerusalem will be yours!

Only the dust and the stones and the wind remained.

The age-old battle raged on. As it was written.

Above and beneath and within these stones, the Prince of Darkness and the King of Light still clashed. And today, kings and soldiers, priests and paupers, heard the whisper: *Bow down! Bow down and worship me! All this I will give you! Jerusalem will be yours!*

While the United Nations dithered about the fate of the Holy City, a handful of half-starved Jewish kids with Molotov cocktails stopped the advance of the Arab Legion into the heart of New City Jerusalem. Meanwhile Jewish defenders trapped in the Old City held on, hoping for supplies and reinforcements.

And King Abdullah of Jordan watched and waited and listened to the voice of the wind.

All this I will give you. . . .

■ ■ ■ ■

Mother Superior stood like a white tower facing Major Luke Thomas, the Englishman who commanded the Jewish defenders of Notre Dame. Sister Marie Claire remained aloof, unwilling to meet the gaze of the soldier. She stood just at Mother Superior's right shoulder with the Arab boy, Daoud, at her side.

The sisters' convent, Souers Reparatrices, was now a heap of blasted rubble strewn across Suleiman Road. It blocked the advance of the Arab Legion into Jewish Jerusalem. With her own hand Mother Superior had destroyed the building. Daoud did not know why the old woman had done it. Now they were prisoners of the Zionists.

"Are we free to go?" Mother Superior inquired.

"Where would you go if I set you free?" Thomas asked the nun.

"Into the Old City. The Latin Patriarchate."

"You would be killed before you took ten steps from Notre Dame. Snipers on the wall. I can't chance it."

"Are we your captives then?"

"You are under my protection, Mother. If there is someplace near . . . a church . . . another order?"

The old woman glanced down at Daoud and placed her hand on his shoulder. "I cannot think."

"The Russian compound?" Luke Thomas suggested. "St. Trinity Cathedral? Neutral territory. So far that neutrality has not been violated."

Mother Superior raised an eyebrow at this irony. She had attempted to keep her convent neutral since the beginning of this mess, Daoud knew. But no one on either side would let her. So now it was over. There was no more French convent. The Zionists and the Jordanian soldiers would haggle over a pile of stones that had once been Mother Superior's home. She would have to find someplace else to pray.

"Our Russian sisters will welcome us," she agreed after a brief moment's hesitation.

"And the lad?" Thomas pinned Daoud in place with a fierce stare. "He'll have to be locked up."

"He goes where I go." Mother Superior looked quickly at Sister Marie Claire.

Major Thomas asked Daoud in fluent Arabic, "Did you come here to spy on us?"

Daoud did not reply at first. There were many English fighting with the Arab Legion. What was this one doing on the other side?

"He is under my protection," Mother Superior said firmly.

The major smiled curiously beneath his thick red mustache. "A spy."

Mother Superior grabbed Daoud's sleeve, drawing him close to her. "He guided me and Sister Marie Claire back through the Arab lines."

"Well, then." The Englishman folded his arms and glowered at Daoud. "What happens if I turn you loose? Eh? You go back to the Mufti and report . . ."

"The Mufti is not in Jerusalem!" Daoud argued. This stupid Englishman knew nothing!

"King Abdullah, then."

"He is not in Jerusalem either!" Daoud retorted hotly. "Only his army. And they also are commanded by Englishmen like you. If you wish to fight your countrymen, you should go back to England and do battle in your own cities!"

"You will tell what you have seen of Jewish defenses?"

"What defenses? You have nothing but boys here and women fighting alongside them. The Legion will trample you here in Jerusalem and break your back in Latrun." Daoud let his scorn for the Jewish defenders show. "You are nothing. Nothing. And now the convent of these kind ladies is nothing because of you."

Luke Thomas glanced up at the Mother Superior with resignation. "You see, Mother? He cannot be set free."

"He stays with us," the nun stated. "I will see to it he does not leave."

Thomas, ignoring the nun, addressed Daoud again. "You did not answer my question. Why did you come out of the Old City?"

"These women are foolish," Daoud spat. "But they are beloved by Allah. I came to watch over them."

Captain Thomas nodded and pressed his lips tightly together in thought. He addressed Mother Superior. "We will take you to the Russian convent. Will you give your word the boy will stay with you?"

Mother glared at Daoud. "If you do not promise to remain with me and Sister Marie Claire, they will lock you up."

Daoud gritted his teeth. What was a promise anyway? He would leave Allah to sort out the truth. "I will," he declared. "I will stay with the sisters."

The Englishman observed Daoud for a long moment. In his eyes flickered the thought Daoud was lying. Daoud knew the Englishman was correct. The Englishman knew. But in the end, Mother Superior, who trusted everyone, won the day.

■ ■ ■ ■

The presence of Rose Smith piloting a small boat full of Jewish refugees in Jaffa Harbor that day was an American story. In the editorial offices of *Life* magazine in New York the old woman and her history were discussed with enthusiasm bordering on awe.

American readers, sick of hearing about war, needed the images of an American heroine to hold their interest.

True, Rose Smith bore a strong resemblance to Tugboat Annie with her grizzled hair tied back in a bun, square, sunburned face, and mouth like a bullfrog. Her arms were thick and strong like a dockworker's, and she had a backside broad enough to tack up a billboard. She was, in a word, not an American beauty, but definitely American. Definitely a heroine. A legend among those who remembered her piloting a canal barge full of kids and wounded soldiers during the fall of France and the evacuation of Dunkirk.

She was someone worthy of a spotlight in Photo of the Week. Absolutely the perfect feature for a public who preferred a magazine with lots of advertisements, big photographs, and a few short captions to propel the story along.

Correspondents from the *New York Times* and the *Chicago Tribune* covered the politics, policies, and sweeping military victories of Egypt, Jordan, Syria, Iraq, and Lebanon against the Zionists. People yawned and used the newspaper to wrap garbage and line their bird cages. If a poll was taken, *Life* magazine would be voted *Most Likely to Be Found on the Back of Every American Toilet.*

Life, however, was a fixture on the coffee table of every doctor's waiting room in America.

Pictures of ordinary people doing extraordinary things guaranteed old magazines a special box in the rafters of the attic.

People like Rose Smith made war worth thinking about again, even a war waged on a tiny scrap of earth in the Middle East.

So it was decided. *Life* magazine would dig into the human interest side of this thing. Rose Smith was good for circulation.

The assignment was cabled to photojournalist Ellie Meyer in Tel

Aviv. Ever since the Arab riots that destroyed the Jewish business district in Jerusalem last November, her images had awakened the curiosity of many U.S. citizens.

In April her uncle had been butchered with over seventy doctors and medical staff in the Arab ambush of a Jewish convoy en route to Hadassah Hospital in Jerusalem.

Her husband, David Meyer, was known to be a pilot flying for the Israeli Air Force.

She was certainly not impartial about who were the victims and who the aggressors in this conflict. But personal tragedy brought passion to her work. Her latest photo showed seven sad-eyed children in a kibbutz kindergarten class gazing searchingly into the lens of the camera. Each child had a tattoo on his forearm.

No caption was needed for the American readership.

According to Ellie Meyer, these kids were what Israel was all about.

■ ■ ■ ■

In the superheated atmosphere of the Old City the measured boom of mortar shells resounded through the narrow streets. One explosion took on the voice of ten. The brittle echo of a single rifle became a fusillade.

"The Arabs are attacking! They have rallied! More defenders to the north perimeter!"

Amid the shouts of alarm from Jewish Old City defenders, Alfie returned to the garden of Gal'ed. Now it was time to get back to the safety of the Hurva shelter. Alfie gathered Abe into his massive arms. Abe perched on Alfie's shoulder fearlessly, as though he could not hear the thunder of explosions, the screams of the injured, and the resonant pop of small arms.

It was, Lori thought, an image like the giant Saint Christopher bearing the Christ child and the weight of the world through the deep waters of Jerusalem.

Abe's gaze fixed on the roses of Gal'ed that crowned the graves of his brother and sisters. "Where we going?" he asked Lori in a piping voice.

"The Hurva," she explained, quickening her pace as a shell exploded and dust bloomed over the tops of domed roofs.

"Flowers." Abe stretched his fingers toward the receding rose garden. "Sister sleeping there."

"We'll come back to visit the roses soon. Visit sister. You need to eat something. The soup kitchen," Lori replied patiently, trying to master her sense of panic. "You see, Abe." She gestured toward the billowing smoke as though it made all things clear.

"Alfie too?" Abe smiled and patted the big man on the shoulder as if he was an obedient draft horse.

"No. You be a good boy. Eat. I got to go, see?" Alfie explained, rounding the corner and coming within sight of the entrance to the courtyard of the Hurva. Five Haganah soldiers ran past, headed for the northern barricade. Two others, supporting a wounded comrade, hobbled down the steep steps of an alleyway. "I got to carry other good chaps. Big fellows. Hurt fellows can't walk, see Abe? I got to carry them 'cause they can't walk."

Abe frowned and tossed his head angrily. "I can carry good chaps too."

Lori ignored Abe's protestations and instructed Alfie. "Those explosions. They are coming from the perimeter beyond the hospital. You will be needed. Tell Dr. Baruch Abe and I will be in the shelter at the Hurva. When he goes to sleep, I will come to the hospital." Lori reached up to take Abe from Alfie. The child resisted, entwining Alfie's hair in his fingers.

Abe's wail competed with the cacophony of the battle. "Not the dark place! No! Not in the dark place no more! Mama's down in the dark place. I want the garden! Flowers! The garden!"

Alfie leaned down. Lori pried Abe's little square hands free and tugged him away from Alfie.

"No! Not the dark place! Not the crying place! I can carry good chaps!"

Lori wrapped her arms around Abe's middle to restrain him.

Alfie laid a benign paw on the struggling boy's head. "Be good, huh? I'll come see you." This assurance made no difference. The pitch of hysteria increased. Alfie scanned the sky and said to Lori, "He's scared, you know? That bomb on his house, see? No wonder. The sky is blue outside."

Lori looked up at the pall of smoke and dust that washed all color from the sky. "He's got to eat."

"Maybe so." Alfie nodded as Abe kicked. "But he's awful scared. Not much light in there. In the cellar. Real hot, too. Lots of people in there. People crying. Maybe out here is better?" He lowered his chin across the square toward the arched open portico of the Yeshiva School. Several dozen refugees huddled there. Heaps of meager belongings provided no real protection. If an Arab shell hit in the open courtyard, there would be no escaping shrapnel.

Just then a geyser of debris spewed up outside the walls of the Hurva compound.

Could she let a child's tantrum dictate where they took refuge? Without looking back she embraced Abe and dashed toward the sandbags that protected the portal of the Hurva.

Abe's once beefy frame was skeletal from months of privation. Like a bird caught in the paroxysm of grief, he had refused all nourishment since the night his family perished beneath the shell that destroyed their home.

"Hannah Cohen will have a good meal for you." Her words were lost as they entered the auditorium beneath the dome of the Great Hurva. Soldiers on the synagogue's scaffolding took aim through lattice-covered windows while Arab snipers on the minaret across the wall pumped bullets into the compound.

CHAPTER 2

Cradling the heavy Speed Graphic camera in her lap, Ellie Meyer perched on a crate and observed the teeming chaos of Jaffa Harbor. Her copper-colored hair was tucked beneath a floppy-brimmed canvas hat that shaded her green eyes from the sun. She wore a baggy British military khaki shirt and trousers that had been cut off above the knees. She had purchased her open sandals on her first day in Palestine less than one year ago.

Ellie glanced down at her feet. How many changes could a single twelve-month stretch encompass?

Then an unknown photojournalist; now renowned for her work.

Then disinterested in Israel, its politics, and its faith; now a fervent Zionist.

Then unmarried; now . . .

Like the combers dashing against the Jaffa jetty, the latest wave in a whole series of breaking emotions coursed over her. David was safe! Her terror and sense of loss at the news his plane had been destroyed were not yet fully erased by the news he was safe. They would not be, she felt, until she saw him, held him.

Raising binoculars to her eyes, she watched the progress of an open boat crammed with refugees as it plowed through heavy seas beyond the breakwater.

"Madame Rose," Ellie intoned as she focused on the tough old lady at the tiller.

A searing east wind whipped the harbor into a dangerous froth. In spite of its historic significance to maritime commerce, Jaffa still had no harbor for larger vessels. All cargo had to be unloaded onto lighters from ships anchored outside the reef, hundreds of yards offshore. Boatmen then ferried supplies past the reef to the quays.

In peacetime this meant that as much as two thousand tons of farm equipment or oranges was landed or loaded in a day.

Today the boats' manifests would show a much different cargo.

Three rust-streaked tramp steamers bobbed on the six-foot swells outside the partially completed breakwater. A fleet of lighters swarmed around them, off-loading guns and ammunition and a ragged host of refugees fresh from Europe's displaced persons or D.P. camps. They were arriving, Ellie knew, at what had been an Arab city only ten days before.

The forty thousand Muslim Arabs who peopled Jaffa fled at the command of their leaders, who claimed the Jews were going to massacre them. An Arab proclamation of the coming annihilation of their Jewish neighbors in Tel Aviv followed.

True to their word, Egyptian bombers pummeled Tel Aviv three times a day. The quays of Tel Aviv were in shambles, making the landing of refugees and supplies difficult and perilous.

For this reason Jewish steamers were redirected to Jaffa Harbor. It was reasoned, correctly, that the Egyptians would not bomb Jaffa since the Arab forces were only twenty miles away and believed they would recapture the city with ease.

This day marked the continuation of a long and dramatic history for Jaffa.

The ancient city, called *Joppa* in the Bible, hung like a squat citadel on the brow of a hill overlooking the harbor. Its streets were tortuous, crammed with the history of past ages.

This was the site of the legend in which Perseus rescued Andromeda from a sea monster.

It was from this port the prophet Jonah set sail, only to be thrown into the sea and swallowed by a great fish.

For a thousand years the Philistines ruled the city. Joppa was not subject to the dominion of Israel until the reign of King David. Under David's son, Solomon, it became the port of Jerusalem, the place where Hiram, King of Tyre, sent cedar logs from Lebanon for the construction of Solomon's great temple.

Throughout succeeding centuries and into the Christian era Joppa continued to be considered the harbor for the Holy City.

At a house on the beach the apostle Peter came to dwell with Simon the Tanner. In that place, stacked high with the cured hides of every kind of beast, the disciple saw his vision of the clean and unclean animals. He was told the promises of God were not only for Jews but for everyone.

The biblical significance of the city made it both the object of pilgrimage and the subject of conflict.

It figured prominently in the wars of Crusaders against Saracens. In 1267 the Muslim sultan Baibars destroyed it and put the entire Christian population to the sword.

From that year onward little was heard about Jaffa until it surrendered to Napoleon in 1799. It was here that Napoleon, rather than endanger his army, executed four thousand soldiers of the garrison who had the plague.

In May of 1948, before being deserted by its frightened citizens, the town's population was three-quarters Muslim Arabs. The remaining one-quarter were Christians.

Tel Aviv, once a suburb of Jaffa, rose from the dunes as a solely Jewish city just after the turn of the twentieth century. Over fifty thousand Jews lived there. Modern Cubist architecture in Tel Aviv was a stark contrast to Jaffa. From its inception, Jews and Arabs had dwelt side by side in harmony . . . until now.

Ellie could plainly see the wisps of smoke rising up over the Jewish city center. From the south came the insistent hum of airplane engines. Two black specks against the sky grew into the unmistakable silhouettes of Egyptian bombers. She studied the aircraft through her binoculars. There was no Jewish aerial opposition to the daylight bombing raids. No Israeli fighters countered the bombers; David did not streak into view like the cavalry riding to the rescue.

Turning her gaze toward Madame Rose and the boatload of ragged people making their way toward shore, she thought again about the wisdom of disembarking passengers in the deserted Arab port.

Swell upon close-packed swell rolled into Jaffa Harbor. Dumping tons of seawater on the unprotected stretches of shore, the Mediterranean was not cooperating with the landing. Approaching the breakwater would require precise timing and careful judgment.

The swells rolling in from Cyprus were met by the gale from the desert.

Wave crests streamed out in the wake of the incoming rollers, the spray resembling the white manes of stampeding horses.

The broad-beamed lighter piloted by Rose Smith was packed with forty refugees, clutching hats and meager personal belongings. Even through the binoculars they formed a huddled mass. Individual faces were alike in anxiety above a shapeless common body.

In contrast a lone distinct figure appeared as the boat swept forward. On the raised platform aft, tiller clamped firmly under her arm and a rigid expression on her face, stood Madame Rose.

Through her field glasses, Ellie watched the woman shout encouragement to her charges. Madame Rose varied the throttle setting of the laboring diesel and cast a glance astern at the following swell. Showing no apprehension, she corrected the course for the set of the current.

Her chin raised into the wind, Madame Rose delighted in the spray the Khamseen tossed off the wavetops and into her teeth. Like a charioteer guiding a surging team, Madame Rose planted her feet and leaned back.

Ellie saw the woman raise her left hand and shake her head. It was an expansive gesture from those ample features. She appeared to be answering someone's query.

Ellie shifted her gaze forward.

From a seat in the bow rose a tall man. No, it was a youth, Ellie corrected. A faded black slicker, much too big for his shoulders, whipped around his thin frame. Clamped firmly on his head and slanted low over one eye was a black beret. He motioned, emphatically, pointing toward his right, away from the jetty.

A sweep of the binoculars disclosed his reason for concern. Near the end of the breakwater churned a maelstrom of froth from a violent clash of currents. Madame Rose's lookout, whoever he was, wanted their course shifted further down the coast.

Viewing the whirlpool, Ellie unconsciously added her agreement and inclined away from the rocks. "Come on," she urged the lighter. "Keep clear of that!"

The first concussions from bombs being dropped on Tel Aviv rumbled through Ellie's back and the soles of her feet. Her gaze flicked away from the harbor. A new tower of dense smoke mingled with shooting orange flames over a field of oil storage tanks.

Back to the boat.

Ellie gasped. Instead of turning away from the crashing breakers, Madame Rose had angled the bow of the lighter toward the point of the jetty. What was the woman doing? Was she crazy?

Nor was the lighter charging ahead into the harbor. Instead the craft was moving at a reduced speed just beyond the line of breakers.

A renewed rumbling from Tel Aviv spoke of another stick of bombs, but Ellie did not turn. Her attention was riveted to the drama on the water. Two waves overtook the floundering craft, then a third lifted its stern perilously high before passing under the keel.

The lighter continued to drift toward the rocks.

"Come on!" Ellie shouted.

Ellie wanted to scream out a warning. Forty people were going to drown on the doorstep of their new land, dead before their new life had even begun.

Snatching up her camera, Ellie snapped a shot, then another. The scene was too far away for the Speed Graphic's lens to capture the horror, but she could think of nothing else.

The roar of engines approached overhead. Men on the quay scattered, running for cover away from the stacks of ammunition and weapons awaiting transport to Jewish defense forces.

Ellie jumped off the crate. Gathering her camera and tucking her head into her arms she crouched low and snapped the shutter as a Dakota bomber swept over.

Machine-gun bullets tore into the beach beyond the harbor, tossing geysers of sand into the air.

The Egyptian plane swooped away.

Ellie raised her head in time to see Madame Rose thrust the throttle forward. Right on the heels of a wave, the craft surged into motion, as if trying to catch up to the roller.

Its acceleration agonizingly slow, the boat labored to regain forward momentum.

The next wave astern raced up, coming on faster than the craft was moving. If the boat lost steerage, it would turn broadside to the surf and be rolled.

The rush of tormented water loomed just ahead. Competing currents boomed. Spray fountained upward three times higher than the jetty.

Snapping the shutter release and cranking the film advance, Ellie framed the scene.

"There!"

Smoothly the old woman thrust the tiller away from her, turning the prow back sharply toward the harbor entrance.

She'd judged the timing of the waves perfectly, lining up the bow so the wave caught the boat from behind. The added impetus propelled it gently forward beyond the rocks of the breakwater and into the calm harbor.

A minute later the diesel chugged to a stop, and the nose of the boat slid up to the beach at Jaffa Harbor. Freight handlers rushed to help. Following the lead of the young man with the beret, passengers jumped from the craft and drew it forward onto the sand.

Then, as Ellie snapped the shutter of her camera, the remaining passengers disembarked. Ragged men, women, and children, a remnant of survivors, staggered through the thin wash to fall on their knees. They kissed the ground in gratitude. Their long journey to the Promised Land had come to an end.

■ ■ ■ ■

Daoud did not like this much. The jeep of the Englishman carried him and the two nuns toward the Russian compound. Once the place had provided thirty-two acres of walled refuge for Russian pilgrims. They were, like the Jews, poor and pathetic. They came for Christmas and stayed through Easter. Even when it got hot, they always wore boots, fur hats, coats, and woolen underwear, which everyone knew they never took off.

The Russians were stingy. Hard bargainers. The women were the worst. Daoud knew that the phrase "as stingy as a bogomolka" meant a Russian woman pilgrim.

Since the Russian church was in exile because of the communists, the Russian compound had been converted to other uses. St. Trinity Cathedral remained a haven of the Russians who had fled from the likes of Stalin.

Of late the British Mandatory Government had used the Russian women's hospital for a prison. Jews had been executed there. Daoud had heard about the hangings from Arab policemen who had seen the bodies swing.

Was this grim place where Major Thomas was taking them? Why were Mother Superior and Sister Marie Claire so calm? Stupid question. They were always calm. They looked death in the eye, made the sign of the cross, and spit on the grim reaper with contempt.

The snow-white Russian cathedral stood aloof from the destruction around it. Ten green domes topped with gilded crosses glistened in the sun. It was too large a target for the Legion guns to miss. Therefore, Daoud reasoned, the Legion did not wish to hit it.

"You will be safe here," the Englishman promised. Then, "Pray for us."

Mother Superior extended her hand and touched the hand of the soldier. "We will pray for everyone in Jerusalem."

"When you hear the shelling on Mount Zion, pray for us."

"You will try again to save the Jews in the Old City?" Mother asked.

"Radio messages are desperate. They are on their last legs. We must try to break through to them."

The woman's head bobbed in acknowledgment, then she added, "Daoud's father . . . Dr. Baruch . . . is in the Jewish Quarter."

The Englishman examined Daoud curiously. "We will do our best to help your . . . father."

The Englishman could see plainly Daoud was no Jew. It did not make sense his father was a Jewish doctor. But there was no time to explain about the way Baruch had saved Daoud's brother, Gawan. And Daoud was tired of trying to explain that he was the son of a Jew *and* a true Muslim patriot and son of Mohammed.

To care for both sides meant he belonged to neither side. He fit nowhere. It was a miserable thing not to hate anybody anymore. He wanted only to return to the Latin Patriarchate to sit with Gawan at the hospital.

They made their farewells to the Englishman.

Here he was, a Muslim Jew, following two French Catholic nuns into a Russian Orthodox convent—the church in exile from communist Russia.

Well, that was Jerusalem for you.

They rang the bell as shelling began again from atop the Mount of Olives. A beautiful Russian nun opened the door and escorted them into a foyer. The scream of a twenty-five pounder drowned most of the woman's welcome. "I am Sister Victoria . . ." She sounded Arab. Local. The sisters smiled at one another as if this was a social call for afternoon tea.

Was Daoud the only sane person? The only one who knew what was going on?

"And we must have a place for the boy," Mother Superior said.

The reply, "A bed in the orphanage," was followed by a *boom!*

Daoud opened his mouth to protest that he did not want to leave the side of the kind 'Mere Superieure. Suddenly being alone was more terrifying than the rain of bombs.

The Russian nun had the face of an angel. Wide brown eyes. Perfect teeth. She put her hand on Daoud's shoulder and said in a refined and precise Arabic, "So many children . . . taken refuge here . . . safe within these walls . . . the promise of King Abdullah . . . the promise of the Jews as well . . . lots of children your own age . . ."

Daoud was indeed a prisoner in the Russian compound. The Englishman had not exactly lied, but he had not explained that Daoud would be separated from the nuns.

'*Mere Superieure* kissed him lightly on the head. Sister Marie Claire cupped his trembling chin in her soft hands. "When this is complete . . ."

Her words were lost beneath the scream of another shell.

■ ■ ■ ■

Talking calmly, soothingly to Abe, Lori hurried toward the steps leading down to Tipat Chalev, meaning "drop of milk," soup kitchen. Heat, oppressive and thick like a steam bath, filled the place. Fewer than ten candles illuminated the space. The hum of voices and weeping of children greeted her ears as they descended. Hundreds of civilians, women, children, the aged, cowered together beneath the stone vaults in hopes that the walls of the Hurva could withstand Arab assaults. Each new concussion was followed by a universal groan. It was, Lori remembered, like the underground London stations on the worst days of August, during the Blitz. At the Hurva, exhaustion and the humidity of close-packed human bodies combined with hunger and thirst to parody the hell from *Paradise Lost.* Every sigh breathed despair into the reeking atmosphere.

When will it end? Never! *When will we see sunlight again?* There is no sunlight. No stars. No moon! *When will the Haganah break through the Muslim vise that holds us fast?* We will die here! The roof will collapse, and we will die. *This place of refuge will be our grave!*

Lori involuntarily held Abe close to her breast and kissed his head. She remembered the sweetness of her own little boy in the garden at Primrose Hill.

Stories in the garden beneath the shade of the plane tree. How he had loved those few short days of sunlight. It was the first summer he could talk and sing. She had spread a red-checkered blanket on the lawn. They had a picnic of cucumber sandwiches and scones with plum preserves. They shared an orange she had saved for such a day. And they lay on their backs and sang nursery rhymes together. Broad green leaves danced in dappled light. He slept with his forehead pressed against her arm. Contentment. Air-raid sirens were nothing more than bees buzzing outside the garden wall.

She had not known the end of summer would soon come forever for him. He would be gone before the turning of the leaves.

Roses! The garden! The roses of Gal'ed!

"You'll be safe here, Abe. Something to eat, Abe. Hannah has been saving an orange . . . an orange, just for you, Abe." Suddenly Abe went limp. His pleas to remain in the sunlight and for the roses of Gal'ed fell silent.

■ ■ ■ ■

"Blow it up, he said!" Haganah stalwart Ehud Schiff peered into the blackness of the crooked subterranean passage. It led from the basement of the Hurva Synagogue and wound away to emerge behind the lines in the Arab-held Old City. "Moshe's instructions were . . . If Dov and he aren't back, he said. He said this is an order, *nu?*"

Rachel Sachar stood resolutely between her brother, Yacov, and her grandfather, Rabbi Lebowitz. Dov's wife, Yehudit, sat unmoving beside the tunnel.

Rachel's head throbbed. Fifty minutes had passed since the blast had silenced the Legion's cannon on the wall.

The Muslim attack had swung around to hit the barricades of the Jewish Quarter with renewed fury. Mortar shells exploded in the streets, blasting Jewish positions.

Since the Arabs captured Nissan Bek Synagogue, the Hurva Synagogue was more crammed with refugees than ever. It was so packed with civilians that the Haganah had moved its command post to the Eliyahu Hanavi sanctuary in the complex of Sephardic synagogues.

The thick walls of the Hurva, sheltering over a thousand civilians, had withstood the assault so far. But if the Muslim fighters discovered the cellar passageways into the Jewish position? What then? There would be no holding them back.

Where was Moshe? Where was Dov?

"A bit longer," Yehudit pleaded. "I don't fancy being a widow at seventeen."

Ehud retorted, "If we don't close off this passage, the Jihad Moquades will come. Moshe told me . . . Moshe said . . . this is our last remaining tunnel leading out beneath the Muslim Quarter. Four blown up. This is the last. It was an order."

Reb Lebowitz placed his hand on Ehud's massive shoulder. "If you see the Grand Mufti or King Abdullah strolling through the tunnel, then blow it up, *nu?* But a few minutes. What can it hurt?"

"The Jihad Moquades will find the way Moshe and Dov came among them to destroy the English cannon, eh? They will disconnect the charges. I will push the plunger, and nothing will happen. Then they will come in through that opening and kill us all in the soup kitchen. That is what it will hurt," Ehud concluded.

Rachel begged, "Moshe and Dov . . . They are coming. Soon. I know it."

"Where are they?" Ehud fretted. "If he is alive, Moshe will think I have sealed the passage. He will say, 'Ehud is a good soldier. He has done his duty. Obeyed orders. Fine chap, Ehud Schiff. Captain of a ship. Understands orders and all that. Better find another way in.'"

The thoughts of each person leapt to the logical conclusion. Moshe and Dov were dead. Or captured, which was the same as dead. Or perhaps they were trying to get back another way.

Grandfather broke the painful silence. "You are in command here in the Old City," he reminded Ehud. "You are needed more at the Eliyahu Synagogue than down in this hole. Leave the box of destruction in my keeping. I will do what must be done when the time comes."

CHAPTER 3

Jordan was a monarchy ruled by King Abdullah, an amiable, educated man, given to chess-playing. He had received his desert kingdom at the conclusion of the First World War as a consolation prize
when the British gave Iraq to his elder brother, Faisal.

Abdullah, not belligerent by inclination and left to his own devices,
would probably have reached an accommodation with the Jews.

Two things conspired to prevent this from happening.

The first was the pressure on Abdullah from the other Arab nations.
He had to assert his military leadership and that of his Arab Legion
troops. The Egyptians in particular could not be permitted to sense any
weakness.

Despite his innate peacefulness, Abdullah had to act more aggres-
sive than the other members of the seven-nation Arab League. The
Egyptians already had been spreading their propaganda that Abdullah
was "soft" on Zionism, a proposition that, if widely believed, would
quickly lead to Abdullah's overthrow.

Compounding this situation were the actions of the British.

Back in the days of the Balfour Declaration, just after the First
World War, the British government fully supported the idea of a na-
tional homeland for the Jews.

If that had remained true, Britain had enough clout in the region to
quell any and all opposition. After all, Jordan received an annual grant-
in-aid from the British Treasury. So did Egypt. Britain truly held the
purse-strings.

If Britain had laid down the law, Jerusalem, instead of being under
siege, would have become an international city dedicated to peace, with
ample room for inhabitants of all faiths. The nation of Israel could have
formed a thriving new state, accepting the poor, the tired, the huddled
Jewish masses clamoring to escape war-ravaged, anti-Semitic Europe.

Israel and the Arab states would have been free to adopt the U.N.-

proposed borders and settle remaining differences across conference tables instead of across minefields and barbed wire.

But the postwar Labor government of Britain had forgotten that the Jewish Brigade fought with the Allies against Herr Hitler while many of the Arabs were cozy with the Nazis.

The British acted like a jilted lover, eager for revenge. If only Winston Churchill had still been directing England, but he was not. Instead the British position in Palestine was in the hands of men like John Bagot Glubb, known as *Glubb Pasha.*

Glubb saw himself as the successor to Lawrence of Arabia.

Millions of rounds of ammunition and thousands of weapons that were supposed to be removed or destroyed by the departing British were left in the hands of the Arabs.

The British-officered Transjordan Defense Force marched out of Palestine one day, turned around, and marched back as the Arab Legion. Serving officers of the British Army acted as more than advisors to the Legion; they actually led Arab troops in battle. This action directly opposed the United Nations partition plan and British law.

The Arab League, meeting in Amman, Jordan, vowed to drive the Jews into the sea and dared the world to make them stop.

Prime Minister Abou Hoda coughed softly one pace inside the doorway of Abdullah's private chambers in his Amman palace.

King Abdullah was at prayer. Kneeling on a red-and-gold brocade rug, his face toward Mecca, the monarch of Transjordan lifted his right hand in admonition. No disturbance was permitted to interrupt his devotions.

The prime minister shuffled awkwardly. A minute passed and then, unable to contain himself longer, he cleared his throat and mumbled an apology.

Abdullah sighed and stretched his back before standing. "It must be bad news," he guessed. "Good tidings always keep until after prayers. What is it?"

"Majesty," the prime minister said, "the attack on the New City has failed. General Glubb is withdrawing the Legion."

"Failed or merely faltered?" Abdullah demanded. "Are we regrouping for a fresh assault?"

"No, Majesty," Abou Hoda reported. "The Jews have dynamited the convent of the French nuns, completely blocking Suleiman Road. At almost the same instant our cannon on the Old City wall, after nearly battering the Jewish position at Notre Dame into submission . . ."

"Yes?"

"It was destroyed by means unknown. Notre Dame continues to dominate the northern approach to the New City. Under the circumstances Glubb has broken off the engagement. He is redeploying the armor to the west of Jerusalem. He says the Holy City will then be encircled and must surrender."

"Today is the twenty-third," Abdullah mused aloud. "The twenty-fifth is the anniversary of my coronation. I must worship in the Holy City on that day. Summon General Glubb here to meet with me."

Abou Hoda bobbed his head, eager to say something pleasing. "He is already on the way, Majesty. He expected your summons. He said he wishes to report to you in person."

"No doubt," Abdullah concluded. "No doubt."

■ ■ ■ ■

Along the Jaffa beachfront a flotilla of boats emptied two thousand passengers unceremoniously onto the sand. They wandered onto the shoreline and collapsed. Survivors of a terrible storm, remnant of a shipwreck, they had at last come to landfall.

Rose Smith, barefoot, clad in denim sailor's trousers and blouse, waded up among Israel's castaways. Squinting toward the carnage of Tel Aviv, she addressed the young man in the beret. "The last of them off the ships. Too few. Too late. That is that, Jerome."

Ellie guessed Jerome was eighteen or nineteen. He was annoyingly cheerful, a regular Guide Friday among the tourists, smacking men and women alike on the back. He offered his hearty felicitations upon their arrival in the Holy Land.

"*Oui!* These fascist terrorists! They are indeed stupid, no? They bomb Tel Aviv, which has no ships and no cargo, but they spare Jaffa." He gestured broadly at the steamers beyond the reef and the quays where heaps of war materials destined for the Jewish front were being loaded into lorries.

"They intend to scrape every trace of Tel Aviv off the face of the earth." The old woman's tone betrayed no real concern. "But Jaffa . . . is Jaffa."

Jerome agreed amiably as he stood in the midst of passengers who were weeping for joy. "Just as you perceived, Madame Rose."

He caught sight of Ellie snapping photographs on the outskirts of the emotional arrival. As if he were posing for a tourist on the Left Bank of Paris, Jerome adjusted his beret over his bushy dark hair and draped his long, thin arm around the shoulders of a sobbing young woman. Drawing her close to him, he grinned wryly for the camera. "Go on. Take the photograph, Madame American! Pay no attention that she is convulsed with this hysteria. To a Jew just come to Israel this is happiness," he explained to Ellie. "You see? Ask her. You are happy, no? Joie de vivre! Oui?" he inquired of the girl. She did not reply. "She is! Indeed! She is so very happy to be here. She cannot help herself, eh?" He gave the young woman a sloppy kiss on her cheek. She laughed through her tears, then kissed him back.

"Did you get that?" Jerome asked.

Ellie had not got it, but she pretended agreement and turned her attention to a couple who knelt in the lapping waves with four stairstep boys, ages eight to about seventeen. A family! Whole, seemingly intact! It was a rare sight among the refugees who flooded into Palestine. Who were they, and where had they come from?

"Russians. The man's name is Sholem. His wife is Katerine. And their sons . . . four of them. Alive. You see? Four sons. A mama and papa. A true miracle, that bunch," explained a male passenger in his late twenties. He carried a mandolin slung over his shoulder. The tattoo on his forearm was plainly visible: 134571.

Ellie snapped his picture as he smiled sadly at her. "And what is your name?" she asked.

"Leon. Leon Pickman. From Sosnowice in Poland." His gaze remained riveted on the Russian family. "They are lucky, no?"

Ellie asked him about the mandolin. A beautiful thing, inlaid with flowers and birds. Was there a story? What did this moment of arrival mean to him?

"I . . . with my family . . . was trying to come to Eretz-Israel in 1936, madame," Leon replied. Fierce words rolled lightly from his soul, composed in a heart-rending poem of loss. "If there had been Israel in 1936 . . . *if only* . . . then my family also would be with me now." He inclined his head toward the billowing smoke over Tel Aviv. "You write this down if your countrymen have forgot . . . tell them . . . Hitler's war against Jews has not an end. It follows us even here. And if we who survived Auschwitz are defeated in this last place . . . maybe . . . there will be no more Jewish sons. Anyone who has not the soul to understand this maybe also believes Hitler and his SS were not such bad fellows, eh? And Treblinka was a holiday hotel. And Vichy, France, was not so bad either. And Mussolini made the trains run on time. And maybe it was us Jews who cause the war, yes, madame? Maybe we brought it onto our own heads . . . Maybe we deserve the killing by the Muslim armies also?" He shrugged. "Write this to remind them. Say to them, please . . . Leon Pickman once had a family . . . a wife. Children . . . I had three children." He paused as the image of their faces danced before him. "So, here is what Israel means . . . there was no Israel when my family needed a place to run. And they . . . my dearest ones . . . who were as real . . . as you . . . they are ashes." At that he turned away from her, not wanting to be bothered by petty questions.

She snapped a photograph of his back as he stared wistfully at the Russian family who embraced one another as they wept. And what if tomorrow or next week there *was* no Israel?

Yes. There was a story here. Leon carried nothing but the mandolin, framed against his tattered coat and thin neck. Beneath a fisherman's cap, ears like jug handles protruded. His brown curly hair needed a trim.

Ellie called out to Madame Rose, hoping to get the old woman to face the camera, full on.

Ignoring Ellie, whom she had met with some irritation in Tel Aviv, Rose scowled and began to issue commands in a half-dozen different languages. "They may not bomb Jaffa, Jerome, but they will strafe!"

Jerome scanned the skies with concern. "Lousy fascists!"

Rose clapped her callused hands, calling her group of forty to attention. "Come on! Time to celebrate later. We've got to get you to a safe place. The Egyptian planes may return. Hurry along! Help one another! That's it. You strong ones, help the others into the lanes of Jaffa's old city. Up the slope there. There is food and drink for you in the hall of the Armenian Convent."

Madame Rose glanced sourly toward a thick-framed, middle-aged man in a jeep who was observing the disembarkation. Rose muttered as she pressed forward, leading her flock first among the hundreds, "I suppose they must."

Ellie, keeping pace with Jerome, who seemed to know everything and was not shy about articulating what he knew, asked, "Who is that? The guy there? In the jeep?"

"American. Like yourself, madame." He put a finger to his lips. "An observer, they say. Observing only. But! A secret, eh? Everyone knows, *oui?* A colonel, they say. Reviewing the troops." He snorted bitterly. "Israel's soldiers hit the beaches, eh? The warlike Jews invade Palestine. A pitiful sight. *Oui,* madame? Here they are. How to say it? Things are . . . the war goes to hell in a handbasket. *Oui?* So this is the army of Israel."

Then he motioned toward the steamers. "And there are her battleships." Another broad Gallic gesture skyward at seagulls wheeling overhead. "As for the air force . . ."

Ellie nodded solemnly and watched as the colonel backed his vehicle from the quay and roared off.

■ ■ ■ ■

In order to meet the attacks rolling over Israel from every direction, able-bodied Jewish men aged eighteen to forty-five were conscripted into the military.

The rabbis argued against the inclusion of Yeshiva students in the call-up. They maintained that after the Holocaust the single way of preserving Judaism's unique contribution to the world was in the lives of the scholars. Yet many slender, pale, eyeglass-wearing Yeshiva students had already exchanged pens for rifles and joined the ranks of "able-bodied" volunteers.

So far the combination of conscripts and voluntary enlistees held at bay the combined armies of five Arab nations. Nowhere was this more evident than in the struggle to possess Jerusalem, where handfuls of poorly armed and barely trained soldiers tied up the forces of the Arab Legion.

Every fragment of time gained by Jerusalem's resistance allowed the rest of Israel to arm, organize, and counterattack.

But how long could the besieged nation continue to hold? There were never enough recruits to meet the threats and replace the killed and wounded. Even the haggard emigrants were pressed into service.

Following a line of bedraggled refugees, Ellie climbed Jaffa's central hill. The procession passed a mosque, a squat, ugly, dull-red building. Beside its minaret was an open-air marketplace. Both were deserted. Striped awnings above the bazaar's empty tables flapped in the east wind.

In the confusing chatter of many different languages, refugees observed and commented on their new surroundings. From what Ellie could decipher, the mood was one of exhaustion coupled with excitement. Their first steps in the Promised Land!

Beyond the Latin Hospice, whose inscription disclosed it had been built in 1654, was the Armenian Convent, destination and first asylum for the emigrants. Once inside the ponderous wooden doors of the convent the talking became instantly muted. The air, with no hint of breeze, was stifling from the number of bodies gathered there, but the changed emotion was not solely due to the temperature.

Solid earth underfoot after months . . . sometimes years . . . of travel, the elation at having arrived was coupled with the memory of those who had not made it to see this day. Women wept openly, crying in each other's arms for those who had not survived. Men, lean-faced, hard-eyed, cynical, turned their faces toward stone walls as tears streaked their cheeks.

One man in particular caught Ellie's eye and lens. Looking more military than most of the Haganah officers, this fellow was dressed in a gray woolen uniform. Sweat poured off his face, but he kept the tunic fastened up to his throat. The sight of a double row of brass buttons suggested a solution to one mystery but left others in its place. He was wearing a chauffeur's uniform; where and how and why had he acquired it? He appeared grim and determined.

More faces, more emotions: uncertainty about what would happen next mingled sometimes with relief, sometimes with suspicion.

What, Ellie wondered, was it like to have had one goal . . . one single-minded dream of reaching Palestine . . . for years? To have thought no further than making the journey and coming safely to a new life? How many of the confused travelers knew what to expect from this moment on?

Madame Rose moved matter-of-factly through the midst of the throng. From a battered pitcher she dispensed lemonade into cracked glasses and tin cups. "Lemons, right out of the orchard," she boasted cheerfully. "Drink up."

■ ■ ■ ■

Human shapes, indistinguishable from heaps of belongings, carpeted the floor of the Hurva. Lori, cradling Abe, stood among them. She covered his head and dropped down. He stiffened in a spasm, then began to shake violently. Was he wounded? Her hands searched limbs, head, and body for some sign of injury. No blood! But was he breathing?

"Abe! Abe, *bitte!*" She rocked him. Pressed him close. "Abe!"

No response. By the yellowed light of a candle she peered into his face.

Eyes were glazed and wide in unseeing terror; his complexion was the hue of ashes.

Was he dying?

"Oh, God! Not this one!" she cried, remembering the lifeless body of her child in her arms.

The night. The night the world had ended. Mad bellowing of animals caged in the London Zoo across the street. The frantic flight of birds released from the damaged aviary . . . She had knelt in the ashes that spilled onto Prince Albert Road. Her son gray as ashes. Eyes fixed. Mouth open in a half smile. All color drained by the glare of the fire that scaled the church spire and gutted the building. Human bodies laid in a neat row on the lawn of Primrose Park. Pools of flame spread out beneath the hill across the great city of London.

As the images of that horror played too clearly before her eyes, Lori cried out, "Not this time, God! Not this child!"

A calming touch fell upon her shoulder. Rachel Sachar stroked Abe's hair and pressed his quaking fingers to her lips. The eyes of the two women met.

"My mother saved a baby bird who fell from his nest. But this one will not survive in this place." Rachel's brow furrowed.

"He did not want to come back here." Lori's reply was choked. "The light, he said. The garden. The roses, He wanted to stay."

The garden. Primrose Hill. Would Lori not have died willingly to save her little boy? Would she not have stayed in the garden beneath the plane tree and spread her arms and sung a welcome as the German bomb whistled down?

"Fall on me, not him! Sky, collapse! Stone and timber make my grave! Earth swallow me! But let him live!"

There was no going back. She could have taken him with her to the market. He would have been with her! Safe! But no! Too late! No going back ever. Unless . . .

Was this not a second chance to die for the life of a child? For love?

"It is not safe for you to go outside," Rachel warned, but both knew it did not matter.

Lori shrugged. She would die ten thousand times if she could sit in the garden and exchange places with her tiny son. And now for the sake of this one precious boy.

"Send someone with rations, will you? Water. Matzo? The orange, you see. I promised him an orange. If . . . when . . . he wakes up . . . he will need food and water. Tell Alfie I have taken him back to the garden."

■ ■ ■ ■

Fighter pilot David Meyer squinted into the glare as his Messerschmitt roared skyward from the Haganah airbase outside Tel Aviv. The aircraft climbed through seven thousand feet with David fervently scanning the southern horizon.

He was anxious to locate his quarry. A pair of Royal Egyptian Air Force Dakotas had been spotted returning to base after bombing Jewish Tel Aviv. David was merely seconds behind them.

David knew but did not dwell on the fact he was the sole airborne warrior of a nine-day-old nation whose existence hung by a thread. Ever since Israel's nativity on the fourteenth of May, 1948, the Egyptians held the mastery of the skies. British-made Spitfires and American-built Dakotas routinely strafed and bombarded newly arrived Jewish immigrants on the Tel Aviv docks.

Captured by Arab forces at an airfield in Galilee, David and his wingman, Bobby Milkin, had escaped only the night before.

David was exhilarated at being aboard the single combat-ready Jewish fighter plane. No longer flying loads of cargo, no longer skulking in thorn-choked wadis evading Arab Legion patrols, David was at last back in his element. This was the fulfillment he had been seeking ever since embracing the cause of a Jewish homeland.

A pair of black dots attracted his hawk-like stare. "Gotcha!" he said aloud, nudging open the ME-109's throttle. Traveling two hundred and fifty miles an hour, David's plane closed the gap separating him from the enemy at three miles to the minute.

The Egyptians, demonstrating arrogant disregard for reprisal, loafed along, conserving fuel. They were no doubt boasting by radio of the havoc they had caused among tattered refugees and helpless women and children.

Since Israel previously possessed no means of retaliation, the Egyptian Dakotas carried no guns and had no fighter cover. "My turn," David said without remorse.

The bombers continued level, straight, and slow. No evasive action; not a single course change indicated he had been spotted.

Diving out of the sun, David launched his attack on the rearward bomber, selecting his wing-mounted twenty-millimeter cannon for the first pass. He was close enough to see the green-and-white Egyptian colors on the tail above a string of Arabic letters.

Cranking the sluggish, manually operated flaps to slow his speed, he aligned the Messerschmitt perfectly for a textbook deflection shot.

David squeezed the trigger.

A burst of three cannon-shells from each gun made the 109 buck slightly, then the weapons jammed.

Repeated crushing compressions of the trigger produced no better result. David glimpsed the terrified face of the Egyptian copilot and a hand jabbing in his direction. The 109 flashed past the Dakota, and the shot was lost. There was no damage to the bomber.

"That's torn it," David said scowling as he brought the fighter out of its plunge. He craned his head around to reacquire a target. The Messerschmitt resisted as he executed a roll. The torque of the engine's tug to port forced him to overcompensate to starboard.

The two Egyptian bombers banked in opposite directions. Both dove for the desert. The lead plane swooped off southeast and the other southwest.

Switching to the nose-mounted machine guns, David opted to go after the same aircraft again. This time he approached from behind. His gunsight centered on the bomber's tail, David intended to walk his fire up the length of the enemy hull.

When he pulled the trigger the machine guns obligingly responded with a deep-voiced roar, but his plane immediately bucked and plunged like a startled horse. Shrapnel hit David's windscreen.

Not properly synchronized!

The bullets, instead of firing through the gaps between propeller blades, were striking the prop.

David was shooting himself down.

Back to the cannon. Maybe the unintended rattling of the airframe cleared the jam. Even before lining up for another attack, David tried the weapon again.

No success, still frozen.

David slammed the 109 into a tight turn as if to punish it for its disobedience.

A crooked W-shape of black specks in the distance resolved into a flight of Royal Egyptian Air Force Spitfires. Doubtless summoned by the Dakotas, the enemy fighter planes screamed toward the defense of their comrades.

CHAPTER 4

Reclining in the desk chair in his Tel Aviv office, Israeli prime minister David Ben-Gurion listened attentively as American colonel Michael Stone described the successful Haganah defense of the Hospice of Notre Dame. It was unknown who had destroyed the Legion cannon on the Old City wall, but its loss demoralized the Arab forces. For the moment Jerusalem's New City was secure.

"So," Ben-Gurion said, "petrol bombs and teenagers. Mysterious explosions? Out of little miracles grows a big one, eh? But this buys us time to break through at Latrun ... more time to resupply Jerusalem ... To rescue the Old City."

Michael Stone frowned. "If the Arabs want to stay tied up with capturing Jerusalem, let them. But we can't. We've got bigger fish to fry."

Ben-Gurion pounded his fist on the glass tabletop. "Bigger fish? The siege *must* be relieved! Jerusalem will *not* be allowed to fall. We *will* break through at Latrun. Look at these cables." He waved a sheaf of dispatches. "Our outpost at Neve Yaakov has surrendered. Atarot is lost. An Egyptian column is twenty miles south of where we are sitting right now. The morale of Israel needs good news for a change. We must lift the siege and resupply Jerusalem. Take Latrun!"

Stone shouted back, "The Egyptians *are* only twenty miles away! If they get to Tel Aviv you can kiss Israel good-bye! Jerusalem served its purpose by holding up the Legion for days. The war's bigger than Jerusalem."

"*Nothing* is bigger than Jerusalem! You are American. You know, 'Remember the Alamo!' Well, that is nothing compared to remembering Jerusalem. Jerusalem holds the secret to our strength. Take a reinforced column and open the pass!" The prime minister struck the table again for emphasis.

Stone snorted. "Reinforced from where? Our boys are tied up in the

Negev with the Egyptians and in Galilee with the Syrians and Iraqis. Do you think I can conjure troops out of thin air?"

"Recruits are arriving every day."

"Boys, and raw, sickly, untrained, undisciplined men. . . . If we attempt to take Latrun with them, they'll all die."

Ben-Gurion said stiffly, "Men, women, and children are *dying* in Jerusalem now! Take Latrun!"

At the next collision between fist and tabletop, the plate glass shattered.

The emotion in the room fell to the floor with the fragments. Ben-Gurion and Stone regarded each other over the wreckage. The two men breathed heavily, like battered prizefighters hanging on the ropes.

Finally Stone spoke again. "We need to know what we're facing. Put someone in a Piper and let him fly recon over Bab el Wad."

"Good," Ben-Gurion concurred. "And since you tell me the Legion advance north of the Old City wall was stopped by boys and sickly men, I want a firsthand account of how. Bring me back someone who was there. Use the Piper for that too."

A secretary tapped on the door. "What?" Ben-Gurion demanded.

"A message for Colonel Stone. He is wanted at the airfield at once. It seems one of our planes . . . our new fighter planes . . . is pursuing Egyptian bombers."

Stone bolted out of the room but not quickly enough to escape hearing Ben-Gurion bellow, "Latrun! Bring me someone who can do it!"

■ ■ ■ ■

Fighting back the urge to imitate the Egyptian bombers and hide among the canyons and sand dunes, David forced himself to review what he knew.

His Messerschmitt had more power, but the pursuing Spits were more agile. His ability to win a game of tag amid the wadis was not promising.

Hauling back smoothly on the control column, David aimed at the westering sun. If he was blinded, then so were his enemies. This was the time to fight for more altitude. If he gave up the advantage of height too soon, the fight was as good as lost. There was no way he could out-maneuver four pursuers.

David's ME-109 ran rough and ragged, its every flaw exaggerated. The flap lever was more recalcitrant. The drag to the left was more pronounced. The throttle setting grew more temperamental, the fuel-mixture adjustment more sensitive.

Every cautionary word he had heard while training at the secret European Haganah base came back to haunt him. *This plane is a wonderful weapon but a potential pilot-killer. It is spiteful, vindictive, and will do its best to murder you if you make a big mistake in it.*

How extreme was the error when the pitch of the prop was damaged by shooting off chunks of it?

How much of the 109's advantage in engine power was already lost?

David took a hasty look at the hunters. Two of the Spitfires were charging up after him while the other two gave chase at a lower altitude. David grudgingly admired the strategy of the Egyptian pilots. The box they constructed could anticipate his every move.

Something about their silhouettes took a moment longer to register, and he shot back another glance to confirm it.

The Spits carried bomb loads slung under their wings.

That made no sense. Why would a commander send up a flight to provide fighter cover weighed down with bombs?

Unless . . . unless the Spitfires had *not* been sent to escort the returning Dakotas. What if the Spits were on a bombing mission of their own, and chance had thrown David into their sights?

David clenched his jaw. More bad luck.

Maybe the bombs' added drag counterbalanced David's struggling prop.

Maybe he could still outrun them.

There was something else.

Maybe he could find somewhere to land since he could not go home.

There was no way he would lead a pack of wolves bearing a thousand pounds of high explosives back to the Israeli air base. All the ground crew and the other half-assembled Messerschmitts would be easy prey.

Now what?

The Spits were gaining.

There was no doubt. They were closing the gap on David.

If his guns functioned he would have engaged the Egyptian fighters, scattered their formation, and escaped in the confusion.

He had no working weapon, not even a slingshot.

Where was another option?

The Egyptian planes were probably stationed at Al Arish in Sinai. They could only carry enough fuel to reach Tel Aviv, drop their bomb loads, and return to base.

Could David keep out of reach long enough to exhaust their fuel before his own tank ran dry?

The 109's engine coughed. The plane shuddered.

David's fingers tweaked the fuel mixture adjustment. He leveled off. The one-hundred-plus heat sapped the lift from the air.

The Spitfires had a higher operational ceiling than his laboring 109. The pair following behind climbed above him, getting ready to pounce.

There was not even a single patch of clouds in which to hide.

The Spits started their run, dropping from the sky like falcons swooping to the kill. The wingman was higher and to the right of the leader.

Having flown Spits during the Battle of Britain, David knew the convergence setting of their guns. He knew when he would be in their target radius. He forced himself to delay his next move.

The sweat on his face was not entirely because of the blistering heat.

Closer. Closer. The Spits also held their fire, waiting for a certain kill.

It appeared they would run over him.

At one-hundred-fifty yards tracer bullets flashed past David's left wing. His hands on the control stick and his feet on the rudder pedals moved at the same instant.

David flicked the 109 into a snap roll to the right.

Inverting, then dropping its nose, the Messerschmitt powered earthward.

The lead Spit tried to follow and flew across his wingman's course. The second pilot, slower to react, jerked up to avoid colliding with his comrade.

David's radio crackled. "Meyer? Colonel Stone. Return to base immediately. I repeat, abort this unauthorized mission and get back here. And avoid Ramat David. RAF base there still active. Acknowledge."

Ramat *David*? A good omen? An RAF base? Royal Air Force meant British, not Egyptian. Was there still an English air base operational in Palestine?

Racking his memory, David recalled a chart showing Ramat David to the northeast of his present position.

Banking sharply, he pulled out of his dive. The 109 streaked into another turn as a Spitfire roared past.

There!

A pair of black strips . . . runways . . . appeared in sharp contrast to the tan desert. Sunlight gleamed off tin Quonset huts and the windscreens of parked British aircraft.

Could he make the Egyptians think he was British? Would they break off the attack?

Was there another choice?

One of the Egyptian Spits was lost, completely out of the action, but the other was on David's tail again. A second pair vectored in from the right, rising toward him.

Machine-gun bullets clipped the 109's tail assembly.

David jinked abruptly left, threw in more throttle, and banked toward Ramat David.

He turned right, then right again, perfectly aligned with a runway.

The 109 plunged toward the British base as if following a homing instinct.

Dropping, dropping, not slowing. With no gear down, the Messerschmitt barreled toward the tarmac.

David could see men on the ground, shading their eyes and gesturing upward.

The parked warplanes were also Spitfires, but LF 18s in contrast to the older LF-9s flown by the Egyptians.

The altimeter spun through five hundred feet, then three hundred, then one hundred. The hand whirled 'round the dial, unwinding the thread of David's life expectancy.

He recovered from the dive at last, a camouflaging storm of grit billowing in his wake. The ground effect uplift provided by super-heated surface air cushioned his leveling off.

The 109 was at a mere dozen feet.

Hills to the west offered sanctuary, and David swung the 109's nose toward a cleft in the brown escarpment.

The muffled crump of explosions never reached him, but the shock waves did.

The Egyptians bombed the British base.

Not one of the Egyptian fighters followed him.

Leapfrogging over the row of low knolls, David observed the action.

Three Egyptian Spitfires released bombs on Ramat David, then returned to strafe it with machine guns.

Flames leapt from two hangars and a trio of parked aircraft.

Two British planes taxied down the runway and bolted upward.

"Let's you and him fight," David suggested.

The Brits engaged a lagging Egyptian fighter with cannon-shells. David saw a wing come off the Egyptian Spit.

"Meyer! You are ordered to return instantly! Acknowledge," Stone's voice demanded.

With a glance at his fuel gauge, David said, "Acknowledged. Returning to base. Meyer out."

■ ■ ■ ■

In the glare of the afternoon sun the spike-shaped shadow of a Muslim minaret fell across the graves of Gal'ed.

Lori could not see the structure that loomed behind the buildings surrounding the little courtyard. Nor could the Muslim muezzin see where she and Abe sheltered in the alcove of a portico beside the garden. The shadow began inching its way across the roses. She could hear the song, calling the faithful to prayer in the adjoining Arab Quarter.

She knew well that an enemy sniper also occupied the prayer tower. For hours she had flinched each time he fired off a round. She thought of bullets finding their mark.

The resonant crack of rifle fire sounded so near that she could not distinguish if it was on the Jewish or Arab side of the barricades. After a time the pop became as normal to her ears as birdsong in a tree.

It was a strange paradox that the call to devotion and the instrument of death could coexist so easily in the minarets, synagogues, and church spires of the Holy City. What did the great and eternal God think when men of all faiths paused in their killing of one another long enough to pray?

Gunfire and Muslim prayer made no impression whatsoever on Abe. Fully shielded in the alcove, Abe played quietly behind Lori. Using two oblong stones as trucks he drove them through a make-believe wadi in a planter box filled with sand. Did he imagine he was bringing supplies to Jerusalem? The child had eaten matzo bread and drunk half his ration of water. In the sparse package of food Rachel brought them, there was an orange that Hannah Cohen had saved for Abe. It now perched on top of a small hill in the box. This was the city, Abe said to Lori, the castle where he lived with his mommy and daddy.

Abe's once hefty frame was skeletal from days of deprivation. Lori was relieved his spirit and imagination had revived after eating. He hummed the tune of truck engines just as little boys did everywhere. The sounds of Abe at play were more holy to Lori than all the prayers of

the saints who had made pilgrimage to Jerusalem. His loud and ener-
getic voice, which had earned him the name of Abe the Obnoxious
among some in the Quarter, was a bell ringing her heart to worship.

And his cries for her attention? "Look, Lori! See here! My truck
comes up the mountain!" Was there anything more important than
truly seeing him? The sight of Abe at play made her stop and think in
wonder of all things ordinary and call them blessed!

She remembered the vision she had carried through the Blitz of
Jacob coming home to her in London at the end of a summer day.

Ordinary? No, sacred!

*There would be no more war. No rationing or blackouts. Maybe Jacob
would drive a double-decker bus or be a plumber. It didn't matter what he
did. They would be together. He would come home, and that was all that
mattered. They would eat cold chicken in the garden and sip Piesporter
slowly. They would listen to Mozart on the BBC as the light faded from the
sky. Later when the clouds chased them indoors they would make love with
the windows open while rain dripped from the eaves. Then they would
sleep in one another's arms as the cool breeze drifted over their skin like a
silk scarf. . . .*

Lori raised her eyes as an artillery shell exploded in the New City.
She studied the lone Haganah outpost on the roof of a nearby building.
From their vantage point they could see across the walls into the New
City.

Was Jacob there?

Was he still alive?

Did his thoughts turn toward her, as hers did to him?

■ ■ ■ ■

A pall of dust and smoke spiraled over Jerusalem. The murky haze
swirled by the Khamseen did not dissipate. It hung above the city like a
dirty winding sheet tangled about a battered corpse.

Part of the Old City's northern battlements lay entwined with the
battered south face of the Hospice of Notre Dame, but at least both
structures remained recognizable. Not so Souers Reparatrices. From
Jacob Kalner's view out a rear window at the Jewish-held position at
Notre Dame, what had been convent now resembled an abandoned
rock quarry. Granite masonry formed a barrier entirely choking
Suleiman Road for a hundred paces in length. In spots the barricade
was twenty feet deep.

At the sound of a groan, he turned from the window to regard his friend, Peter Wallich. Wallich commanded the youth brigade that had successfully defended Notre Dame against the Arab Legion attacks. In the climax of the battle he received a rifle wound in the left leg. Though the bullet missed bone and artery, he had lost a significant amount of blood.

Sixteen-year-old Naomi Snow changed the compress on the wound and examined the stitches, but Jacob knew she was hiding the depth of her feelings for Peter.

Major Luke Thomas was also present. "I said, the Legion armor is pulling out," he repeated when Jacob appeared not to have heard. "The route into the New City is blocked. You have done it. For the moment at least, the north flank of Jerusalem is secure. You are needed in Tel Aviv."

"But I don't see why I should be the one to go," Jacob said. "Peter is out of action, and this place has to be held against mortar fire and infantry. And we must save the Old City."

Major Thomas gestured toward the sling around Jacob's arm that supported his recently dislocated shoulder. "Wallich is not the only one who has seen plenty of action," he suggested. "The High Command . . . by which I mean Ben-Gurion himself . . . wants to know how you turned back the Arab Legion's armored cars and cannon. Who can give the report better than you?"

But Jacob's thoughts were on his wife, Lori, trapped inside the Jewish Quarter of the Old City. Being flown out of the fighting to Tel Aviv would take him further away from her. When he spoke again what he said was, "I don't even know if any of the rest of the men I joined up with . . . the Spare Parts Platoon . . . I may be the only one left. For their sakes I should stay and fight to the end."

Thomas cleared his throat, but it was Peter Wallich who spoke first. In a voice so weak as to be barely audible above the rifle fire that cracked outside, Peter corrected, "It is for their sakes that you must go. Don't let anyone give up on Jerusalem, Jacob. Tell them what a handful of us did and make them try again to lift the siege. Otherwise everything we have fought for here is wasted."

■ ■ ■ ■

Buses would come soon and take the refugees out of Jaffa. That was the rumor.

Take them where?

There was no front to this war. No rear. No clear battle lines. All was a muddle. Pockets of people fighting other people. Word had come early that Jaffa was no longer a safe place for Jews. The Egyptians were advancing rapidly from the south. There still was a strong Muslim presence in Ramle, just on the fringes of Jaffa. So where would these new citizens of Israel go?

Refugees in the Armenian Convent milled about in the courtyard, sheltering from the sun beneath the arches of open cloisters. Conversations hummed in the babble of a score of languages. People clustered in groups by country of origin. One-quarter were Polish. The remaining nationalities were divided more or less equally. Russian. Czech. Latvian. German. Dutch. French. Italian. Greek and Turkish.

Ellie could spot the Russians because, as Leon had explained, they were the only ones in family groups. Husbands. Wives. Grandparents. Children. She spotted Sholem, Katerine, and their four sons together beside a dry fountain.

Beyond them was the easily recognizable man in the chauffeur's uniform and the fellow with the mandolin.

Ellie attempted to make conversation with the family but was ignored with a distant smile and gaze that told her she was outside and could not come in.

Rose Smith, however, fluent in English, French, Dutch, German, Polish, and Italian, moved with ease among them all. Ellie simply watched her for a time.

The burly old woman did not seem American. Thick forearms and tough leathery skin . . . everything about her connoted the physique and mannerisms of a Parisian laundress. Ellie commented on this to Jerome, who clearly was French.

Jerome, wearing his wool beret in spite of the heat, leaned jauntily on the stone pillar where Ellie stood. He told her everything he knew about Madame Rose, which was not much.

"Look at them. They love her already, this old lady! By tonight . . . you will see . . . the children . . . they will wish to curl up on her big lap. Mothers will speak to her about how their babies are getting the teeth or have a sore behind or . . . you know, Madame! Everything they will tell her! You and I could ask these people ten thousand questions, but they will not tell us anything. *Oui?* They all think she is a Jew also!" Jerome shrugged. "Catholics think she is Catholic. Protestants, of whom there are countless varieties, think she is one of their own sort. Muslims know she is not . . . but they do not care. That is how she is. A saint, I think."

Jerome Jardin and his younger sister, Marie, had come into the Paris orphanage of two American spinsters, Madame Rose and her sister,

Betsy, in 1940. How these two old American ladies came to take in French foundlings on the Left Bank of the Seine was a mystery to Jerome. But he knew they supported the home by taking in laundry. They had often done the laundry of such literary notables as Ernest Hemingway and F. Scott Fitzgerald! No one starched the way Madame Rose starched. Such famous clients were gone by the time Jerome came on the scene.

In the late spring of 1940 France was collapsing and Paris was about to surrender to the Nazis. The children of the orphanage escaped France on a wretched canal barge piloted by Madame Rose. They also rescued many Englishmen and French soldiers at Dunkirk. Rose was a fine sailor, though Jerome did not know how or where she had acquired such an unusual skill.

Nowadays sister Betsy, who was extremely frail, lived in a hospice in England. Rose said sadly about her that "all the lights are on but no one is at home." Madame Rose believed perhaps the war had done it; sapped everything out of Betsy.

As for Jerome's sister, Marie, she was attending a fine girl's boarding school in England. She was learning to be a proper young English lady, Jerome said in wonder. And Ernest Hemingway paid her tuition! This was an amazing thing, was it not? Proof that no one had starch like Rose Smith. She usually got what she wanted. She never wanted anything for herself, however.

"But how did she . . . and you . . . come to Palestine?" Ellie asked.

Jerome gestured around the courtyard. He let his admiring gaze rest on Rose as she knelt to speak into the attentive face of an unhappy four-year-old.

Jerome's grin faded a bit. "Look at them," he said. "She is always where they are."

"They?"

"Children. She says, you know . . . It is always the little ones, the innocent ones, who suffer the mistakes of politicians and nations, is it not?" He sighed and appeared almost thoughtful for an instant. Turning his face toward the blue square of sky he added, "And with these people . . . 'God's Chosen,' she calls them . . . she loves them like she loves her Jesus . . . The world has made so many mistakes. Too much suffering, *oui?*"

"And why are you here?"

The wry grin exploded. He laid a hand on Ellie's arm. "She is not as strong as she was, you know? She needs me to carry things now. I am eighteen years old. Clever enough, but school is not for me. If it was, Hemingway would be made to pay for my tuition also. So I have no one but Madame Rose who ever loved me. Except my sister Marie, perhaps. But being wholly French and male . . . I would not be welcome to live with Marie in an English girl's boarding school."

CHAPTER 5

The Khamseen howled through the Old City lanes around the Hurva Synagogue where most of the fifteen hundred civilian population of the Jewish Quarter sheltered. The floor of the synagogue was a babble of parched misery.

Three hopes remained alive. The first was for an international cease-fire that would stop the fighting and preserve this last foothold for the Jews of the Old City.

The second was for miraculous rescue from the Palmach and Haganah outside the walls.

The third was that Moshe Sachar and Dov Avram would return through the tunnel and rally the few remaining troops to stand until the first two hopes could be realized.

Rachel sat on the steps of the sub-basement beside Yehudit. By the yellow light of a candle she gazed at Grandfather. The detonator box was wedged between Grandfather's feet. Grandfather recited psalms in an almost inaudible whisper.

Where were Dov and Moshe? Where was salvation for the ancient Yeshivot? Wouldn't this be a fine hour for Messiah to come?

Behind Rachel, Yacov explained the politics of the Middle East to the two Krepske brothers who had also come to wait for the return of Dov and Moshe.

"King Abdullah does what the English want. They hate us. We hate them. They want to come back to Jerusalem, but we don't want them here. That's why they help the Arab Legion and the others kill us, *nu?* They tell Abdullah, who's a *smartut,* a rag, what he should do. They give him Glubb Pasha to see that Abdullah does as he's told!"

Leo Krepske asked, "So. You think Moshe and Dov are dead or what?"

Yacov did not reply.

Mendel Krepske silenced his brother with a clear smack. "Shut up!" he hissed. "There's Rachel. *Nu!* and Yehudit . . . *almona* . . . ! The widows!"

Yehudit, who heard the question clearly enough, had been thinking the very thing.

Moshe and Dov are not coming back. How could they have survived the destruction of the Arab cannon on the wall?

Yehudit covered her face with her hands and began to weep silently. Rachel placed an arm around her shoulders and said at last to Ehud, "If . . . if . . ." She faltered, afraid to speak of the probability that Moshe and Dov would not return. So many she had loved had said good-bye, promised to see her again, and never come back.

■ ■ ■ ■

Despite the renewed fighting, the mood in Misgav Ladakh, the Old City Jewish hospital, was jubilant. The destruction of the Arab cannon on the north wall and the successful defense of Notre Dame was greeted with cheering. Wounded soldiers, lying in the corridors because the beds were filled, celebrated the victory. With the dreaded Arab Legion juggernaut stopped, the war was as good as won!

What followed was a riot of outrageous rumors, each one more euphoric than its predecessor. "The Arab Legion is running," called a sinewy Palmachnik, elated despite the throb of his head wound.

"Our boys are pursuing them toward Jericho," avowed Manny Rheinhart. Manny smiled broadly, even though a second shrapnel wound in two weeks had returned him to the infirmary. "We'll be in Amman before the week is out."

The building rattled with the report of an explosion somewhere to the east.

"I heard Arab snipers warning each other! Truly! Arab soldiers are rebelling and murdering their own officers."

"The Muslim Brotherhood fired on the Egyptians south of Bethlehem."

"The British bombed Cairo and will depose King Farouk."

"The Americans have landed tanks at Tel Aviv. General Blood-and-Guts Patton is leading them toward Jerusalem because the American president Truman is Jewish!"

Sixteen-year-old Daniel Caan observed the other patients coldly. With phantom pains in his amputated foot, he turned his face toward the wall, wishing he could shut out the cheerful nonsense. He wanted to yell, "Shut up!" Daniel knew the Arabs were not so easily discouraged.

Even if they received a temporary setback, they still had British bullets and British bombs and thousands more men to throw at Jerusalem. Eliminating one cannon had not won the war; it had not even guaranteed one more day of life for the Jews in the Old City.

A series of reverberations caused Misgav Ladakh to shudder. The new explosions also came from the east, toward the Haram.

"See? See!" Manny asserted. "Now our mortar bombs from Mount Zion are dropping on their heads. Our boys will be here again by nightfall!"

Ehud, Dr. Baruch, and Alfie appeared in the doorway. A cheer arose. Questions fired from every corner of the ward.

"How long until we are relieved?"

"Have our fellows broken through Zion Gate?"

"When will they get us out of this stinking hole?"

Ehud shouted, "Listen!" The cry of the muezzin echoed from a nearby minaret, calling the Muslim faithful to prayer. "No one is coming to save us! Not today, anyway. Moshe and Dov did not return!" He stopped to let that grim news sink in, then continued, "Commander Shaltiel has sent word. Maybe tomorrow we'll get reinforcements. *If* we can hold on till then. Tomorrow, *maybe* they will come, *if* they can break through the Legionnaires holding Zion Gate. But for now, there is no one but us to hold the Old City!"

The jubilation fell away. The somber crump of shells falling on the New City replaced the chatter. Ehud jerked his thumb toward the sound. "The Haganah in the New City is busy, true? There remain fifteen Arab Legion cannon on the Mount of Olives, eh? Four batteries minus the one gun Moshe and Dov knocked out."

"But they gave up," a quavering voice protested from the back of the room. The celebration died hard; these desperate men were unwilling to exchange a mood of triumph, however deceptive, for harsh reality.

"They only stopped to regroup. But they gave us time to reinforce the weak points since Nissan Bek is lost," Ehud replied. "With Moshe and Dov both . . . away . . . I am in command here. We need anybody . . . any one of you who can move and shoot. We need you back out on the barricade."

A long silence followed. No one volunteered.

Then Daniel shouted, "Me! I'll go!"

Dr. Baruch shot him a scornful look. "It is too soon for you."

"You will have to be able to move," Ehud said.

Daniel struggled to sit. He held the stump of his leg up. "Put me on the front line. See? It's a sure thing I won't run away."

Nervous laughter from other patients rattled around the room.

Baruch shook his head. "Your wound is too serious. You cannot be moved. Cannot be exposed to . . ."

"Please," Daniel begged. "I got to . . . I'll rot away in here. Sentry duty. Anywhere. I can shoot, see? You got to let me out of here."

Ehud and Baruch exchanged a look. Where could Daniel Caan be of use?

Daniel repeated, "I can shoot!"

At his pleas, the arms of fifteen less seriously wounded patients rose.

"Me."

"I'll go."

"Me too."

■ ■ ■ ■

David Meyer's stare was fixed on the floor of the stifling office. Twice he raised his eyes to meet Colonel Stone's, just to receive blasts of reprimand for even looking like he would offer an excuse.

Surely the walls of the windowless cubicle were bulging outward from Stone's heated words and the volume of his angry censure.

Despite the fact Stone had coldly ordered David into this private space in the hangar, surely everyone on the Jewish airfield could hear the dressing-down.

Maybe everyone in Tel Aviv could hear it.

"Do you have any idea what an idiotic thing you've done?" Stone demanded. "Throwing away the element of surprise to no purpose! The plan was to keep the existence of our 109s a secret till we could jump the Egyptians on the ground at Al Arish . . . smack them down good without any warning. Now this!"

"I . . ."

"Shut up! Don't you think Weizman and Allon and the other fighter pilots want a crack at the Spits? Do you think it's easy for any of us to let the docks get pounded without retaliating? But everyone obeys orders except you. What sort of out-of-control cowboy are you?"

"It won't . . ."

"You're right it won't! When the boss hears about this, I don't know if we can keep you in the country, let alone flying."

Bobby Milkin gingerly poked his head around the door frame as if expecting to have to dodge a missile. "Radio intercept," he offered, extending a flimsy slip of yellow paper.

"Save it!"

Milkin bravely demurred. "Think you oughta see this," he argued. Then pressing on before Stone could respond he said, "I'll read it to ya." Clearing his throat, Milkin intoned, "Radio traffic between Ramat David and British Command, Cyprus: 'Request instructions. Base attacked by Egyptian Spitfires at 1500 hours. Two 18s destroyed on ground. Two more damaged. Air combat downed two Egyptian fighters, and a third observed descending, trailing smoke. Please advise.'"

Stone stopped ranting and turned thoughtful. His silence encouraged Milkin to continue.

"There's more. One 'Gyppo' pilot reported that his flight was pursuing an *unidentified* aircraft when the Brits attacked *them*. There's no mention of a Messerschmitt."

"Meyer," Stone said.

"I ain't done," Milkin objected. "That third Spit the Brits say they potted? Went down near a kibbutz close to Latrun . . . same one where we came out of the hills and they thought we was Arabs, right, Tin Man? Plane and pilot survived. Both captured. Prob'ly those same farmers with their pitchforks." Milkin gave a mock shudder at the memory.

"Near Latrun," Stone repeated speculatively. Then as if recognizing Milkin for the first time he added, "Come in, Milkin. Here, both of you sit down."

Without speaking, David and Milkin agreed Stone's unexpected outbreak of politeness made them more nervous than his tirade.

"You two were captured. How'd you get away?"

Grateful to see the subject change from David's unauthorized flight, Milkin and David alternated describing their exploits. For the next twenty minutes they explained in detail their crash landing in Galilee, their apprehension by Arab Legionnaires, and their subsequent escape by night past Latrun and out of Bab el Wad.

"You say there's a path south of the road that avoids the Arab villages. Could you find it again?"

"Sure," David said with a shrug. "Not much of a path. I could fly you over it."

Stone corrected. "Lousy poker strategy, Tin Man. Never tip your hand to your opponents. No way we'll let the Arabs know we care about anything south of the highway. Okay. So take me there. But on foot. And since you're so keen to fly, take the Piper to Jerusalem right away.

There's a Haganah soldier there by the name of Jacob Kalner. The boss wants to meet him. On the way back fly recon over Latrun. Give Kalner a good look. He'll be fighting his way through there, God help him."

David was stricken. "The pass is full of British officers. And Arabs with machine guns. Daylight recon and then a foot patrol? So shoot me."

"Meyer," Stone said, "after that dumb stunt with the 109, everybody on *our* side wants your hide, remember? I may be able to sell this to the boss, but you better not argue."

Milkin interrupted. "Way I see it, Tin Man is the first Israeli ace. After all he's responsible for three downed 'Gyppos' and . . ."

"Get out!" Stone roared. "Meyer flies to Jerusalem in ten minutes. Go!"

Outside the door David said, "Great stuff, Milkin, but you don't know when to quit, do you?"

Bobby Milkin was miffed. "I wasn't the one gettin' reamed out," he said archly. "By the way, Zoltan says you got three bullet holes in your tail."

"Yeah," David concurred. "Feels like it too."

■ ■ ■ ■

Lori sat cross-legged with Abe upon her lap. The arched portico of the courtyard reverberated with the chaos of retreat. Throughout the Old City, buildings collapsed like the husk of an empty cocoon beneath hammer blows.

Hard to believe such fragile dwellings have ever contained life! How easily they crumble!

The three rosebushes trembled with each concussion of falling shells.

Had it been like this when the Romans leveled the city 2000 years earlier? The Assyrians before them? The Crusaders after? The Saracens? The Turks? Were such scenes of destruction embedded in the great blocks that groaned and tumbled inward on themselves? Was the image she saw simply the reflection of unending grief projected like a film onto the hewn stones? Did the picture reveal an eternal, unending judgment of Jerusalem and her cursed inhabitants?

Lori knew the scenario all too well: the screams of the wounded and those who try to help them escape the assault . . . the acrid scent of cordite.

Many voices cried out for help.

"Pull back!"

"Wounded to hospital! We need help here!"

"Please . . . oh, God! Save me!"

Next week an Arab with a long stick would fish out pots and kettles from beneath smoldering beams. He would take the prizes home to his wife. Someday he would make pilgrimage here and tell his children that Jews had lived in this place once. His children would not believe him. They would climb the heap of rubble and plant a flag. They would run and scramble and scream with the enjoyment of their games. They would not hear the echo of Jewish cries trapped beneath the meaningless heap.

Expecting each minute to be her last, Lori laid her cheek on Abe's head. She covered his ears against the punch of shells detonating.

But he acted unaffected by the panic taking place beyond the walls of the garden. His eyes remained fixed on the blooms. He did not flinch when the dust from an exploding mortar clogged the passageway and drifted across the graves of Gal'ed.

There would be more Jewish dead to bury before the battle ended.

Lori was certain she would be among them. And this boy whom she had saved from death would be among them, too.

She reasoned that she had given little Abe Kurtzman only a few more days of life.

Had she saved him in vain? Did it make an eternal difference that he had not perished in terror three days ago beneath the fallen house?

He would surely die now, in her arms. They would die beside the roses of Gal'ed with no one left alive to gather the pieces in a basket and bury them.

At least Abe was at peace, unafraid. His last memory of life on earth would not be of terror.

His lack of fear had nothing to do with courage or bravery. Both of these qualities required self-control in spite of the urge to panic. During the Blitz Lori had often acted courageously. She knew firsthand that facing death bravely meant overcoming the terror that boomed like a bass drum in her heart.

But here among the roses of Gal'ed, Abe was calm even in the shadow of death. He did not either summon courage or resist cowardice. Like the aged nuns of Souers Reparatrices, marching unafraid through the hail of bullets on Pentecost, his soul was innocent. He never suspected he would be blasted to pieces. Or if he knew, it no longer mattered. His soul was drawn toward an invisible light by inaudible voices singing a hymn with lyrics that Lori longed to understand but could not.

Somehow three-year-old Abe Kurtzman trusted the promise God made in the budding of a rose.

Lori, though frightened, found courage in this. Courage to remain calm in the midst of pandemonium. To sit while others ran. To be silent while the world cried havoc to the dogs of war.

Whatever fragment of life they had left would be spent in a garden.

CHAPTER 6

On the north wall of the Old City, between the crenellated towers of Damascus Gate and St. Stephen's Gate to the east, was Herod's Gate. Named for King Herod the Great, builder of temples and slaughterer of innocents, it was called *Bab es-Zahire,* meaning the "Gate of the Flowers," by the Arabs.

Though this late May day was technically part of spring, there were no flowers at the market. The Khamseen withered any trade in blossoms.

Ahkmed al-Malik, captain of the Jihad Moquades, stood atop Herod's Gate, alongside Arab Legion major Tariq Athani. Though he was prepared to advance his own ambitions by cooperating with King Abdullah's Legion, al-Malik did not like the Jordanian king or his soldiers. Besides, he felt the Arab Legionnaires were puppets of the British.

Major Athani, commander of a portion of the Arab Legion forces under the British officer John Glubb, talked about the necessity of permanently cutting the Jews' supply route through Bab el Wad to the sea. The Babylonians, the Romans, the Crusaders, all had used siege tactics to subdue Jerusalem. Impatience cost men and equipment, Athani said. The Legion's battered armored cars would be of more use in open country, like that around Latrun, than in crooked city streets.

The infantry assault had already been renewed as more Arab Legionnaires arrived from Ramallah to join the Jihad Moquades in conquering Jerusalem.

A battery of six-pound cannon, which had delivered ineffectual fire at the granite monolith of Notre Dame, were hitched to the armored cars to be trundled out of Jerusalem. The Arab heavy artillery on the Mount of Olives continued to hammer the New City of Jerusalem, but the more portable lesser guns were leaving.

Al-Malik caught at Athani's elbow. "Major," he said, "since you have so many guns with which to punish the Zionists at Latrun, why not leave one here? For the use of our combined forces in capturing the Jewish Quarter?"

"What use will it be from outside the Old City walls?"

"How about if it is inside them?"

"Maneuver it through the tiny passageways? It can't be done. Besides, we have already expanded the assault on the Jewish Quarter and our rifles are more than enough to overpower the Jews. Then we can break out of the Old City and conquer the New City at will."

Athani had himself argued for one more attack on Notre Dame, one last attempt to break through the Jewish lines north of the Old City wall. The Legion major was convinced the Haganah had exhausted their resources. One more charge would carry his infantry into the heart of the New City. But in this he had been overruled by General Glubb, over-all commander of Abdullah's forces. The Old City must be taken first.

His remarks were interrupted by an aide who saluted and presented a white-skinned British captain. The newcomer was in full dress uniform despite the blistering winds. "Sir," the aide said, saluting, "Captain Gerald Kerry wishes a word with you."

Kerry shaded his eyes against the glare. Though lower in rank, he spoke to Athani as though addressing a waiter about an unsatisfactory meal. "See here, Athani," Kerry said. "You've got to do something immediately. This won't do. Won't do at all. Your armored cars parked east of Damascus Gate are drawing machine-gun fire from the Yids right where my infantry is bivouacked. A good thing the Jews lack mortar shells, eh? Anyway, you'll have to move the guns at once."

Ahkmed al-Malik made no attempt to hide the smirk on his face, though he avoided Athani's dangerously flashing eyes. Al-Malik stared off toward the skull-like knob of rock where some believed the prophet Jesus had been killed by the Jews.

"We are already moving out," Athani replied tersely.

"Oh, good show," Kerry replied with satisfaction. "Knew we could count on your cooperation. I was saying to John the other week, 'That Athani is a very able man.' Just . . . plan a little better next time, eh?" The Englishman turned on his heel and departed.

Al-Malik wanted more from Athani than just watching the Legionnaire's chagrin. He bit his lip to keep from speaking.

Athani leaned over the wall. "Sergeant Khatibi," he called, "detach gun number six and its crew, together with two caissons of shells. They will remain here to aid in our capture of the Old City."

"*Ya Allah*," al-Malik offered with approval. "You have the soul of an Arab after all, Major."

"Just do your part," Athani said tersely. "Press them hard and the Old City Jews must surrender. Meanwhile we at Latrun will keep the Haganah from getting mortar shells to drop on your head . . . or Captain Kerry's."

"*Insh' Allah*," al-Malik intoned. "As Allah wills."

■ ■ ■ ■

In a rubble-choked alleyway between the Great Hurva and the three Sephardic synagogues were Yacov and the two Krepske brothers. Leo, Mendel, and Yacov gathered there to escape the worries of their elders and the chores handed out by feisty Hannah Cohen.

Sitting on a chunk of masonry, Leo sifted through the fallen plaster with his toe. From the debris he plucked a shilling-sized rock. Fitting the stone to the pocket of his slingshot and drawing back the scavenged strips of inner tube that served as bands, he launched his missile over the enclosing walls. In clearing the roofline the projectile disturbed a pair of pigeons. "I hope it comes down . . . *smack!* . . . on an Arab," he said.

"Or Rabbi Akiva," his brother put in.

Yacov unfolded a bit of paper and removed his food ration: a square of sheet-metal-strength matzo. The top of the unleavened bread was smeared with a mixture of crushed matzo and olive oil, dubbed "monkey fat." "Guess what we have today," Yacov said glumly.

Leo launched another lump of limestone. "The windows are busted out," he noted, peering around at the shattered frames. He shot a rock through one of the gaping holes. "Hannah Cohen would have whipped me for that two weeks ago. Can you imagine what she would do to the Arabs if she could reach them?"

"Maybe we shoot her over the walls and see?" Mendel suggested.

The three boys snickered at the vision of pear-shaped Hannah Cohen first arcing above Jerusalem and then dragging Arab Legionnaires around by their ears.

Yacov nibbled the edge of his ration. "It doesn't taste bad if you talk about something else while you eat it," he said. "What shall we talk about now?"

"Max Birnbaum says Moshe Sachar is not coming back. He says Moshe and Dov Avram are dead," Leo said.

"*Momzer!*" Mendel said, yanking the band of the slingshot and popping his brother on the hand. "Idiot! Moshe is married to Yacov's sister."

"Ow!" Leo complained, shoving Mendel. "So? I didn't say it. Max Birnbaum did."

"Maxie is a *momzer*," Yacov said, trying to interfere before the brotherly riot really got rolling. "What does he know?" Then, "This matzo tastes like plaster."

■ ■ ■ ■

The wind at his back, Jacob Kalner waited on the British Mandate cricket field that served as Jewish Jerusalem's airstrip. Major Luke Thomas, tall and sunburnt, shielded his eyes against the westering sun. "There he is."

Thomas pointed toward a black speck that bucked the current of the Khamseen. The plane moved so slowly it seemed suspended in the sky.

"I thought it was a crow." Jacob shifted his weight nervously. He had never flown. The thought of going up in something so insignificant made fighting the Arab Legion with Molotov cocktails a small thing.

The buzz of the engine preceded it. Thomas cleared his throat. "Piper. Quite small. Two-seater. Enough room for a bit of mail. Kibbutzniks call it a *Primus* because the motor has the sound of a Primus kerosene stove." Thomas rocked back on his heels and clasped his hands behind his back. Bags of mail and official dispatches rested beside a boulder.

"This is what I will ride in to Tel Aviv?" Jacob inhaled raggedly and scoured his ear with his finger. "I flew kites bigger than this when I was a kid, you know?" Then he admitted, "I have never been in an airplane. Not any airplane at all, you know, and . . ."

"Ah. Well then. You've got nothing to compare this experience to. Good. Twenty-minute flight to Tel Aviv in a Piper. Quite safe, I assure you," Thomas remarked, but he did not look altogether confident. "David Ben-Gurion himself has gone up in it."

"Yes. But he is . . . Ben-Gurion. I am . . . you know . . . just Jacob Kalner." From the east the sound of Arab arms popped an unfriendly greeting for the insignificant aircraft. "And they are shooting at it." Jacob's stomach churned. The flyspeck buzzed steadily closer.

Thomas acted pleased. "Hard to hit something that size. Ideal aircraft for these forays from Tel Aviv to Jerusalem. A bullet would have to kill the pilot to knock it down. Steady on, Kalner. Doesn't matter who the passenger is. It's the pilot that counts. American pilot. The most experienced, most polished of the branches of the volunteer forces, these Yanks. You'll be in professional hands from the instant of takeoff. Safe as a baby in a pram."

Jacob pivoted away toward the smoke rising over the Old City. Lori was somewhere in there. He had not imagined he would leave Jerusalem without her. "Someone else would be better to send than myself."

"Nonsense." Thomas clapped him on the back. "They need you for the raw recruits."

"But you see, my wife remains in Jerusalem and I . . ."

"How many languages do you . . . speak?" The Englishman's voice faltered. His face was strained as the Piper banked in a slow-motion arc, skirting Arab-held Jerusalem. The crack of hostile fire increased. The aircraft, unstung, hummed into its approach.

It was a fragile thing. Painted blue, the wings were marked with a star of David. The Israeli Air Force incarnate, Jacob thought. A paper kite without a string. All hope and little substance.

And then it swooped down on the cricket field like a moth lighting on a daisy. It bounced four times, then rolled to a stop within yards and swung around.

"Well done!" Luke Thomas snatched up the wheel blocks and sprinted toward the aircraft.

Jacob, taking up the mail sacks, followed. The propeller kept spinning. Clearly the pilot did not plan on staying long enough for the Arabs to get him in range. The thin metal of the fuselage was riddled with bullet holes. So, the Jihad Moquades had been trying very hard to kill the pilot and thus knock down the plane! Maybe this would be their lucky day. Jacob balked and stood motionless in the prop wash as Luke Thomas flung open the panel of tin that served as a sort of door.

"Jacob Kalner, meet the renowned fighter ace, Tin Man. David Meyer."

Jacob's eyes widened as he glimpsed the pilot. Was he supposed to recognize the name? Tin Man? Fighter ace? American? Professional? Polished? The grizzled, filthy fellow glaring at him from the pilot seat resembled more a drunken derelict recruited from a back street slum.

Meyer exchanged several words with Luke Thomas, but it was plain he was in a hurry.

When Jacob did not move, Meyer shouted angrily over the roar, "Get in!" Then to Thomas, "What's wrong with him?"

"A bit nervous. Never flown." Thomas tossed the mail bags into the back.

Meyer grinned diabolically. "Oh. Is that it?" He crooked his finger at Jacob like the devil summoning Faust to his final doom. "It'll be over before you know it."

Jacob hung back. *Oh God! Will anyone tell Lori what has happened to me?*

Thomas shoved him hard toward the plane. "Don't keep the prime minister waiting."

Jacob stuttered, "My wife. In the Old City. Lori Kalner is her name! Remember to tell her! Tell her Jacob . . . Lori Kalner . . ."

"Right. Right. In you go." Jacob was crammed into the seat, which was less supportive than a beach chair. The door panel slammed, bounced open, then closed again with the hollow rattle of insubstantial corrugated metal.

Jacob found himself beside the filthy, grinning lunatic, inside a vibrating tin can attached to a lawn-mower engine that began hurtling down the cricket field toward a precipice.

Then Tin Man, who appeared relaxed with this scenario, remarked, "This won't hurt a bit." He hauled back on a lever, and the Piper lifted into the teeth of the Khamseen. An Arab bullet pinged against the skin of the aircraft as it climbed slowly over the city and circled toward Bab el Wad and the sea.

■ ■ ■ ■

Abe was asleep in the shade of the portico.

The shimmering heat of the Khamseen distorted Lori's view of the Haganah outpost on the roof opposite Gal'ed. Four men, mostly concealed behind sandbags, trembled like leaves in the wind.

Thirst swelled her tongue. She contemplated the glass jar containing her water ration. It was already half gone. Still there was the rest of the afternoon and the long hours of night before morning water rations were distributed. She resisted the need to quench her thirst.

One sentry in the Haganah nest raised up and waved broadly in her direction. Was he signaling her?

Footsteps rounded the building. The voice of Alfie Halder hailed her softly. "You still here, Lori?"

In his arms Alfie carried Daniel Caan. Daniel's stump oozed fresh bright blood through the bandage. The young man, fierce-eyed with pain, clutched a rifle to his chest. Lori remembered him from the hospital. Although pain often made people unpleasant, she had the sense Daniel Caan had a personality problem before he lost his foot. Why had they brought him to her?

"Here?" Daniel demanded.

"Doctor Baruch said." Alfie addressed Lori. "The roses, he said."

"What about her?" Daniel snapped. He flashed Lori a hostile look.

"She can change your bandages, Doctor Baruch said. And you will protect her and the boy, huh?" Then to Lori, Alfie said, "You hear that? Doctor Baruch says . . . he says you should look out for . . . infection, see? Gangrene, he says. Get word to Doctor Baruch if the leg gets to stinking too bad." With that he unceremoniously deposited Daniel in the alcove beside Abe.

Daniel scowled at the child. "What is this place? A kindergarten?"

Lori replied, "A grave. The boy's family is buried there."

"I am guarding a grave?" Daniel challenged.

"Put it this way." Lori's eyes narrowed in resentment. "If you die, we will not have to drag you far, eh?"

Both fell silent as a high-pitched hum was added to the intermittent discharge of sniper fire.

Over the Haram swept a light aircraft, tossing on the surging Khamseen like a feather.

Lori turned hastily, checking to see that Abe was sheltered under the stone arch. What additional terror was about to be unleashed on the Old City? "Theirs or ours?" she wondered aloud.

"Listen to the Arab rifles," Daniel said scornfully.

The noise of gunfire from the Muslim-held portions of Jerusalem increased in volume, swelling to a crescendo until the airplane flitted away toward the west.

■ ■ ■ ■

For an instant the Piper hung motionless in the air. Its engine all sound and no fury, it was grasped by the harsh fist of the Khamseen. And then, as dust stung Jacob's eyes, the plane swooped to the right and spiraled upward above the holy mountain.

Seconds of terror evaporated into rapt fascination as the panorama spread out beneath them. This was, Jacob reasoned, Yerushalayim, "Vision of Peace," as the angels saw it. *A city on a hill cannot be hidden.*

Roadblocks, rubble, death, and destruction were remote and unreal from this high vantage point. There were the landmarks: the King

David Hotel opposite the YMCA buildings. Mount Zion and the Church of the Dormition. Zion Gate. The Mosque of Omar. The Hurva Synagogue.

Houses in the New City settlement of Mea Shearim gleamed in the afternoon sunlight. Jacob strained to see the structure of Mandelbaum House where he and the others first fought the Legion's armored cars. There was the broken hulk of an Arab vehicle, small and toylike, insignificant now where it rested.

His gaze fell on the battered structure of Notre Dame. Next to it the ruined Convent of Souers Reparatrices spilled across Suleiman Road, halting Arab encroachment into the New City center.

He studied the ramparts of Suleiman's Wall. Jacob knew it was thirty-eight feet high, forming an irregular quadrangle some two-and-a-half miles in circumference. There were thirty-four towers and eight gates, all currently under control of the Muslim forces. Within that powerful ring was a city compressed into a paltry 210 acres.

In peaceful days the main streets, lanes, and byways saw an endless parade of tourists, sheep flocks, and camel caravans headed for the bazaars. Old Jerusalem was churches, mosques, synagogues, convents, belfry towers, and soaring minarets. It was a teeming contrast of dark hovels and wide sunny courts; English tea and sorbet; tourists, pilgrims, Jewish rabbis, and Bedouin drovers. Medieval ruin rubbed shoulders with modern wretchedness.

The wall encircled the holiest sites of three faiths. All that was sacred to Muslim, Jew, and Christian was crammed together in an area taking up less earth than a farmer's cornfield.

Perhaps, Jacob reasoned, the nations of the world somehow believed the wall encompassed God himself, holding up the Almighty's trousers like a belt. Whoever possessed the ramparts controlled how God was perceived and worshipped. Hebrew. Roman. Saracen. Crusader. Muslim. Turk.

How many millions had perished over the centuries in this endless battle to cram the infinite, omniscient, omnipresent God into a finite space bordered by mankind's politics and intellect?

Such philosophy had extinguished the light of Judaism in all of Europe.

And now? Of the sacred 210 acres, a mere scrap remained the last toehold of the Jews. In this religious football match, the God of Ishmael was going to outscore the God of Isaac and Jacob.

Lori! Trapped in the Jewish Quarter!

Smoke from captured Jewish positions rose like the tendrils of a vine from the Old City.

"Really something, huh?" David Meyer remarked as they glided over every hostile line and barricade with the ease of a bird.

"My wife is there." Jacob pointed toward the Hurva. "A medic in the Jewish Quarter."

At this the pilot lifted his chin in acknowledgment, banked in a steady spiral until they floated high to pass directly above the enormous synagogue. "It's okay. We're well out of range of small arms."

Jacob craned his neck to see. On the roof of the Hurva, the ant-like figures of men nested in a circle of sandbags. The defenders turned their faces skyward toward the plane. There was a flurry of color, blue and white. Someone held up an Israeli flag, its corners stretched and held taut by four defenders. It sent a message. *We are still here. Holding on. When will help come?*

Did the sight of the Jewish-marked plane give them false hope?

What if they could witness what Jacob saw? Beyond the constricted borders of the final Jewish stronghold, Arab soldiers flowed through the choked tributaries. Jacob knew the end must be near for the Jewish defenders of the Old City.

What would happen to Lori?

Would the Palmach manage to break through once again and drive off the attackers?

Jacob was helpless, floating above Lori like a silent spirit. Unable to warn her. Unable to save her from what must surely follow.

He put his hand to his head in despair. He muttered, "So the angels see Jerusalem and weep." And then it came to him that maybe he would never see her again. Had he brought her here, only to lose her? She had not wanted to come. Had his decision to fight for Israel killed her? *Oh God! Lori! I'm sorry. There's nothing I can do.*

Tin Man frowned and turned the nose of the aircraft toward the sun. He cleared his throat awkwardly. And then, too cheerfully, he tried to comfort Jacob. "But look. This is what the boss wanted you to see. The pass of Bab el Wad. See? Open the road from Tel Aviv to relieve Jerusalem, and that'll put a stop to it. Down there. Have a look. The boss specifically said you should memorize it. I hear you're coming back to Jerusalem through that pass, and bringing supplies with you."

■ ■ ■ ■

The Piper swooped off toward the west. Circling over Jerusalem it was already high enough for Jacob to see the sparkling blue waters of the Mediterranean, some thirty miles away.

"It's so close," Jacob murmured.

"Huh? Oh, the sea?" David queried. "Yeah. Twenty minutes even in a toy plane like this with a rubber band for a motor. Five minutes in a real one. An hour or hour and a half by car, if the bad guys would step aside."

Jacob pushed open the top glass panel of the sandstorm-etched window. Extending his arm, he studied his outstretched fingers. "From here my hand covers the entire highway," he noted. "If only it were that easy to move supplies and ammunition . . . lift them over the pass and set them down in Jerusalem. Why not? Can't you move supplies by air?"

David lifted his shoulders in a shrug as an updraft of super-heated air lifted the delicate craft a hundred feet higher in a single vault.

When David recovered control of the gyrating Piper and Jacob recovered control of his stomach, David explained, "Someday maybe, but not now. Jerusalem needs hundreds of tons of supplies a day. A single crate of ammunition weighs fifty, sixty pounds. Carrying the two of us, the Piper is about maxed-out except for a couple of sacks of mail. With me this rig can tote maybe two hundred pounds of cargo. You do the math."

Squinting downward, Jacob repeated, "You say I am coming back through the pass with supplies. Can you take me lower? I have only seen the road once, by night. I have to know what I am facing."

Descending as lightly as a falling feather, the Piper flitted along the outline of the gorge that was Bab el Wad.

Arabs hold both sides of the canyon," David noted. "They can shoot right down on the road . . . chuck grenades without exposing themselves to return fire. And take a look at that."

Jacob found his attention forcibly diverted by an abrupt dive and bank to the right that lined up the nose of the plane with a hairpin turn in the road. It appeared that a landslide had fallen across it. "The Arabs have blocked the road," he said grimly. A stretch of the two-lane highway was buried under rubble.

"Yeah, and that means they expect to be attacked," David observed.

"So how many are 'they'?"

"Knew you'd ask. Harness cinched up? Here we go."

Diving to build up speed, David aimed the Piper into the gorge.

At the instant it seemed they would crash into the limestone escarpment, David hauled back on the control stick and the Piper bounded upward, skimming the crest by what felt to Jacob like mere inches.

On the plateau beyond the knife-like ridgeline was an Arab village. "Deir Ayub," David said, naming the place. "You count. I better drive."

In a dirt square surrounded by flat-roofed, one-story houses, Jacob saw a half-dozen trucks. There were at least a hundred men. A few of them waved. Others merely pointed or stared, but several more snatched up rifles and sighted toward the aircraft.

The side-to-side jinks into which David threw the Piper made it difficult for Jacob to concentrate, but he noted at least ten more vehicles parked on dirt tracks. As the plane darted across a copse of trees, Jacob glimpsed movement within the thicket and the flash of sunlight on metal.

Then Deir Ayub was behind them and they were over the narrowing point of the headland. The land beyond the terminus fell off sharply on three sides.

A larger village loomed up. To the north of it Jacob saw the bulky forms of two substantial buildings shimmering in the haze.

There appeared to be three times as many Arabs and five times as many trucks as at Deir Ayub, and those were merely the ones easily spotted. Jacob also noticed armored cars and mortars before another precipitate bank and sideslip shut out the view.

"That's Latrun," David said. "Looks like they're expecting us."

There were no friendly waves or curious stares now. A concerted chorus of rifle and machine-gun fire erupted from all points.

"Hold on," David warned, but Jacob had anticipated the stomach-churning drop this time and was prepared for it.

As if by magic, a row of penny-sized holes appeared in the fabric of the starboard wing. The line stopped less than an arm's length from Jacob's window.

Men on the roofs of the pair of fortress-like structures tracked the dancing Piper with heavy weapons. Gunfire blazed, and a cloud of dust and smoke eddied up to curl over the parapets like a brown and blue ocean wave.

"Time to go," David remarked tersely.

The Piper dropped suddenly one more time as it plunged over the edge of the precipice. Then the shooting was behind them, and they soared off across the Valley of Ayalon toward Tel Aviv.

"You got your work cut out for you," David said.

Jacob agreed, then said, "I'd rather be on the ground than do what you do. Up here there's nothing to hide behind."

Scoffing good-naturedly, David said, "This pleasure cruise? Nothing to it."

"Oh?" Jacob returned, motioning at the floor by the rudder pedals. Through a bullet hole between David's feet the ground could be seen rushing by. Then Jacob pivoted his finger to point upward at a matching exit perforation that existed over David's head.

CHAPTER 7

It was the waste of it that bothered Lori more than anything.

There was Alfie, with Abe on his knee.

Alfie, crumbling up his matzo and, for the pleasure of the child, throwing it out onto the ground beyond the sandbags. Very near the roses.

Daniel chided him. "Are you crazy? Why aren't you eating?"

Alfie did not look at Daniel but placed crumbs in Abe's hand and said, "Throw it far. Like this." He flicked the boy's arm and fragments scattered.

Lori said, "Alfie, that's all you have to eat, and you've not taken a bite."

Birds on the eaves skipped down to the wall and watched with interest.

"I'm not hungry," Alfie said, tossing another bit into the wind.

Three birds fluttered like dry leaves among the rosebushes and began to peck.

Abe laughed and clapped his hands, oblivious as machine guns tatted in the distance.

"Do it again," the boy urged Alfie.

"Sure." Alfie repeated the gesture. Anther bird, a pigeon, joined the sparrows.

Daniel cried his protest. "Listen, you *dummkopf!* I'll eat it if you don't want it! Give it to me!"

"Alfie, really," Lori instructed. "He's right."

Alfie ignored their prating. "I'm training them to come," Alfie said softly. "Do it like this. Throw more close each time. See, Abe? Soon they will hop right to you. Sit in your hand."

Daniel snorted in derision. "Sure."

Alfie reached over the sandbags and placed his hand near the birds. Cocking their heads in curiosity, they hopped even closer.

A huge twenty-five-pound shell shrieked overhead on its way to the New City.

Alfie was smiling that *dummkopf* smile of his. There was no reason the birds should not come closer.

A tympany boom sounded from somewhere in the west.

"Shhhhh," Alfie warned Abe.

A brave sparrow twittered up, hesitated, then hopped onto Alfie's fingers.

Abe cooed at the wonder of Alfie's magic.

Lori thought that if Alfie stayed there long enough, an angel would fly down and gobble up this stale, pathetic meal from his palm and call it blessed. "Cast your bread upon the waters," she murmured.

"Just what do you hope to accomplish," Daniel demanded, "throwing good food away?"

"They like it," Alfie said.

"I like it too," Abe agreed.

"I am training them, see?" A fat, assertive pigeon trounced, then scattered the sparrows. They retreated to pout and watch jealously as it feasted.

"Training them for what?" Daniel spat.

"To come," Alfie explained. "Later they'll give back the bread."

"Like hell," Daniel snapped.

"They'll go away, make Abe a pudding, or maybe a stew. Then they'll come back."

Abe patted his stomach and licked his lips.

At this Daniel gave a bitter laugh. He rolled his eyes.

The clatter of returning fire came from the rooftop opposite. The birds fled in terror.

The game was over.

■ ■ ■ ■

On Sunday night Egyptian radio boasted of the fall of Yad Mordechai and other Jewish settlements on the coast between Palestine and Egypt. The kibbutz, near Gaza, had been captured by the Egyptian army.

What Radio Cairo did not mention was that it had taken the Egyptians five days to reduce the Jewish stronghold. Five days in which Jewish defenses north of the beleaguered settlements were strengthened . . . five days the Haganah used to fortify the approaches to Tel Aviv.

While perhaps but a footnote in the history of war and battles, the defense of Yad Mordechai was significant. It helped enable Israel to enjoy one more day of existence by keeping the Egyptians from joining forces with the Arab Legion and dividing Israel between them.

How desperate was Israel's situation when it celebrated a delayed loss as a kind of victory?

Another night raid by Egyptian bombers over Jaffa and Tel Aviv left fuel tanks ablaze on the docks, illuminating the Jewish state's vulnerability from the air.

The water in the harbor reflected the flames as if even the sea were burning.

So, Jacob thought when he watched its eerie glow, *the Arab High Command will drive us into a lake of fire and finish what the Nazis began.*

Since Haganah High Command was determined to save the Messerschmitts for a massive, unexpected blow against the Egyptian planes on the ground, there was still no air defense of Tel Aviv. Egyptian Dakotas continued to bomb the power stations and the fuel tanks with impunity.

This fact enraged David Meyer, who, Jacob could tell, was not a patient man. "Four fighters with ammunition and cannon could put a stop to this."

But there were not four fighters . . . yet.

The road from the seacoast to Jerusalem would have to be won without the benefit of air cover. The old way, Ben-Gurion explained. The hard way. Any help Israeli soldiers could expect from the sky would have to come from heaven.

Ben-Gurion held up a Jerusalem Command dispatch that David Meyer had flown to Tel Aviv. "You see how desperate the situation is! We cannot turn a deaf ear to the pleas of Jerusalem!"

"Arab Legion from the north and east and Egyptians from the south," David reported to Ben-Gurion in the meeting that included Michael Stone. "The road is pinched in two at Latrun." David squeezed his fist shut to demonstrate.

Jacob involuntarily copied the motion with his injured arm, making the shoulder throb again.

Stone jabbed an ink pen at a map illuminated by a kerosene lamp. The chart lay spread out across an oak table marred by splinters and cigarette burns. "Show us," Stone commanded.

David traced a fortress-like ridge that overlooked the Tel Aviv to Jerusalem road. The promontory on which Latrun was located extended from the Judean hills like a bony finger pointed toward the Mediterranean. The terrain, overlooking the highway for a long stretch, fell off dramatically on either side of the crest.

To the north on the map block letters spelled out "Valley of Ayalon." Beyond Latrun lay the pass that zigzagged up to Jerusalem. Smaller print read "Bab el Wad."

"These two buildings," David said, pointing to black dots on the ridge at Latrun, "are where I saw the Arab Legion vehicles and where we took the automatic weapons fire."

Stone observed, "The police station and the monastery. Built like forts. From there the Legion can see any movement along the road or across the wheat fields for miles. Any attackers will have to fight their way uphill, in the open, without cover."

"So?" Ben-Gurion said with a shrug. "We attack at night." The prime minister waved his hand, and shadowy fingers danced on the walls.

Michael Stone coughed, then glared at David.

At the instant Jacob understood what Stone wanted. David Meyer was to assist him in talking the prime minister out of launching a frontal assault on Latrun. But without Latrun the road was impassable. Without the road the surrender of Jewish Jerusalem was inevitable.

Jacob considered what he would say if anyone asked him about fighting for the road. It came down to the life of one person trapped in Jerusalem. For Lori he would fight his way to hell and back.

"Any approach from the west is suicide," David said. "Closest point unseen would be two miles off. That's a long walk in the dark. I also bet they have artillery hidden in these trees." David gestured again toward the topographic map, at the contours of a hill shown to the east of Latrun. "The road itself is not simply barricaded. The Arabs piled boulders on it. There's a stretch maybe fifty yards long strewn with boulders. Like a rock quarry. You'd need a tank to get across it. It'll take a bulldozer to clear it. Even if nobody was shooting at you the road is really messed up here."

Silence.

Not one tank was available to the Israeli army.

Ben-Gurion spoke. "*Today* that is the most important road junction in Israel. It must be captured . . . *tomorrow.*"

Again palpable quiet enveloped the room. It was Ben-Gurion who ended it. "Young man," he said, addressing Jacob, "they tell me you held Notre Dame against cannonfire. Against armored vehicles. You accomplished this miracle with rifles and Molotov cocktails."

Jacob recounted the progress of the battle. He refused to take credit for himself, instead speaking of the heroism of Peter Wallich, Uri Tabken, Naomi Snow, and others.

Too many of them were dead. Too many more were wounded.

"The cannon was beating us to pieces. We were out of rockets for the bazooka. We were almost out of grenades. We could not have held out one more time."

"But you did hold out," Ben-Gurion insisted. "You stopped the Legion."

"We were lucky. They gave up."

"Luck like yours we need."

"Cannon, ammo, and trained men we need more," Stone corrected. "Let us try to outflank the Arab Legion at Latrun; surround them."

"No time for that. Jerusalem . . . Jerusalem is waiting for our help. Head on. That is the way we will take Latrun. Like a bulldozer, eh? A ship was docked today with rifles and ammunition for this operation," Ben-Gurion said. "And you, Jacob Kalner. You were in a D.P. camp. A British prison kept you out of Eretz-Israel."

"Interned in Cyprus," Jacob replied.

"How long?"

"Too long. I was waiting to fight, you know. A long time."

"You are the example of what can be done by new recruits, eh? Israel will be saved by fellows just off the boats. Like you. We will show the men how to fight and how to beat the Legion, yes?"

Jacob looked at David and Michael Stone. From David he saw sympathy, from Colonel Stone resignation. "I must get back to Jerusalem," Jacob answered truthfully.

Stone interjected, "At Notre Dame they were defending, not attacking," he said. "They had no choice but to hang on . . . or die."

"Or run away," Ben-Gurion corrected. "So we will offer the Legionnaires of Latrun such a choice and see if they do not choose running instead."

Hearing a weary sigh, Jacob watched Michael Stone make one last attempt at thwarting the inevitable. "Give me seventy-two hours to get an assault coordinated," he said. "Hit them from three sides at once."

Ben-Gurion dismissed the notion with a shake of his ponderous head. "Hit them from above and below, too, if you wish. Call down the ten plagues if you can manage. But I will agree to a delay of just twenty-four hours. By midnight Tuesday I want Latrun in our hands."

■ ■ ■ ■

In Amman, Jordan, the delegates of the Arab League were going all out to present a show of unity. There was much smiling and posing for group photos, but it was merely for public consumption.

King Abdullah went nowhere without bodyguards and not because he feared a Zionist attack either. He recognized that the real threat was from Egypt's Farouk. The hand that wielded the knife or the bomb might be Syrian or Iraqi or a henchman of the Grand Mufti (who was pointedly not invited to be present at the meeting), but the assassin's pay would certainly come from Egypt.

But this internal dissension did not keep the Arab League from presenting a unified front to the world when the matter of a Jewish state was raised.

The Security Council of the United Nations proposed a cease-fire in Palestine. It called for a cooling-off period of reexamination and reflection.

The Arab response was contained on a single typed sheet.

The Arab League categorically rejected the United Nations' demand for any truce with the illegal Zionist invaders.

Then the League responded with an ultimatum of its own: since the Security Council insisted on meddling in the affairs of Palestine, the United Nations was allowed forty-eight hours from midnight Monday in which to redesign a new Palestinian nation . . . omitting any reference to or future plan for a Jewish state.

Midnight plus two more days advanced the calendar to Wednesday, the twenty-sixth of May . . . the two-year anniversary of King Abdullah's coronation.

General Glubb's uniform chafed because of the dried sweat and fine grit that were the pervasive gifts of the Khamseen. The combination turned the inside of Glubb's collar to sandpaper. Running his finger around the neckband did nothing to ease the annoyance. At times like this he was sorry the Arab Legion had adopted British military fashion. How much cooler and more comfortable were flowing robes. How much more practical for this climate.

Glubb had been waiting an hour for his audience with King Abdullah. The king was closeted with Prime Minister Abou Hoda, reviewing the Arab League's ultimatum to the United Nations. Glubb fretted over the delay. It was a long drive back to the front lines.

There were troop dispositions to be made around Latrun. The British officers commanding Arab Legion armored columns and artillery batteries awaited his orders.

Positive the Jews would mount an attack to open the road to Jerusalem, Glubb wanted to be present in person to direct preparations.

If the Haganah committed to a major offensive in Bab el Wad, then its defeat would bring a swift end to the war. Jerusalem was as good as finished if it could not be resupplied. The concentration of Jewish forces at Latrun would weaken the Jews elsewhere, especially south of Jerusalem and on the coast south of Tel Aviv. The Egyptians would certainly break through in one or both places.

That would leave isolated settlements in the Negev and those in Galilee in the north to be mopped up; the campaign would be finished.

Glubb was disappointed that Abdullah was placing more importance on political jockeying than on strategy. Politicians should know that wars first had to be won before the spoils could be divided.

The door opened, and Abou Hoda beckoned Glubb to enter.

"Glubb Pasha," Abdullah said graciously, "I am truly sorry to have kept you waiting. The affairs of state are so pressing. Can you imagine what behind-the-scenes bargaining takes place before five Arab countries agree on one simple statement?"

Glubb ducked his head guiltily as if Abdullah had been reading his thoughts. Their meeting had not even begun, and Glubb already felt defensive. "Majesty," he said, trying to regain the initiative, "the campaign is going splendidly. We have gathered our forces above Bab el Wad. The armored units have been concentrated there. I have moved the entire Fourth Brigade and the reserve artillery from Ramallah to Latrun. Our batteries command the road and all approaches, and our armor has room to maneuver properly. Once the Jews commit themselves I have a surprise for them. We will blunt their advance and then counterattack. Once they are rolling backward, we will slash through *their* lines."

"And . . . what of Jerusalem, General?" Abdullah's words were gentle, but his eyes offered a challenge.

"Anticipating your wishes, I have transferred additional infantry to Jerusalem. The city is ready to collapse," Glubb replied without flinching under the king's direct gaze. "Our intelligence indicates the Jews are critically short on water, and almost as desperate for food and ammunition. Moreover their lines at Latrun are stretched thin and will break like twigs at our counterattack. Then the encirclement of Jerusalem will·

be complete, and the city must surrender." Glubb paused, then added defensively, "Further headlong assaults on the position at the Hospice of Notre Dame would waste our men and equipment to no purpose."

"To no purpose . . . except securing the Old City area so I may go and pray on the Haram. This I have sworn to do on Wednesday. I do not make vows lightly, John, nor is it my will that anyone prevent me from keeping them."

"It is Your Majesty's right to ask for my resignation," Glubb replied stiffly. "I will deliver a full report to whomsoever you chose to replace me."

"Peace, John, peace! How can the English have a reputation for self-control when they are so precipitate and headstrong?"

"Majesty?"

"Go to Latrun. Secure the road. Obviously we cannot allow Jerusalem to be resupplied. But also redouble the artillery fire directed at the New City. Perhaps there are Jews who would rather surrender than die. If they are both endlessly bombarded and hopelessly cut off, their hearts will falter."

"Exactly my belief, Majesty."

"Good. And redouble the ground attacks on the Old City Jewish Quarter. See that it surrenders by Wednesday. You may go, General."

■ ■ ■ ■

The hot breath of the Khamseen fell away. The gibbous moon glided like a billowed sail across the sky above Jerusalem.

Faint and fragmentary, the notes of Mozart's horn concerto drifted over the Old City walls.

Souls strained to hear the language that spoke to all hearts.

Had Daniel Caan finally fallen into exhausted sleep? Lori could not see his face.

Little Abe slept with his head on Lori's lap. She ran her fingers through his hair and inhaled the scent of roses. Resting her head against the wall, she closed her burning eyes and listened to the high distinct notes that carried above the strings. She let herself pretend it was summer evening in Queen Mary's Rose Garden at Regent's Park.

Elisa playing with the Chamber Orchestra. Wicker hamper packed with cheese and bread. Bransom pickle and a cold bottle of Gewürz-traminer. Mother beside Aunt Anna and baby Al on the blanket. Mother smiling as she carefully doles out the bounty of our picnic.

Lori smiled.

Her heart hummed with the memory of actors on the stage of the Open Air Theatre. Jessica. Lorenzo. *Merchant of Venice* in the final act.

How sweet the moonlight sleeps upon this bank! Here we will sit, and let the sounds of music creep in our ears. Soft stillness and the night become touches of sweet harmony. Look how the floor of heaven is thick inlaid with patens of bright gold . . .

Lori fixed her gaze on the brightest star in the sky. She remembered clearly how in awe she had been when a teacher quietly explained to her the meaning of this passage of Shakespeare's poetry.

You see, a paten was a golden dish used to serve Holy Communion. And so he was saying that God had filled the stars with His glory and set them in heaven to share with us the bread of eternal rejoicing!

The heavens declare the glory of God. A lovely image, isn't it?

For a time after that Lori had worshipped beneath star-filled skies and shared in the Eucharist of creation's praise.

But the day came when the glory, love, and beauty of the Creator turned distant and cold. She lost the sense of awe that was as natural as breathing for a childlike heart. Without the oxygen of praise, her hope had shriveled, hardened, and dried.

When was it she had begun to believe that she walked alone through life? That the world was a fearful place? That beauty and joy were illusions, accidents of nature, doomed in the end to be overcome by darkness? When her father was imprisoned by the Nazis? When she was separated from Jacob? Perhaps she had chosen hardness over love in order to survive. *Much easier not to believe. Much easier not to feel.*

Yet the music and the stars awakened longing again!

The hoarse voice of Daniel broke her reverie. "Kol Jerusalem," he remarked wistfully. "We used to listen to them on the wireless. In the mess hall. All of us . . . Now they are playing in the street. By moonlight. It must mean the transmitter is finally gone. No more lights. No more wireless concerts."

Lori sighed and looked toward the star-frosted sky. "I rather like the night without street lamps."

"It means, you know, we're at the end."

Lori cleared her throat wearily. "Listen." The horn reached joyful crescendo. She searched her memory for the passage she had chosen to memorize in her study of the English language when they came to London. She spoke aloud,

"*'Look how the floor of heaven is thick inlaid with patens of bright gold. There's not the smallest orb which thou beholdest but in its motion like an angel sings, still choiring to the young-eyed cherebins . . .'*"

"What does it mean?" Daniel asked.

"That God offers us a feast of beauty. That all things in heaven and earth sing praise to God. Man alone is deaf to it. . . ." She continued, "*'Such harmony is in immortal souls, but whilst this muddy vesture of decay doth grossly close us in, we cannot hear it.'*"

The two listened for a time without speaking. Then Daniel whispered, "I think maybe kids hear it, you know? I remember a time . . . I was little and . . ." He paused. "But now? I am never happy when I hear sweet music. Sometimes at the kibbutz, when the concert played, I would have to get up and leave. Leave everyone because I . . . I am buried with such longing when I hear it."

Lori nodded, understanding. The clear strains of Mozart, Bach, or Handel made her ache inside as though she would break.

She replied, "It means your spirit is attentive."

"My mother . . . we had a phonograph in the shop. The tourists would come, and she would play this one record. A woman singing like an angel. *'And he shall feed his flock . . . like a shepherd . . . and he shall gather the lambs with his arms.'*" He stirred, moving closer. "Do you know this? *'And carry them in his bosom . . . and gently lead.'*"

"Yes," Lori answered.

"I have not heard it since the morning we left the shop. Left home. Left . . . my mother and father, you know? And me and my baby sister . . . we left everyone and finally came here."

Such pain in the memory! Lori pictured this bitter young man as a small boy saying good-bye forever to his family. Had they perhaps shared the same ship to England?

"It is hard," she said. "I was on a ship, too."

"You?"

"Yes."

He thought about this revelation. "I did not like you much . . . I mean, I was a pain in the hospital."

"You were in pain." Her comment forgave him for hating her.

"Thank you for . . . helping." Then, awkwardly, "I have not heard such music since the day I said good-bye."

"Handel. *The Messiah.*"

"Messiah." He tried the word on. "Yes. Well then. It would be. Sometimes when we were very alone at night, even with so many other children around, Suzannah would cry for Mama. And I would sing this to her. *'And he shall feed his flock . . .'*" He sang words as though he heard them every day. "I thought it was a lullaby, and I would sing until she went to sleep. Then when I could not sleep I would think about it myself. Remember. I would hope for this shepherd to feed the longing of my heart."

"*'Such harmony is in immortal souls,'*" she mused, repeating Shakespeare's poetry. And then, "I feel it too when I hear the music. Longing to know God, I think. To be loved by Him maybe? To be sure even when everything is so . . . so . . ."

"Yes," he agreed. "Yes."

"Maybe that's what creation sings about . . . praises we can't hear? I don't know. I wish I could hear the words behind the melodies of worlds and stars and . . ."

Daniel picked up the thought eagerly. "Crickets. Birds. The rush of water in a stream."

"Rain."

"Colors!"

"Yes. There must be melody in a rainbow."

"Wind in the wheat fields . . ."

MONDAY

May 24, 1948

"I will lead the blind by the ways they have not known,
along unfamiliar paths I will guide them. I will turn the
darkness into light before them and make the rough places smooth.
These are the things I will do; I will not forsake them."

Isaiah 42:16

"This is what the Lord says—
Israel's King and Redeemer, the Lord Almighty: I am the first and I am
the last; apart from me there is no God . . .
Do not tremble, do not be afraid. Did I not proclaim this and foretell it
long ago?"

Isaiah 43:6a and 8a

CHAPTER 8

David Meyer closed his eyes and lifted his face to the moon early Monday morning as the jeep sped along broad Tel Aviv Boulevard toward the hotel.

Clutching an unlit stub of a cigar in his teeth as he drove, Bobby Milkin cautioned, "Colonel Stone is nuthin' compared to what's comin'. You know that, don't you, Tin Man? You ready for it? I told you not to get hitched. A fighter pilot's got no business gettin' hitched, I said. A worried wife is an angry wife."

"Who says?" David scowled.

"My mama. Somethin' like that anyway. A worried mother is an angry mother, she said. But you know, a guy's got no choice. Everybody's got to have a mother. But with a wife you got a choice."

"She'll be glad to see me." David shifted uneasily in the seat. He had not thought about his reunion with Ellie until the mechanics at the airfield said she had called a million times to ask if there had been any word.

"'Course she'll be glad to see you. Then she's gonna kill you."

"She's a sport."

"Yeah, sure. She *was* a sport. Used to be one, you know. You crashland in Galilee and survive, she's a sport. You get captured by the Arabs and escape, she's a sport. You make it back to the airfield, she's a sport. But then! You get back here A-OK, and three seconds later you're in a fighter? Goin' after the Gyppos? Get your tail shot up? I'm not talkin' about how stupid it was tactical wise, you know? I'm your friend, Tin Man. It worked out, didn't it? Egyptians bomb the British. The Brits shoot down Egyptians. Everybody's mad in Cairo and London. I say, well done Tin Man! But you know, I'm talkin' about somethin' else here. And I'm warnin' you here. You didn't even call her, see? You go flyin' off like that. Twice! And all this before you so much as give her a jingle to say, 'Hi honey, I'm home'? Naw. Tin Man. Nawww. Ellie's gonna kill you herself."

David considered Milkin's warning. "Huh. Yeah. Probably."

"So. Yeah."

"So?"

"You gotta have a strategy, like."

"Like what?"

"Make her feel sorry for you . . . Limp."

"I am limping."

"Good. That's good. And don't take a shower until she sees you like this. Man, you stink. Make it look like you been in a real . . . a real . . . thing . . . you know . . ."

"A war."

"That's it. Like you was almost killed or somethin'. I mean, if you take a shower, and she comes in and you're there shaved and smilin' and in your clean aloha shirt . . . well, she'll kill you. And why not? Whereas . . . just let her get one whiff of you like this. Pitiful. Pit-i-ful. You'll have her eatin' outta your hand."

David glanced down at his hands. They were sore from the thorns of the orange grove where he had hid from the Arab massacre of the passengers. "She has a right to worry, I guess."

"I'll say. As for me, every dame I meet I tell her I might be dead to-morrow. You know the line . . . 'Gee, honey, if only I had met you sooner. But we got tonight, don't we?' That's what I'm sayin'. Real love is . . . it's a scary thing . . . to love somebody who might . . . you know? I knew this dame in Croydon married an RAF pilot in '43. Dreamed her husband burned to death, trapped in the cockpit. Dreamed it every night. Saw him burn, you know. Just heard him screamin'. And then it happened the way she dreamed it. She went nuts, just nuts. Slept with every guy on the base. Called everybody by this dead guy's name. Nuts. Better off single. But as for my mama? She thinks I'm flyin' freight in Panama, you know?"

"I should've called," David muttered as Milkin brought the jeep to a halt in front of the glistening edifice of the Park Hotel.

"You better tell her from here on you're haulin' freight."

"Sure. Thanks." David glanced apprehensively at the open doors of the lobby. The interior of the Park was swarming with news correspondents.

"Courage." Milkin slapped him on the back and sent him, limping, into the thick of it.

To David's surprise, the hotel clerk informed him that Ellie had not returned from Jaffa. She sent word to say she was following the story of the refugees and did not know when she would get in.

David fell asleep between relief and concern . . . and all the time he had pictured her worrying about him!

■ ■ ■ ■

Ellie's thoughts were filled with David. Somewhere in the twilight between sleep and wakefulness, she pictured him as he had been when she first fell in love with him. A wounded fighter pilot, he had come home to Southern California to recover. She remembered the first time they made love as the waves rolled onto the beach.

How desperate and self-centered they had been in those months together. She had not spent one unselfish hour of her life before she came to Palestine. She had never imagined suffering or known true courage until she met the Jews who had survived the war and come to Zion.

Even now her thoughts longed for life without conflict or pain. What would things have been like if David had not returned to fight in this crazy war?

Kids and a little house with a yard. David flying cargo planes from Burbank to Sacramento!

It was a sweet dream.

And what dreams did the people gathered in this hall have for themselves and their children?

She considered Leon, who had nothing left of his life but a mandolin. How had he lost his wife and children?

And then there was the Russian family: Sholem and Katerine, who huddled together beside the fountain. How had they managed to save four sons? Would they survive the desperate struggle ahead?

What about Jerome Jardin, who had never been loved by anyone but an old woman who loved everyone equally?

Perhaps the longing of every heart was the same. Perhaps they, too, desired merely a day, a week, a month, in which each second was like the last. No heartache. No good-byes. No adventure. No surprises. Ordinary life. This was the blessing each longed for.

But an existence of peaceful obscurity was a remote possibility. Especially with the thunder of artillery booming in the distance.

Where was David now, Ellie wondered: Probably back at the hotel in Tel Aviv. Would he find the note she left for him on the bed table?

Would he be upset she was not there to be with him after his ordeal? Would he be in Israel when she finished her assignment? Or would they send him back to Czechoslovakia to pick up anther load of disassembled fighter planes? And by the time the armament and men reached Israel, would there be a Jewish homeland left to fight for?

She shifted uncomfortably against an archway in the Armenian Convent. A jagged-edged stone pressed into her spine. Each time she fell asleep she slipped sideways. Moving that fraction of an inch jabbed her awake. She was, she supposed, fortunate to have anything to rest against in the packed hall. Most of the immigrants were propped on each other, bumping and elbowing their way through a night's rest. Through bleary eyes she noted that none of them had the least difficulty sleeping. Probably all were grateful to be off the steamer and on solid ground.

Despite persistent scuttlebutt about how and when the refugees would be transported to more suitable lodgings, no buses had arrived before nightfall. Since it was Ellie's intention to photograph the entire journey from arrival to settlement, she stayed with the group, sharing their supper and sleeping arrangements.

The meal had been a strange contrast of scarcity and abundance. Sandwiches . . . grape jelly for those who kept kosher and bologna for those who did not . . . were made of rock-hard matzo. Jerome quipped it must have traveled forty years with Moses in the wilderness. A handful of raisins and half a chocolate bar completed each sack lunch. But added to this unimpressive diet were oranges and limes, bushels of them; take as many as you want. It was the first fresh citrus many of the younger migrants had tasted, ever.

Some of the children would be sick tomorrow, Ellie knew.

With food had come drowsiness and a suspension of anxiety about what the future held. There were no answers, but everyone seemed content to leave off fretting for a time.

It was nearly 3:30 A.M. Ellie opened her eyes as Rose Smith slid down to sit beside her. This was the first time she had seen the old woman stop to rest. Did Madame Rose ever sleep?

She whispered to Ellie, "Jerome said you wanted to talk to me. You have been patient with all this. We'll have to talk in fits and starts, I fear. Ask the most important questions first, my dear. That way if we cannot get back to it . . ."

"Why are you here? Why are they here?"

Thoughtful in her response, Madame Rose replied, "They are here because God is calling them home, and there is nowhere else for them to go."

"And you?"

"I am here because I also hear God's calling when I look into their faces." Her wide mouth turned down as she chose her words carefully. "Jesus said, 'If anyone offers a cup of cold water to one of my children he has given it to me.'" The old lady smiled gently. "The Messiah is here. Look around you. He is here among them. I gave him lemonade and a bit of matzo."

"Why here? Why these people, when there are so many in need?"

"The children of Israel are the heart of God. The apple of his eye. They ask simply for a cup of water. Not a sermon about hellfire and damnation. They have been to hell, you see. They know about suffering. No. That is not the way. They don't need a Scripture lesson in morality or the evils of Darwin. No. A cup of water. A bit of bread. Someone to listen to what they are going through. Someone who loves them. Love is an action verb. It means saving by serving. That is the heart of the gospel. Only the spirit of God's love can change a life. Jesus said all the rest is simply for show. Religion without active love has no more life than a mannequin in a shop window."

The conversation came to a sudden end. There was a disturbance at the door. A trio of men appeared, wearing military drab. The third, younger than the other two, rubbed his face and yawned. He looked as if he was much in need of sleep himself.

Ellie chafed her own eyes and peered at her wristwatch. The only illumination in the hall were a half-dozen candles smoking fitfully in wall sconces. By the dim glow of the one over her head Ellie made out the time: 4:00 A.M.

Surely the transport could not be here now?

Madame Rose stood and strode to confront the men. In a commanding whisper that carried over the dome and down to Ellie's ears, Madame Rose wanted to know their business.

"Recruits must report at once," the one wearing the thick glasses snapped. "No time to argue. Men, ages seventeen to fifty."

Ellie watched Madame Rose's back straighten. The large woman appeared to gain another four inches in height. "Absolutely not," Ellie heard her say. "These people have just arrived. They need rest. You will not interrupt their first night's sleep in Israel."

Despite the conversation being carried out in hushed tones, here and there around the hall refugees stretched and sat up.

The second of the two older military men spoke with an American accent, making Ellie regard him with interest. She recognized him as the man in the jeep who had watched the arrival of the refugees.

"My name is Michael Stone," he said. "This is Commander Menachem of the Irgun. And you are Rose Smith. We met in London during the war." Madame Rose acknowledged the earlier encounter. "It is critical," Stone said, "or we would not be here. The prime minister himself gave the order."

So this was the famous American colonel Stone who had been a New York city judge and a politico with a promising future. Now, it was said, he was prepared to buck even the U.S. government in his support of Israel.

Others in the room awakened.

The males scowled, and the women darted anxious looks at each other. All the suspended apprehension came flooding back. What would happen next?

Madame Rose blustered, but Menachem had had enough. "Attention," he shouted loudly, clapping his hands. "Able-bodied men must accompany us now." No one moved. *"Now!"* he said again, forcefully.

Stone stepped forward. "Welcome to Israel," he said, translating the phrase into three different languages before resuming in English. "I am sorry we could not greet you with a brass band and speeches, but we are dealing with troublesome neighbors."

A nervous chuckle ran through the crowd.

"This young man," Stone said, grasping the third member of the trio and drawing him, unwillingly, Ellie thought, to the fore, "is Lieutenant Jacob Kalner. He has come from the fight for Jerusalem. He can tell you how desperate that struggle is."

"It is true," Jacob noted. "We stopped the Arab advance . . . barely. Jerusalem remains surrounded and cut off. The Old City may fall at any moment," he said, then hesitated. "My wife and I came to Israel ten days ago, from camps, like you, on a ship, like yours. She is in the Old City. She and my best friend . . . many others . . . are trapped there, waiting for the breakthrough that will lift the siege."

"Jerusalem . . . the Holy City . . . needs you," Stone summarized. "Prime Minister Ben-Gurion asks, 'Who will go and fight to save the Holy City?'"

"I will go," offered Leon Pickman, standing up and straightening the strap of the mandolin where it hung across his back. "What is the point of coming all this way if there is not an Israel?"

"And I," said Sholem, the Russian Jew. "I fight for Jerusalem." His sturdy, seventeen-year-old son, Ivan, already stood beside him, nodding.

"And I," piped the next younger son, a boy of perhaps fifteen.

Katerine, his mother, grabbed his sleeve and said something to him, but the boy defiantly yanked his arm away from her.

Sholem studied the boy, then Katerine's pleading eyes. He pushed him back down. "You must care for the family," he said.

Around the hall men stood and repeated, "I will go. I will fight for Jerusalem," as though taking an oath of allegiance.

A fellow missing his right arm stood, his remaining limb awkwardly encircling the neck of a thin-bearded young man. The twenty-year-old returned the hug, then stepped toward the door.

"You tell this Ben-Gurion to be mindful of my son," the one-armed man called. "Lain is the last. My last of six. You tell him this for me!"

Jerome Jardin approached Madame Rose. Ellie heard him say, "My mother . . . I was not old enough to fight the fascists in the last war. But this time I am old enough."

Madame Rose stiffened. Did serving God mean also fighting for Israel? Offering the child she had saved and raised to manhood?

The old woman searched Jerome's face for a long moment, then nodded. She said nothing but opened wide her powerful arms to embrace him.

Jerome laid his head against her shoulder. "You know I must, 'Mere."

Rose still did not speak but kissed Jerome on his cheeks and, with other women in the crowd, watched him to into the darkness.

The flash of Ellie's camera popped as she recorded tearful farewells.

Michael Stone spotted her and came to her. "It's best you not get my ugly mug in any of these shots. I'm an observer. Not really here. Unofficial."

"So is my husband," she replied, not looking at him. "None of us Americans is really here, are we?"

"You're David Meyer's wife, aren't you?"

She snapped one last shot of Leon with his mandolin as he ducked into a troop lorry. "David Meyer?" She pretended not to know the name.

"He's on the ground. Safe."

"I know." She asked, "What about them? Where are they going?"

Stone did not answer the question. "Nothing more will happen tonight. David is back at your hotel. I can give you a lift to Tel Aviv, if you like."

■ ■ ■ ■

Yehudit slept with her head against Rachel's shoulder. The two women huddled on the bottom step of the sub-basement room. They had passed the night waiting and praying for the return of Dov and Moshe. Rachel pressed her cheek against the cool stone of the cellar wall. Above them, in the dimness of early morning, all was still.

Grandfather, his back to them, waited before the open hole that led to the tunnel. It was as if the old man sat Shiva for the dead, Rachel thought. Throughout this longest night she thought she heard him whispering the prayers of the Amidah and then the reading from Lamentations.

"This is the hour of *avaylut*. The mourning time between the death of the beloved and the funeral. . . ."

When she opened her eyes to look, the old man was unmoving and silent. Perhaps she heard his heart? Did he mourn for Moshe or for what had come upon Jerusalem?

Or was it another voice she heard? A memory from her childhood that spoke to her own longing for the safe return of the man whose love had made her whole again?

And what if he was not coming back?

Rachel closed her eyes and tried to sleep. Tried to shut her hope away until the instant she saw his face again.

How long would that be?

A lifetime?

Yehudit stirred and raised up. She stared, bewildered, at the pinpoint of light from the candle.

"Dov isn't coming back," Yehudit said in amazement after a long time, the way one speaks when the report of a death has been newly received. Then, "I am going to the hospital. To do what I can." She rose stiffly and placed her hand on Rachel's shoulder before ascending the steps.

Rachel remained rooted, sick with the certainty that Yehudit somehow knew the awful truth.

She stared at Grandfather's back. Was he awake?

He inhaled fully, then cleared his throat.

"What time is it, Grandfather?"

"The candle is nearly out."

"Dawn?"

"Another hour."

"I thought . . . if they . . . Moshe . . . could escape, they would come in the night. Darkness to cover them."

The old man nodded, affirming he had imagined the same thing. "So, maybe there is a reason."

She studied her dirt-caked hands. No water to spare for washing. How much longer could they expect to hold out here in the Hurva? So little water. Hardly any food. House by house the Muslims advanced. She knew Moshe would be here to fight for the last square meter of soil if he could. Rachel glanced at the detonator box. How much longer could they wait until the tunnel was sealed?

"How long?" she asked.

The rabbi did not reply. "I will need another candle," he told her, never looking away from the hole. Then he said kindly, "While it remains dark, take rations to Lori Kalner and Abe Kurtzman. Be strong, eh? Have courage."

"But I am afraid . . . afraid all of us are at the end . . ."

"It is important for the others . . . even if you are afraid . . . that they think you are not afraid. This is what courage is, *nu?* Going on even when you think you can't."

"How long can we keep hoping?"

"Even when everything looks hopeless and at the end. Even when the heart is broken. This is also what we call faith."

Her voice cracked. "I fear the worst."

"The worst thing is never the last thing. This is what we believe. Why we keep living. And you . . . Rachel . . . your mama and papa and . . . Moshe would expect this of you. Yes?"

CHAPTER 9

Moshe jerked awake.

How long had he been asleep? How could he have let himself drift off? And what had awakened him?

Solid blackness surrounded him. Moshe's back tensed with the effort of straining to listen for footsteps. His fingers touched the butt of his revolver, lying on the floor nearby.

There was nothing. The silence, like the darkness, was total.

It had been day when they entered. Now there was no gleam from where Moshe remembered the stairs to be.

Moshe's legs were numb below where Dov lay across them.

"Dov?" Moshe whispered hopefully. "Are you awake?"

There was no reply, apart from Dov's uneven, hoarse breathing.

The explosion that successfully destroyed the Arab Legion cannon . . . how many hours ago? . . . had been followed an instant later by a second, larger blast.

Escaping amid a throng of panicked Jihad Moquades, Dov was struck on the head and felled by a chunk of stone.

He had not been awake since.

At first it was all Moshe could do to get his friend clear of the stampede and the rampage of enraged Muslim militants that followed.

Then, while crouching directly opposite, cradling the injured Dov, he'd seen it: a doorway, a roll-down steel shutter with an imperfect seal at the bottom.

Crawl through! Drag Dov in after!

It was a candlemaker's domain, long since emptied of its stock and its proprietor. Bare shelves retained the aroma of wax. A basement workshop, likewise abandoned except for tin molds and a ball of twine for wicks.

Staying out of the grasp of the Jihad Moquades had been the first priority. *Wait for nightfall; then sneak back into the Jewish Quarter.* That had been the plan.

But Dov had not regained his senses. Instead his breathing became more shallow, more ragged. Carry him? Drag him upstairs and carry him through the alleys of Jerusalem? Half a mile and more?

Moshe was afraid to move him.

And how long had it already been? Ehud, good friend that he was, understood the danger to the Jewish district if the tunnel entrance remained unblocked. He might have already destroyed it.

■ ■ ■ ■

Tel Aviv was awash in the muted blue light of pre-dawn. Waves lapped the sandy beach that stretched out beneath the balcony of the Park Hotel. For the moment, the war was remote, a bad dream from which Ellie had awakened.

Ellie rested her back against David's chest as the two soaked together in the cool water of the deep bathtub. The air had softened, but this was the only real refuge from the heat.

Ellie thought about the refugees, packed together in the sweltering atmosphere of the Armenian Convent. She remembered besieged Jerusalem. She remembered what Madame Rose had said about a cup of water. Right now water was the most valuable commodity in Jerusalem. More precious than bullets. How could the Jewish population of Jerusalem hold out if they were dying of thirst?

And here they were, the two of them, luxuriating in forty gallons. She did the calculation.

"Enough for water for 160 people in Jerusalem. For an entire day."

David sighed and said in a drowsy voice, "Don't do guilt, Ellie." He kissed the back of her neck and slid his arms around her. "This is the first time in days I've felt good, you know?"

The curtains stirred, announcing the Khamseen was awakening. Daybreak would once again bring unbearable heat. She cupped the soothing liquid in her hands and drizzled it over her shoulders.

David kissed her again, then asked, "Where did you go?"

"I was thinking about . . ."

He stroked her back. "Don't think. It doesn't change anything."

"How do you know what I was thinking?"

"You were thinking about water. Feeling guilty about this. About how they are dying of thirst in Jerusalem and here we are soaking."

"I wasn't."

"Then what?"

"I was thinking about how long it's been since I ironed. We're all so . . . rumpled," she countered.

"You were thinking how messed up everything is. About this wind sucking everything dry." He kissed the nape of her neck.

"How do you know?"

"Because that's what I was thinking."

"If that's what you're thinking, then I'm a failure." She clasped his fingers and guided his hand to her breast.

"I mean, off and on, I think about . . . you know . . . how. . . ."

"Let me guess." She closed her eyes and sighed as he caressed her. "You were thinking you'd like to stay in bed with me for a couple weeks?"

"Good. That's good. And . . . the tub. A month."

"Call room service once a day?"

"Maybe . . . if we don't have to get up to eat."

■ ■ ■ ■

Hours of staring into unrelieved blankness played tricks with a man's vision, Moshe knew.

When the first dingy gleam of light crept around the doorframe at the top of the stairs, Moshe did not trust it.

Dov stirred, groaning. "Water. Is there water? Moshe?"

"Yes, Moshe . . . no, no water. But Dov! I thought you . . . I'm glad to hear you speak."

"Grenades are blowing up in my brain. What happened?"

Moshe explained about the aftermath of the cannon's destruction and the blow to Dov's head.

"How long ago? It's night now?"

Shooting a glance toward the stairs, Moshe saw that two sides and the bottom of the door were fully outlined with bluish light. He could even make out the wobbly railing of the cellar steps.

"Can you open your eyes, Dov?"

A note of fear entered Dov's voice. "They're open!" His hands clasped Moshe's arm with surprising strength. "They *are* open! Moshe? I cannot see!" Dov's body jerked, and Moshe had to hold him down.

"Easy! It will pass!"

Dov said earnestly, "Leave me! Get back to the Quarter. Tell Yehudit . . . I love her."

"We'll go back together," Moshe argued. "We're safe for now. We'll figure something out." Easing Dov's shoulders off his legs, Moshe waited for circulation to get restored before standing. "But we need water, eh? Something to eat. If I can find anything. You lie still."

A search of the candlemaker's shop turned up nothing apart from the stub of a candle that had rolled under a workbench. Reporting this to Dov, Moshe added, "It's early. A quick trip and I can bring water, at least."

Though Moshe was prepared or renewed panic from Dov, the man kept control of his tone. "Good. And you must scout a route for us to get home . . . especially if Ehud has blown the tunnel."

Gripping Dov's hand firmly, Moshe said, "I'll be back soon. Try and rest."

■ ■ ■ ■

The base camp for the Third Battalion of the recently formed Haganah Seventh Brigade was outside Kibbutz Hulda. A farming community, Hulda was ringed by barbed wire fences and pinned to the coastal plain by a central guard tower. The kibbutz, marked by a stand of pine trees, stood at the mouth of Wadi es Sarar.

The wadi, known lower down its course as the *Valley of Sorek*, infrequently brought Hulda streams of water, but more reliably produced raiding parties of Jihad Moquades. It connected with Bab el Wad five miles furthest east.

Latrun brooded over the road above the juncture.

On the dusty, bumpy bus ride from Jaffa to Hulda, Jacob had plenty of time to contemplate not just the surroundings but also his comrades.

And they him.

With his grand total of ten days' experience, Jacob was the veteran. He was the old hand, the seasoned warrior whose expertise would calm their fears and save their lives.

It was a fearful responsibility.

Jacob remembered his first battles as a member of the Spare Parts Platoon. Although *spare* referred to being left over from regular units, it also meant expendable.

It had also meant anonymous.

Men had died fighting beside Jacob. He had known nothing about them beyond a name. Not who they were, not in any meaningful way.

He vowed not to let it happen again.

He struck up a conversation with the man seated next to him. Jacob had seen this fellow be one of the first to jump up and volunteer to save Jerusalem. Was he an ardent Zionist? He wore no kippa or ritual fringes. Was he religious?

Rudolf, responding to Jacob's accent, volunteered that he also was from Germany. "I went to synagogue twice a year," he said. "And I never thought of going to Palestine. Before the war I owned a printing business in Höhenschwangau."

Höhenschwangau was a picturesque village in a beautiful setting.

It was also in Bavaria, cradle of Nazism.

"I was interned very early," Rudolf said.

Jacob noticed Rudolf's overused stooped shoulders, sunken chest, and wire-rimmed spectacles. Such a man did not look capable of surviving as slave labor. The man appeared to need encouragement, so Jacob urged him to go on.

His voice lowered to barely above a whisper, Rudolf resumed his tale. "I was not sent to a work camp. Instead I was taken to a KZ near Berlin. There I and a hundred other Jewish prisoners operated a printshop for the Nazis . . . making counterfeit money and documents. British pounds, Allied travel passes, you know."

Jacob understood Rudolf's reluctance to speak. He had survived by serving the purposes of the Nazis. It did not matter that refusal would have meant death. The man plainly carried a load of guilt and had borne it for years. Once begun he anxiously poured out his past, as if Jacob were a priest hearing his confession.

"We were not mistreated. We worked fifteen, sometimes eighteen hour days, but we had plenty to eat. We tried to put deliberate errors into each document. Not obvious ones. We could not be blatant. Also . . ."

The furtive looks around the bus told Jacob that Rudolf was nearing the heaviest, most troubling part of his narrative.

"Once I met Himmler," he said at last.

Heinrich Himmler was the head of the Gestapo, the Nazi secret police. Next to Hitler himself, he had been the most feared man in the Reich. He was also the author of the Final Solution, the intended death knell of the Jews.

"Himmler was visiting the secret facility. He congratulated my team on the good work being done and asked if I wanted any reward for my men."

Rudolf stared straight ahead, but Jacob knew the man did not see the plowed fields of Israel. Once again he was inside a Nazi concentration camp, confronting evil in human form.

"Where the courage came from, I don't know. Over the printing presses was a banner: *Work Is Freedom.* I waved toward the last word and said that is what my men wanted most."

Rudolf pushed his glasses up on his forehead and rubbed his eyes. "Himmler replied, 'Soon, very soon.' Then he laughed and passed out cigarettes. I was shaking with what I had said. Whenever any one of my section grew ill or got hurt, they simply . . . disappeared. No one ever came back from hospital. That is what Himmler meant. That is what he intended for all of us."

His shoulders hunched up, Rudolf subsided for a time. Then, straightening his boney frame, he said, "That is why I am here . . . Israel, I mean. Why did others die and I live? I don't know. But there must be a place for Jews to live in freedom. I must do what I can to make it real."

The first view of Hulda reminded Jacob of the D.P. settlement in which he had been interned on Cyprus. There was no shade. The buildings stood dismally in the unflinching glare of the dawn sun. Nor was the sentry post the lone reminder of life in a concentration camp.

There were also the people: Jacob's comrades-in-arms of the Third Battalion.

Seventh Brigade was the cobbled-together product of three battalions who had never ever trained together, much less been in battle together. But at least the first two elements had a degree of instruction in drill and the manual of arms.

First Battalion was drawn from Palmach units previously guarding Tel Aviv.

Second Battalion had, until two days before, been the cadets of the Haganah Artillery School. The school commandant, Chaim Lascov, became the battalion commander.

Third Battalion, to which Jacob was assigned, was altogether different, altogether worse off.

Of the 425 men in Third Battalion, about sixty were conscripted off the streets and docks of Tel Aviv. Cab drivers and stevedores, bakers and day laborers, none had any military training, nor had any ever held a rifle before.

But the other 365 who arrived with Jacob on the buses from Jaffa were even less prepared.

Of this year-long ration of lives who had arrived on the Turkish freighter *Bonbel,* some had been homeless for nine years.

These paltry gleanings left behind after the reaping of the Holocaust were all, in varying proportions, sickly, suspicious, angry, furtive, and frightened.

Jacob found them duplicates of his fellow inmates back on Cyprus.

As each passed inside Hulda's wire fence, Jacob surveyed his responsibility with dismay. "How long did you say it was before these men must go into battle?" he asked Michael Stone. "Six months? Three?"

"Eighteen hours," Stone reminded him, "unless I can convince Ben-Gurion to give us more time."

"God help us," Jacob murmured. "I could knock down any five with one blow of my fist."

Menachem shrugged as it was of no consequence. "It does not matter if they live or die as long as they kill Arabs."

■ ■ ■ ■

Grandfather's study table faced the opening of the passageway. The detonator box was within reach. Light from a kerosene lamp spilled over the open scroll of the Torah.

At the top of a sheet of paper he had written Hebrew letters:

alef lamed vav   heh lamed dalet   dalet resh

Isaiah 42:16: I will lead the blind by ways they have not known, along unfamiliar paths I will guide them; I will turn the darkness into light before them and make the rough places smooth. These things I will do, I will not forsake them.

Rachel glimpsed this and a list of Scriptures as she brought his ration to him. Three slices of matzo. A bottle of water.

He thanked her, then glanced up from the portion he was searching. "Give my bread to someone else." He pushed the ration away.

"You need to eat," she urged. Above them the structure of the Hurva quaked at a trio of explosions. Dust sprinkled down on the page.

"I am fasting."

Rachel knew well that no amount of coaxing would make the old man eat or drink if he had made a vow to refrain. She could not scold him or encourage him to break it. Reluctantly she placed the matzo back in the basket.

"When should I bring you food again?"

His lips curved in a smile behind his beard. "I will tell you when."

"You are studying."

"For some time I have felt the presence of a Lamedvovnik among us. Do you understand my meaning?"

"One of the Righteous." Rachel knew Grandfather was referring to the tradition that thirty-six righteous souls, the Hebrew number *lamed* and *vav,* lived upon the earth in each generation. For their sake God held back his judgment. Perhaps it was merely a legend and yet Rachel had often wished it was true. Wished that in a world so overpowered by evil she could talk with someone whose pure heart effortlessly accepted and walked in goodness.

"I am sure of it." The rabbi did not raise up as he traced a line with his finger.

"Will he save the Old City?"

Grandfather did not reply. He tugged his beard. "He cannot save. Only Mashiyah, the Messiah, can save. 'Not by might nor by power, but by my Spirit,' says the LORD." Then he considered her with a sad expression. "I hear shells falling like rain."

"There are about fifty defenders left in the Quarter who aren't wounded."

The rabbi inclined his head as though he knew already. He muttered, "A few days more."

"If only Moshe was here." She hesitated, hoping Grandfather could give her insight, a fragment of hope. "Will I ever see Moshe again, do you think?"

"The answer is here." He swept his hand over the scroll. "Every answer is here."

"What does it say?"

"That the Creator of heaven and earth has not forgotten His promise to Abraham nor forsaken the Holy Word He gave to Moses on Sinai."

"But what does it mean to me, Grandfather, if I am left to live my life alone? Alone? Without Moshe?"

"You have taken his name. Rachel Sachar. Wife of Moshe. The answer is in the name," he replied cryptically.

She sank down beside him and clasped his arm. "Don't talk riddles to me, Grandfather! The reality is this: I survived by selling my soul to men who murdered my family. Not a riddle. Not an allegory. I survived, but at what a price! Moshe's love bought back my soul. Helped me believe again that God cared for me in spite of everything! Forgave me. I saw myself through the eyes of Moshe's love. If I lose him now..." Shame and fear welled up in her. She began to cry.

Grandfather put his hand on her head. "Your worst fear then. Losing Moshe?"

"My one fear."

"The answer to your heart's longing came when you took Moshe's name. True? But not in the way you think, Rachel."

"More riddles. Another puzzle for me to wonder about." She stood abruptly and turned away. "Akiva is stirring up the people. A revolt. Demanding surrender. Poor Ehud. How can he fight the Arabs and Akiva too? Ehud believes if the Palmach troops on Mount Zion do not succeed tonight . . . if they can't break through to us again . . . the Old City will fall." Her questions remained unspoken. What would that mean to them? Would they be slaughtered like the people at Kfar Etzion? Or would they simply be driven from the Jewish Quarter?

And what about Moshe? As the hours crept by, she had stopped believing she would ever see him again. The ache in her heart was perhaps the greatest burden she had ever carried.

"We will pray tonight." Grandfather returned to his passage. "Pray that the Palmach breaches Zion Gate again. Or that Ehud is wrong and we can, with the Lord's help, stand."

CHAPTER 10

lfie brought the day's ration to the trio at the rose garden on Gal'ed Road. He carried the food supplies for thirty defenders. His burden was light.

Each received one liter jar of water and a tiny stack of brittle matzo bread. Two flat, tasteless slices per person.

"This is what we've come to," Daniel remarked, rubbing his eyes against the fading starlight. "Not enough to keep a bird alive."

Alfie, his broad, unshaven cheeks hollow from starvation, instructed, "Hannah says this is it for today. You know? Save the water, she says. It has to last the day, she says." Pausing, Alfie stooped to peer at the sleeping child. Removing another half slice of matzo from the pocket of his shirt, he placed it beside Abe. "For the sparrows," he whispered. Stretching out his thick square fingers in a gesture that proffered a sort of benediction over the fragment, he muttered, "He sees even sparrows . . ."

"Alfie," Lori scolded, "you can't give away your ration."

"I'm okay," Alfie replied, not looking at her.

"When did you eat last?"

He was haggard. His once substantial form had become angular and awkward.

"Don't matter," Alfie replied.

"If you don't eat, Alfie, you will get weak. You won't be strong anymore. Won't be ableto help like before. Carry things, I mean."

Daniel interjected forcefully. "He's not eating. Look at him! My God!"

Lori snatched up the scrap of matzo and held it out to Alfie. "Eat this. I want to see you take a bite."

He jerked his head up sharply, searching her face with an amused expression. "When Jacob comes back. Then." His lips were cracked and dry. "Hannah Cohen says make the water last. There ain't no tea anymore."

Lori put a hand on his forearm. Thin as a spindle. She remembered the first time Hannah had seen Alfie in the soup kitchen. In exasperation the cook had exclaimed that it would take food for an army to feed such a big man and that the Jewish Quarter could not spare it. Had Alfie taken those harsh words literally?

Lori probed. "Alfie, tell me when you ate last." It came to her that in the time they had been trapped in the Old City she could not recall Alfie accepting any nourishment. Had he also been denying himself water?

She asked. He would not answer.

"I got to go." He waved to the sentries on the roof opposite. Then he turned his eyes toward the Dome of the Rock and addressed the air. "Jerusalem, Jacob! They know you're coming, see? They're up there, watching. Knowing. They been warned . . . And then there's Jacob . . . waiting. Everybody waiting. Scared. Hungry. All that grain, but no bread. Today. The wind. In the wheat field . . . Everybody thirsty, you know?"

"Alfie . . ." Lori clasped his hand, knowing he was seeing . . . *something!*

He shrugged her off and shook his head, clearing his vision. Patting her tenderly, he kissed her cheek. "I got to carry this . . . Everybody's waiting." With that he jogged away clumsily.

The first hot breath of wind followed after him as the Khamseen awakened.

■ ■ ■ ■

His hair was full of rock dust, and his face cut and bruised. With a scrap of bloody robe tied over one eye to simulate a bandage, Moshe had no trouble passing as an injured Jihad Moquade.

Gunfire crackled behind him, north along the battlement, but it was without intensity. Clearly the battle for Suleiman Road and the New City of Jerusalem had moved on.

More ominous was the renewed flurry of shots in the direction of the Jewish Quarter. The bicker of machine guns was accented by a thunderous crash of explosions echoing at regular intervals down the crooked byways. Too loud for either grenades or mortars. Were the Arabs dynamiting their way into the Jewish District? Was the situation already so desperate?

A block from Grandfather Lebowitz's abandoned dwelling near the Wailing Wall, Moshe stopped.

The house was intact. No column of smoke as would follow the tunnel's demolition rose overhead. Instead, a line of Arab Legionnaires, interspersed with Jihad Moquades, carried obviously heavy crates into the entry.

Moshe was seized with alarm. Had the tunnel been discovered? Was an assault being prepared right in front of him?

But the carriers were not armed. Minutes after entering the Lebowitz dwelling, they emerged again, their hands empty.

Grandfather's house was being used as a storage depot.

The existence of the underground passage remained a secret.

Retracing his steps toward Dov's lair, Moshe entered the Triple Bazaar, marketplace for foodstuffs in the Muslim Quarter.

The plenty available on the Muslim side of the fighting was overwhelming. Certainly some stalls had been vacated by Arab families frightened away from Jerusalem. But what remained was stunning: heaps of dates, raisins, and dried figs competed with mounds of pale-red tomatoes and bundles of dark-green dill and silver-green mint. In an adjacent corridor, stacks of pita bread braced against each other above saffron-streaked mounds of rice.

It was still too early for many shoppers to be in the marketplace, but in the mix were several hardy local Arabs, Jihad Moquades, and a number of uniformed Jordanian Legionnaires.

Ducking his head under the Crusader-built archway, Moshe rested for a time against a mottled stone column recycled from a Byzantine-age structure. How could the Jews, starving for food and water, desperately short of medicine and ammunition, hope to hold out against such bounty?

In his despair Moshe lost his deliberate air of swaggering menace.

An elderly Muslim shopkeeper, stepping around the low brick wall that marked the boundary of his premises, offered Moshe a glass of tea, which Moshe swallowed gratefully.

"You are hurt?" the shopkeeper asked.

"It is nothing," Moshe returned with a shrug. "But I must obtain food for a wounded comrade." Reaching inside the pocket of his robe, Moshe withdrew a handful of Mandate pennies bearing the image of King George VI of England.

The clerk scowled down at the pittance, then took the coins. Into Moshe's hands he thrust a pound of dates and a thin deck of pita.

"We need water also," Moshe insisted. "I have nothing in which to carry it."

"You desert wanderers are all alike," the shopkeeper scolded. "You come to Jerusalem expecting to live off the plunder." Rummaging under a canvas the merchant extracted two chipped glass bottles. He handed the empty containers to Moshe. "Fill them from the cistern by the northern door."

■ ■ ■ ■

The U.N. Security Council, in a transparent attempt to ignore the harshness of the Arab League's position, renewed its call for a truce in Palestine.

No one expected it to be heeded.

Though many prayed for the peace of Jerusalem, no one expected that either.

The door at the top of the candlemaker's stairs creaked as Moshe gingerly shouldered it aside. "Dov," he hastily called. "It's me."

"I knew it," Dov replied in a shaky voice. "No Moquade could be that quiet."

As Moshe cradled the two water bottles and the food, a date escaped from the packet and bounced down the steps. "How about your vision?" Moshe asked, knowing his form was outlined against the halo of light around the door.

"Better," was the terse reply.

But Dov started when Moshe touched his shoulder, indicating he had not seen Moshe's approach. "Still not good?" Moshe asked.

"Light. I can see light, but it makes my head throb," Dov acknowledged. "What did you find out?"

Recounting the result of his expedition, Moshe spoke of what he saw at Rabbi Lebowitz's house.

"So that return route is out," Dov summarized. "Ammunition is sure to be guarded."

"But it also means that the tunnel is intact," Moshe reminded him. "One thing at a time. Here is water." He thrust a bottle into Dov's outstretched hands. "Careful of the rim."

Dov slurped noisily. "Smells like rancid olive oil," he noted. "Best water I ever drank."

His thirst partially slaked, Dov eagerly accepted pita bread and dates. Moshe reported the results of his expedition.

"Destroying the cannon on the wall was an important triumph. We succeeded in stopping the Arab Legion. They have withdrawn their armor. Bazaar gossip says a big battle is coming at Latrun, a siege instead of a direct attack on the New City."

Moshe let this good news sink in, then added, "But the Legion and the Jihad have renewed the assault on our Quarter. From what I saw they are preparing a big push."

There was silence in the cellar. The men knew the situation in the Old City had reached a critical stage. It was urgent they return there as soon as Dov was able, by any means possible.

■ ■ ■ ■

Leo Krepske unfolded his ration, examined it, and made a face. "Want to trade?" he asked Yacov.

"Why?" Yacov returned. "They're the same. Matzo and monkey fat."

"I know, but maybe it tastes better if you trade for it."

"*Meshugge*," his brother put in. But the comment was without conviction, as if even the Krepskes were too tired to fight.

Yacov broke off a piece of his matzo and gave the corner to his shaggy dog, Shaul. "Shaul is so skinny," he worried aloud. "See how his backbone sticks out?"

"Have you looked at your own?" Leo asked.

Shaul quivered and wagged his tail-less behind. He sniffed out the tiniest crumb that fell to the pavement, then licked the oil from Yacov's fingers.

Mendel, who had made himself a slingshot like his brother's, shot a chunk of rock into the sun and said, "We used to use matzo to scoop up chicken and rice."

"Or falafel," Leo put in.

"Don't start," Yacov warned. "It makes it worse."

Mendel would not be put off. "Chicken and rice. I dream about it, you know." He launched another rock toward a trio of pigeons perched between two uprights of a shattered balustrade.

The pigeons bolted into the air, then joined a flight of ten or twelve more circling overhead.

Conversation stopped. The three boys stared at the spiraling birds.

"Do you suppose . . . ?" Leo said.

"Do you think we could . . . ?" Mendel added. "Why not? There's hundreds of 'em."

Yacov looked at the monkey fat and shuddered. "Pigeon and matzo would be better than matzo and matzo," he noted.

"Who's the best shot?"

"Shh! Don't scare them again."

"Here," Yacov said, grabbing his dog's collar before crumbling another corner of iron ration into a pyramid atop a fallen building block. Get back in the corner. Come, Shaul."

Leo picked through the rubble and came up with a perfectly uniform half-inch cube, painted blue on one side. It had been part of a mosaic before being blasted loose.

Now it was ammunition.

It took five minutes of breathless waiting for the pigeons to zero in on the bait. When they finally came, two settled to pecking the crumbs at once, then these were joined by three more.

"Easy," Mendel cautioned. "Don't miss!"

"Shut up!" his brother hissed, drawing the rubber cords back to his eye.

He fired.

The flock exploded upward, except one bird, which was knocked into the far wall of the alley.

Shaul bounded forward.

"Stop him!" Leo yelled.

"Jackal! Hyena! Get away from our bird," Mendel shouted, snatching up a rock to throw.

"Wait!" Yacov insisted, jumping in front of the Krepskes. "Watch. Here, Shaul. Here."

The dog, which had raced the length of the alley, trotted back obediently.

And laid a dead pigeon at his master's feet.

■ ■ ■ ■

When gathering his assigned company at Kibbutz Hulda, Jacob Kalner counted the different languages being spoken until he reached seven, then gave up. Many of the Europeans spoke Yiddish and others understood English. Jacob assumed the training would be done in one of those two languages.

"Hebrew!" Menachem shouted. "Irgun officers issue commands in Hebrew! Line them up!"

Not one of Jacob's company of recruits spoke a word of Hebrew.

By pointing and pushing, Jacob managed to get his one hundred charges into a semblance of order. A twenty-five-year-old Palmachnik named Joseph Lavie was the captain of Company Aleph; Jacob was his lieutenant.

When the four companies composing Third Battalion were finally placed in rank and file, Menachem stalked across the front of the formation. Through thick-lensed glasses he eyed them critically, not even bothering to hide his contempt.

They in turn stared back at him, not knowing who he was or what was about to take place.

Jerome Jardin was certain he understood what was happening. Turning to a fellow countryman, he remarked confidently in French, "This fellow is the commissar, a communist, you see. Like my father knew back in Paris. He is going to make a political speech."

"The first commands everyone must know are Left and Right," Menachem announced. "Repeat after me: *Smali! Yemani! Smali! Yemani!*" With each repetition of the two words, Menachem became more and more animated.

Jerome, beret askew but grin firmly in place, clearly thought the whole experience was ridiculous. What was this highly charged fellow going on about, his expression asked.

"Something is wrong with him," Ernst Hersh, the man in the chauffeur's costume, suggested to his comrades. "Maybe he's having an attack or something."

Jacob pantomimed repeating the words. When Menachem bellowed *"Smali!"* Jacob shouted the term and indicated for his neighbors to do the same.

Soon the improvised parade ground of Kibbutz Hula's central square echoed with *"Smali! Yemani!"*

It also resounded with Poles inquiring in Yiddish, *"Vas?* What does it mean?" And with Dutch asking, *"Begrijpen?* Do you understand what this is about?" And the Czechs querying, *"Rozumeti?* Does anyone comprehend what he wants from us?"

"Silence in the ranks," Menachem bellowed. "No talking except to repeat the commands!"

The order for quiet was repeated by the Irgun officers.

Jacob went from recruit to recruit, helping each make the connection between left foot, *"Smali!"* and right foot, *"Yemani!"*

"Why didn't he say so?" Leon, the mandolin player, wondered aloud in Yiddish.

The question went unanswered.

"Now!" Menachem roared. "We will march to the far fence. *Halach! Smali! Yemani! Smali! Yemani!*"

No one moved.

Menachem had neglected to teach them that the Hebrew word meaning "advance" was *Halach*.

Furious, the Irgun commander bounced up on his toes. *"Halach! Halach!"*

Dutifully the battalion responded, *"Halach! Halach!"*

Rudolf, the forger, even obliged by bouncing on his toes.

But no one moved forward.

A fleck of spittle appeared on Menachem's lips. "You are idiots! As stupid as cows! *Parah!* All of you, *Parah!"*

"Parah!" Third Battalion repeated.

■ ■ ■ ■

Daoud supposed that everyone in Jerusalem had gone to ground somewhere. The Russian Orthodox Church first protected its own Russian congregation. The safety of Arab Christians was of secondary concern. Muslim Arabs of the Druze sect also lived within the sanctuary.

The cathedral was organized something like a giant passenger liner tossed upon the seas of war. Russians who had fled the Bolshevik Revolution and settled in Jerusalem were given first priority. They occupied the more comfortable sanctuary, where they set up housekeeping in the side chapels. Living beneath the watchful gaze of crooked-necked, serene-faced icons, they had their own toilet facilities, one for men and one for women. They also had access to a private water cistern.

Second-class passengers on this ship without a country were four hundred Christian Arabs. They lived in the passageways and storage rooms. They shared one toilet, alternating hours with six hundred Druze Muslims.

The Druze were consigned to steerage.

The Druze sect, despised by the mainstreams of Muslim thought, had tried to stay out of the conflict between the Grand Mufti and the Zionists. Their founder had split from the main body of Islam in the eleventh century.

He disappeared one night, likely murdered because he preached tolerance of other religions. His disciples believed he would return in one thousand years to bring peace to the world. From that day his followers had likewise taught tolerance.

And how they had suffered for their beliefs! Centuries of persecution at the hands of the other branches of Islam, as well as by Christians, had left them decimated.

Still, they clung to their belief in open-mindedness.

Not many Muslims in the Middle East openly supported the establishment of the State of Israel. But to the Druze, democracy, religious freedom, and the prosperity of a Zionist state, was a beautiful dream. When Ben-Gurion gave the call, Druze men went to the aid of the Zionist forces. Their wives and children gathered their belongings and fled to St. Trinity Cathedral.

Here they sheltered in a tin Quonset hut, which had once been a dormitory for the poorest pilgrims. Supposed to offer shade, it was more like an oven. Water was doled out by the cupful.

Daoud, being neither Christian nor Druze, was nonetheless placed among the Druze orphans.

Daoud hated the Druze. He had been taught the Druze were neither this nor that. They accepted beliefs not found in the teachings of the Koran. True, they had no God but Allah, but they rejected the calls to Jihad. And they were alongside the Jews, fighting against Arab princes, because Ben-Gurion promised they could vote in the next election!

The hut into which the Druze were crammed gave evidence of the contempt everyone in the Middle East held for them. They were outcasts. Perched on their mattresses and baggage, they fanned themselves and comforted wailing children as the barrage continued from the Mount of Olives.

Daoud was shown to a sort of pen made of piled-up belongings where twenty-two motherless boys from the ages of six to twelve bullied one another. Druze tolerance did not extend to Daoud's arrival, either. A blind man could see Daoud was not a Druze. Was he a follower of the Mufti? A supporter of the Iraqi army who used holidays and birthdays as an excuse to slaughter whole villages of Druze people?

Two of the toughest-looking boys approached Daoud.

"Where are you from?" The eyes of the biggest boy squinted.

"The Old City." Daoud coughed nervously and hunted for a place to sit. There was none.

"Fighting on the side of the Mufti?"

"My brother is in hospital. At the Latin Patriarchate."

"You're not Christian," challenged the second-in-command.

Daoud shrugged. "I came here with the French nun."

"Why did they put you with us?"

Daoud did not know why. They were crazy, these Russians. The Druze boys hated him maybe more than he hated them. "The Russian nun said you might like to play . . . soccer . . ." The concussion of an exploding mortar shell dispelled the idea of a game of soccer. "Maybe not, then. I am not staying long. After nightfall I am going back to the Christian Quarter with the old French nun."

The Druze boys looked at one another like Daoud was crazy. "Nobody is going in or out of there unless they are fighting or dead."

Daoud replied, "I come and go as I please."

The younger Druze walked around him, eyeing him. Then he asked, "You have seen the fighting? Up close?"

Daoud nodded. "My brother was wounded by a bomb."

This sparked interest. Hostility was replaced by curiosity. "Yes? Tell us what is happening there. Nobody tells us anything. Just these cannons booming, and we don't know which side is winning."

"Sure." Daoud sat down in exhaustion. "The Jewish Quarter will not last. They say King Abdullah is coming to the Haram any day . . ."

He figured he would tell them stories, and then they would probably kill him because he was not tolerant. Maybe he could escape after dark.

CHAPTER 11

The formation of recruits at Kibbutz Hulda broke apart. Jacob found a spot of shade at the side of the mess tent. The view before him was reminiscent of the D.P.'s compound on Cypress. Anxious, confused men gazed through the barbed wire and wandered about the settlement. Though frightened, each had made a commitment to fight for the survival of Israel. What did it mean when Menachem, their leader, stalked off the parade ground? Were they actually going to fight? When? What about the training they were supposed to receive? When would they get weapons?

One of the most anxious and confused was Jacob. He sought out Captain Lavie, who fished a cup of water from a barrel nearby.

"Menachem is through with the training?" Jacob asked Lavie. "He will work more later?"

Lavie tossed the ladle into a bucket. "Commander Menachem answers to nobody, see?" Lavie stared into the brown hills in the direction of Latrun. "He thinks these men merely disobeyed, he thinks, you know . . . they were having him on."

Jacob retorted, "Having him on, is it? He thinks he can make everyone understand Hebrew because he wants it to be so! Use Yiddish, maybe. English even. But Hebrew! Colonel Stone would find a better way I think. The Americans . . ."

Lavie whirled around. "Never, ever, say that again! Stone is an American observer. He has no authority here. Try to understand. Sure, Haganah and Palmach have their jealousies. But Menachem and the Irgun . . . they are something else again. They make their own rules and cooperate with the rest of us when it suits them. Ben-Gurion got Irgun help with this operation by offering Menachem a command. This battalion, eh?"

Gesturing at the knots of men in the compound, Jacob suggested, "Irgun is the same as saying gangster. That massacre . . . you know the one . . . The Arab village . . . Irgun did it. yes? On Cypress I heard the Tommies speak about Irgun. Killing English soldiers. Other stuff. Blowing up the King David Hotel in '46 . . ."

"Lower your voice! You want somebody to hear?" Lavie said urgently. Peering around first to see if he could be overheard, Lavie offered, "I did not say this, okay? Ben-Gurion is trying to keep the whole ball of yarn from unraveling. Yeah. Maybe the Tommies knew something. Menachem does what he wants. It's a war, you know. Innocent people die, he says. Then he personally kills a few. Murder is the word. But the Irgunists know weapons; they have weapons. They know explosives; they have explosives. They are ruthless. Menachem is no kind of leader, but to get the collaboration of the Irgun in other operations, we are stuck with him in this one."

"So? You speak Hebrew."

"A few words."

"I don't," Jacob admitted. "If we're going to translate every Hebrew order into Polish, Dutch . . . French . . . my God . . . what else? Aleph Company better have men who know Hebrew, or we're going to die."

The pre-dawn scene in the Armenian Convent flashed into Jacob's mind. The one-armed man and his son were dressed as Hasidic Jews. Surely they were Hebrew speakers. Moreover the son . . . Lain, his name was . . . had shown his eagerness to fight.

Jacob located the fellow by the eastern fence of the compound. The tassels of Lain's ritual garment emerged from below his coattail. "You speak Hebrew?" Jacob inquired in German.

"Ha?" replied the twenty-year-old, cupping a hand beside his right ear and leaning forward. Then in Yiddish, Lain asked, "What is that you are saying?"

Terrific, Jacob thought. *I find one person who understands Hebrew and he's deaf.* "I said," Jacob repeated loudly, "Do you know Hebrew?"

"Of course," Lain responded in a normal tone of voice, bobbing his head as he spoke. "And you do not have to be shouting. I'm not deaf. Hebrew? *Ja.* I am studying with my grandfather and father."

With his thin fringe of beard, pasty complexion, gold-rimmed spectacles, and incessant nodding, Lain appeared every inch the stereotype of a Talmudic scholar.

"Good! You're hired!"

"Ha? what is that you are saying?"

■ ■ ■ ■

Because of the shrinking boundaries of the Jewish Quarter, there was no longer much need for couriers.

This freed Yacov, Leo, and Mendel to continue hunting.

Giving up their matzo for use as bait . . . no sacrifice they thought . . . the three intrepid hunters stalked and dispatched scores of pigeons.

Perhaps hunger sharpened the boys' aim. Or perhaps the pigeons were also hungry and therefore careless. Whatever the causes, the take of slaughtered birds soon filled a pillowcase.

The two Krepskes and Yacov marched into the Hurva and, for the first time ever, instead of avoiding her, went in search of Hannah Cohen.

"Where have you been?" she demanded. "A whole list of chores . . . what's this?"

Yacov upended the bag. Pigeons tumbled onto the kitchen floor.

A miracle!

"Pigeon stew!" Hannah proclaimed.

The boys beamed.

"Now what's needed is for them to be plucked and cleaned."

Leo and Mendel looked askance at each other. Plucking and cleaning a heap of pigeons would take forever. Suddenly pigeon stew sounded less appetizing. "I'll get the water boiling," Hannah said, "and . . ."

"No," Yacov replied, surprising even himself.

Leo and Mendel put distance between themselves and Yacov, certain a Hannah explosion was imminent.

"No," Yacov repeated. "We are the hunters. We do not pluck or clean. We hunt."

No one ever crossed Hannah Cohen.

Ever.

She opened her mouth, then closed it again without speaking. She raised a perilous index finger, then lowered it. Putting her hands on her hips, she seemed to be contemplating plucking and cleaning Yacov.

Then the most amazing thing: she laughed.

Another miracle!

"You are right," she said. "Hunters do not have to prepare the game. Hunters hunt. Go, bring me back another bagful."

Leo, Mendel, and Yacov were already backing toward the door. They did not want to push their luck where Hannah was concerned.

"But be careful," she called after them. "The Eternal bless you, boys!"

A blessing from Hannah Cohen unaccompanied by swat or scolding? Greatest miracle yet!

■ ■ ■ ■

Abe played quietly enough. He was a three-year-old. He lived in a world peopled by his imagination. He did not always need Lori in his world, although he wanted her near.

And then there was Daniel. Sixteen. Hating life. Hating everyone. Living in a world people by his disappointments. He imagined he did not need anyone ever, least of all Lori Kalner.

Lori unwrapped the bandaged stump at the end of Daniel's leg. The wound was healing properly enough, the incision pink and healthy. She washed it with a mixture of soap and water. There was no disinfectant.

Daniel pointed to the nest of three Haganah defenders on the roof opposite the sheltered garden of Gal'ed. "You know why they put me down here with you?" His voice was caustic.

"It doesn't matter." Lori dreaded his bitterness. He was so young. Did such rage come from being young, she wondered? Or from losing a foot? Or was there something else?

She proceeded to rebandage the stump.

"I'll tell you why," Daniel said. "They put me here with you and the kid because I am useless. Because unless all three of those guys up there die . . . and a flock of Arabs overrun that position, I have nothing to shoot at. We are safe here."

"Good." Lori shrugged. "I'm glad for that."

"I can shoot as well as the next man. My foot being in a garbage heap has nothing to do with how well I can shoot. My eyes are fine. Doctor Baruch put me here with a woman and a kid because he doesn't think I can be of use anywhere else."

"He put you here because there is no room in the hospital, and you're everybody's worst pain in the ass."

He inhaled. "Why couldn't I be up there? With them? Doing something?"

"They don't want you. You're too unpleasant." She finished the bandage. She wondered if her husband, Jacob, was as eager to get into danger as Daniel Caan. The thought made her shudder.

"Well . . ." He almost smiled. "Thanks."

"You're welcome." She patted him. "Now shut up. I'm going to read." She took out her copy of Rilke's poems.

He scooted back into the shadow. She felt his envious eyes on the spine of the book and lifted the volume higher to conceal her face. She was not reading. Simply enjoying the fact she had excluded Daniel from the book.

After a while he cleared his throat in a manly way and said to her, "I wouldn't mind if you want to read to me."

"What's that?" She pretended she had not heard.

He knew she had. "I said . . . I would . . . like it if you would read."

"Ah." She thumbed through the slim book. "Anything in particular? You are familiar with Rilke?"

"German. That's what I know. Sometimes . . . well . . . my mother liked his stuff. And later . . . my sister, Suzannah. For her birthday . . . got . . . a copy. From somewhere. I don't know."

"You have a sister?"

"Had."

"Ah." Lori would not ask about the mother or the father. "Shall I pick out something?"

"Please." He settled back. The sentries on the roof were quite well. Occasionally a shot zinged into their position, but Daniel was not needed at present.

Lori scanned the pages, lighting at last on a poem that might have been written about Daniel Caan. "Der Panther," she began. "Shall I read in German?"

A single jerk of the chin.

> "Sein Blick ist vom . . .
> His vision, from the constantly passing bars,
> has grown so weary that it cannot hold
> anything else. It seems to him there are
> a thousand bars; and behind the bars, no world.
>
> He paces in cramped circles, over and over,
> the movement of his powerful strides
> is like a ritual dance around a center
> in which mighty will stands paralyzed.
>
> Only at times, the curtain of the pupils
> lifts quietly. An image enters in,
> rushes down through the tense, arrested muscles,
> plunges into the heart, and is gone . . ."

Silence. The rushing of the Khamseen above the rooftops. Lori peeked over the pages to see if Daniel heard himself in Rilke's words.

His face was covered with both hands. Like a toddler thinking he could not be seen. Shoulders sagged a bit.

Lori knew he was crying.

What image had entered in and plunged into his heart?

■ ■ ■ ■

Major Francis Burr of the British Highland Light Infantry, but attached to the Arab Legion, stood atop the wall of the police station crowning the promontory at Latrun. More fortress than civil government building, the compound boasted thick stone walls. A massive steel door blocked the single entrance. Built by the British, the citadel commanded the approaches to the heights from north or west.

It overlooked the road to Jerusalem.

A cat could not cross the wheat fields stretched out below Latrun without being picked off.

The blockade against any Jewish convoys was total.

Two heavy machine guns were mounted at opposite corners of the parapets. In the central square Burr had placed squads with three-inch mortars that could fire over the walls. Also located within the structure were a pair of armored cars, ready to issue out for the gate as needed. Two more armored vehicles lurked in the shadows of the village of Latrun. A final pair were hidden alongside the Trappist monastery a few hundred yards away.

Burr was in radio contact with a battery of six-pound cannons hidden in the trees a half-mile to the east on what was called *Gun Hill*. He could call down high-explosive rounds on any movement ahead or to either side of his position.

Though the Arab Legion lines at Latrun were lavishly supplied with weapons, the major still was not satisfied with their placement. With newly arrived Legion major Athani at his side jotting down notes as his subordinate, Burr studied the steep hillside that fell away below the peninsula. "Two more machine-gun nests," he said for Athani's benefit. "One back of those boulders and the other behind that clump of trees in the old trench." He indicated the locations, and Athani used red ink to mark the positions on a map.

The dust-clogged trenches were a legacy of the time when the Turks had held the heights of Latrun against the British general Allenby. These emplacements Burr had ordered renovated. To them he added his own refinements of barbed wire and anti-personnel mines.

The most important aspect of the defenses of Latrun was yet to be mentioned. Fifteen hundred soldiers of the Arab Legion's Fourth Regiment occupied the police station, monastery, village, trees, and were spread along the perimeter of the ridge.

Four hundred Jihad Moquades and local villagers had been organized in auxiliary companies. These were held in reserve near the artillery battery. Another three hundred Arab Legion infantry had recently arrived from Jerusalem with Athani or were en route to Latrun from Ramallah.

The total of Arab forces defending Latrun exceeded two thousand men. They were well dug in, well armed, and well supplied. As Burr noted, his army had numerical superiority over any organized Jewish force in Palestine.

They also held the high ground and, though Burr did not mention this to Athani, they had the added benefit of being led by scores of British officers in varying ranks and capacities. Over two hundred Englishmen served with the Arab Legion.

The Legion's oldest-serving Arab officer had eight years' experience.

Some of the Brits had double that and more, and had seen action in Europe against the Nazis.

Athani remarked, "The Jews know we are here and have been fortifying and reinforcing. They would be fools to launch a direct attack."

Cupping his chin with his hand, Burr replied, "You are right. And the Jews are not fools. When they review the reports of their recon planes, they will know it is hopeless."

Athani was too disciplined a subordinate to question a superior officer, but his quizzical look expressed his quandary.

"You want to know why we are digging in?" Burr asked. "General Glubb is on his way here from Amman. There may not be any Jews within twenty miles of this place, but I have promised the commander to leave nothing undone. This may never be witnessed by any Jews, but to Glubb, this hill will bristle with every spine we possess. Ah," he said to Pipe Major Duncan who approached with bagpipes in hand. "Give us 'Scotland the Brave.' And Duncan," Burr added, "beginning tomorrow morning I want you to pipe the dawn, like a regulation post. The commander will like that."

Duncan filled the bag with air, punched it, and squalled his way through the requested tune.

When Burr was not watching, Athani gritted his teeth. He hated the sound of bagpipes!

■ ■ ■ ■

What a mountain of feathers!

What tiny bits of meat a cut-up pigeon reduced to!

Hannah Cohen decreed that to make the provisions stretch as far as possible, the birds would be stewed, bones and all, in a base of onion soup.

Soon the savory aroma drifted up from the kitchen of Tipat Chalev and over the hungry inhabitants. Everyone inquired what that delicious smell could be.

All the meat, seething together, only filled two large kettles. The second decree was that the first of the new ration would be for the wounded, young children, and the elderly. One half cup each.

Yacov received two half-cup allotments. One was his own, the second for his grandfather.

The boy raced down the steps into the Hurva's sub-basement. After his eyes adjusted to the dimness, Yacov saw Reb Lebowitz bowed over a scroll. Despite the sphere of light surrounding the single candle, there was barely enough illumination to see Grandfather's features, much less make out faded gray script against a tan and amber background. Grandfather could not possibly be reading. He must be wrestling with troubling thoughts.

Yacov waited patiently, expecting the stew's fragrance to speak for him.

If the aroma did not rouse Reb Lebowitz, it certainly did Yacov's stomach, which growled.

Grandfather responded to the growl. "Eh? What is it?" He did not look up.

"Grandfather!" Yacov said proudly, extending a cup. "Pigeon stew. Leo, Mendel, and I killed the pigeons, and Shaul retrieved them. Hannah Cohen even spoke kindly to us."

"*Mazel tov,*" Grandfather said absently. But he did not take the soup.

"I brought this for you," Yacov said, raising the chipped enamel mug.

The old man did not reply. It was as if he had gone deaf. His eyes were riveted to the page.

"Pigeon stew," Yacov ventured hopefully.

Grandfather raised his hand, commanding quiet.

Yacov waited. He raised the brew to his nose and inhaled the steam. His stomach rumbled again. "*Nu.* Grandfather?"

"Not now, Yacov," the old man mumbled. "Not . . ." He did not finish.

"Should I leave it for you?"

"Not now." The old man was not even interested.

Yacov tucked his chin. "Sure." He turned to go. But then Grandfather held out his right arm, beckoning Yacov to his side.

Yacov sighed with relief and went to him. Still Grandfather did not glance up from his studies. He did not accept the nourishment. But he embraced Yacov. "You have done well, Yacov."

"Taste it." Yacov brightened.

"When Moshe comes back. Then we will sup together. Go along."

Yacov understood then that Grandfather had made a vow. He was fasting, and not even pigeon stew would tempt him to break it. No food until Moshe returned safely.

But what if Moshe never came back?

CHAPTER 12

A file of transport vehicles rolled into the compound at Hulda. The men of Third Battalion stepped aside to let them pass, then crowded around to watch. Drivers and their assistants flipped aside the canvas covers off the truck beds and exposed a cargo of wooden crates. These were pried open with crowbars and hammers to reveal . . .

"Rifles!" Commander Menachem bellowed, coming out of his tent. "Line up! Your equipment is here."

Excitement rippled through the compound as his words were translated.

Now it was real! Now they would be soldiers!

Eagerly the recruits jostled into two queues and walked down both sides of the column of trucks.

Rudolf, the forger, was handed an oblong object wrapped in brown, oiled paper. A rifle! He reached out enthusiastically, then fumbled when it turned out to weigh more than expected. He darted an embarrassed glance at his comrades.

"Heavy, eh? I have not ever held one before." Hurriedly retrieving the weapon from the ground, he cradled it awkwardly across his arms and walked forward to the next lorry.

On the other side of the truck ahead, Leon Pickman juggled his mandolin over one shoulder and his new rifle on the other. From the cargo bed a pair of cupped hands reached toward him.

"Here," said the driver. "A rifle is no good without bullets, eh?"

"Where do I put them?" Leon asked.

"You have pockets," he was told.

Michael Stone prowled the file of vehicles from one end to the other. Jacob followed at a discreet distance. With each step Stone's scowl deepened. Reaching the last truck in the column, he rounded on his heel and hurried toward Menachem. "There's more than this coming?" he demanded.

Haughtily Menachem retreated inside his quarters. Stone followed. Jacob, standing nearby, overheard the exchange that ensued.

"I said, where's the rest of the supplies?" Stone repeated.

"That's everything there is," Menachem returned.

"Helmets?"

Menachem shook his head.

"Cartridge belts?"

Another negative.

"Boots? Rations?"

"Brand-new, Czech-made rifles," Menachem boasted. "I insisted and Ben-Gurion agreed."

Stone ignored this. "Canteens?"

"They are going to fight. Not have a picnic," Menachem retorted.

Jacob stood with his back to the flap to hear the exchange. The canvas flew back as Stone and Menachem emerged.

Stone's voice was low and intense, barely audible as he spoke to the Irgun commander. "You see the wheat fields?" Stone gestured toward the acres of rustling golden stalks stretching away toward Latrun. "Do you? Last week they were green. Now they're brown. The wind, see? And the heat. Toasted the whole Valley of Sorek. It saps moisture out of everything, this wind. Hear me? Including men. You expect them to fight with no water?"

"We attack by night," Menachem responded. "Surprise attack. By night. By the time the sun comes up, they'll be drinking from the Arab wells in Latrun. And eating Arab rations."

"Commander Menachem," Stone said. "Leading an army is about more than fighting. Supplying and resupplying is 90 percent of it. Even the best-trained soldier is only as good as the tools he has to use. That means all the necessary tools. Helmets. Sturdy shoes. Good food, and plenty of it. And . . ." He pointed toward the merciless sun already baking Palestine's coastal plain. "Lots of water. I was told you have 250 canteens. Two thousand men. It's nuts to send these guys out without water."

Menachem pursed his thick lips. "Colonel Stone, you were allowed here as an observer," he said. "You have observed. You say you are an advisor . . . your advice we don't need. Go carry tales to Ben-Gurion, but we have a battle to win. Tell Ben-Gurion we will drink from the Arab wells before sunup."

■ ■ ■ ■

Rabbi Akiva found Ehud Schiff in a storeroom of the Eliyahu Hanavi Synagogue.

Ehud, his fingers clutching a handful of beard, was lost in thought. Since the defense of the Quarter had devolved on him, he struggled with how to allot the shrinking provision of men and bullets. Allocating grenades was no problem: the remaining explosives had already been distributed.

The defensive perimeter of the Quarter extended from Misgav Ladakh Hospital across to the Street of the Jews. The southern boundary was the open space between the Jewish district and the Old City wall.

It was the northeastern sector that presented the largest problem. With the loss of Nissan Bek Synagogue, the warren of streets in that part of the Old City was almost impossible to protect. Arabs, using bazookas like cannons firing at point-blank range, blasted through the common walls between houses. Any defender still functioning after the concussion was unable to respond when the enemy burst through the opening, firing rifles and tossing grenades.

House by house, room by room, the Quarter was being lost.

Only the propensity of the Arabs to stop advancing in favor of looting allowed the Jewish soldiers time to catch their breath and regroup.

But there were so few undamaged houses left, and just so much loot remaining.

The struggle could not last much longer on the present terms.

Ehud was not in a good mood, nor would he have been pleased to see appeasing, troublemaking Rebbe Akiva at the best of times.

"What do you want?" Ehud growled.

"I will come straight to the point," Akiva said brusquely. "Sachar convinced people in the Quarter they would be massacred if we surrendered to the Jihad Moquades, that we must wait for the Legion. So we waited, and more of our people died. The Legion came, but still Sachar refused to discuss surrender. More died. Now Sachar is dead. You are not even from our Quarter. You know it is hopeless. Let us surrender while some remain alive."

"Go away," Ehud said. "I do not have time for this."

■ ■ ■ ■

The attack on Latrun was set to be launched after sunset, Monday, May 24, still many hours away.

For Jacob it could have been that many days into the future and there still would not be enough time to prepare Aleph Company for what they would face.

The Czech-made rifles of which Menachem had been so proud arrived full of packing grease. Each had to be dismantled, swabbed with cleaning fluid, and reassembled, by men who had never before handled a firearm.

Gathering a group of eager recruits, Jacob sat them in a circle, demonstrating the cleaning procedure. As he painstakingly reviewed each step, Lain, the Polish Hasid, conducted a class in Hebrew commands.

"*Hifsik,*" he said. "In Yiddish, *Opschtel.*"

Leon Pickman wiped a drop of sweat from his nose. He struggled to tug a rag on the end of a string through the muzzle of his weapon. A glob of grease spattered his mandolin.

"In English, *Halt!*"

Dutch-born Ernst, and Rudolf, the German, recognized the English version, as did Jerome Jardin.

The Russian father and son, Ivan and Sholem, conferred. "*Astanofka,*" they decided.

It was Jacob's intention that by educating a cadre in the basic commands, each could in turn help his countrymen make the connections.

"*Hifsik!*" the assembly repeated, committing it to memory.

The laborious process continued, going through *Halach* for "Advance," *Himtin* for "Wait," and *Matah* for "Drop, Get down!"

"So," Jerome inquired, "now we have weapons, and we can shout Hebrew words like any kibbutznik. Does our attack have a name, so we can tell our grandchildren about our famous victory?"

Grandchildren? Jacob wondered how many of his comrades would be alive at this time tomorrow, let alone for years enough to have grandchildren. "Operation Bin Nun," he answered, holding Rudolf's rifle up to the sky and sighting through the bore. Shaking his head, he returned it for further scrubbing.

"What's that you are saying?" Lain bent his ear toward his cupped hand. "But this is quite right and proper."

No one asked why. The Hasid would tell them whether they wanted to know or not.

Lain waved toward the valley that narrowed as it ran eastward. "That . . . the very place . . . is the Vale of Sorek." He waited expectantly for expressions of recognition or at least curiosity. When none followed, he seemed disappointed, but continued, "Sorek. It is meaning 'desperate need.' When the Philistines, great oppressors of our fathers, are ruling Sorek, they are planting grain just as you are seeing today. Then Samson . . ."

"Ah," Sholem remarked to his son. "He who had great trouble with naughty women."

Lain continued, "Yes. Whatever. So! Because of this naughty woman, Samson is revenging himself on the Philistines. Three hundred foxes he is trapping. Then he is tying torches to their tails, eh? Turning them loose in the dry wheat. And *pfffft!*"

Jerome laughed, cocked an eyebrow, and glanced admiringly toward the valley and the wheat fields. "Foxes."

"The Philistines are not laughing," Lain corrected sternly.

Everyone in the circle of recruits chuckled at Lain's seriousness, and finally he relented and smiled as well.

"Onward," Jerome encouraged.

"The Valley of Sorek is leading to the Valley of Ayalon," Lain continued. "The Ayalon Valley is where the Almighty is making sun and moon stand still at Joshua's request."

"This is before or after the wheat is burned?" Jerome eyed Lain doubtfully.

"Before. Much before. So this Joshua is beating the evil Amorites, in battle. And with the longer day it is becoming a . . ." He extended his arms when the greatness of the victory defied words. "Victory."

Leon Pickman plucked a chord on his mandolin. "Operation Bin Nun," he said, strumming to underline the words. "Joshua's family name. Clever fellows, our commanders. Hoping Joshua's good fortune will spill over on us. Yes?"

"There is one problem," Ernst Hersh said quietly to Jacob, working the bolt of the unloaded rifle he held beneath the third row of buttons on the chauffeur's jacket. "Our attack is at night. Darkness is what we need, not light."

Captain Lavie appeared at the edge of the circle. His arms were loaded with empty Coca Cola bottles.

"Collecting them for the penny deposits?" Jerome teased. "Are they for us to shoot at?"

"We do not have enough canteens to go around," Lavie said, chagrined, as he handed one to each man. "And so . . ."

■ ■ ■ ■

The day was like a clock face without hands to mark the time.

Lori could not tell one hour from another; all were the same.

Sunlight turned orange behind the dust of the wind. Daniel, feeling tension emitted from the other side of the wall, sat with his rifle resting on the sandbags. He fingered his three bullets. *Clink, clink, clink.*

He would be ready when they came. Three bullets in his hand. One in the chamber. That was what he would have to turn back the hordes.

A legless David against the Goliath of King Abdullah's army.

Alfie snored in the shade. Like a big dog on its back, his enormous feet were propped on the pillar. His mouth was open. He did not notice when Abe used his legs as bridges to drive imaginary trucks over.

Abe grew bored with playing trucks and building houses in the sandpile. With a crash of his fist he smashed the houses and crept over to Lori, begging a story.

She obliged. One story turned to two. Another followed, and then another.

When the sound of fighting near Misgav Ladakh Hospital increased in volume, the child pressed his ear against her breast and asked to hear her heartbeat.

And then Yacov came, darting in and out of shadows. Stooped over like Groucho Marx running through a bad comedy, he carried something in both hands.

Tin mugs.

He was grinning broadly even as he dodged potential bullets.

He crouched the last yards, then entered the shelter of the courtyard.

"Shalom!" he cried exuberantly. "I brought you something!"

He passed Lori four mugs, half-filled with a weird brownish concoction.

She inhaled the aroma. Onions and . . . what? Bits of meat. It smelled wonderful.

Alfie awakened from his dreaming and sat up. "Something smells good," he said.

Abe clambered over to Lori.

Daniel left off vigilance and scooted toward the feast.

"Pigeon stew!" Yacov cried exultantly.

Abe gave a loud, shrill, sustained shout of joy. He pounded Alfie on the back in happiness. "They brought back the bread! The pigeons brought it back!" the child cried.

Yacov gave Abe a sideways glance. Of everyone who had received the blessing, no one had been as joyful as Abe Kurtzman.

■ ■ ■ ■

It was not auspicious news to receive right before planning an attack. Another key piece of the defense of Israel was lost. The village of Ramat Rachel, practically a southern suburb of Jerusalem, had fallen.

Embattled Jerusalem had even less outposts.

The noose around the Holy City drew ever tighter.

The necessity for success at Latrun loomed ever larger.

The briefing for Operation Bin Nun took place in Kibbutz Hulda's kindergarten classroom.

It was, in Jacob's view, a singularly appropriate choice, given what he had seen in the way of training and equipping.

One-word Hebrew commands!

Undoubtedly the battle strategy would also be painted in broad strokes, like a child's first experience with drawing a picture.

In this expectation, he was not disappointed.

Captain Lavie warned Jacob that he should not speak unless asked a direct question.

Commander Menachem swept into the room at half past three. Lavie nudged Jacob, urging him to stand. The assembled officers held themselves rigidly at attention until Menachem's aide remarked, "Be seated."

Menachem indicated a map posted on the wall. It hung below two kindergarten drawings. One showed a wobbly, blue, six-pointed star on a white banner. The other was a bird, in form like a chicken, but bearing an unmistakable olive branch in its beak.

At the outbreak of the war, the youngest boys and girls of Kibbutz Hulda had been evacuated to Tel Aviv.

Would the kindergarten classroom ever again be occupied by Jewish children?

In eight years of marriage, Jacob and Lori had never known a world without war or some sort of conflict.

Would there ever be a place and time when they could raise babies in peace and safety?

Would either of them live to see such a time?

Flicking a British officer's swagger stick against the chart's center, Menachem snapped, "Latrun village. Police station here. Monastery here. First Battalion will capture the monastery. Second will attack and neutralize the police fort. Our job is to capture the village. After that Seventh Brigade will hold a three-mile length of the Jerusalem road so that the supply convoy waiting near Rehovot can pass."

Just like that, Jacob thought. *He waves his hand and makes it so.*

Continuing with the briefing, Menachem noted, "They will not be expecting an attack. The enemy holds the ridge . . . his exact numbers are unknown. We will field fifteen hundred men. He may have artillery, placement and number likewise unknown. We will also have artillery brought up to support the attack."

The commander's tone and manner suggested that such details were pure formality, inconsequential to the outcome of the engagement.

A messenger arrived, saluted, and handed Menachem a communiqué.

The Irgun leader frowned at the interruption, scanned the memorandum, crumpled it in his fist, and threw it to the ground. "There is a bridge here," he said, tapping the silver tip of the swagger stick on the red line that represented the Hulda to Latrun road. "It is two miles below Latrun. Far enough that the enemy will not hear our approach."

Jacob leaned forward but could see no indication of a bridge.

"Third Battalion will be transported by lorry. We will form up at the bridge and advance from there. Aleph Company will lead. Remember, surprise is everything. Any questions?"

Before anyone could respond, Menachem exited the classroom.

Amazed no one had opened his mouth, Jacob blurted out to Captain Lavie, "I saw this from the air, but even I don't know if there are Arab patrols between here and the bridge. Do we already hold it? How far is it from the bridge to our objective? I saw open fields. Is there cover? Fortifications?"

Lavie shook his head. He had no response to those or any of the hundred other pertinent questions. "Do you know the most important issue?" he asked. "It is, will Ben-Gurion change his mind and give us more time to prepare? The rest we will find out for ourselves . . . whether we like the answers or not."

As he left the building, Jacob's toe brushed the message discarded by Menachem.

Retrieving and unrolling it, he read: *Enemy convoy estimated at thirty troop vehicles plus armor and artillery left Ramallah yesterday. Believed heading for Latrun. Suggest you expedite attack before additional enemy forces can deploy.*

■ ■ ■ ■

Fawzi Chabbaz was the eldest son of the muqhtar of the little Bab el Wad village of Yalu. He had gathered around him a group of men from Yalu into a band of Arab Irregular soldiers.

To date Chabbaz and his men had accomplished nothing noteworthy. His troops had ambushed and burned Jewish trucks in Bab el Wad, but there was not much glory in that. There had been raiding parties carried out against Kibbutz Hulda and other Jewish farming communities, but the Jews had been too well-prepared for Chabbaz's force to achieve anything except long-range sniping.

One reason for their early lack of success was his father. Muqhtar Chabbaz the Elder had always lived in peace with Yalu's Jewish neighbors. It was only after it became apparent war was inevitable that his father consented to the raids.

Later, after Deir Yassin, he could not have prevented them.

But now the war was truly coming to them. Instead of a nighttime foray, an opportunity was approaching for real battle. Chabbaz would personally lead his men and achieve a great victory. The growth of his reputation would be assured.

Chabbuz was told to place his men under the command of Major Tariq Athani of the Arab Legion.

Hating the Jordanians as arrogant invaders, Chabbaz and his father hated the British even more . . . but the British offered them weapons.

Chabbaz and his second-in-command went to meet Major Athani on the hillside below Latrun. The major was giving orders to his subordinates. "What is it?" he asked.

"When do we attack?" Chabbaz said eagerly. "My men are anxious to be in the front of the battle."

"Your assignment," Athani returned, "is to remain in reserve at Yalu. You will be directed to move your men if they are needed. But only," Athani stressed, "when I say, and then you will place them where I tell you."

Chabbaz was shocked. Before he could express his outrage, Athani continued, "As for missing the battle, you need not worry about that. There will be no battle here. The Jews will never attack in the face of such powerful defenses. We will hold here until their revised direction is clear, and then we will move. More likely they will see that this war is hopeless, and they will accept King Abdullah as overlord. Then we can go home."

"But what if the Jews attempt to surprise us? What if they do attack?" Chabbaz insisted. "Let me lead a night patrol to spy out the land beyond the wheat fields. You know," Chabbaz said, waving toward a cluster of red roofs on the horizon, "those are Jews there. The place is called *Hulda.*"

"I know it is Hulda!" Athani snapped. "If we can see them, don't you think they can see us and what we have built here? There will be no patrols," he ordered flatly. "Especially not at night. The roads are mined. The fields of fire of machine guns, mortars, and cannon are fixed precisely. No inch of the ground remains unmarked. All that would result from such a movement as you describe is for Arabs to shoot Arabs. The Jews would stay safe in Hulda, laughing at us. Go away and leave me to my work!"

Chabbaz did so, but not without muttering to his friend, "They are so arrogant! They and the English are consumed with overconfidence. Abdullah as king over us? Never!" Studying the terrain one more time, he fixed in his mind a path that zigzagged down the slope and connected to a dirt road that skirted the standing grain. The track ended at a stone bridge over which ran the highway leading toward Kibbutz Hulda. With or without permission, Chabbaz contemplated yet another nighttime foray.

CHAPTER 13

For the first time Colonel Michael Stone's expression matched his name. Stern-faced and scowling, he roared onto the Haganah airfield in a battered jeep.

David, coveralls spotted with grease as he and Milkin worked over the engine of a 109, spotted Stone stalking into the Quonset hut office.

"What's with him?" David wiped sweat from his brow, leaving a streak of oil over one eye.

"He's an observer," Milkin remarked, turning his attention back to the carburetor. "He observed. Things don't look so good."

Zoltan, peering out from behind the air intake of a turbocharger, grunted. "I am hearing they make Menachem, the Irgunist butcher, to be in charge of taking the road to Jerusalem. Tonight they are attacking Latrun."

David gave a low whistle. He had seen the fortifications of Latrun. "So soon?"

Zoltan shrugged. "Sure. Menachem says Stone is . . . something. I forget. But Menachem don't like American much."

"Don't like anybody much," Milkin added.

Moments later Stone strode out toward David and Milkin. His scowl deepened. "Come on," he said. "We're going for a ride."

The sun slid down a ramp of milky haze into the Mediterranean as the two pilots followed him to the jeep. Stone shoved Sten guns into their hands. "You know how to use these, right?"

Looking askance at the American officer, David inquired, "Another low-level bombing run?"

"More low level than that. Let's go find your Roman road."

Milkin's brow furrowed with concern. "What're you thinkin' . . . if you don't mind my askin'."

The fury in Stone's demeanor faded a bit. Once again a grin cracked his features. "You guys were the ones who told me. You followed an old road out of the wadi on the backside of Latrun, right?"

"Yeah." Milkin didn't get it. He scratched his neck and pondered.

David understood perfectly. "We'd have a better chance in daylight. Take the Piper up. Have a look."

Stone shoved the jeep into gear. "We covered that before. We take the Piper over that wadi, every Arab and English officer's going to see us. The moon is full tonight. We'll drive it. Walk it, if we have to. But we'll find it."

■ ■ ■ ■

The last English-language radio broadcast of Kol Yerushalayim, the Voice of Jerusalem, trickled to a halt in midsentence when the last of the petrol powering the generator ran out.

Like the trickling stream of water that came from the tank trucks . . . like the shrinking distribution of tinned food and hard bread . . . the life of the Holy City was trickling to a halt.

Jewish Jerusalem lay athwart the path of the Legion and Abdullah's ambitions, but it had been reduced to the silence of near exhaustion.

It was quiet in Jerusalem except in the tin shed of the Russian compound. The shanty resonated with snores and whispers and here and there a child's cry. Worse than that, the orphaned Druze boys lay awake, competing to see who could pass gas with the loudest explosions.

In all of this they insisted that Daoud continue his horrific stories of severed Jewish ears and men blown to bits by Dajani's bombs. At last came the part where Gawan was wounded by the metal shard through his neck. The old gardener had come and carried Gawan to the hospital at the Patriarchate where the Jewish Dr. Baruch had saved his life.

"And after that I did not wish to fight Jews any longer," Daoud concluded.

"So you came here?" asked the elder Druze.

"Something like that," Daoud said. He was hot and tired from talking so much. He wanted air.

There were hours of story yet to be told: how Mother Superior had blown up the convent and stopped the advance of the Legion.

But he did not want to tell them. He wanted to sleep, to breathe.

"That can't be everything," persisted one of the younger boys. The others chimed in with a babble of questions. Irritating.

It came to Daoud that he had not slept since yesterday. It was no wonder that the Russians put the Druze out in the tin Quonset building. Foul, stinking, and they never shut up! They would not let him sleep.

Daoud was suffocating.

"Where is the toilet?" he asked.

"You'll have to wait. This hour the Christians have it. Tell us more," answered the younger Druze.

Daoud grimaced. "I can't wait an hour." He stood abruptly and climbed over the barricade of bundles. Picking his way around sleeping adults he heard a boy call to him. "Hurry back! We want to hear about the battle of Notre Dame!"

He stepped out into the night and inhaled. He smelled flowers. He had not seen flowers when he arrived at the compound, but they were blooming somewhere. And there were stars in the sky. He had almost forgotten the clean look of stars in a night sky.

For an instant he glanced back at the shabby structure. Hot. Airless. Stinking like farts, dirty feet, sweat, and unwashed baby bottoms. He imagined what even one mortar shell would do to an atmosphere so full of gas.

Was he better off dying in such a way with six hundred Druze in a tin hut?

Or just staying in the open and waiting for an errant shell to find him? If he went back to the pen the Druze boys would drive him mad with questions.

He would die from lack of sleep.

"They're crazy," he said aloud. "Everybody in Jerusalem is crazy."

With that he walked down a path toward the sweet scent of flowers.

■ ■ ■ ■

With David riding shotgun and Milkin bouncing about in the rear, Stone piloted the jeep up the highway. For weeks Haganah leaders had been kicking around the thought of finding a back road to Jerusalem around the Arab blockade in Latrun and Bab el Wad. David had heard their discussions. He and Milkin had been told to keep their eyes peeled for any route . . . even goat tracks . . . circumventing the Arab positions.

David had not believed another road to Jerusalem was possible. Then he and Milkin had stumbled onto a moonlit track out of the Judean wastelands. At least part of a centuries-old passage existed in a boulder-strewn wadi, hidden from Arab positions by a ridge of hills.

Past the kibbutz where David and Milkin had emerged after escaping their Arab Legion captors, Stone turned onto a rough dirt track into the hills. Ahead was a band of Israeli Palmach soldiers in a lorry. A jeep and an armored car bristling with nine armed Druze Arab troops waited for Stone's arrival.

David knew that the Druze sect of Palestinian Arabs had been loyal to Zionist Jews from the beginning. Of the Arabs within the borders, the Druze population had suffered most in the conflict. Over eighty Druze leaders, pleading for harmony and supporting the establishment of a Zionist state, had been assassinated by fellow Arabs who backed the rule of the Mufti.

With Ben-Gurion's appeal for coexistence the Druze population rallied behind Israel. These Arab men felt that the armies of neighboring nations were the invaders. They joined the Haganah to fight side by side with the Jews for a homeland in which Jew and Arab could live as equals.

Michael Stone slowed and stopped. Without a word or a signal a tall, dark-skinned Druze wearing sunglasses and military khakis climbed into the jeep beside Bobby Milkin. Stone drove on.

The word *enigmatic* came to David's mind. No one spoke for a mile. At last the Druze bent forward and said to David in a perfect British accent, "I am Bashir."

Introductions were made all around. Bashir and Stone were old friends. Bashir had been educated at Cambridge and fought beside British general Montgomery.

Milkin lit up. "Basher!" The nickname was pronounced. "Basher! I'm glad you're on our side."

Bashir was indeed on the side of a Jewish homeland. A local, as homegrown as a Zionist orange, he resented the intrusion of tens of thousands of Arabs from Syria, Jordan, and Lebanon into Palestine.

He commented simply, "They came to pick oranges and stayed. Now they want the orchards for themselves. And a foreign king in Jerusalem. I am for a parliament. Democracy. A rather terrifying concept to the kings and sheikhs and Muslim imams who now invade us."

Bashir knew the terrain of the bleak Judean hills as well as anyone alive. He too had seen bits of Roman road exposed after a windstorm when he was a boy. It had run out halfway up to Jerusalem. Whether the track could be found and used to circumvent the hostile Arab blockade was another question.

Bashir said to Stone, "The Legion forces at Latrun are commanded by Francis Burr. A good soldier."

David and Milkin exchanged a glance. "We know Burr," David said.

"Yeah," Milkin confirmed. "We didn't plan it, but we was his guests."

Bashir continued, "With Menachem commanding part of the attack I fear this may not go well. I'm keeping my lads out of it."

Seventh Brigade's surprise midnight assault on Latrun was proceeding without Stone's participation and over his protests. So finding an alternate route of resupply for Jerusalem was uppermost in Stone's mind. He wanted food for the Holy City, regardless of the outcome of the battle.

Darkness fell over the brushy lower slopes, but almost instantly a bright moon sailed aloft. It beamed down into the canyons and wadis, casting long shadows and picking out the trace even better than the jeep's cat's-eye headlights.

The trail was not broad enough to accommodate the entire width of the jeep. As Stone steered into a hairpin turn, the vehicle leaned awkwardly. David felt the tug of gravity lifting the frame as the two right side wheels momentarily parted from the ground before slapping back down.

The front end dropped into a rut, then bounded out again.

Bobby Milkin, nearly thrown out with the violent bouncing, hooked one arm around a machine-gun mount and hung on with Bashir.

At the next abrupt corner the uphill wheels lifted off the ground again. David heard Milkin's intake of breath. The jeep's angle worsened, and the steering wobbled drunkenly.

Milkin and Bashir threw their weight onto the uphill side. Perching on the frame, half of their bulk resting outside the jeep's body, they acted as if the jeep were a sailboat and they a counterweight.

The wheels finally dropped again.

Stone did not slacken his pace. He drove as if he could take out his anger and frustration by assaulting the trail, whipping it into submission.

A steep downward plunge appeared ahead. Facing them was an even more precipitous ramp upward.

Knowing the jeep would need all possible momentum to climb out of the gully, Stone let the engine roar and powered downward. It flew up the ascent, wheels slipping in loose sand.

There was nothing beyond but blackness.

The edge of the world.

Stone spun the steering to the right.

The jeep tilted, on the verge of rolling over.

The right side lifted off the ground again.

Could they stop before plunging over the brink?

Wheels churning, the jeep fought for traction, then the left rear tire dropped off the edge and jammed against a boulder.

The jeep perched on the rim of the drop, rocking.

"You three stay put," Stone said as he set the brake.

As much as they might have wanted to get off the potentially fatal teeter-totter, David, Milkin, and Bashir knew that any movement could tumble the jeep into the void. Through gritted teeth Milkin said, "Hurry, okay?"

A brief look and Stone was back. "Here's the deal," Stone said. "The rock is loose on the slope. If we roll back a hair, it'll clear itself. 'Course we have to blast forward when it does."

Bobby Milkin gulped.

"Go ahead," David said.

Releasing the hand brake, Stone slowly lifted his foot from the pedal. David heard a trickle of sand grow to a shower of gravel and a cascade of stones. The jeep started to slide backward.

The engine bellowing, Stone released the clutch and stomped the accelerator.

The vehicle vaulted clear, coming to rest twenty feet past the precipice.

They heard the boulder hit the bottom of the canyon.

Bashir pointed to the right. "That way. There was a pond. A spring, I remember."

Fifteen minutes later Stone steered the jeep into a sandy depression tucked at the base of two hills. The pond was dry, but a stand of date palms marked the place as a onetime oasis.

■ ■ ■ ■

The pink flowers of the hydrangea bush stirred. Daoud opened his eyes to see the face of the Arab gardener peering curiously down at him. The old man smiled, a patchwork smile of missing teeth.

"*Salaam.*"

"You," Daoud said

"Why are you hiding?"

"I want to go home. To see my brother. The Old City."

"It is not safe for you there."

"Yes. I know. Al-Malik will kill me if he finds me. I am a deserter. I do not hate the Jews as I must to be worthy. I am tired of hating."

"So you are hiding."

"I am thirsty," Daoud said miserably.

The old man carried a skin of water tied to his waist. He poured a tin cup full and slipped it through the branches and blossoms to Daoud. Daoud guzzled it down noisily. It dripped down his chin. He drained the cup and gave it back to the gardener, then wiped his face with the drops that had spilled. He felt better.

The old man asked, "Is there no place else for you to go? No family?"

Daoud thought. "My father's brother used to live near the village Beit Susin."

"In the hills beyond Latrun. I know the place. Why do you not go?"

"Me and my brother would have gone there long ago except for the war. One must travel through the pass of Bab el Wad to get to Beit Susin. There is always fighting there. One side or the other. We could not go."

"Why did you not travel the other road?"

"There is no other road."

"Indeed there is. I have walked it myself many times on my way to the sea."

"There is no other way to the sea except Bab el Wad. Everyone knows this. That is why the Jews in Jerusalem are starving to death."

"If they ask me I will show them the way."

"Next time I see Ben-Gurion I'll tell him you said so."

"There is a path. They would not be hungry if they knew the way."

"I'm hungry."

"Come out of the hydrangea bush, boy. Here is bread. I am going to the seacoast for a while. I will take you to Beit Susin on the old road. There is a spring in the wadi nearby and date palms. A grove of fig trees where pilgrims ate as they made Aliyah. I have been there many times."

■ ■ ■ ■

The halt at the oasis was brief.

"From here on," Bashir said, "I will walk ahead. You follow in the jeep."

"Suits me," Milkin agreed, grateful to believe Stone's maniacal driving would be controlled.

In the moonlight Bashir's khaki-clad form drifted ahead like a floating pillar of sandstone.

They passed through a grove of fig trees without difficulty, then came to the base of another knoll. "Wait here while I check ahead," Bashir said.

Hanging onto the machine-gun mount, Milkin relaxed.

Bashir's voice floating down from above instructed, "All right. Come to me."

With a clash of gears, Stone gunned the jeep up a grade steeper than any they had yet ascended. Narrowly avoiding running head on into a giant boulder, Stone swerved to the left. When the vehicle bounced over another rock only slightly smaller than the first, the jeep became airborne . . . and so did Bobby Milkin.

He turned a complete somersault, landing on his back in a thornbush.

Picking himself up more embarrassed than injured, Milkin suggested, "Think Basher could use help with the scoutin'." He limped uphill after the Druze soldier.

CHAPTER 14

Progress up the Roman road was slow. Every ten yards of forward was a team effort. Each gain was accomplished with Bashir scouting, Stone driving, David sweating and pushing and Bobby Milkin sweating, pushing, and grousing.

"You and me come down this?" Milkin groaned to David. "How come it seems so much steeper now?"

"Maybe because we weren't carrying a jeep?" David suggested.

The moon, serene and unperturbed, soared above, lighting the hillsides.

"It's so bright out," Stone noted with a tone of dismay. "Gonna be hell for our guys at Latrun if they are attacking in the open."

"That valley is a couple miles over those hills," David remarked, pointing north.

Stone stared northward as well, then said, "Come on, another ten yards. Let's go."

When they reached the top of another rise a dog howled in the distance. Blocky, clearly man-made shapes occupied the moon-bathed hilltop visible across the gap of a mile.

"Beit Susin," Bashir commented. "From where we are I think the old road goes there. It may be deserted, but we can't take the chance of going over there tonight. We must leave the jeep here and circle around on foot."

Stone gave the village-crowned knoll a last thoughtful study. "We'll have to do something about it if it is occupied," he said. "Can't leave them on our flank like that."

Bashir shrugged. "We don't even know if the road is passable beyond this point."

"Beyond this point?" Milkin queried. "You mean it's been strictly legit up to now? Guess those Romans weren't such hot stuff after all."

■ ■ ■ ■

When the four explorers left the jeep and continued on foot, they left their voices behind. Though Stone issued no order to cause it, conversation was carried out in whispers, and they placed their steps carefully. The mosquitoes buzzing around their ears made more noise.

By the time the moon was high overhead, the Khamseen was entirely silent. Blistering day was replaced by a sweltering night.

No wind howled down the gullies Bashir, Stone, David, and Milkin struggled up. The absence of the breeze did not mean the night was fully noiseless. Cicadas whirred and crickets chirped. Distant dogs howled and barked. Once the faint echoing report of a gunshot froze everyone in place, but no further disturbance followed and the procession continued.

Panting as he trudged up yet another steep incline, David listened to his heart pounding in his ears and the gravel crunching under his boots. He tried to entertain himself by computing the temperature with a method learned as a Boy Scout: count the cricket chirps, multiply, add something . . .

David mopped his forehead. The total he reached, four hundred degrees, felt possible.

He started over, lost count, then bumped into Milkin, who had halted abruptly.

"What's the matter?" David hissed.

"Dunno," was the reply. "I remembered what you said about them Roman soldiers . . . trampin' up this road . . . and what Moshe Sachar told me about them other old dead guys . . . Hittites, Amberkites, whatever Shites . . . and I swear I can hear 'em."

"Who?"

"Dead guys, marchin' along beside me."

"Get a grip," David said. "How can a big, ugly lug like you get the willies? You're the scariest thing out here."

Stone and Bashir were also conferring. "We are near the highest ridge east of Beit Susin," Bashir said. "Do you feel that?"

"What?" Milkin asked. "You too?"

"An updraft of air," Bashir explained. "We are approaching a ravine."

Directly in front of the party was an expanse of exposed shale. David and Michael Stone scrambled across it, their boots slipping on the smooth surface.

A heap of boulders crouched at the head of the shale. In the moonlight the pile of rocks had a troll-like form. "Not natural," Stone noted.

The stacked stones marked the edge of a sheer drop. Though near and far rims shone in the moonlight, overhanging outcroppings and brush combined to obscure any view into the depths of the canyon.

A silver bowl, five hundred yards across, swimming with black ink.

"How deep you think?" Stone asked Bashir.

By way of reply, Bashir hefted a baseball-sized rock and tossed it into the wadi.

A long wait . . . five seconds that lasted like that many minutes . . . and then the stone clattered against the bottom.

Instantly the sounds of crickets, cicadas, and mosquitoes ceased.

"Don't do that again, okay?" Milkin suggested.

"Four hundred feet," Stone said. "Spread out. The path came right to this spot, so there must be a way down. Find it."

After searching for half an hour, the four men regrouped at the marker cairn.

"Nothing," Stone said with frustration.

"Me neither," Milkin agreed.

David shook his head. "We aren't gonna find it tonight."

Bashir concluded, "I know what that pile of rocks means. It's a monument to the death of Jerusalem."

■ ■ ■ ■

The engines of the transports that would carry Third Battalion to the jumping-off point for Latrun began rumbling at 9:45.

That was the time appointed for the men to embark.

Jacob's company, toting unloaded rifles to prevent accidents, climbed aboard.

In struggling over the tailgate, Lain's waterbottle snagged. Breaking loose from the loop of string that secured it to his belt loop, it fell to the ground. The stopperless container emptied with a gurgle. Lain apologized profusely and asked Jacob's permission before going to refill it.

At 10:15 there was still no order to move out, so the men of Company Aleph sat in the canvas-enclosed cavern, expecting at any moment to get underway. Even with the rear flap open wide, the interior soon brimmed with the stench of sweat. There was no breeze to cool the close-packed troops.

Ten-thirty arrived and nothing happened, except the order came through to shut off the engines.

The waiting continued. What had happened? Why weren't they moving out?

Nerves, already stretched with the anticipation of battle, frayed further. Each man brooded over whether he would live or die.

Jacob knew this to be true because he felt it himself: a nagging foreboding that this night would be his last.

Beyond that, each confronted the possibility that his fear would get the better of him, that he would freeze up under fire and be useless.

Jacob's thoughts turned again and again to Lori. If existence in the New City of Jerusalem was so tenuous, what must she be living through in the Old City?

He tried to focus on the upcoming battle to break through and link Jerusalem with resupply from Tel Aviv.

What if Lori's life depended on what he did tonight?

The Jewish leadership sent the call, the demand, to save Jerusalem!

Jacob could think of nothing except saving Lori! Faced with the reality of losing her, nations and wars were insignificant.

And what of his own life?

By this time tomorrow he would be dead. He sensed it.

He did not fear the end, but he had so many regrets. By tomorrow night the end of his world would have come in an obscure wheat field in Palestine. Who would remember him? Who would know he had once lived and hoped like other men? That his heart longed for a life, a woman to spin out his years with, to bear his children . . . *Lori!* There was not even a pencil or a scrap of paper for him to scribble a hasty good-bye.

Lori! I love you! I feel I will never see you again. That all the hopes we shared once will end here in Latrun. And if it is so, please remember my last thought will be of you! My last act on earth will be to reach out to you! I am sorry! When I think what you have suffered in loving me . . .

Jacob shifted the weight of his rifle and tried to focus on what he must do to stay alive, and how to keep his men alive. Had the others under his command also resigned themselves to dying?

The morose silence in the back of the lorry worried Jacob. He needed to get them talking again.

Even in the semidarkness, the brass buttons of Ernst Hersh's chauffeur's uniform gleamed. As Jacob watched, the Dutch Jew rubbed each in turn with his sleeve, removing fingerprints from the shiny surfaces. "A fine suit of clothes," Jacob remarked.

"Ernst," Jerome warned, "those buttons could get you killed."

"Such good shots the Arabs are? They can hit coat buttons?" Rudolf, the forger, asked.

"Shut up, Rudy," Leon suggested without rancor. "Jerome is saying, why give them any better target?"

"Rub on a layer of grease," Jacob suggested. "You can polish them again later."

"*Meshugge!*" Leon added. "It's two hundred degrees already. Why not take the coat off altogether?"

"No!" Ernst responded vehemently.

"Ernst looks more like an officer than the officers do," Jerome noted. "No offense, Jacob."

Leon persisted. "Why not take it off?"

Unbuttoning the coat, Ernst replied, "I'll show you why."

Did the thick fabric hide some deformity? Jacob wondered. The scars of torture?

Parting the lapels of the double-breasted jacket, Ernst revealed the black-and-white striped top of a prisoner's concentration camp pajamas. "This is my one shirt," he explained. "When the Nazis came to Amsterdam, they made me wear the yellow star. Later, when they started rounding up Jews, young priests of the Sacred Hearts of Jesus and Mary . . . my friends . . . hid me and my family in the attic of their seminary." Ernst continued, sadly, "We were betrayed."

No one asked any questions in the blank space that followed this statement; everyone there knew what it meant to be betrayed.

Jacob thought to himself that if this conversation was meant to cheer everyone up, it was a miserable failure.

Ernst plucked at the ragged shirt. "For three years this is what I had to wear. After the war there was nothing and no one to go back to, so I ended up in a D.P. camp. I got this uniform from a barrel of cast-off clothing. Traded one prison for another, yes?"

Once again, there was no commentary, nor any need.

"I vowed I would not discard the shirt until I could live free forever. Then I will *burn* it," he added fiercely.

"Jacob Kalner," Captain Lavie's voice called from outside.

Jacob thrust his head out the back. "Here," he responded.

"Orders are sit tight," Lavie said.

"So . . . when?"

"Soon."

"Something up?"

"Mines. The road. They're clearing it." Lavie moved off toward the next truck to continue passing the word.

"Mines!"

The news exploded around the company.

Jacob recognized the urgent need to deflect the conversation away from Arab preparation. "Sholem." He addressed the Russian Jew. "You and your wife. You got four boys here alive. Tell us."

"For Jews in Russia? The war, it did not bring us the yellow star," Sholem said in an apologetic tone. "I am teacher of agriculture on the collective farm. I am not taken to fight when the Germans attacked. My boys . . ." He patted Ivan affectionately on the back. "They are too young then to fight, so we all live, not well, but we live."

Ivan added, "The food we grow is taken to the front. We are left with turnips. Our soldiers too were starving. But they outlast Hitler. Then after it is over . . . Papa, tell them . . . trouble."

"Yes, trouble," Sholem agreed. "Stalin, you know. Pogroms come again to Russia, like in old, bad times, so we decide we go to America . . . Brooklyn. I have an uncle there. So we go."

Father and son conferred, then Ivan said, "I think, maybe, we walk a thousand miles to the ship. Picking up others as we go."

His father added, "And someone tells me there are collective farms in Eretz-Israel. Kibbutzim. What's the difference, I think? Brooklyn or Palestine, eh?"

Ivan thumped Leon Pickman on the back. "It was that stupid song that made Papa decide." He laughed. "Polish Jews teach us to sing *Wir Muzen Boyen a Yiddish Land.* You know this song?"

"Sure. Everyone knows that stupid song." Leon nodded, thought a minute, and then the flutter of rapidly strummed mandolin strings overflowed the enclosure.

It was true. This was a tune everyone, regardless of nationality, knew.

Jacob's company began to sing. Other men in the lorries before and behind picked up the melody. It swept down the line until the entire convoy joined in.

> *We must build a Jewish land.*
> *Listen! Your heart is telling you so.*
> *We'll fill it with laughter and songs of joy*
> *Where evil can't tell us no.*

It was a fine sentiment, Jerome remarked when the singing faded away. If only someone would teach the words to the Arab Legion!

■ ■ ■ ■

It had been a savage day and savage night for the Jews of Old City Jerusalem.

Daoud followed the old gardener through the tombstones and monuments of Mamillah Cemetery, which was no-man's-land.

Bright green flares splashed light above the ongoing battle as the Palmach brigade once more attempted to take back Zion Gate from ten thousand Syrian, Iraqi, Arab Legion, and local forces who swarmed the Arab Quarter of the Old City.

Red and yellow tracer bullets knifed the air between the Old City wall and the tenuous Jewish positions on Mount Zion.

Lorries of Jewish civilians rumbled through the streets of New City Jerusalem. They were headed for the British Ophthalmic Hospital where the Palmach had launched their attack. From the roof of the hospital a metal, coffin-sized box hung from a cable where it slid across the Valley of Hinnom to carry supplies and reinforcements to Mount Zion one man at a time. The thick-walled Church of the Dormition received double-barrel mortar blasts. Machine guns tacked rambling patterns into stone and flesh.

Daoud said, "Poor Jews. Poor stupid fellows. They will never break through to the Old City a second time."

The cacophony of assault and counterattack unwound like the rattle of a chain dropping a drawbridge. Daoud knew there was no bridge for the Jews to cross. There were only heroic last efforts. Useless. Hopeless. If the Jews of the New City were starving and low on ammunition, what must it be like for the Jews inside the tightening noose of the Old City walls?

Daoud knew the old rabbis would surely be massacred. He had heard it shouted in the streets by Damascus Gate on the morning the Jewish terrorists butchered the people of Deir Yassin.

Vengeance was everything.

The Mufti of Jerusalem declared that one hundred Jews would perish for every Muslim murdered! That would mean Dr. Baruch. Lori Kalner. Rachel Sachar.

Daoud's friend Yacov would surely die, as would his grandfather, Rabbi Lebowitz.

Daoud wished it could be different.

Daoud thought all these things as he jogged to keep pace with the old man.

The gardener did not deflect from his single-minded purpose. His gait was steady, unchanging, tireless. His stride devoured the mile and a half through Jewish New City Jerusalem.

The flash and the boom of mortar fire receded.

"Where are we going?" Daoud asked.

The gardener did not reply. He made his way through the neighborhood of Rehavia, streets full of Jewish houses. Maybe the old man had tended the gardens in Rehavia, Daoud thought. Lightless and shuttered, the homes seemed deserted. But Daoud knew there were people inside hiding from the shell bursts, praying for deliverance, measuring their water, counting grains of barley and eating white, tasteless slabs of matzo bread to survive. If they peered out through the slats of their shuttered windows, they would see an old Arab man and a child trailing after him. But the Jews were too afraid to look, and so Daoud and the gardener passed unseen and unknown through Jerusalem's heart.

TUESDAY

May 25, 1948

"Who foretold this long ago,
who declared this from the distant past?
  Was it not I, the Lord?
And there is no God apart from me,
  a righteous God and a Savior;
  There is none but me.
Turn to me and be saved, all you ends of the earth;
for I am God, and there is no other . . . I have sworn . . . in all integrity
a word that will not be revoked:
  Before me every knee will bow;
  by me every tongue will swear . . .
'In the Lord alone are righteousness and strength.'
. . . In the Lord all the descendants of Israel
will be found righteous and will exult . . ."

Isaiah 45:21–25

CHAPTER 15

The hillside below the Haganah-held British Ophthalmic Hospital was steeped in shadow. But even in the night anyone trying to cross the intervening space between the eye clinic and Mount Zion by vehicle or on foot risked his life. Arab machine guns on the Old City walls and Arab mortars east of them had long before zeroed in on that stretch of territory.

The cable strung across the Valley of Gehenna was the lone way to safely resupply the Palmachniks holding Mount Zion . . . and only after dark.

The coffin-shaped iron box made as many nightly flights as its operators could manage. It carried food, bullets, Davidka mortar shells, and bandages to the handful of Jews in the fortress of the Church of the Dormition, a stone's throw from Zion Gate.

A shrinking handful of defenders.

Despite Dormition Abbey's sturdy walls, ten days of pounding by Arab cannon and nearly continuous sniping had taken their toll.

Nor was defense the only cause of wounds.

The Palmachniks knew the desperate condition of their fellows inside the Old City walls. Since the night of the breakthrough on May 18, they had made three more attempts to carry Zion Gate and reopen the lifeline, including one already tonight.

All failed, leaving the Palmach with more injuries and less ability to succeed the next time.

Return flights of the box carried the more seriously wounded out of the battle.

Luke Thomas placed boxes of rifle bullets inside the chest. "No mortar shells?" he asked.

Palmach Commander Nachasch shrugged. "We asked for more but received none."

Thomas substituted rolls of bandages instead. "If we are so badly off out here," he said, "what must things be like for them in the Jewish Quarter?"

Nachasch grunted. "You do not need to say more. I know what brought you to my post, and I agree: another week has passed. If we cannot rescue the Old City tonight, I don't think they will last. We will hit the gate again . . . about three in the morning. But I make no promises."

■ ■ ■ ■

The truck carrying Jacob and his squad of Aleph Company troops twitched forward yet again. After a gain of less than five yards, another crunching stop was accompanied by a squawk of brakes. The jerk tossed the occupants around, spilling Rudolf onto the floor of the lorry and landing Lain on Jacob's lap. Leon bashed his head into the cab when he expended more effort protecting his mandolin than himself.

"Do these drivers work for the Arabs?" Jerome sputtered. "Are they trying to kill us?"

"How far have we come?" Rudolf wondered as Ernst extended a hand to help the man up.

"And how many hours is it?" Lain asked.

Jacob did not know the answer to either of the serious questions. The convoy of trucks, traveling single file, nose to tail like a column of elephants, had been lurching about for what seemed like days. Despite the moonlit surroundings the procession was incapable of sustaining forward movement.

So far a flat tire, two overheated radiators, and a minor collision had conspired to disrupt any progress.

The vehicles behind each breakdown were temporarily trapped. They could not turn off and motor around the stalls because just the road itself had been cleared of mines . . . not the fields on either side.

Time was passing.

The hour of the planned midnight attack had long since come and gone.

If anxiety had earlier been replaced with camaraderie, the good feelings had evaporated. The emotions dominating the cargo space of the lorry were boredom and misery due to muscle cramps and bladder cramps.

As the latest halt stretched beyond a quarter-hour, Jacob decided to exercise the single privilege conveyed by his rank. "Stay here," he ordered. "I'll see what's up."

Grateful to stretch his legs, Jacob strode along beside the column till he reached the cause of the latest delay. He joined Captain Lavie and others in heaving at a broken-down jeep towing what appeared to be a length of sewer pipe on wheels.

"Busted axle," Lavie grunted.

When the vehicle was dumped in a ditch and the roadway cleared, Jacob peered at the trailing object, a cannon.

The field gun, Lavie explained, was half of the Haganah artillery.

Two cannons of French manufacture constituted the entire battery. The guns were so primitive that they were aimed by sighting along the barrels like giant rifles.

"We call these 'Napoleonchiks' in honor of their first owner," Lavie joked. "Don't share that. I don't think our recruits would find it funny."

■ ■ ■ ■

Daoud stood beside the old gardener on the lip of the world. The thunder of Jerusalem's suffering throbbed behind them.

In the moonlight, hills and canyons tumbled downward toward the sea. White boulders resembled sheep grazing.

But there was no road.

"Where is the road to Beit Susin?" Daoud asked the old man. He was beginning to doubt.

"For four days the Khamseen has been blowing from the east," replied the gardener. "Blowing dust from the bones of Israel." He turned unexpectedly and walked along the ridgeline toward a heap of stones.

Daoud followed. "But where is the road?"

The old man did not reply. He stooped beside a white rock that was shaped like the head of a mortar shell. Rounded, man-made. He extended his hand to Daoud. "Come. Put your hand on it."

Daoud obeyed. It was a sort of marker. "But where is the road?"

The gardener said, "Here. Paving stones. There was a house over there."

"What is this place?" It was a ruin, a desolation, scrubbed clean by the ages. As Daoud watched by moonlight, a breath of east wind swept aside a layer of sand from paving stones like a hand turning back the sheets on a bed. And there, beneath the sand, was the promised road. Or at least part of a road. Twenty broad yards of pavement stretched westward from the place where Daoud knelt beside the marker.

"Come," said the old man. "I will show you the rest."

■ ■ ■ ■

The man who guided Daoud along the long-hidden way descended mountain passes with the stamina and confidence of one who knew the road well.

Daoud stared away into the chasm of a canyon. It was like a dream. He thought that perhaps he was yet in the bushes of St. Trinity, dreaming about walking, and seeing what was not there.

When he glanced back, he was astonished to notice that the stooped posture of the old man had straightened.

"How much further?" Daoud heard his own voice ask.

They had already walked so very far. Daoud's feet hurt. He was tired. "This is a rough and narrow path."

The man slackened his pace and said, "I know you are tired, but you must keep on. The salvation of Jerusalem depends on it. You will show them the way."

Daoud hesitated. Could this be the same old man who had found him in the hydrangea bush? The one who had taken Gawan to the hospital in a wheelbarrow?

In the colorless light of this moonlit night, Daoud's eyes played tricks on him. This fellow was not the elderly gap-toothed gardener, but someone strong and young!

"Where is the old man?" Daoud asked, searching for the gardener. Perhaps exhaustion and lack of sleep had confused Daoud's senses. "Are you the one who found me in the garden at St. Trinity?"

"I am."

"I thought you were someone else . . . someone old . . . Am I dreaming? Was there an old man with you?"

"We have come far, Daoud. You are tired, boy. Come climb on my back. I'll carry you."

His broad forehead and the arch of thick eyebrows bore the unmistakable stamp of a noble race. He was perhaps thirty years old. Handsome and dark. Though he wore the striped caftan and keffiyeh of a nomad, he was not a Bedouin as Daoud first imagined. No. Something else. Kindly brown eyes examined Daoud with a solemn anguish. It was the same expression Daoud had seen when Dr. Baruch first laid eyes on Gawan's wounds. Compassion for suffering.

Had this fellow also suffered?

The mouth was wide and straight and ordinary behind his beard. The forehead was unlined, except beneath the hem of the head scarf

Daoud could see the marks of wounds on the brow. Moonlight glistened on drops of blood. Or did the light come from within the wounds?

"I am dreaming," Daoud mumbled, feeling weak. Suddenly he could not remain conscious. Sleep descended like a weight. "A dream." His knees buckled, and he collapsed on the ground.

A voice whispered to him, "Daoud, son of Baruch. Son of blessing. It is written, 'A little child will lead them.'"

Daoud was vaguely aware of strong arms bearing him up, cradling him like a lamb, carrying him down and down and down the treacherous ravine in safety.

■ ■ ■ ■

When the truck stopped again, Jacob did not move.

Nor did any one else, apart from those who stretched to ease kinked backs.

Ernst sat in morose stillness. Ivan dozed against his father's shoulder. Lain and Rudolf talked softly. Jerome slept soundly, his long legs and thin arms drawn up into a tight ball. Others drowsed.

Jacob squirmed uncomfortably on the hard bench. How he wished *he* could sleep. He had done what he could to keep the squad from giving in to fear.

What about his own fear?

What if the night evaporated before the Jewish attackers ever reached the bridge? There was hardly time left to march on to their assigned spot and launch the assault before daybreak.

Surely Menachem would know this and call off the operation.

It was Tuesday, May 25.

Jacob had been in the Promised Land for less than two weeks.

Four pitched battles in eleven days.

How many men near him had died in those days?

It might have been him. Why was he left alive?

His guts churned with fear. Jacob had no delusions about being immortal, about having a charmed life.

How much longer could he survive?

What difference had his life made to anyone?

Leon read his thoughts. Bending closer the musician said softly, "Maybe by this time tomorrow we will know . . . something, eh?"

An expression of comprehension passed between the two.

Leon said urgently, in an almost inaudible voice, "Tell me what you think. Someday will we soldiers stand before God, I wonder? Souls like tattered rags. Bits and pieces of lives. And with one voice we will cry judgment on kings and generals who sent us to be killed when we were not ready to die? You think so, maybe, Jacob?"

Jacob considered his reply. "They tell us to fight. Maybe even die, you know? But my soul's my own. And if my soul is not ready I think, maybe . . . no one's to blame but me."

"Hmmm. Yes. I have thought about it a lot. Wondered. Maybe it will be a relief to finally know."

Where would he be at the end of the day? And if he never left the field? If this was the hour his soul would stand before Almighty God, what could he say about his life?

Captain Lavie poked his head through the canvas flap. "Out! Everybody out and form up."

Astonishment from the sleepy men followed this command.

Ivan was one of the first to collect himself. But before he could clear the tailgate, his father caught his arm.

"If I should . . . not make it," Jacob heard Sholem say to his son, "you must take care of Mama and your brothers."

Ivan was angry. "Don't even talk like that," he said.

"Promise me," Sholem repeated. "Say it."

Jacob wondered who would take care of Lori.

In the confusion, Captain Lavie offered Jacob one word of advice: "Concentrate on this squad. If you nine get it right, the others will follow. I'll be with the next squad back."

The night was a sea of babbling voices. The dreaded chaos connected with having so many different languages surfaced, doubled and redoubled by the darkness and fear. The Valley of Sorek hummed with human voices.

Ahead stood a row of trees, sentinels at the lower end of the Valley of Ayalon. The grove was beside a dry creek bed and a bridge. From there it was a two-mile hike to the assault point.

Two miles was too close to the Arabs, Jacob thought. This jabber must carry that distance and more. Could surprise yet be possible?

Aleph Company was the first to tramp across the bridge. Three more infantry companies of Third Battalion followed, then Second Battalion and First. Finally fifteen hundred men of the infant Seventh Brigade were on the other side.

They advanced a hundred yards further when a figure loomed up in front of them.

"Youqif! Halt!" a voice demanded in Arabic.

Before Jacob could reply or raise his own weapon, the muzzle blast of a rifle split the night.

A bullet whined off into the gloom.

Aleph Company threw itself to the ground as one man.

Not one of them fired a return shot.

There was a flurry of movement and the sound of running feet disappearing into the distance.

After a time spent listening to the hum of insects and hearing nothing else, Jacob crawled forward to investigate. There was no trace of the enemy.

He returned to report.

"Bedouin shepherd," Lavie guessed.

"Right. Without a flock," Jacob retorted. "Anyway, no chance of surprise left. What now?"

The message was passed along the column to Menachem.

From the commander returned the order: "Proceed as planned."

■ ■ ■ ■

The Palmach attack against the south wall of the Old City was launched precisely at three.

Thunder and hail combined with the crash of waves and the rumble of earthquakes would not have matched the furious noise that followed.

It was 4:30 in the morning when a concluding Arab mortar shell ignited a fire in Gehenna.

4:35 when the last brilliant red flare floating down over the fifteenth-century walls showed no one left alive in front of Zion Gate.

4:50 when a final nervous Arab Legionnaire scraped machine-gun fire across the blackboard of the Jerusalem night.

Without receiving an official report, Luke Thomas already knew the Palmachniks had again failed to smash past Zion Gate and into the Old City.

He and Nachasch tugged at the messenger cable, hauling the iron crate back over the finally-silent valley.

At the midpoint of its flight the box sagged, as if exhausted.

Retrieving the crate from the lower elevation of Mount Zion to the higher eye hospital always meant hauling it uphill. Having the circuit droop made the effort even more difficult.

As the box neared the summit it groaned.

When it reached the crest, blood dripped from it onto Luke Thomas's shoulder.

"Gently!" Nachasch ordered curtly. "Lower it carefully!"

Within the iron hamper was a wounded Palmachnik.

The worst hurt were always evacuated first.

Major Thomas did not recognize the man; knew simply he was young. His face was without color, and he had lost his right leg at mid-thigh. A tourniquet cinched high in his groin was what kept the Palmachnik's soul in his shattered body.

"We tried . . . I swear it, we tried!" he raved. "Three times. The last I touched the gate . . . Zion. Mortars, I yelled."

"Hang on, lad," Luke Thomas said. "We'll get you help."

The Palmachnik's head shook from side to side. "No help! No more shells! No grenades. Always the Arabs have . . . I'm so sorry," he said. "Sorr . . ." And he died.

■ ■ ■ ■

Though it was not yet dawn, Major Francis Burr stood atop the parapet at the Latrun Police Station. The report of a shot being heard from the direction of Hulda had roused him, and now he and Major Athani stared across the darkened wheat fields.

"There is something moving there," Athani said. "It is within the range of our guns. Shall I radio the battery?"

"Not yet."

A Legionnaire approached, accompanied by Chabbaz. "This man," the trooper said after saluting, "wishes to speak to the major."

Chabbaz did not wait for permission. To Athani he said, "The Jews are attacking! Many, many Jews are approaching. Even now they are across the bridge. We must fire at once!"

Athani gestured toward Major Burr. The Englishman was in command; it was his decision when to open the battle.

Chabbaz frowned. Did the Englishman even understand what he had said? What was he waiting for?

"So it was you who fired the shot?" Burr asked in perfect Arabic.

"Yes," Chabbaz replied proudly. "I discovered the approach of the Jews and came to bring warning."

Burr turned back to studying the Jerusalem highway through his binoculars. A thin, black line stretched halfway up the valley from the bridge.

"Many, many Jews," Chabbaz repeated. "A large army."

Nodding, Burr did not thank Chabbaz, nor did he give the order to unleash the artillery. "I don't understand it," he said at last, "but we are fortunate. We *want* them to keep coming! Major," he said to Athani, "give strict orders that no one fires until they hear the signal. And Major," he added, "keep this man under your direct supervision."

■　■　■

Throughout the shelters of the Jewish Quarter the voices of rabbis in prayer rose and fell beneath the obbligato of enemy machine-gun fire.

Rachel, alone in the Hurva basement with her grandfather, listened as the old man prayed for hours and watched the underground passageway for sign of Moshe's returning.

His voice was a melody. "Blessed are you, Adonai, our God, and our ancestors' God: Abraham's God, Isaac's God, and Jacob's God, great, mighty, and revered God, Supreme God who acts most piously, who is master of everything, who remembers the piety of our ancestors, and who brings a redeemer to their descendants for the sake of His Name in love."

After these words he stopped. The sounds of fighting were louder to Rachel without the comfort of his voice.

Why had he stopped? Did he hear something? She strained to hear if there was human sound in the passageway. But there was nothing.

"What is it?" she asked.

"How is it with Abraham? I must know. Is the little boy going to live?" He did not look at her but continued to stare into the tunnel.

"If any of us lives through this, Abraham will survive."

"Well spoken, Rachel." The rabbi smiled enigmatically at her reply. "So. From your mouth to God's ears. Where are they?"

"In the garden. Waiting beside the grave for our deliverance." And then she asked, "Grandfather? Do you think Moshe is alive?"

"I will pray."

"How long will you wait?" She glanced at the detonator box at his feet. She noticed he had taken off his shoes as if he was in mourning.

"Three days is long enough for God to rescue his beloved from death."

Three days! What did the old man know that she could not understand? Had he seen a vision as he prayed? Had the Word of God answered his heart?

"And if he's not here?" She winced at the thought of it.

The old man sighed deeply and shifted on the crate. "There are things I must have, Rachel. Send Yacov to fetch the man who carried Abraham to the garden. The big man with the heart like a child."

"Alfie Halder?"

At the mention of Alfie the rabbi smiled again. His expression brightened. "The exact name I was thinking of."

CHAPTER 16

It was the monastic hour of Lauds.

The monks of the Trappist monastery on the ridge of Latrun gathered in their chapter hall to chant praises for a world about to be reborn in the approaching dawn.

The angel of Lauds, waiting for the sun, floated above the earth and watched as the men of Aleph Company marched clumsily toward death.

The moon hung in the west, casting colorless light over the fields below Latrun.

Would it ever set? Jacob wondered.

In barely an hour the sun would rise.

There would be no darkness to cover their advance. The transition from night to day would happen, but the movements of the advancing troops were as clear as a black-and-white movie projected on a screen.

Moonlight shadowed the eucalyptus stands on the ridge ahead, illuminating black groves against rocky slopes. The top of the bell tower of the monastery was a perfect position for sentries and snipers. Had they spotted Jacob's column moving ponderously forward?

The face of the bluff below Latrun glowered down like a skull with hollow eye sockets.

Jacob turned to look at his men. The features of each member of his company were distinct:

Leon, carrying his rifle lightly, as he had carried his mandolin.

Rudy, the forger, with moonlight bright on his thick spectacles.

Jerome, the gangly French kid with a grin fixed immutably on his face.

The Russians, Sholem and Ivan, father and son.

Lain, the Hasid, whose crippled father had buried five other sons.

Ernst in his chauffeur uniform, buttons concealed by axle grease.

And Captain Joseph Lavie.

Besides Jacob, he was the one other man in the group who had ever fired a shot.

Lining the path beside him Jacob could clearly make out individual stalks of wheat, like thousands of spearpoints barring the way toward the objective.

What was the view like from the heights of Latrun? Against the backdrop of the wheat field how could the Legion miss seeing the snake uncoiling directly in their view?

Everything was happening so slowly!

Since the element of surprise was lost, when speed was everything, the advance felt stalled.

You are too far west, they were told. *Move further east.*

Then again: *you are still out of position and in the way of Second Battalion's route. Move east another five hundred yards.*

What had happened to the Arab patrol? Surely they had reported the earlier encounter. They . . . those unseen watchers hidden within the skull . . . they knew the Jews were coming.

Why was there no response from Latrun?

The buzz of insects carried in the sultry, motionless air.

There was not even any breeze to rustle the trees and cover the noise of their movements.

Jacob could hear the shuffle of Leon Pickman next back in line, and Rudolf, behind him, and Jerome, behind him. There was no tramping of footsteps. Everyone sensed how exposed and vulnerable he was. Each tried to move with a minimum of noise.

Somewhere to the southeast a dog barked.

Jacob halted and the line bunched up, then remembered their instructions. They backed up to regain the proper spacing.

Was the dog sounding the alarm?

Was he baying because he sensed the coming of Aleph Company, or was he responding to some other disturbance, such as the approach of a band of Arabs?

Where was the noise coming from?

Jacob had been told there was an abandoned Arab village in that direction. *Don't worry about it,* he was told. *There's no one living there now.*

The barking ceased. There was no sequel. No one raised a warning cry. No shots were fired. The cicadas resumed their humming.

Motioning with his hand, Jacob waved the troops into advancing again.

This was it: the spot Jacob recognized from the map where a dirt path turned off from the main route. It marked the extent of the movement eastward. It was time to turn north, face Latrun, and get the assault underway.

The shuffling noise of steps on a dusty lane changed in an instant to the rustle of grain being crushed underfoot.

In the stillness it sounded like an enormous threshing machine, crunching, churning.

"Safeties off!" Jacob hissed to Leon. "Pass it on."

"Safeties off," he heard repeated three times.

Then Lain's voice, an apologetic whisper: "How is it you are doing that again, please?"

Fifty yards across the field toward the slopes. One hundred.

No sign they were discovered.

Were the Arabs so deaf? Was it possible Latrun could still be taken by surprise? Had the news of reinforcements been false? Had the enemy already conceded the position?

Voices floated downward from the ridgeline. Melodious, not alarmed or alarming. Singing a hymn.

The Trappist monastery, celebrating Lauds.

The brothers were giving thanks for passing in safety through the night, anticipating the glory of another day, worshipping the Creator.

Another sound was added to the scene.

A high-pitched, flute-like tone, accompanied by a low drone. The tune felt familiar, recognizable, yet Jacob could not quite name it. He was caught between trying to figure out what was making the music and what the melody was.

Recognition was accompanied by unreasonable fear.

He was hearing a set of bagpipes. No Arab played the pipes! The monks?

The air was something he had heard once. Not a march or anything military. It was a comic air.

There was a little man and he had a little gun.

A British soldier—awake, on duty, and playing to announce . . . what?

The first mortar shell screamed overhead, landing twenty yards behind the file of men.

"*Down!*" Jacob cried in English. Then in Hebrew, "*Matah!*"

They flung themselves into the rustling stalks of grain.

Glass waterbottles clattered against rifle stocks.

Someone's breath was coming in short gasps.

"Leon, you hurt?"

"All right," was the wheezing reply. "Landed on the bolt."

The second shell landed in front of them but further back along the line.

Shrapnel scythed wheat and men.

"I'm hit," Joseph Lavie called. "My leg! Kalner, do you hear? I'm hit!"

Jacob raised up long enough to see that everyone else had head buried in hands and body plastered into the terrain.

"Keep down!" Jacob yelled. "Hug the ground! Don't even look around!"

The third shell fell, and the fourth and the fifth.

A machine gun added its rasp to the crump of exploding mortars.

They were seen, located, and bracketed.

And they had not fired a single shot.

■ ■ ■ ■

The shelling stopped finally.

Jerome lifted his head to peer around.

"Keep down!" Jacob ordered. "This isn't. . . ."

He had not time enough to finish the thought before the whistle of incoming rounds resumed.

The Legion gunners had changed their fuse settings.

The next three shells were airbursts.

Thunderous explosions overhead were followed by shrieks of pain.

White hot slivers of steel radiated downward, piercing anyone caught underneath.

"Move!" Jacob shouted. "We can't stay here."

"Retreat?" someone called.

"No! It's as dangerous to go back. Crawl forward! Ernst," Jacob bellowed. "Help Captain Lavie. Everybody crawl!"

What was the Hebrew word for *crawl*?

The word? They did not even know *how* to crawl, how to push their weapons ahead of them, to move on elbows and toes without raising up.

Sholem struggled to his knees, dragging his rifle by its muzzle.

"No!" Jacob yelled. "Keep low!"

An arc of machine-gun bullets sluiced across the field.

Ivan threw himself across his father's shoulders. His weight thrust the older man back to the ground, but a fifty-caliber slug tore off the top of Ivan's head.

■ ■ ■ ■

The line of Third Battalion fractured into tinier and tinier pieces as the exploding shells eliminated any semblance of order.

Close to four hundred men in a line of four companies were pinned down in the wheat field. There was no organization left, no united effort in groups larger than six or seven.

Three battalions . . . fifteen hundred lives stretching from near the entrance to the pass of Bab el Wad all the way around the point of Latrun's peninsula . . . splintered and subdivided into fightened clumps unable to save their closest friends.

Aleph Company, at the furthest east point of the the Jewish advance, disintegrated into fragments.

Men jumped up to flee, only to be cut down by bullets.

Others, equally panicked, trampled on their fallen comrades.

Cries for help doubled and redoubled as soldiers stopped to assist the wounded, then were themselves shattered by shrapnel.

Here and there a few fired their weapons, but accomplished nothing.

Rudolf thrust his rifle in front of him, waved the muzzle toward Latrun, and squeezed the trigger. He did not aim.

No one wanted to raise his head to aim.

Not many knew how.

What was there to shoot at anyway? The enemy was the whining slugs and the bursting mortar rounds, not the vague shapes glimpsed high on the hillside.

"Keep them . . . moving . . . Jacob," Captain Lavie grunted in short exclamations that plainly cost him great effort. "A ditch . . . halfway across . . . shelter."

Jerome and Lain dragged Sholem away from the body of his son.

Ernst lay on his back, flailing his arms like a dry land swimmer to gain a yard. After each advance he then reached out and helped Captain Lavie struggle to join him.

Unnoticed amid the detonating shells, the sun had crept up the margin of dawn. Its fiery ball burst over the Judean hills like the biggest explosion yet.

A wave of heat rushed down Bab el Wad, propelled by the east wind.

The Khamseen, no longer content to whisper from the rooftops of Jerusalem, howled instead through the Valley of Ayalon: *Bow down and worship me!*

■ ■ ■ ■

And so they waited. Jewish women, survivors, mostly strong and young because the old ones had been butchered, milled about the open spaces of the Armenian Convent in Jaffa. They gathered at the washtubs beneath the shaded porticos that ringed the courtyard.

Freshly washed laundry flapped like colorful banners on lines above their heads, giving the gathering a festive appearance. Red woolen underwear. Frayed white shirts. Trousers. Knickers. Bloomers. Long and short socks of an infinite variety of sizes and colors danced above their heads.

"Soap and water," Madame Rose intoned wisely to Ellie as she looked on with satisfaction, "does a world of good. Nothing like a washboard. Helps them feel human again. Takes their minds off the men. Off the war. The wondering."

Ellie followed Madame Rose's gaze to the Russian woman, Katerine, as she attacked a heap of dirty clothes. Her three boys, stripped to the skin, bathed in a bucket behind a partition of blankets. Wrapped in towels while their trousers dried, they lounged in the sun beside a fountain. Other children played tag around them.

There is a woman," Rose said of Katerine, "with a load to carry today. To have kept her husband and sons alive through everything and now. . . ."

Ellie nodded mutely and thought of David. Wondered when she would see him again.

She took a picture of Katerine worrying over the stain in a white shirt. The Russian woman rubbed soap into the fabric, scrubbed it, then held it up. Her wide-set brown eyes brimmed.

Was it Ivan's shirt? Or Sholem's? Was she remembering the time the fabric was marked? A meal perhaps? A cup of tea spilled? What had they said to one another then? Where had they been? Ellie wondered.

Wherever it was, they had been together. A family. Four boys. A mama and a papa. It was a sort of miracle, was it not?

Katerine rinsed the shirt, looked again at the stain for a long moment. Then she shook her head and held the garment tenderly to her cheek.

Ellie averted her eyes quickly as if the woman's pain somehow entered her own heart.

Madame Rose, her face full of pity, furrowed her brow. "Poor woman. Waiting is always the hardest part. They have all been waiting so long." The brawny American linked arms with Ellie and led her back to a storage room, which had been set up as a temporary office. "So," she said, offering Ellie a chair opposite her own. "What is it you have come for?"

"An assignment . . . American magazine . . ."

Madame Rose waved off the reply as though she was brushing away a fly. "No. Why is it you have come? Here. To this little war. Your husband? The pilot?"

"I stayed because of him."

"But you came here for another reason?"

Ellie pondered the question. "I came to Jerusalem not knowing, really, anything about this. Stayed with my uncle. I'm a photographer, so I took pictures of people . . . of these . . . day after day. And things got hard for them. Very hard. And in the darkroom, with their prints all hung up like laundry, I studied their faces. Their eyes. Longing, searching. And in their suffering I saw the face of God. The heart of God loving his children. Am I making sense? I don't know . . . In a thousand gestures . . . like that woman caressing the shirt and thinking, maybe her husband would never come back to wear it again. Loving. Wanting him to come back to her and wear this shirt, see? And God wanting his children to come home to him. Each of them. Each life a love story. The ones who survived are miracles. Their hearts are wounded, broken, but they are miracles just the same . . . and I feel God's love for them." Ellie lost her place. She was rambling. There was so much she wanted to say but where were the words?

"And so," Madame Rose inhaled as if she were breathing in Ellie's emotions, "you stay for them?"

"For myself, I think. Because they are . . . everyone. Everyone who's suffered and not known why. The wandering. The suffering. The homecoming. It's somehow a story about us and God's love, isn't it? About me, too. I haven't got it sorted yet." She shrugged, embarrassed. "I'm just a photographer."

■ ■ ■ ■

Flushed and sweating with heat and the importance of his assignment, Yacov held Alfie's hand, urging him toward the Hurva basement where Grandfather and Rachel waited.

Shaul, the dog, a mere skeleton covered with fur, whined at Alfie's heels and licked his huge hand.

The boy commanded the animal to wait at the top of the stairs as he and Alfie descended into the chamber where the rabbi prayed. "You are forever mighty, Adonai: giving life to the dead, you are a mighty Savior . . ."

Rachel moved aside as the enormous man and the boy stood patiently waiting for Grandfather to finish his prayers.

Alfie was gaunt, bearded, and filthy, and his clothes tattered. But he bowed his head and clasped his hands respectfully like a child saying grace before a meal. His large, square head perched upon the spindle of his neck.

Yacov, slingshot protruding from his back pocket, shifted impatiently from foot to foot.

Grandfather said the last *Omaine,* glanced up at Alfie, and then at Yacov. "Yacov, go upstairs and wait."

The boy scowled. "Do I have to wait?"

"Yes," the old man replied sternly.

Yacov shrugged and ascended, leaving Alfie and Rachel alone with Grandfather.

The old man queried, "Do you know who I am?"

Alfie answered, "Sure. Rachel's grandfather."

"Rabbi Schlomo Lebowitz is my name."

"Sure. Schlomo. Like Solomon, huh?"

"This is good," the old man said, "Alfie. That is your name. Halder, is it? You are here among us, though you are not a Jew."

"I am here to carry."

"Yes. And how is Abraham?"

Alfie replied mildly as he wiped sweat from his brow, "Alive. Waiting in the garden."

"Where are you from?"

"I came with Jacob," was the simple reply.

"A friend of yours?" Grandfather probed kindly and yet insistently, as if this information was important.

"Sure. We was in Germany when the Nazis came. They killed the boys in my hospital. They wanted to kill me too, because I'm *dummkopf.* Like they wanted to kill Jacob because he was a Jew. You know? But I heard the voice and got away out the window."

"The voice." The old man inclined his head and considered Alfie's story.

Alfie raised his eyes upward. "Sure. Like you talking then."

The rabbi's eyes widened. "Alfie." He paled and muttered the Hebrew letters, *"Alef lamed vav."* And then, "Halder . . . *Heh lamed dalet . . . Dalet resh?"*

"Alfie Halder. My name. *Ja,*" Alfie responded cheerfully.

"A good name. A good name. So . . . where did you go?"

"I hid. In a tomb with Joseph. Then after that, I left from there with Jacob and the others. Later we was trying to come to the Promise Land. But we couldn't because they kept us out. Put us in prison. Then the D.P. camp. Then the boat across the sea. We traveled a long time. But we are here."

"Where is your friend? Jacob?"

"Fighting, I think." Alfie scratched his head. "Trying to save Jerusalem, I think."

"And will he? Will Jacob save Jerusalem, do you think?"

Alfie shook his head as the boom of a mortar shell exploded in the distance. "Not all."

Grandfather's eyes blinked back tears. His voice trembled as he asked in a hushed, almost hostile tone, "Why have you come to the Jewish Quarter? To fight?"

"I can't fight. A *dummkopf* don't fight. I help carry," Alfie replied somberly.

"Carry."

"Things. Lots of things. Whatever I'm told. See? Medicine. Food. Sometimes people. Wounded. Hurt. Maybe scared. Like Abe. I carried him on my shoulders. I am supposed to carry. On my shoulders. That's all."

Overcome by emotion, Grandfather covered his eyes with his hand and swayed as though he had seen a vision in Alfie's simple words.

Rachel rushed to his side. "What is it?" she asked, studying the entrance to the tunnel and then Alfie.

Alfie was smiling, oblivious to the old rabbi's grief. "He wants me to carry something," Alfie said. It was not a question but rather a certainty in the simple man's mind.

The rabbi's chin raised up. "Yes. You are here to carry. I understand. Yes." He drew a deep breath. "I will stay here until the last. I need a study table. Pen. Ink. Paper. And . . . Rachel, go with Yacov and Alfie to the library. I need a copy of Torah. Psalms. Isaiah. The Midrash. Alfie must himself carry Torah to me here."

■ ■ ■ ■

By the time the remnants of Aleph Company reached the furrow in the center of the stand of wheat, its strength was two-thirds of when it left Kibbutz Hulda. Some soldiers, running from the battle, were picked off by snipers or blown apart by shell bursts. Wounded and killed scattered across half a mile of Ayalon's plain, and the sun had barely risen.

The survivors prayed Joshua's miracle would *not* be repeated: *God, don't let the sun stand still this day. Bring darkness to hide me. Let rocks cover me. I cannot shelter behind stalks of wheat.*

The ditch was no more than a crease in the wheat field's palm, a lifeline a scant six inches lower than the surroundings.

"Dig!" Jacob ordered. "Dig faster! Pile the dirt up in front of you!"

Mortar rounds continued to burst behind them. Bullets, aimed, deliberate shots, slapped around them.

The Khamseen walked through the field, flattening the wheat, revealing victims past and future.

A black cloud, wafted along by the breeze, settled over Ayalon. It drifted into the lowest folds in the terrain.

No shovels, no helmets, not even knives.

Bare hands tore out clumps of wheat, scratched at the loosened earth.

Lain used his waterbottle as a spade. So did Rudolf and Jerome.

Of the soda bottles, just Leon's remained full. Ernst had slopped out half of his water but preserved the rest by stuffing his thumb in the opening.

Jacob and Captain Lavie had full canteens.

The others had either lost or broken their bottles, or spilled the contents.

CHAPTER 17

Rosebushes.
   Thirty-six roses, bud and bloom, crowned the graves of Gal'ed.

They were dying, wilting in the blast of the Khamseen.

Abe noticed it first. He sat crossed-legged beside Lori. His eyes peeked above the sandbags.

"They are sad," he said.

Around the base of each bush was a thin layer of red petals. The rosebuds, yet unopened, drooped at the ends of their stems. The edges of leaves withered.

Daniel said to Abe, "They're thirsty, kid. Like us." He took a swig of his water.

"Yes. Thirsty." Abe frowned at the jar containing his water ration. And what could be done about it?

Abe took Lori's hand and tugged. "Give them a drink, Lori."

"I can't," she said. "There's not enough water."

"But they'll die," he pleaded. "Give them a drink."

"We have to save our water for people, see?" she tried to explain. "If we don't drink, we will be like the roses."

Abe's face clouded. He frowned toward the roses and then at the murky water drawn from the Hurva cistern. Turning away he scooted toward the makeshift sandbox that was against the back wall of the portico. Soon he was humming truck engines and pushing stones across imaginary roads.

Lori hoped he would not think again about the roses of Gal'ed as they faded away.

■ ■ ■ ■

Jacob saw a puff of smoke appear near the monastery's tower. A second later a crash rolled over his head. The Haganah artillery was returning the Arab fire!

A second thunderous bang tumbled down from the ridge. The antique "Napoleonchiks" found their marks.

"Now!" Jerome exulted when the word was passed. "Let it fall into their laps!"

The Legion mortar fire lifted, sought out its opponents far back across the wheat, and the artillery duel gave Aleph Company a chance to breathe.

"What happens next?" Leon asked. He peered along the barrel of his rifle and grunted as he squeezed off a shot.

Jacob crawled down the ditch to Captain Lavie. He checked the bandage knotted over Lavie's leg wound, then repeated the question.

"Our armor will hit Latrun from the other side of the ridge," Lavie replied. "That will draw the Arabs away from us. Then we can attack again when our reinforcements come up."

Everyone approved of this tactic.

No one believed it.

Jacob, and all of Aleph Company, realized there was no one behind them but those for whom the battle was already done.

There were no reinforcements.

Jacob slapped his neck as something stung him.

Scooting back along the line, he gave each man a drink from his canteen and reminded them to check the muzzles of their weapons for dirt.

Rudolf, brushing at his forehead, found his rifle plugged with a bristling head of wheat. He unclogged it with one hand, while vigorously wiping his eyelids with the other.

The Arab guns were tossing bigger explosives than mortar rounds toward the Jewish battery. Twenty-five-pound shells that made the earth shudder detonated back down the road.

Sholem was huddled in a heap. He made no attempt to hold, let alone aim, his rifle, which lay on the ground beside him. Jacob stopped to console him, to rouse him from his grief.

The back of the man's thin shirt was covered with mosquitoes that he made no effort to dislodge. Jacob, swatting them, saw the outline of his hand appear in blood on Sholem's back.

"What is this?" Jerome said, smacking himself on the cheek and then the ear.

Barkaches, they were called. Minute, biting insects, driven by the Khamseen to seek moisture wherever it could be found.

Hacking and coughing, Jerome spat. "They are getting in my nose and mouth!"

Those who had bandannas, bandages, or cleaning rags arranged scarves as best they could. For exposed arms and necks, they sacrificed part of the precious water to make mud with which to cover themselves.

Every bit of cloth that flapped above the level of the ditch drew a shot from the hillside.

A large column of smoke erupted in the direction of Hulda where Arab rounds scored direct hits on the Haganah artillery emplacement.

Thereafter no more Jewish shells fell on Latrun.

■ ■ ■ ■

By removing the rear seat from the Piper and carrying a minimum load of fuel, David was able to get the single-engine craft airborne. Michael Stone was in the copilot's seat; Bobby Milkin sat stuffed into the back.

David gritted his teeth on the inordinately long takeoff roll. The soaring temperatures removed the lift from the air. The tail wheel of the Piper barely cleared the row of locust trees growing in the wadi east of the airport.

"Sheesh, Milkin," David said once the plane climbed out of danger, "you need to lose weight, buddy."

"Yeah? Comin' on this joyride wasn't my idea, remember."

"We have one chance to get this right," Stone said, leaning forward and peering into the brown hills. "More of us searching means a better chance of finding."

A second unspoken reason for the hasty survey flight was the battle for Latrun.

David guessed that Stone, though banished from the actual fight, felt compelled to observe firsthand what was happening.

His touch light on the controls, David danced the Piper in and out of canyons, giving them a closer view of the terrain. It also made them less likely to be spotted and shot down by Egyptian warplanes.

A few minutes' flying time took them over the Gaza road. "Look sharp," Stone cautioned. "That's Beit Jiz." He pointed out the Arab village across a row of low hills from the Valley of Ayalon.

Nodding, David swung the nose of the Piper onto a heading of one hundred five degrees. "Should be seeing the second village about now."

"Got it," Milkin confirmed, pointing. "And there's where we was last night. Goat trail is right! See how narrow: for two camels to pass they'd both have to exhale."

A crosswind out of the north tossed the Piper sideways, throwing Milkin against the roof. The landscape below traveled from right to left in front of the windscreen.

"Perfect!" Stone exulted. "Right on the lip of the ravine! Hold it like this."

David shot a hurried look over his shoulder, warning his friend not to reveal the truth: the Piper's sideslip had nothing to do with David's piloting. The Khamseen pushed the aircraft around like a toy.

"There's where we were last night. Where the track ends," Stone reported. "See that? Now, is there a way down and across?"

The wadi drifted out of view. "Too far," Stone complained. "Take us back upwind."

The Piper struggled to regain the lost ground, eventually vectoring in at the head of the canyon. The same breeze funneling through the gap in the hills blew them away again. The road that had carried the chariots of Rome to the walls of rebellious Jerusalem two thousand years ago seemed lost forever to ages of landslides and erosion. Gone. Hope of relieving the Jewish population of the Holy City through this route vanished.

"Nothing," Stone muttered. "You?" he said to David.

"Negative."

"Me neither," Milkin put in. "Rocks, cliffs, and sticker bushes. A real dead end."

"One more pass?"

David checked his gauges. "One more," he said.

The banked turn carried the three men over the canyon one last time, but revealed no continuation of the ancient Roman road to Jerusalem. That meant the one route for Jewish convoys was through Bab el Wad. If Latrun was not taken, Jewish Jerusalem was doomed to fall.

When the Piper escaped the grip of the Khamseen, they were over the mouth of Bab el Wad, two miles east of Latrun.

The east wind hurried them down the valley, from which columns of smoke rose.

Bobby Milkin whistled shrilly. "Man," he said. "Like when Patton pounced on the Afrika Corps."

Banking tightly for a better view, David commented, "Yeah, except those are our guys getting their butts handed to them. Look!"

The blazing wheat field was littered with burning wrecks, fleeing men, and the dark clumps of bodies. At the eastern end of the valley a group of khaki-clad troops massed for what must only be an Arab counterthrust.

"They're gettin' murdered!" Milkin said. "What idiot told 'em to attack in broad daylight?"

"What idiot is right," Stone observed. "Get me back, pronto. The dam is about to burst. We have to plug it before it floods Tel Aviv!"

■ ■ ■ ■

In the distance Jacob saw a light plane buzz over the hills. He had a fleeting moment to wish he and the rest of Aleph Company could also take flight.

"One mouthful and pass it on," Jacob said, handing his canteen to Rudolf.

Sholem, paralyzed with grief over the death of his son, ignored Jerome's prodding. The young Frenchman gave the water to Lain instead.

The mortar fire stopped, but no one in Aleph Company moved. Here and there, down the length of the valley, refugee recruits could no longer bear the torment of mosquitos, thirst, and suspense.

They broke from cover and ran.

Not one of them made it out of the wheat field.

At last the promised attack by the Haganah armored unit rumbled out of a grove of oak trees at the extreme western end of the valley.

Firing machine guns as they advanced, six armor-plated jeeps moved to outflank the Legion position. Sixty Haganah foot soldiers followed after. They ran crouched over, trying to remain sheltered by the vehicles.

A portion of Gimel Company, a hundred yards from where Jacob and his comrades lay, attempted to join the assault. They rushed up the slope toward Latrun.

There had been no order to attack, at least none Jacob had heard.

Frustration at being pummeled without being able to respond drove them forward.

Muslim mortar fire began again at once, as did the heavy artillery.

A Haganah armored car disappeared in a direct hit. Jagged pieces of its metal skin sliced into the ranks following, killing ten.

Another armored car stalled. Smoke poured from underneath. Men popping out of the blazing interior were catapulted into the air by the force of a second blast.

Rudolf fired his rifle and worked the bolt. "Come on," he urged. "We'll die if we just stay here!"

Ernst agreed with him. Rising to his knees he sighted and pulled the trigger. "I got one," he said with satisfaction. "I. . . ." A bullet hit him in the left shoulder, spun him around. Blood soaked the tunic of the chauffer's uniform.

Jerome, Leon, and Lain half rose from the ditch.

"Get down," Jacob bellowed.

The remaining four Jewish armored cars reversed direction, retreating toward the grove of trees.

One of them made it to shelter.

A smoking two-inch mortar shell landed in the trench without exploding. It fell between the two wounded men, Ernst and Captain Lavie.

"Shell!" Lavie called in English.

What was the Hebrew for "mortar shell"?

Lain, the scholar, the rabbi's son, the linguist who could not remember how to work the safety of his rifle, had not fired a single shot. He threw himself across the explosive device.

The detonation, muffled by his body, injured no one else, though it shredded him.

His spectacles, unbroken, landed a few feet away.

Gimel Company met streams of machine-gun tracer rounds. Streaking lines of bullets crisscrossed in midair like giant knitting needles. Bodies tumbled over backward or pitched headlong, woven into the fabric of death.

Then the blazing tracer shells set fire to the wheat.

■ ■ ■ ■

Major Burr watched the fall of his battery's shells. The far hills were lashed by mortar and cannon fire. From his vantage point, at each impact the earth erupted from underneath. The bodies of Jewish soldiers were tossed into the air. Twenty yards from a concussion fleeing men crumpled, speared by shrapnel.

The Jewish artillery, which had done scant damage to the Arab positions, had been silenced. Their puny armament was no match for his twenty-five-pounders and mortars.

The feeble attack by Jewish armored vehicles had not even come close to breaking the Legion lines. The Jews had sacrificed their armor and accomplished nothing.

The furthest point the Jewish advance had reached was the vegetable garden of the Trappist monastery. Some of the Haganah soldiers remained alive there, hugging the poles of bean plants and hiding behind tomato vines . . . waiting to be diced, like their comrades.

Burr admired the courage of the Jews who attempted to advance into the ravening mouth of the Legion's guns . . . and had nothing but contempt for the officers who had ordered such a bloodbath.

"It is time," Major Burr said to Athani. "The Jews are running. Order Fourth Regiment to execute a flank attack from Deir Ayub against the easternmost end of the Jewish line. Tell our men that speed is the important thing. If we do not allow the Haganah a chance to regroup, we can break through their lines . . . perhaps push all the way to the sea. At the least we will link up with the Egyptians."

Chabbaz was eager to speak. "My men are ready," he urged. "Let us join this pursuit. We will not stop before Jaffa."

Burr frowned. He did not trust the Arab Irregulars and thought them little better than brigands. Glancing at Athani, Burr sought his opinion without voicing the question.

Athani shrugged. How could they refuse?

"Go then," Burr agreed.

Chabbaz dashed away.

"Pipe major," Burr bellowed. "Give us another tune. 'Lord Randal' will suit."

> O where hae ye been, Lord Randal, my son?
> O where hae ye been, my handsome young man?
> I hae been to the wildwood; Mother make my bed soon,
> For I'm weary wi' hunting and fain would lie doon.

■ ■ ■ ■

Landing the Piper back at the Haganah Air Base, David powered the craft through an abrupt turn and taxied directly to the hangar where his Messerschmitt was being repaired. Michael Stone leapt from the hatch before the plane stopped rolling. Yelling for his jeep and driver, he demanded to be taken to Tel Aviv. "Stay close," he hollered back at David and Milkin. "We'll need recon if the Legion breaks through. Have to set up a line of defense."

"Recon?" David shouted in return. "Defense? What about saving the guys who are already . . ."

But Stone was in his vehicle and roaring away.

"Zoltan!" David bellowed for the Czech mechanic. "How soon can the 109 be ready to launch?"

Emerging from behind the dismantled tail assembly of the Messerschmitt, Zoltan rubbed grease from his hands. "You are making joke, yes?" he suggested. Waving the oil-streaked rag toward the disassembled fighter plane he said, "Holes in tail, in rudder, in ailerons. Intakes full of sand . . . come back in a week."

"No, man." Milkin joined in David's anguished plea. "How about the two new Messers? The Cowboys are surrounded by Injuns and the cavalry has to ride to the rescue, see?"

"American cinema," Zoltan said, "is not Palestine. Unless maybe you can fly without engines. New fighters is not builded yet."

David's mind was racing. "Okay, so we do this the hard way," he said.

"Tin Man," Milkin intoned suspiciously, "this ain't a crapshoot. What hard way?"

"Zoltan," David commanded, ignoring Milkin's look of mistrust, "refuel the Piper and bring me a crate of grenades, on the double."

■ ■ ■ ■

When Samson set fire to the Philistines' wheat, it was the foxes who bore the brunt of his joke.

The Khamseen, laughing with pleasure, clapped its hands and juggled balls of flame.

Bundles of blazing stalks sailed aloft, spilling drops of fire across the field.

A clump landed beside Aleph Company, then another behind them.

Sheets of flame rushed skyward, scorching whoever was nearby.

A soldier of Bet Company, next in line to Jacob's men, screamed and ran. The back of his tunic was smoldering. One of his comrades tried to grab him and was shot. The man flailed futilely at himself, spinning in agony till he collapsed.

"Gav! Gav! Achoranit!"

The Hebrew words for "Get back! Retreat!"

No one needed a translation.

"Listen!" Jacob said fiercely. "Don't run or we die! We withdraw, firing as we go."

He looked around at the group. Who was the steadiest, the least likely to panic?

Leon carefully folded Lain's eyeglasses and put them in his breast pocket, buttoning the flap over them.

Somehow that action made up Jacob's mind. To the mandolin player he said, "Leon, you and I will cover the retreat. Everyone else, back twenty paces, then drop flat on your bellies. Keep shooting at the ridge. When Leon and I get to you, we do it again."

"What about Captain Lavie and Ernst?" Jerome asked.

"Never mind me," Captain Lavie said through gritted teeth. "But you lead them, Jacob. Leon and I will cover you."

Ernst was conscious. His left arm dangled uselessly. "All right," Jacob agreed. "Sholem, you help Ernst. Sholem!" Jacob slapped the Russian, hard. "I said, help Ernst." Sholem managed a nod, but his eyes were wild as he gaped toward the holocaust where his son's body burned.

"Give me Lain's rifle and ammo," Lavie directed. "Leon, you take Ernst's."

Bagpipes skirled, a silly tune, mocking them with a frivolous sport.

Black smoke, swirled by the wind, drifted across the slope. It hid them from the watchers above.

"Move out!"

Fighting the urge to turn and run at full speed was as difficult for Jacob as for any of them. Yet he knew that if he gave in to the temptation, all of them would break. His rifle at his shoulder, Jacob trudged backward deliberately, counting the paces. The muzzle of the weapon searched out targets above the line of the smoke, fired, drove the enemy to cover.

Sholem, sobbing, supported Ernst.

Jerome and Rudolf backed away together.

Lavie was not down in the ditch. He lay across its rim, propped on his elbows, blasting up into the eucalyptus trees. When he emptied one rifle, he threw it aside and grabbed the other.

At the opposite end of the furrow knelt Leon, firing and working the bolt.

Twenty steps. "Down!" Jacob shouted. They had made it that far. "Come on!" he yelled.

Leon made it back. He flung himself beside Jacob. "Need a second to reload," he said, rummaging in his pockets for bullets and stuffing the magazine of the rifle. "Then you can move again. Where is Lavie?"

The captain was obscured by a wall of smoke.

When it cleared he could no longer be seen.

"Why aren't they shelling us?" Jerome wondered. "We are out in the open again."

"There's the reason," Rudolf urged, pointing and then shooting off to his right.

A wave of Legionnaires swept down from the east in a flank attack. If the Jewish line was hit on end, it would be rolled up and crushed entirely. No one would get out of the Vale of Ayalon alive.

CHAPTER 18

The road back to Hulda for the fleeing Jewish army was also the road to Tel Aviv for the attacking Arabs.

Beyond the ruins of Seventh Brigade, there were no Jewish reinforcements nearer than twenty miles away.

If the Arab Legion overran Hulda, they would realize no defensible Jewish position existed between Latrun and the seacoast. A sizable thrust by the Legion could not be stopped. They and the Egyptian army would link up, severing Israel into two fragments.

Not merely the battle but the entire Israeli War of Independence could be lost at that juncture. Not only would besieged Jerusalem be forced to surrender . . . so would the nation.

There was not a single second available for indecision. The battle for Latrun was already a staggering defeat for the Jews. If it was not to become a rout, a disaster of overwhelming consequences, the flank attack had to be stemmed at once.

Jacob and what was left of Aleph Company were the end of the line, the key to staving off catastrophe.

"That hill," Jacob said, pointing to a conical rocky knoll across the road that skirted the wheat field. "That's where we dig in."

But how to get there? The Arab Legion troops were not rushing headlong down the Ayalon valley, but they were sweeping steadily nearer.

Ernst, his chauffeur's jacket stained a dark, oily black from neck to waist, was the first to recognize what was needed. *"Kiddush Hashem!"* he cried to Jerome. Clamping his wounded limb under the opposite armpit, he cradled the rifle in the crook of his elbow and ran toward the enemy. "Go!" he yelled over his shoulder. "I'll buy you time!"

Shouting *"Atah!* Now! Now!" and *"Halach!* Charge!" Ernst fired his weapon, worked the bolt, fired again.

At half the distance to the advancing Muslims, Ernst was wounded a second time and knocked down. Jacob saw him drag himself upright and keep going.

Was it a Jewish counterattack, the Legionnaires wondered? Surely one man would not charge headlong into superior forces unless a greater number followed.

They hesitated.

Ernst, kneeling and shooting, confronted twenty Legionnaires.

The splat of bullets dogging their steps, Jacob led Rudolf, Jerome, Sholem, and Leon in a dash out of the stand of wheat and up the slopes of the knobby hill.

"Pile up the rocks!"

Digging frantically with their bare hands, the scraps of Aleph Company built a makeshift barricade.

His rifle resting in a stone groove, Jacob sighted and fired. His carefully placed shots dropped two Legionnaires, but Ernst was nearly surrounded.

"Ernst!" Jacob yelled. "Get back! Come on!"

Amid the whiz of bullets there was no way to know if Ernst ever heard him.

Jacob saw Ernst reload his weapon, then charge again toward the Arabs. He wounded three more of them before he was riddled with gunfire, fell, and did not reappear.

■ ■ ■ ■

The little band on the rocky hilltop across the smoldering wheat field from Latrun withstood two Arab Legion charges.

The second assault reached the foot of the knoll before being driven back.

The sun beating down heated the boulders so they could not be touched with bare skin.

A mortar round passed overhead, bursting on the reverse slope of the knob.

Another landed in the rocks at the base of the hill. It deafened the defenders, but did no injury.

"Will they shell us out of here?" Rudolf wondered.

Jerome pointed to another massing of Arab soldiers. "They won't wait that long," he said.

The Khamseen sucked the remaining moisture from their already parched bodies.

Jacob passed his canteen around again; he got it back empty.

"How much ammo do you have?" he asked Jerome.

"Twelve shells," was the reply.

Rudolf had ten, Leon, six, Sholem twenty.

Jacob was out.

They pooled the cartridges and shared them. By unspoken consent, they skipped Sholem.

Each man had twelve shots left.

Jacob possessed four grenades that would be useful if the fighting became hand-to-hand.

"One, maybe two more charges," Leon observed. "That's all we can stand. Is it enough?"

Gazing westward toward Hulda before replying, Jacob said, "What choice do we have?"

From his vantage point above the plain, Jacob saw the highway was a ribbon of the limping, crawling, and fallen of the Jewish army. Heat waves made the images multiply into tortured images of genuine agony.

Fifteen hundred men had gone into the Valley of Ayalon.

How many would get out alive and unwounded?

The rain of mortar shells stopped.

"Here they come," Jerome reported.

The Arab Legionnaires, no longer as arrogant as before, were anxious to exploit their victory. This time they came in three waves, leapfrog fashion. Those who were not advancing knelt and fired up at the hilltop.

The shooting was disciplined, dangerous, continuous.

A bullet plowed into the boulder sheltering Jacob and screamed off into the sun. Ducking to his right, he snapped off a shot, then rolled to the opposite side. "Keep moving around," he urged. "Don't give them a target."

A bullet nicked Jerome's ear the same instant he aimed.

A rattle of machine-gun fire pinned Rudolf behind his rock. Shots straddled his position so he could move in neither direction.

From a different angle Leon picked out Rudolf's tormentor and silenced him.

Jacob heard a high-pitched hum augment the crackle of gunfire.

Not a bagpipe, this time.

What was it?

A shadow darkened the hilltop and the hum increased to a ragged roar.

A light plane, swooping out of the sun, pounced on the Legion-naires.

As Jacob watched with amazement, he saw the same Piper aircraft that had plucked him from Jerusalem descending to his aid.

A burly, dark-haired man, leaning out of the right-hand window, tossed a grenade into the front rank of Legionnaires. The plane, facing into the Khamseen, moved so slowly over the ground that it almost hovered. The bombardier took the time to unpin and toss three more grenades before the Piper turned downwind and glided away.

Jacob did not have to order his men to shoot. With the arrival of the unexpected assistance, each refugee soldier redoubled his efforts to drive back the Arabs.

Startled, beset from above and confused, the Legionnaires wavered.

Leon picked off one, Jerome another.

The attack faltered, began to fall back.

The Piper dove in again, this time from behind the Arab line. Heed-less of the tracers being fired from Latrun, the airplane unloaded five more grenades on the Legion troops, who fled.

The pilot . . . Jacob recognized David Meyer . . . waved, and the Piper soared off to the west.

Minutes passed.

There was no further assault.

No more mortar rounds fell. Instead, the high undulating cry of Arab victory punctuated the air from the ridge and on the battlefield.

"Look," Jerome suggested, stanching his wound with a torn-off shirttail.

The fire in the wheat field had nearly burned itself out.

Through gaps in the columns of smoke Jacob saw Arab women in long black robes gliding, stopping, stooping, gathering, and moving again.

Human vultures, gleaning the field of battle, Jacob thought.

"They are stripping our dead," Jerome remarked bitterly.

Sunlight glinted. A knife? A man's scream followed, long and sus-tained.

"Oh, God!" Rudolf muttered. "They are killing the wounded."

Leon fired wildly at the woman and missed, worked the bolt, and discovered he was out of ammunition.

"Come on," Jacob said. "Let's get out of here."

As they fled, Jacob glimpsed three black specters approach Ernst's body. The buttons of the chauffeur's uniform flashed in the sun as they stripped the corpse of the Dutch Jew. Then the stripes of Ernst's prison shirt fluttered like a bloody flag above the dead man for an instant.

Jacob saw the garment tossed onto a heap of burning stubble where it sparked, flared, and rose in scorched fragments on the wind.

■ ■ ■ ■

Bobby Milkin's olive complexion was ashen as they passed beyond the bloody scene of Latrun. Hundreds of Jewish dead and wounded littered the wheat field. "Five, six hundred of our guys down there. Dead. Wounded. We gotta . . . do somethin'." The Piper bounced on the wind.

"How many grenades we got left?"

Pawing through the crate that sat on his lap Milkin reported, "Six. Plenty of firepower."

Sunlight streamed into the cockpit of the Piper. The windscreen was a blinding expanse of glare. Despite the rush of air outside, the temperature heated up noticeably. Banking to change his viewing angle, David peered out the side window. Tendrils of smoke curled skyward behind them as they skimmed over the low Judean hills. "I'll swing around. Make another pass."

"There's our canyon." Milkin noted the chasm where the Roman road dropped away. "No way. I think Jerusalem's in trouble."

David concurred. "Those poor schmucks on the ground aren't getting past Latrun today."

As the nose of the Piper swung toward north once more, David's attention was diverted below. A zigzag pattern, like the flash of a lightning bolt, appeared, blazoned among the boulders on the far side of the ravine. A thin ribbon of a path traced the slope leading to the heights and Jerusalem. "What's that?" David wondered aloud, dipping the nose of the Piper toward the sight.

"You mean *who's that*," Milkin said, jerking his chin toward the ridgeline at the apex of the jagged streak.

A pair of figures stood at the edge of the precipice. Though they appeared poised on the edge of the abyss, their feet were clearly planted on a trail that wound into its depths.

So there was a remnant of the Roman road that led from the coast to Jerusalem!

David fixed his attention on the man and boy who gaped up at them.

A whoosh of wind, like a miniature tornado, buffeted the Piper. A menacing shape roared past, banked, and climbed into the sky.

"Egyptian!" Milkin yelled.

"Spitfire!" David warned. "Hang on, Bobby. I'll go Split-S to evade."

"Split-S!" Milkin gulped. "Tin Man, not in this tin can . . ."

A Split-S was an aerobatic maneuver combining a snap roll with a dive and a recovery in order to make an immediate about-face at a lower altitude. It was a common action during a dogfight.

But a Piper was not a fighter plane. Underpowered at the best of times, the tiny aircraft was never designed for such a move.

The light plane faithfully executed the roll but did not have the guts to right itself. It flew upside down, motoring toward the ground without enough torque to pull out. The engine screaming, the tachometer needle redlined, David grabbed for throttle and fuel-mixture adjustment. "Gotta save the engine."

"Forget the engine!" Milkin protested. "Save us!" Grenades falling from the crate hit him in chin and nose and rattled against the Piper's roof.

The aircraft dropped toward the line of trees and boulders. His eyes glued to the inverted horizon, David demanded, "What altitude?"

"Two thousand!" Milkin cursed. "Roll us out of this!"

They descended toward the boulder-strewn floor of the rugged wadi. The airframe groaned and creaked as the fuselage flexed with the competing pressures. "Can't!" David retorted. "We'd bust in half!"

"Spit's on our tail! Here he comes!"

Pulling up on the control column so the Piper was diving more sharply toward the ground, David coaxed the plane into a loop. "Come on, baby," he crooned as the Piper convulsed and rattled.

The nose had not reached straight down when the aircraft body warped further.

Doors popped open.

Grenades tumbled out, lazily falling into the abyss.

A double line of tracers flashed past the sides of the plane.

"Treeline!" Milkin wailed. The tops of the one-hundred-twenty-foot-tall pines appeared to be scarcely inches lower. "We're not gonna make it!"

"Yes, we are!"

"We're not gonna . . ."

"Come on, baby!"

"We're not . . ."

"Atta girl. Come on . . ."

A circle of flat-roofed houses showed up in a clearing ahead. Robed

Arab villagers stared and gestured at the plunging apparition. One lifted a rifle to his shoulder.

"Two hundred feet!"

"She can do it . . ." The Piper's nose passed vertical, then climbed the other half of the loop with agonizing slowness. "That's it, baby." Finally the Piper came right side up as the enemy roared in for the kill.

The Egyptian Spitfire, intent on his quarry, failed to account for the low altitude and the velocity with which he overtook the Piper. Jinking away from a midair collision at the last second, the fighter plunged past the Piper and exploded in the center of the Arab settlement. A geyser of orange and oily black flame billowed skyward. The villagers scattered and ran for cover as the Piper was buffeted by the shock of the concussion.

Milkin sat rigid, frozen in terror. His mouth was wide in a soundless scream.

He did not move as David eased the Piper back to level flight and readjusted the carburetor and throttle settings. "Close your door," he instructed Milkin.

"Can't," his copilot noted, forcing himself to breathe. "Frame is sprung."

"Yeah, mine too."

Back on the ground minutes later, David taxied toward the hangar. The Piper rolled as if it were limping. Each bit of uneven surface made the aircraft bump and bounce so much David expected the belly to hit the runway.

Zoltan watched them arrive. "Ahhh!" he exclaimed in a strangled tone. "What did you do?" Dancing around the plane as if the ground were blazing hot underfoot, he pointed toward creases in the Piper's skin. "This and here and see!"

Stepping out and turning back, David saw that the aircraft's spine resembled a swaybacked horse. Nose and tail nodded toward each other. Reaching out, he stroked the furrow of wrinkled fabric above the bent frame. "I dunno," he said. Then to Milkin, "Wasn't it always like this?"

CHAPTER 19

The crump of artillery resounded in the wadis beyond Latrun. The battle was raging, Daoud knew, though in the direction of the village of Beit Susin, he could see nothing but smoke.

Daoud's uncle was not in the village. As a matter of fact, nobody was there except one dog and a trio of stray chickens. And it was plain to Daoud that everyone had left in a hurry.

"My uncle has gone."

"Beit Jiz is also deserted," said the gardener.

"Where is everyone?"

Daoud's guide offered, "The battle in Latrun." He inclined his head toward the pillars of smoke beyond the next range of hills.

"And the plane crash," Daoud concurred as he wondered if the dead Egyptian pilot was yet in the wreckage somewhere.

The beehive-shaped ovens of Beit Susin were still warm. Daoud, whose stomach growled back at the scruffy dog, inhaled the smell of baking bread. His mouth watered as the man retrieved loaves of fresh hot bread from the oven and placed them in a canvas sack.

"Where will I go?" Daoud asked, tearing off a chunk of bread and stuffing his mouth.

"There is a sheepfold below this ridge. A short walk from here. Follow me, and I will tell you what you must do."

■ ■ ■ ■

It was a simple discovery that kept the pigeon stalkers safe.

Whenever the day rolled around to the Muslim hours of prayer, the shelling stopped. As long as no one tempted fate by lingering in an open space, even the Arab snipers were less of a danger.

As Yacov noted, "We can kill pigeons when they are not killing Jews."

The pursuit soon expanded beyond the three friends to include the boys about their same age: big enough to be away from mamas and too young to be on barricades with rifles.

A contest followed.

According to Yacov, whoever racked up the highest count of birds during a single Muslim prayer time was entitled to claim the matzo ration from everyone in his group.

"Why?" Leo Krepske challenged. "Nobody wants it anyway."

"Exactly," Yacov responded. "That way, no one feels bad losing, and the winner won't mind sharing if someone actually gets hungry enough to want it back!"

Pigeons, it seemed, were not very bright. Even though each team of hunters had a favorite location to which they resorted over and over, the birds never learned which places were fatal to their kind.

A handful of matzo crumbs invariably attracted a quarry.

The expertise of the boys soon extended to advanced skills: launching multiple stones with one snap and knocking over more than one bird with a single shot.

They also attempted wing shots, but no one ever got really good at it.

Yacov actually knocked a bird out of the air, but even he admitted it was not the one he had been aiming for. It had simply flown into the path of the rock!

For his part in retrieving birds, particularly capturing those that were merely stunned and might have otherwise escaped, Yacov argued that Shaul be allowed a share of the food.

No one, not even Hannah Cohen, objected.

Of course Shaul relished the bits no one else would eat.

■ ■ ■ ■

Eliyahu Hanavi, the synagogue of Elijah, was once a hall for Torah studies belonging to the Ben Zakkai Synagogue next door. As the Jewish population of the Old City expanded after the expulsion of Sephardic Jews from Spain in 1492, the classroom was converted to a sanctuary.

But the name came later.

Once an epidemic stalked the city, and people were afraid to leave their homes. Morning prayers could not be held because not enough men came to form a minyan.

At last a tall, spare-framed stranger with piercing eyes arrived, and the service proceeded.

That morning marked a turning point in the ravages of the disease.

When the prayers for deliverance were answered and the plague abated, the stranger could not be located. In fact, no one knew his identity, or acknowledged having seen him either before or following that one morning's prayers.

That night his name was revealed to the rabbi in a dream.

He was Elijah, the prophet. The same man who had defeated the priests of Baal in the contest on Mount Carmel. The same Elijah whose return to earth was said to herald Messiah's approach.

A chair for Elijah, should he choose to visit again, stood near the ark containing the Word of the Almighty. A candle was kept perpetually burning near it.

Under this flickering light Ehud Schiff pondered the condition of the Quarter.

On the positive side, pigeon stew had extended the starvation rations, at least as far as those with the greatest needs were concerned.

On the other hand, after the last desperate radio message pleading for reinforcements and ammunition, Haganah High Command had responded, "Give us two hours."

That had been forty-eight hours ago.

Ehud looked up.

In the doorway was Rabbi Akiva. Beside him was a child from an ultraorthodox family. The boy had left his thumb in his mouth. With the finger of his right hand he played with the silken ringlet of earlock that hung down his cheek.

Ehud rubbed his eyes wearily. He had not slept in those same forty-eight hours. Or was it seventy-two? A visit from Reb Akiva was never a pleasant experience. What now?

"Schiff," Akiva said. "I have come to apologize. I was wrong."

This was so totally unexpected that Ehud could think of no reply.

"You are as much in danger here as any of us," Akiva continued. "More, because you are exposed to bullets and bombs. Nor, I think, did you choose to be a soldier. The sea is your home, yes?"

Ehud nodded.

Akiva shifted the boy around so the child was directly in front of Ehud. "This is Gabriel Rivlin," he said. "He is two. His father was killed by a sniper in April. His mother died last week. He has no other family." Akiva patted Gabriel's shoulder with his pudgy hands. "He is the last of a line of Talmudic scholars whose lineage here in the Quarter goes back centuries. He is the treasure worth preserving. He is our future."

Ehud could see where this discussion was heading. "Reb Akiva," he said, "I am sorry for the boy's losses, but it was the Arabs who killed his parents. Not me . . . not Moshe . . . not the Haganah. If we received the state we were promised, we would not be at war and no one would be dying. If you can get the Arabs to stop shooting at us, then I would agree to stop shooting at them!"

Akiva shoved Gabriel aside. "Do you want his blood to be on your head?" he thundered. "Do you? The Legion has promised civilians safe passage to the New City as soon as the Quarter surrenders."

"And did King Abdullah tell you this himself?" Ehud said, barely able to control his anger. "You look like a Jew, but you speak like a Muslim. Take the boy and go!"

After Akiva's departure, Ehud glared at the vacant chair of Elijah. "So, you couldn't manage another visit to stop this plague, could you?" he said. "Or if Messiah came tonight, that would be fine." He stared with despair at the inventory figures of guns, ammunition, and unwounded defenders. "*Oy*," he said. "Just send Moshe back. This job makes my head ache."

Daoud jogged to keep pace with the quick stride of the one who had led him from Jerusalem to the deserted village of his uncle. And now? What would he do since he had no family at Beit Susin?

Halfway down the trail that stretched from the villages to the oasis, the great storm began. A wall of dust, hundreds of feet high, was carried on the Khamseen. It roiled down the mountains from the east, from Jerusalem.

Daoud watched as date palms bent with the force of the wind. Then they vanished behind the curtain of grit. Daoud covered his head and face with his robe against the sting of gravel. The villages were lost behind a brown curtain.

The figure of the one was a phantom image far ahead of Daoud now, walking on, unperturbed, into the teeth of the storm.

Daoud struggled to keep up. What if he got lost? What if the one who had carried him that far left him behind? Without help Daoud would wander off, blindly, into the desert blizzard.

"Wait!" Daoud cried, but his voice dissipated beneath the howl of the Khamseen. The drumming of cannonfire over the hills could not be heard above the rumble.

He stumbled forward along the trail. His eyes burned. The heat was like a furnace blast. Tripping on a stone, the boy fell to his knees, scraping his palms and forearms bloody. "Wait!" he called again, afraid. "I'm lost! Help me! Sir! I am lost!"

Moments passed as Daoud crouched on the path. He anchored his hands on rocks as the storm tore at his clothes. He had been left! Deserted! Forgotten! The Khamseen could blow like this for a week. Daoud would die of thirst. His body would be found by a shepherd months from now. He dared not move forward on a path he could not see.

"I am lost!" he called out. "Find me!"

Misery. Why had he ever left Jerusalem? Why had he followed this gardener who was not a gardener? Who was, indeed, not at all what he first appeared to be?

The air was too thick to breathe. Daoud cupped his hand over his mouth and nose to filter the grit. His eyes squeezed tight.

"Please." His voice was weak. "Come back for me."

Daoud gave up. He would die. Even strong men perished in the wilderness when the Khamseen blew. He lay down flat and covered his head. He was tired and miserable. He began to weep. His brother, Gawan, would never know what had become of him. He would simply dry up and blow away like the dust of Palestine!

"*Ya Allah!*" he cried. "Oh, God!"

And then, amazing thing! For the second time the strong arms of the gardener gathered him up to carry him as he had been carried through the night. A broad hand shielded his head from the fierceness of the sand. Daoud tucked his face into his savior's shoulder. He could not see where he was being carried, but it was as though the storm did not trouble the one who carried him.

Minutes passed. Daoud could not say how long the trek was. And then the man put him down in the lee of a stone wall. A sheep pen. The force of the wind whistled above his head but did not penetrate the shelter. A date palm rattled overhead.

Daoud's rescuer stooped beside him. His cloak was lowered over half his face so only the piercing wounds in his brow and deep-brown eyes were visible. Kind eyes, but terribly sad. Daoud knew without being told that he was going away.

"Wait here, Daoud, son of Baruch."

"But where are you going?" The boy barely choked the words out.

"Three men will come here. You must show them the way back."

"But where are you going?"

The man stood, towering over Daoud. Sun broke through and shone around him, blinding Daoud.

"The wheat fields," came the reply. "Remember what I have told you. Peace be with you." And then, turning into the whirling wind, he was gone.

■ ■ ■ ■

At the same time as the Jews were attacking Latrun, elements of the Arab Legion assaulted and captured a twenty-seven-hundred-foot-tall promontory north of Jerusalem. Called *Radar Hill* because of the British-installed aerials on its summit, the mountain overlooked the road between Jerusalem and Ramallah.

The Legion also tried to conquer Abu Ghosh, a Haganah-held village on the other side of that same road, but failed.

Stalemate.

But lacking in men and supplies, it was a standoff the Jews could not afford to sustain for long.

They had to break through to Jerusalem, or every Jewish post in central Israel would be forfeit.

And in the meantime, the lone thing dividing the attention of the Arab Legion was another standoff: the Old City.

"We are losing the Jewish Quarter!" Luke Thomas punched the wall of the eye hospital with his fist. "Losing it!"

Nachasch stared coldly at Jerusalem commander David Shaltiel. "We had but fifteen rounds for the Davidka last night," he said. "And half of them did not explode. What kind of war is this when men lay down their lives but don't get the support they need? Palmach is bleeding to death . . . the Palmach is dying!"

Shaltiel took off his glasses to rub his sunken eyes. He appeared to have aged twenty years in two weeks. "We may lose more than the Old City," he said. "Nachasch, you did not have more shells because I had none to send. We are down to twenty-five mortar shells in all of Jerusalem."

Luke Thomas waited. Shaltiel had not come up to the British Ophthalmic Hospital from his headquarters solely to talk about mortar shells.

Shaltiel continued, "Latrun. I had a report from Tel Aviv. We failed to open the pass. Our dead number in . . . hundreds."

"That's it, then," Nachasch said flatly. "You have pissed away my men's lives trying to save the Old City, when we cannot even save the New."

"The message said they will attack again and that they are trying to open an alternate route. . . ." Shaltiel's voice trailed off in misery. No one believed help for Jerusalem could come in time.

"I will not attack again," Nachasch concluded. "You cannot force me to kill more Palmachniks. We will hold Mount Zion, but I will not watch any more of my people die. You, who had it in your power to send us reinforcements when we held the gate open! You have killed the Old City, and now it falls back on your own head!" He stalked out of the room.

■ ■ ■ ■

Despite Zoltan's protest that they had "already wrecked too many equipments," David and Bobby Milkin commandeered a jeep and roared off toward Kibbutz Hulda to find Michael Stone.

The road between Hulda and Tel Aviv was jammed with traffic. David steered into the eastbound line behind a troop lorry bringing reinforcement up from Jaffa. Every time he poked the nose of their vehicle out from behind the slow-moving truck he had to jerk back to avoid a head-on collision.

The traffic heading west was all ambulances and other motor vehicles pressed into service as medical transport. "Must be as bad as it looked," David remarked to Milkin.

Despite their near disaster with the Piper, it was the images of the heaps of bodies lying amid the wheat field that haunted David.

"Worse," Milkin returned as a bus clattered past. Every seat was occupied, and every occupant bandaged and hollow-eyed.

They located Stone in the schoolroom at Hulda. A group of Haganah officers pored over a map, talking in hushed tones. Stone and Menachem were in the corner away from the others. Their voices were anything but hushed.

It was apparent at David's first glance that only the width of the flat-topped teacher's desk prevented the two men from being at each other's throats.

"Ben-Gurion ordered this attack personally," Menachem snarled. "Even you could not change that."

"He did not order you to go ahead with it after the sun was up and all chance of surprise was lost," Stone barked back. "How many did you kill? Five hundred? Six? For what?"

Menachem said coldly, "This is no concern of yours. I am summoned to the prime minister's office tonight. I will make my report directly to him. Leave me alone. I have orders to issue for the revised defensive perimeter."

"I will also make a report to the prime minister," Stone said.

Menachem stared at Stone, then turned toward the map table.

David signaled to Stone, who joined the two aviators.

"You guys did good work up there," Stone said. "Crazy stunt, dropping grenades, but it worked."

"Yeah?" Milkin said doubtfully. "We saw how bad our side was gettin' plastered."

"With your help, one unit managed to hold the east flank," Stone explained. "Kalner. Same guy you brought down from Jerusalem, David. Anyway, it kept the Legion from overrunning the field. We've got a new line, along with mortars and armored cars, between here and the bridge. We can hold 'em there, but the road is no nearer open than ever . . . maybe less since they know how bad we want it."

"You ready for good news?" David asked.

"Anything."

"We found it, up at the canyon. A way across."

"A kinda path," Milkin put in. "Zigzag down, zigzag up."

"You sure? Not just a vein in the rocks?"

"Saw two people at the top on the far side," David explained. "Why would they be there if there was no trail?"

"What people? Arabs?"

David shrugged. "We didn't really get a good look at them."

"Yeah," Milkin added. "We got real busy about then, you know?"

Stone pondered, then said, "Okay, here's the drill: Another 109 is coming in tonight. Milkin, you stay and help uncrate it. David, you and me pick up Bashir and up we go. Rush trip, so I get back to meet with the boss. There may be hope in this mess after all."

■ ■ ■ ■

The mood on the heights of Latrun was a mixture of elation and chagrin.

The Arab Irregulars like Chabbaz's men were celebrating. At a cost of a handful of wounded and none killed they had plundered much of value from the dead Jews. Of this loot a large amount had already been sent home with the women, before the Jordanian soldiers could insist on a share.

Chabbaz was pleased that many weapons had fallen into his hands. He had heard that as many as two hundred brand-new rifles had been left on the field by the retreating Jews. His own band had carried off forty-seven of them.

Across the square the Legionnaires who were not on guard were lined up in somber ranks. Major Burr dealt them a severe reprimand. "The door was open!" he shouted. "The path to Tel Aviv was in front of you. Victory was in sight. You had your enemy in full retreat, and yet you did not take advantage of it!" he said scornfully. "You allowed a few men . . . a mere squad at most . . . to act as rearguard, and the door has been slammed in your faces! Because of your failure, the war will be prolonged. More of your comrades will die. Perhaps you will die. If we get such an opportunity again, you will not stop; you will not slow down; you will pursue and pursue and pursue until your enemy at last turns to fight because he has nowhere left to run . . . and then you will annihilate him! Dismissed!"

Burr drew a frowning Athani aside to speak with him. "You think I was too harsh with them?" he inquired.

"No," Athani responded. It had been a defensive victory, but wars were not won by defense. A greater triumph had been possible but had eluded their grasp. "Women and villagers came out of the wadis to strip the dead," Athani suggested. "We could not fire without hitting them. Do you really think the Jews will come again after today?"

Burr showed Athani a box of personal effects retrieved from the plundered bodies. "The Jews desperately want this pass," he said. "Look: there are papers here in every European language. We found rifles with the safety catches on. Muzzles jammed with dirt. They threw their rawest recruits into this fight, without regard to the cost." He stared across the smoldering stubble. "Do I think they'll come again? Oh, yes. They'll come."

Burr stalked away.

Athani pondered how he would have spoken to the troops. Perhaps he would have reminded them of the time when the hero-warriors of Saladin had swept down from these heights and hacked their enemy to bits on the plain below.

Then again, he likely would not have used that example in front of Burr. After all, the enemy decimated by Saladin's men had been the Crusader knights of the English king Lionheart.

■ ■ ■ ■

Daoud awakened, alone, within the stone enclosure beneath the shade of a date palm. It took him several minutes to get his bearings. The wind had died. The dust settled. The wadi, like the villages, was deserted.

Within Daoud's memory was the gorge into which the man had carried him from Jerusalem. They had crossed the chasm, climbed up the opposite grade, then walked miles to Beit Susin and Beit Jiz. The dust storm had come, and Daoud had been left here.

Waiting.

Turning toward the north, Daoud saw the low hills on which the towns perched. The scattered wreck of the Egyptian fighter plane pocked the terraced fabric of the ground between the tiny settlements.

Beyond the ridge smoke rose up from the wheat fields around Latrun. Daoud guessed the battle had been terrible. But he could not see it, nor could this secluded spot be seen from the fortress of Latrun.

The gardener had gone away to the wheat fields, Daoud remembered. Did he join the battle?

This was a place where shepherds kept their flocks by night.

There was an old well in addition to the stone sheep pen. The ground beneath the date palms was littered with dried sheep dung.

The well was covered with boards. A bucket dangled from a hook on a post, inviting the thirsty traveler to drink. Daoud lifted the cover and let the bucket down into the well. It echoed hollowly in its descent. He filled it, hauled it up, and drank deeply of the cool, clear water. Splashing his face, he drank again.

Everything about the long trek from Jerusalem was clear to Daoud, as clear as any dream could be. It seemed he had slept a good bit of the way, and even the parts when he had been awake seemed dreamlike. He remembered every step, each turning of the switchback and the ascent of the Roman road.

Daoud puzzled over it.

The savior who had carried him through the storm said he must wait here.

Three soldiers would be sent to find him. Then he would have to show them the way back to Jerusalem.

The gardener was nowhere to be seen. Why had he left the task of leading others back to Jerusalem to Daoud? Daoud felt very worthless. What if he forgot the way? What if he got lost and misguided the others?

Daoud scanned the surrounding hills for movement. He wondered if his uncle had gone off to fight the Jews at Latrun.

The wind was up again. Fluttering, not raging like before. Daoud lifted the bucket from the lip of the well and closed the plank cover to keep sand from blowing into it.

Glancing toward the tower of smoke rising beyond the hills he wondered if the Jews had won or if the Arab Legion had turned them back. He thought about the souls of the dead, hovering barely above the earth. Did they regret leaving, he wondered?

He drank again, his thirst finally quenched.

Then he settled down in the scant shade of the well to wait.

CHAPTER 20

T he mood among the soldiers returning to Kibbutz Hulda from
the defeat at Latrun was grim.

Officers shouted commands at fresh troops conscripted
from civilians in Tel Aviv and later refugee ships.

The rumble of lorry engines drowned out conversation as these reinforcements moved forward to hold the line against an expected Arab
Legion push to the sea. Taxi drivers and shopkeepers, armed but dismally unprepared, gawked at the survivors as though they had returned
from hell and could reveal what to expect.

Jacob and four others in his squad staggered past the troop lorries
and found a place in the shade of a budding almond tree. He had been
informed that they would be left to lick their wounds for a while but
that their assignment was far from over.

Sholem lay on his back, staring up through the branches. The blood
of his son splattered his clothing. He had not spoken in hours, and even
the tears had stopped. Jacob reasoned that Sholem would be no use to
anyone. He should be sent back to join his wife and sons at the Jaffa
Convent.

Rudolf, the forger, had stripped to his waist in the heat, revealing a
pale, soft, unsoldierly paunch. And yet, somehow, courage under fire
had proved Rudolf was not a counterfeit as a man.

Leon, inscrutable, recovered his mandolin from the schoolroom,
then returned to join his squad beneath the tree. He found refuge in his
instrument. Making eye contact with no one, he plucked the strings in
sad, dissonant melody.

Jerome had lost his beret somewhere in the wheat field. Brown,
matted hair tumbled over his brow. His long, thin face appeared angry
as he studied the other knots of devastated men gathered within the
barbed wire of the enclosure.

Jacob, certain he could not survive if he was sent to fight even one more time, thought of Lori. He had been a fool to bring her here. To believe in miracles and prophetic promises. Where was God when men were dying in the wheat fields to open the road to Jerusalem? Surely, with this failure, Jewish Jerusalem would be lost. Probably the dream of Israel would also die.

Fifty years from now all of this would be forgotten, an insignificant footnote in history.

Jerome spoke at last to Jacob. "Look at him." He inclined his head slightly toward Sholem. "He's gone. He just lies there. The brains of his kid all over his shirt."

Leon did not stop in his playing. "He needs to sleep. He will come back after he sleeps."

Leon spoke as one who knows about such things.

Jerome grimaced, then asked, "Did you see what they did to Ernst's chauffeur's uniform? Those vultures."

Rudolf said, "They burned his KZ shirt. Did you see? He said when he was finally free that he would burn the prison shirt."

Leon nodded.

Jerome clasped his hands around his knees and rocked back. "Suicide going back like that. He was yelling something when they killed him. . . ."

Leon answered, "*Kiddush Hashem.* That is what he was yelling. It is forbidden by Jewish law for a Jew to commit suicide. The exception is *Kiddush Hashem,* when a person takes his own life rather than transgress against the Lord. It means, 'Sanctify the Name.'"

"He knew he would die." Jerome considered the information. "All of them. So many. Does it make any difference?"

Leon plucked out single notes and then began to sing almost in a whisper,

> *Overcome all obstacles and straits.*
> *Don't falter through the depth and heights*
> *   of the rebellion.*
> *Carry a torch to burn, to ignite.*
> *Since quietude is like mire.*
> *Risk your blood and your soul*
> *For the glory that is unseen.*
> *To conquer the mountain or die.*
> *Yodephet. Masada. Beitar.*

Jacob at last joined the conversation. "What are Yodephet, Masada, and Beitar?"

Leon's thin lips curved in a sad smile. "Three towns that fought heroically against Rome. In the end, they fell. But they did not surrender. *Kiddush Hashem!*" He studied Sholem's blank expression. "One day Sholem will wake up and say, 'My son died to save Israel.' He will understand that Ivan's death is a holy death. And Ernst gave his life so we could live. To Sanctify the Name. *Kiddush Hashem.* As Abraham offered his son to the Lord, so the Lord offers His Son, the Messiah, to redeem Israel. In Torah and the writings of the prophets there is nothing more holy in the sight of the Eternal than this. And also we may die so Israel may live. Those of us who survived Birkenau and Auschwitz and Treblinka know about *Kiddush Hashem.* The world may forget. But we cannot. That is why we will win or die."

Jerome replied quietly, "So. Ernst is free now."

■ ■ ■ ■

Several hours passed.

Daoud sat on the stone wall and munched bread and dates. Sweat trickled from his forehead.

If the clamor from the British guns at Latrun was any indication of the way things were, Daoud figured the seacoast was more dangerous than Jerusalem. He decided that at twilight, when the land cooled a bit, he would begin the long trek back to Jerusalem even without the three men.

He had stopped looking for the three mysterious travelers to find him. He wanted to go home. Here was bread enough to last him a week. He would fill the skin with water. Walking up the pass would be slower than coming down, but he could be back where he started in two days. Maybe he would somehow get back into the Old City to see his brother. He had nowhere else to go.

Everything was still. Superheated air rising from the hard stone floor of the wadi created the illusion of lakes of water on the horizon. He would have liked to plunge into a pool of water, but contented himself with the bucket from the well. Ladling out handfuls, he splashed his shirt extravagantly. The water evaporated within an instant.

He glanced up and on the trembling horizon spotted two jeeps bearing three figures. They grew steadily more distinct as they moved toward him. It would be another twenty minutes' driving over rugged terrain before they arrived at the wadi.

He took another bite of bread, then drew another bucket of water from the well and filled the water skin.

He was ready when they came at last, sweat-stained and tense-eyed to the oasis.

One Arab, young, strong, and confident, dressed in military garb, sat in the passenger side of the first jeep. Daoud guessed from his keffiyeh and features that he was a Druze. Not a Sunni like himself, nor a crazy Shiite, as were many of the most rabidly anti-Jewish.

The vehicle was adorned with a Star of David. So the gardener had sent Jews for him to guide. So be it. As Allah willed. It made sense. He should have known. The Arab Legion could drive to Jerusalem on the main road any day of the week. Only Jews would be hunting for another way.

Since the gardener had saved him, Daoud was in his debt. He would guide these Jews up the pass as he had been told.

The driver, a young, sandy-haired, sunburned man, jumped out of the vehicle and glared at Daoud. He carried a British Sten gun and was wearing the sort of boots Daoud and Gawan had seen once on American cowboys at the cinema. He did not have a hat. A foolish thing in such a place as this. His nose would blister.

The second jeep was driven by a middle-aged man, bull-necked and thick around the middle. He was fit enough. Wearing sensible shoes for a long walk, he was dressed in khaki and wore a floppy canvas hat like an English tourist.

The three men considered Daoud with suspicion.

"*Salaam,*" Daoud greeted them.

The Druze returned the greeting.

The cowboy, not knowing Daoud spoke English, said, "Ask the beggar what he's doing here. Ask him where everyone in his villages have gone."

The Druze opened his mouth to ask, but Daoud thought there was no time to waste.

Daoud addressed the cowboy in English. "Sir? Where is your hat?"

The American replied roughly, pointing the gun toward Beit Susin. "Are you from up there?"

Daoud answered in Arabic to the Druze. "I speak English. Why does he not ask me himself? I am no fool. I used to speak to the English soldiers in the Old City. I can talk. This American you are with is rude. He did not offer me the sign of peace. Who are you? Why are you with him?"

The Arab replied, "My name is Bashir. We have come looking for . . ."

The American interrupted, "Ask him where his people have gone."

Daoud frowned and passed the water skin to Bashir, who bobbed his head politely, blessed him properly, and drank.

Bashir asked, "What is your name, boy?"

"Daoud. Son of Baruch."

"A Jew?"

"My father. He is in the Old City."

"The villages seem to be deserted."

"They are. When we came this morning they were empty. I took this bread from the ovens for the journey. Still warm. They ran away in a hurry. The plane crash, I think. Or maybe the sound of the fighting. There will be plenty enough bread if we are going to ride in a jeep."

The driver of the second jeep spoke, "Where is he from?"

Daoud perceived he was also American. He was likewise rude and did not bless the well or Daoud as he drank from the skin.

Daoud would not speak to either of these Americans. He perceived also that they thought he was an ignorant boy. Why had the gardener sent them to him?

Daoud said to Bashir, "I will very much like to ride in a jeep."

"We cannot take you with us, Daoud," said Bashir. "It is very dangerous where we are going."

"A bad road. I know this." He narrowed his eyes in appraisal and studied the width of the vehicle. "But I do not think it is too narrow."

The driver of the second jeep asked again, "Is he from one of the villages?"

Bashir replied, "He says he is from Jerusalem. His father is a Jew."

Daoud snapped in English, "I am from Jerusalem. I came here last night from Jerusalem with the gardener to look for my uncle because my father Baruch is in the Jewish Quarter and my brother Gawan is wounded in the Latin Patriarchate. And I would like to go home to Jerusalem. I should not have left. I was told you would come and that I should show you the road and you would take me home. But I will not show you if you make me walk. I shall wish to ride to Jerusalem in your jeep!"

■ ■ ■ ■

From the top of the cliff where Daoud and the three men stood there was no evidence of a path down four hundred feet to the bottom of the wadi.

The cowboy, who was called Tin Man, peered over the rim and said to Stone, "Not without wings we don't."

Bashir put his hand on Daoud's shoulder in a friendly way. "Ask the boy. Ask him where he came from last night."

Stone eyed Daoud with interest. "All right. The straight of it. Did you walk from Jerusalem?"

"I did," Daoud replied. He glanced toward the heap of boulders that marked the start of the footpath.

"He wasn't alone," Tin Man interjected. "I saw a man with him on the other side."

"The gardener," Daoud agreed.

Bashir queried, "Who is this gardener?"

Daoud explained, "He wanted to come to the sea, he said. He was tired of Jerusalem, I think. He showed me the way. Brought me here. You must know him. He said you would come, and I must show you the road back to the Holy City."

The three men exchanged doubtful looks. "Sure," Stone said tentatively. He winked broadly at Tin Man. "You know, the gardener? The fella who told us to come find Daoud?"

Daoud had the feeling Stone had never met the gardener, but never mind. The three men had come and wanted to go to Jerusalem.

"Show us," Bashir said to the boy. "The path down. Where is it?"

Daoud pointed. "Under your nose."

The trio followed Daoud to the place. He walked over the flat natural stone platform where the trail began. The rock was worn away slightly from centuries of footsteps, but it was impossible to see the path unless someone knew where to look. Daoud stepped off and began the steep descent.

The trio followed, scouting the terrain.

"But can a donkey make it?" Stone asked.

Bashir eyed the ravine and the switchbacks. "This side? Any day."

"Camels?"

"Yes. But not that side." He pointed to the opposite wall of the ravine. The path was a slender thread stitched into the stone edifice.

Tin Man asked Daoud, "On the other side? How's the path at the top?"

"For three miles it is not so good. But enough for camels and donkeys. After that a jeep can climb it."

"Is the way clear?" Stone demanded. "Were there soldiers on the road?"

"The Haganah holds all of west Jerusalem," Daoud replied. "King Abdullah's soldiers are in the Old City. Or they have gone to Latrun to fight. I did not see any men of Jordan's Legions on our way to this place."

Bashir remarked, "Jerusalem. If Haganah can send men down from there . . ."

Stone hesitated and frowned up toward the mountains. In a solemn voice he whispered the phrase from *Merchant of Venice*, "Who chooseth this, must give and hazard all he hath."

Tin Man nodded. "Everything depends on it. If it doesn't work . . ."

"We lose Jerusalem," Bashir concluded.

"And if we don't try?" Stone asked.

Tin Man answered, "We lose Jerusalem. Maybe Israel."

Stone grinned. "Fair enough. Jerusalem needs a transfusion. We can do it! It's a beginning. Bashir, you come back to Tel Aviv with me. We'll need to commandeer every freight animal we can get our hands on. Tin Man, you and the boy go up the pass. Tell the Haganah commander in Jerusalem what we're doing. Bring camels. Donkeys. Wheelbarrows. Anything. And a couple hundred men from that side who can haul supplies up from the bottom of the ravine by hand." He passed canteen and Sten gun to Tin Man. "We can get a trickle of supplies through to Jerusalem this way while we're building the road."

"Build a road?" Tin Man gave a low whistle.

"Under the noses of the enemy?" Bashir asked.

"We'll have help. The waters parted when our backs were against the sea, didn't they? So, we need another miracle. A road is not so difficult after the Red Sea, is it?" Stone chucked a rock into the chasm. It arced into the void and tumbled toward the bottom.

■ ■ ■ ■

Ben-Gurion, no stranger to loud exchanges himself, nevertheless required that his subordinates control their emotions. He had already quelled two violent outbursts in his Red House office between Stone and Menachem; he was losing his patience. "I want to know the facts," he announced. "How many?"

The other men understood the import of the question.

"Stragglers are coming in," Menachem said. "Many of the raw recruits ran at the first shots . . . threw away their weapons and ran. Many are no doubt back in the Tel Aviv cafés by now."

Stone snorted but made no comment.

"How many?" Ben-Gurion repeated.

"Perhaps . . . seventy-five killed," Menachem suggested.

Unable to contain himself longer, Stone exploded, "Seven hundred fifty, you mean! Shot, bombed, burned to death! Wounded men knifed where they lay. Shot in the back by Arab villagers while trying to escape this fiasco."

"See?" Menachem interrupted. "Dumped their weapons and ran."

Stone said through gritted teeth, "If half of Seventh Battalion survived, I will be amazed. Even less of Menachem's Third Brigade."

Ben-Gurion bowed his massive head into his hands. "So many as that?"

Stone gripped the arms of the chair. He lowered his voice again, but his words shook with emotion. "Some died of thirst! Thirst! Collapsed from heatstroke and died."

Protesting, Menachem said, "We were not supplied enough canteens. . . ."

Quartermaster Brigadier Shotter opened his mouth to protest, but Stone beat him to it.

Whirling toward Menachem, Stone snapped, "It is the commander's duty to see to equipment."

"There was no coordination between the columns," Menachem said, changing the subject. "We asked for support from the armored cars, but they did not come."

The commander of Second Battalion, Chaim Lascov, admitted that his armored cars had been unable to achieve anything useful.

"We asked for artillery assistance, and it was ineffective," Menachem continued. "There should have been an overall commander, and then these mistakes would not have happened! I am already working on a better plan to take Latrun."

There was truth to the assertion that Haganah efforts were uncoordinated and in need of being synchronized by a higher authority.

Clearly Menachem was suggesting himself for the position.

Ben-Gurion eyed Menachem, but his gaze returned to Michael Stone. "I will carefully consider your suggestion," he said at last to Menachem. "But meanwhile, Jerusalem must be saved. What is to be done?"

"There is another route; a way to resupply Jerusalem that does not go through Bab el Wad," Stone said.

Ben-Gurion, who had been slumped in his chair, pulled himself upright. With more energy that he had shown since the news from Latrun he said, "Tell me."

Stone elaborated on the first attempt to trace the Roman road by night, of David's locating the connecting path across the ravine from the air and the recent trip to reconnoiter. "It is there," he said. "I have seen it, walked it. Jeeps can make it easily as far as Beit Susin. From there we haul supplies over the wadi . . . manhandled if necessary . . . then reload them for the run to Jerusalem."

"Then we call off any other attempt on Latrun."

Shaking his head, Stone said, "No, on that Menachem's right. We must keep the Arabs off our backs if the alternate route is to succeed. We have to make them think we remain desperate to open the pass."

Ben-Gurion closed his eyes. Though he had not been present in the wheat fields, the horrible images were too vivid. "Not like today," he said with a weary sigh.

"Not like today," Stone agreed. "Here's what we need immediately: Picks and shovels. Bulldozers, if we can find them. Men, women, and boys to clear and widen the road. A force of at least brigade strength for sentry duty and patrols, and every jeep, donkey, and camel you can round up. We can do it," Michael Stone asserted. "We can have supplies in Jerusalem by Saturday without going through Bab el Wad."

"Ha!" Menachem sneered. "By camel? By donkey? Jerusalem needs . . . what did you tell me, Prime Minister? One hundred fifty tons a week for starvation rations. And what about ammunition to fight a war, or has the American forgotten that Jerusalem must also fight? Latrun! Latrun is the key!"

Stone was ready to strangle the Irgun commander, but he only said, "We can do it. But we must have men. Lots of them. Road-building equipment and operators, of course, but mostly lots of men. Let me have the rest of Third Battalion and as many more as you can spare. Attack Latrun again, yes, but a feint to hold the Arabs in position. Make them *think* we still need the pass."

"We do!" Menachem said. "Do not waste men and time! Give me the resources this time, and I will give you Latrun."

Second Battalion commander Chaim Laskov cleared his throat. "I have heard that the United Nations is again pushing for a cease-fire. Is this so?"

Ben-Gurion acknowledged the truth of the assertion. "Whatever the Arabs hold when the cease-fire begins they will arm and resupply. That will be fatal for Jerusalem unless we resupply it first."

His thoughts clearly divided, Ben-Gurion wanted to believe that

Stone could do the impossible. He wanted to be spared the horrors of another disaster like the first assault on Latrun.

But more than anything, he wanted to achieve a breakthrough to Jerusalem, by any means possible.

"No more fighting men for the road," he declared. "You can have volunteers from Third Battalion and the civilians we round up from Tel Aviv and bring down from Jerusalem."

Menachem smirked with delight.

"But I am not yet ready to name a Jerusalem Front commander," Ben-Gurion declared. "I want to see results first."

The lines were clearly drawn, the contest begun.

■ ■ ■ ■

It was evening when the American colonel Michael Stone arrived among the Latrun survivors at Hulda. He disappeared into Menachem's schoolhouse headquarters for five minutes and then emerged with the news that one hundred volunteers were needed to patrol the ridge between Latrun and a desert wadi where a hidden road to Jerusalem was being built.

Seventy-three volunteered to go. To a man, the remainder of Jacob's squad stepped forward. Leon, Jerome, Rudolf, and finally, with evident weariness, Sholem.

It was clear to Jacob that Sholem would be of no use to the squad as they patrolled the heights above the secret road. His lack of interest in anything after his son was killed made him a liability. In his present condition he was no soldier. But perhaps years of moving earth on a collective farm in the Soviet Union made him a candidate for road building.

Jacob explained this quietly to Stone, who agreed. He then took Sholem aside and told him he would be needed elsewhere. Stone was driving back to the refugee camp where Sholem's wife and three sons were. Members of the road-building crew would be drafted from among them.

Sholem took his new assignment as a kind of disgrace. He would not meet anyone's eye.

Troop lorries arrived to transport the seventy-two soldiers into the hills of Beit Jiz and Beit Susin.

Jacob waited beside Michael Stone at the jeep as Sholem made his farewell to the other members of the squad.

"Build a good road." Jerome slapped him on the back.

"Yes." Sholem said solemnly. "Shoot straight."

Leon passed the mandolin to Sholem. "Take care of this for me."

Sholem's lip quivered. "Yes."

"And give this to Lain's father." From his pocket Leon took the spectacles of Lain, the fallen Hasid. He gave them to Sholem. "You both lost sons. Tell him his boy died bravely. Say to him Lain died '*Kiddush Hashem*'."

Sholem could not reply. He fingered the eyeglasses of the young Hasid. "I will. I will tell him." He embraced Leon, then Jerome, Rudolf, and finally Jacob. "So. Next week in Jerusalem." He held up the instrument and attempted to smile. "Then we will sing together."

Leon called after him, "Next week in Jerusalem!"

Sholem climbed into the back of the jeep and was gone.

CHAPTER 21

oshe Sachar grew more and more anxious with each passing hour.

The advantage gained by the destruction of the cannon on the wall was slipping away. Even in the depth of the candlemaker's basement, the rasp of machine guns could be heard, supplemented by periodic explosions.

Moshe knew the vise around the Jewish Quarter was tightening.

How could he get back?

Dov lapsed in and out of consciousness. He was barely awake at the best of times.

Taking Dov would mean carrying him across blocks of hostile territory, without even knowing if the underground passage was open.

At sundown Moshe decided he could wait no longer.

Moshe's arm linked through Dov's elbow, they navigated the crooked streets.

The Muslim Quarter pulsed with the arrival of soldiers intent on freeing Jerusalem from the presence of Jews forever. Many of the Arabs who fled after the sabotage of the cannon returned.

Excited conversations revolved around two topics: King Abdullah intended to keep his promise to enter Jerusalem on the anniversary of his coronation.

"Truly," said a white-turbanned Muslim cleric to an eager audience. "The king will come. He will worship on the Haram. Then everyone will acknowledge him as the proper ruler."

For the local Arabs of Jerusalem, peace would be a welcome visitor, no matter who was proclaimed sovereign.

More disturbing was news about a battle to open the road at Latrun. The details Moshe picked up were sketchy and often contradictory, but the consensus was that the Arab Legion had won a decisive victory over the Jewish attackers.

"Two thousand Jews lie dead in the wheat fields," boasted a peasant wearing crossed bandoleers.

"Were you there?" inquired an old man leading a donkey loaded with sticks.

"No, but my cousin was. Never was such a slaughter, he says. Many weapons were taken from the dead, and he gave me these." The speaker indicated the bullets around his shoulders.

So the Haganah attempt to force open the road had failed.

No breakthrough at Bab el Wad meant no resupply for the Jews holding New City Jerusalem. The siege was intact.

No supplies and no reinforcements lessened the chances of saving the Old City, perhaps eliminated any remaining hope altogether.

Moshe pressed on.

Dov shuffled his feet as if he were a hundred years old and barely able to walk.

They reached the far end of Bab el Silsileh.

The entrance to the tunnel . . . if it still existed . . . was two blocks away.

Moshe and Dov turned the corner.

Even in this Arab-controlled sector there were no lights for fear of Jewish snipers, but there was moon enough to reveal a knot of uniformed men up ahead.

Keep going, Moshe told himself. *We're so close.*

A snatch of conversation reached him.

English!

"Latrun is impassable. Jewish Jerusalem will fall. They have no more mortars in the New City. The Old City will soon be reduced to throwing stones. But we don't have time to wait for starvation to have its effect. The safety of the king is our primary concern, you understand."

Moshe recognized the voice and then the face! British major Francis Burr, now of the Arab Legion.

Moshe had met the man several times during the years of British Mandate. Burr had an interest in archaeology and had sat in on Moshe's lectures at Hebrew University.

Burr continued, "I'm returning to Latrun tonight. You have fourteen of the finest British officers at your disposal to finish the job."

Could Moshe trust that darkness and disguise would be enough to get them safely past?

"The Old City must fall tomorrow. The next day at the latest,"

Moshe heard someone else say in guttural tones. "After the new gun is in position King Abdullah will expect it."

Ahkmed al-Malik! One man who could unfailingly identify Moshe at a glance.

That settled the idea of continuing forward.

Moshe turned around. Dov swung like the dead weight of a drunkard at the end of Moshe's arm.

Three paces.

Five.

No alarm raised.

Retracing his steps, Moshe rounded Bab el-Silsileh, and plunged into the arms of an Arab Legionnaire sergeant.

"What are you doing here?" the Legionnaire demanded in Arabic. "This area is off limits for security reasons until after the king's visit tomorrow."

"My brother," Moshe returned in perfect Arabic. "He is wounded. We seek medical attention."

Security for the king's visit! Abdullah's arrival in Jerusalem meant escaping through the tunnel had gotten more difficult, if not impossible!

"Well, you are lost, then," the sergeant continued. "The closest infirmary is at the Rawdah School, back the other way."

"*Salaam,*" Moshe thanked him.

Dov mumbled the name of Yehudit, then Chaim.

"Thank you," Moshe repeated hastily. "I can find . . ."

"No, I better help you," the sergeant said, grasping Dov's other arm. "Orders are that anyone moving in this area in another half-hour may be fired on."

■ ■ ■ ■

"Majesty," General John Glubb said, reporting to King Abdullah, "I have news. A Jewish attack on our position at Latrun has been decisively defeated."

When the king made no comment but merely nodded to show his comprehension, Glubb took this as a signal to elaborate. "The Jews were routed. Their operation was ill-planned and poorly executed, and launched in full view of our guns. They left eight hundred dead and large amounts of weapons and other materiel on the battlefield."

"And the number of prisoners taken?" Abdullah inquired.

Glubb examined the ceiling as if the required sum was written there. "No prisoners were taken," he replied at last.

"I see," said the king quietly, then, "and how have we followed up this success?"

"Regrettably, our forces did not aggressively pursue the retreating Jews. There was . . . some confusion," Glubb concluded lamely, chagrined. "But we are reorganizing even as I speak in order to achieve a conclusive victory."

The king studied his general for a time. "I also have news," he said. "I will go to Jerusalem tomorrow, as planned."

"Majesty," Glubb said, raising a cautioning hand, "I don't think . . ."

"The United Nations," Abdullah continued as if Glubb had not interrupted, "is demanding a cease-fire. We must assert our mastery over Jerusalem, *even if* we have not yet *fully* achieved it."

Generalship was not enough. Warfare also involved politics and diplomacy.

Glubb knew King Abdullah held him responsible for failing to finish the conquest of the Holy City, yet Abdullah would show the world he was already king there.

"There is yet another reason for urgency," Abdullah added. "What you have not yet heard is that the U.N. pressures your English government to withdraw the British officers seconded to our Legion."

"Withdraw? How many?"

"All of them."

Glubb sputtered. "But Majesty, the brigade commanders are English. The commanding officers of three of our four infantry regiments are English. The trained artillery officers are English. . . ."

"And you are saying the Arab officers are incapable of taking over command?" Abdullah chided.

Glubb avoided answering that question directly. Instead he replied, "The artillery units have been operational for just three months. There has not been time to adequately teach . . ." This response was not an improvement, since Glubb was admitting he had failed to properly train the officer corps.

Abdullah let Glubb flounder, then said, "One further communiqué concerns yourself, my general. You are, it seems, going to face a charge of violating the British Foreign Enlistments Act since you accepted employment by me without His Britannic Majesty's permission."

Snorting, Glubb said, "Then His Britannic Majesty is suffering from memory loss!"

Abdullah put his hand on Glubb's shoulder and smiled. "Of course," he said. "But you see the pressing issues we face. The date spoken of for British officers to stand down is May thirtieth. There are two things I know: I *will* go to Jerusalem tomorrow. Here is the other: when the cease-fire comes, the picture of who will rule Palestine may not be complete, but the whole of *Jerusalem* must be in *our* hands."

"Jerusalem cannot be resupplied, Majesty," Glubb said. "And since it cannot, it will fall into our hands within the week."

■ ■ ■ ■

On the horizon to the north the flashes of a distant battle flared and subsided, then flashed again. Galilee? Ellie wondered. Too far away for the sound to reach her, it was like watching a forest fire on a summer night in California when she was a kid. The terror of its destruction was lessened by its fearful beauty. People were dying out there. Even as she snapped a photograph of the devouring light, heartbeats were stilled and voices cried their last.

So far away. Who was winning?

Madame Rose leaned against the balustrade of the Jaffa Convent. "Like lightning in a storm at sea," she remarked quietly. "Beautiful to behold. Nothing you want to be caught in."

Everyone had some image.

The rooftop parapet was crowned with other spectators. They talked among themselves in languages Ellie could not understand.

Katerine and her three boys murmured, and Ellie caught the mention of "Papa" and "Ivan." Perhaps they imagined husband and brother together in the conflict.

Just then a man's cheerful voice echoed in the courtyard of the Armenian Convent. "*Shalom!*"

A lantern flared. Ellie instantly recognized Michael Stone, and with him three others including Sholem, the husband of Katerine. He was holding a mandolin. Ellie wondered at the fate of its former owner.

Katerine cried out at the sight of him. "Sholem!" A shout of joy and relief.

The three boys called, "Papa!" and bolted for the steps.

Michael Stone glanced up toward the ruckus and then, as the Russian father was reunited with his wife and sons, he explained about the road.

"The path traces the wadi up the back way to Jerusalem. . . ."

Madame Rose whispered to Ellie, "The father is back, but the son is not with him."

Sholem led his wife and sons to an uncrowded place beside a broken pillar.

Ellie watched the drama as Stone's message was translated.

". . . workers to build the road . . ."

Sholem covered his face with his hands. Weeping. Shaking his head.

". . . the back way . . ."

Katerine, already knowing, grasped his fingers and tugged his hands down, revealing the tears.

". . . to relieve Jerusalem . . ."

Sholem touched her cheek, then struck his own chest with fury. Why had it not been himself, the gesture cried.

". . . Our troops were turned back at Latrun . . ."

Turned back?

Katerine wrapped her arms around Sholem and cradled his head against her shoulder.

The next oldest boy clenched his fists and turned away in fury.

The two younger children clung to their father and mother.

". . . We must make another way . . ."

From the shadows came the Hasidic Jew with one arm. Ellie recognized him as the man whose son had gone to fight with Sholem and Ivan. He had called after them, "Take care of my son! He's all I have left."

Cautiously he approached the grieving family. Was there news?

He ducked his head, sorry to intrude. But he must know. Must . . .

Sholem looked at him in anguish. *Sorry. So sorry!*

The Hasid knew without being told.

Sholem removed a pair of eyeglasses from his pocket and held them out. At first the Hasid would not take them. And then he reached for them. Received them. Held them in his hand as one would hold an injured bird.

Michael Stone, his voice forceful, did not see any of this.

". . . If we cannot relieve Jerusalem, everything will be lost . . ."

The knees of the Hasid buckled. He fell slowly, so slowly. It was as if his human form melted with news of his son's death. He lay very still, a dark pool at Sholem's feet.

■ ■ ■ ■

As Moshe and the Legion sergeant struggled to propel Dov through the darkened roads of the Arab Quarter, Moshe's mind was racing.

The Rawdah School had long been headquarters for the Muslim

forces in Jerusalem. Previously occupied by the Mufti's Holy Strugglers, it was now obviously under the control of Jordan's Arab Legion.

There was no comfort in that.

Either Burr or al-Malik could identify Moshe if they saw him there. It did not matter whether he was picked out by one of Haj Amin's creatures or by a British officer in an Arab Legion uniform.

Either meant summary execution as a spy.

To go into the Rawdah School was suicide.

But how to escape without causing suspicion? Dov was visibly in need of medical attention. Refusing assistance would cause instant alarm bells in the Legion officer's mind.

The Muslim School of Kuliat Rawdat el-Ma'arif stood on the site of an ancient fortress. When the Roman conquerors of Judea wanted to demonstrate their military presence in Jerusalem, they did so by building the Tower of Antonia as a visible symbol of their might.

The would-be rulers from Jordan occupied the same location.

Even the present structure suggested a desire for dominance. Built on rock and elevated well above ground level, a flight of stone steps climbed to the entrance.

His foot already on the bottom tread, Moshe sagged as if he could go no further. "Your pardon," he said to the Legionnaire. "I must rest. I am myself unwell."

Moshe sat abruptly, forcing the sergeant to release his grip on Dov.

A rusted metal plaque affixed to the wall across the street identified the spot as part of the Via Dolorosa, the Way of Sorrows for the suffering Savior.

If I leave Dov, he'll be found out and they'll kill him. If I stay, we'll both be killed.

"Come in," the sergeant urged. "Just a few more steps and then help for your brother."

■ ■ ■ ■

Three Iraqi brigades attacked Tulkarm in north-central Palestine. The latest attempt to cut Israel in two nearly succeeded . . . but not quite. As with the Legion in the center and the Egyptians in the south, the Israelis demonstrated unexpected resilience and tenacity.

Arab predictions of a war that would be over in three days . . . five days . . . a week . . . were replaced with suggesting a conclusion at the end of two weeks.

But the voices were not as confident as they had been.

Ellie found Michael Stone as he encouraged refugees who piled into the arriving trucks. The very old and very young he turned back. Everyone else was drafted for duty.

"Colonel Stone? We met in Jaffa. You know my husband." She reintroduced herself as David Meyer's wife.

"Of course. Spouse of the infamous Tin Man." Stone had a gleam in his eye. "Avenger of the sky."

"I haven't seen any Israeli planes. I was wondering."

"They're works in progress. But in due time." Stone cheerfully waved a line of lean, sunburned women into a lorry. "That will keep morale up."

"Where is David?" she asked.

"By this time? Jerusalem I hope."

"He's flying the Jerusalem–Tel Aviv route?"

"Nope. No planes for Tin Man for a while. He's walking, dear lady. The whole long way. As Judy Garland sings in *The Wizard of Oz*." He hummed and grinned. "Something . . . something . . . yellow brick road. I'm not sure of the lyrics."

"He's coming back?"

"I sincerely hope so. With an army of Munchkins. Come along, and you may meet up somewhere in the middle."

■ ■ ■ ■

Moshe's mind churned as he searched the shadows for a way of escape. There was none.

Perversely, his thoughts turned to Rawdah School's historic past. It was at the Tower of Antonia that the apostle Paul was rescued by the Roman tribune Lysias from rioters who would have killed him.

Likewise, Moshe and Dov needed a miracle of intervention to save their lives.

The door at the top of the Rawdah School steps banged open.

"You there," called a booming voice in English. "What are you doing hanging about?"

Moshe believed this was the end. He could not escape without abandoning Dov. He was unwilling to do that.

The Arab Legion sergeant responded to his British superior, "There is an injured man here, Captain Kerry. He is a soldier of the Irregular forces. I am assisting him and his brother."

"Well, assist yourself back on duty," ordered the Englishman. "Sergeant Shaba, is it? No time to waste with riffraff. After what happened at

Latrun today, the Jews will be desperate. Bloody well may try something when King Abdullah enters the Old City tomorrow. Leave off playing Good Samaritan. Get over to the Church of the Holy Sepulchre. Report to the chief of security for tomorrow's ceremony."

With that the British captain turned on his heel and reentered Legion headquarters.

"Rest here as long as you need to," Shaba said softly to Moshe in Arabic. "Your brother will recover, *Insh' Allah*. And someday, *Insh' Allah*, we Muslims will recover from the rule of these English Christian pigs! *Salaam.*"

Moshe breathed a prayer of thanks as the soldier vanished into the darkness. They were reprieved from death.

Moshe hoisted Dov onto his shoulder and carried him around the nearest corner on the route back to their basement hiding place.

■ ■ ■ ■

Dov was no worse . . . and no better.

His life, like Jerusalem's, hung by a cobweb fine enough to be parted with a single breath.

Moshe's thoughts revolved from Dov to the Old City and back again, without resolution.

If he did not return soon to the Jewish Quarter, he would be too late to make any useful contribution. There would no longer be a Jewish Quarter to reenter.

Besides that, the returning life animating the Muslim Quarter suggested their hideout might not exist much longer. At any time the candlemaker might return to his shop and evict them.

And Dov, if he was to survive, needed more medical help than Moshe could provide.

Even waiting for another day to pass might be too long.

But how? The area near the tunnel was being patrolled.

In his inability to find an answer, a cloud of despair settled over Moshe.

I have failed, he thought. *Can't do any more. Like the dead men at Latrun. I have failed the people I love . . . Rachel. Our coming baby . . . our children. What will happen to her when the last wall goes down? No miracles left.*

Something nagged at Moshe's memory. What else had he overheard?

The streets nearest the Jewish Quarter had been cleared to keep as-sassins from threatening King Abdullah.

Abdullah was going to be on the Temple Mount tomorrow, Wednesday.

Security would be tight throughout the Old City. The Englishman at Rawdah indicated the Legion had a chief of security at the Christian Church of the Holy Sepulchre.

Why? Thus far the remaining Christian presence in Jerusalem had tried to remain neutral in the fighting.

Why was an Arab Legion officer needed at the church? Unless Abdullah intended to visit it as well!

Suddenly something clicked.

Abdullah was going to pay a visit of respect to the Christian shrine!

Attention would, for a time, be focused on the northwestern section of the Old City . . . away from the Jewish Quarter!

It might be the chance he had been looking for.

It might be their last chance.

The cellar of the candlemaker's shop smelled of wax. It was cooler here than the floor above. Dov stirred and reached out his hand. Moshe took it and kissed his fingers as if he were a boy in need of his father's comfort.

"Papa?" Dov asked weakly.

"No. Moshe."

"Where is Papa? Where is Chaim?"

He called for his father and brother, both of whom had perished in Warsaw.

"They aren't here," Moshe replied gently.

Dov moaned. "It wasn't a dream then. They are gone!"

"You're in Jerusalem, Dov. Jerusalem! You're hurt."

"The fire. The fire. I couldn't carry them out. Papa's legs shot up. Chaim shot through the spine. The fire coming up the stairwell! I tried to drag them. Tried! The tank gun aimed at the window."

"That's finished. A long time ago."

"No! I carry it with me! Every day!" He clutched Moshe's shirtfront. "The fire coming up the stairs. Papa shouting at me to live. To run. Chaim shot through the spine. And me so scared because the tank has us in its sights!"

Moshe soothed, "It's Jerusalem, Dov! May, 1948! You're alive!"

"So scared. I was . . . I left them. Papa and my brother. Chaim screaming he was scared to die. I crawled out the door. The smoke so thick! My God! Chaim screaming. Papa yelling I should go! Why didn't I die with them?"

Dov's eyes were wild with grief and resurrected terror. Moshe held his hand. "It's over, Dov. You're here. Jerusalem. You have a wife to live for. Yehudit. Remember? Yehudit is waiting for you. Praying for you to return. *Shalom!* Peace, Dov! You must be still. The Arabs will hear you!"

Dov turned his face to the wall and replied with a racking sob, "Go. Leave me, Moshe. Like I left them. To die. Please go."

"I'm staying," Moshe said. "We'll get out of here together. Sleep. God will find a way for us, Dov. We will live."

WEDNESDAY

May 26, 1948

"I will go before you
    and will level the mountains . . .
I will give you the treasures of darkness,
riches stored in secret places,
so that you may know that I am
    the Lord,
the God of Israel, who summons you by name.
For the sake of Jacob my servant,
    of Israel my chosen,
I summon you by name
and bestow on you a title of honor,
though you do not acknowledge me . . .
I am the Lord, and there is no other;
apart from me there is no God.
I will strengthen you,
though you have not acknowledged me,
so that from the rising of the sun
    to the place of its setting,
men may know there is none
    besides me."

Isaiah 45:2–6

CHAPTER 22

Long hours passed until Dov finally reawakened.

"What happened?" he asked hoarsely.

"We are in the candleshop," Moshe said, trying to disguise his disappointment.

Just then came the boom of another wall being blown.

"Leave me." Dov groaned.

"I'm staying." Moshe winced. If he went back, could he rally the defense of the Jewish Quarter?

"What's the use? With me you can't get back."

"I won't go."

"I'm a dead man. All . . . everything . . . what's the use? I should have died in Warsaw. With the others. With my brother. My father."

"I'm staying with you. Hear me. The Arab Quarter is swarming with soldiers. But listen! We stopped the advance of the Legion into the New City. Remember, Dov? You did it."

Dov squeezed his hand. "I was never afraid of death."

"God will help us. We'll get you to a Jewish hospital. . . ."

"For a long time I thought, you know, that there was nothing after death. I'd die like my father and Chaim, and all would be darkness."

"No. Not darkness, Dov. Life! *Chaim!*"

"Jerusalem! The air hums with everything that ever was! I hear it. I'm afraid of what I hear. All around. Death. Something after this life . . . I heard voices. Not of this world, but close. Like behind a screen. On the other side of a door."

"What do they say?"

"No hope, they say. You're lost, they say. Your life is nothing. You mean nothing. You are nothing. You deserted your own father. You killed your brother. Left them to the Nazis and the flames. Voices whispering to me. Everything I ever did. Despair. The law of Moses. Every commandment I've broken. God can't forgive me."

"He does forgive, Dov! God is love."

"But I've hated him. In my heart I've blamed God. For all the things that were done to us. To me. My family. I hated God."

Moshe placed his hand on Dov's brow. He was burning with fever. Hearing things. Imagining. What was God doing to bring Dov Avram to such an end? To let him die in the cellar of a Muslim candleshop? Dov Avram, the hero who rallied a handful of Jews in Warsaw to stand against the Nazi Panzers? The spiritual anguish was more powerful than any physical pain he was experiencing.

"*Chesed!*" Moshe whispered the Hebrew word for God's mercy, for loving-kindness. "Only ask."

"How can I ask? I can't believe."

"Believing means sometimes trusting what you don't understand completely."

"Help me, God! *Chesed!* Mercy!" Dov's cry broke into sobs. Helpless, Moshe held his hand until Dov lapsed into an uneasy sleep.

■ ■ ■ ■

The hike out of the ravine was a struggle. His boots slipping on loose gravel and his hands clutching at scrubby brush to keep from sliding backward, David was grateful when that much of the journey ended. Once the crest was reached, the remaining trek over the rolling hills toward Jerusalem was easy by comparison.

There was one problem: Daoud was too exhausted to go any further.

"*Ya Allah,*" he said, squatting down beside the trail. "My feet have not walked this far in all my days on earth put together."

David smiled to hear such a groan of age come out of the mouth of one so young. "No problem," he said. With a swoop that startled Daoud, David swung the boy atop his shoulders. "You can ride awhile."

Daoud decided right then that he liked this cowboy, this American. "When the Bedou wish to start their camels they say 'Hut! Hut! Hut!' How do cowboys make their horses go?"

"Giddyap."

"So! Gi-dy-ap!"

Giddyap was fine for the first mile and a half, but after that even Daoud's slight mass weighed on David's shoulders and back. He had a crick in his neck, and his pace dragged considerably.

Colonel Stone had emphasized what David already knew: speed counted for everything. When the convoy of supplies reached the ravine they had to meet the means to move the supplies on to Jerusalem.

Panting, David lifted the boy off. "Is there any way to reach Jerusalem that isn't on foot?" he asked.

Daoud shook his head, then brightened. "Perhaps . . . a donkey or a camel?"

"Super," David said. "Okay, scout. Where do we get one of those?"

"Follow me," Daoud said. "I know a place. I passed it on the way down with the gardener."

Thirty minutes brought them to the outskirts of a collection of whitewashed, flat-roofed houses. "Whoa, hold it," David said, grabbing Daoud's shoulder and dragging the boy behind a thicket of dry reeds. "I thought you meant a Jewish place. You might be okay here, but me they'll shoot."

Daoud appreciated his new friend, so he did his best not to sound scornful when he said, "No, this is a village of Christian Arabs."

"How can you tell that?" David asked, raising up enough to peer over the brush. "By the color of their sheets? What?"

"Because there are people in this village," Daoud explained. "We are on ground held by the Jews. If these were Muslims, they would have run away when the Mufti told them to."

"Oh," David said. Then he spotted something. "A car! Now we're talkin'."

"I do not think the muqhtar of this village, whose auto that must be, would hand it over to someone who appears at night in his village," Daoud said doubtfully.

"No problem," David returned. "If it's got gas and it's got juice, then it's mine."

Daoud did not have a clue what the crazy American was talking about, but it was fun.

No dogs gave the alarm when they approached.

Upon closer inspection, David was not quite as enthusiastic. The car, a 1928 British-made Humber, had no glass, no unbroken lamps, and little rubber on its tires. A probe of the petrol tank showed fuel, which David reasoned meant it had at least been running not long before. "Get in," he said.

Daoud watched from inside as David did something mysterious in the engine compartment, then slid behind the wheel.

The cowboy ducked under the panel and manipulated several wires. "Get ready to hut, hut, hut!" he said. He pressed the starter.

The Humber's motor clattered to life, and with a jerk that jolted Daoud back in his seat, they roared away.

Daoud was impressed. His new acquaintance clearly had some useful skills!

■ ■ ■ ■

Was there anyone in Israel who did not have someone to mourn for, Ellie wondered?

And yet, there was no time to grieve. To pause and reflect meant death would overtake the mourner.

That fact was evident in the stony expressions of Sholem and his wife, Katerine, when they climbed from the back of the lorry. They did not say it out loud, but Ellie guessed their thoughts: *"For Ivan's sake we will reach Jerusalem. Break through to Jerusalem. Our boy will not have died in vain."*

Perhaps that desire and that motivation was on the heart of every mourner. Just the name of the one who died was different. Six million names. *Six million beloved! They cannot have died in vain!*

Ellie experienced a peculiar sense of excitement as she joined Madame Rose and her refugees. They were a tiny part of a vast contingent of laborers who flooded the wadi below Beit Jiz.

Bulletins were sent to the building trades in Tel Aviv and the surrounding countryside calling for stonecutters and anyone with a strong back who could lift, haul, dig, or rake.

Hundreds came.

By morning, Ellie, Madame Rose, Sholem, Katerine, and their sons were immersed into a force, a people who intended to claw aside the waters of the Red Sea one drop at a time.

■ ■ ■ ■

Dov awakened as the sound of shelling lapsed. "You're still here," he muttered. "You're an idiot."

"Maybe," Moshe answered.

"Peace."

"They've stopped shelling. It is the Muslim hour of prayer."

"I wasn't talking about cannons. My heart. I long for peace."

Moshe closed his eyes and prayed for the words to help his friend find his way in the darkness. "We've all failed to live as God would have us live. As the law of Moses says we should live. But God is merciful."

"Where was God's mercy when Papa and Chaim lay dying? When I ran from them? When I left them to burn to death so I could live?"

"Your father wanted you to live."

"I wanted to die with him. It's a punishment to live! I have studied Torah. The law God gave Moses on Sinai. I am condemned by what they say."

"Torah tells of God's mercy. *Chesed!*"

"The books of Moses accuse me. And now? I will die beside a man named Moses who is a linguist . . . Mosheh . . ."

Moshe laughed and squeezed Dov's hand. "Then I'll tell you the truth behind the name I inherited, eh?"

"Truth," Dov whispered. "Is there such a thing?"

"In every letter of Torah truth and meaning is embedded. I will begin with the name of Mosheh."

"Mosheh. Teach me, rabbi."

"You must think. Focus your mind, Dov."

"It will pass the time."

Moshe hoped it would also keep Dov from drifting away into delirium and despair.

"Mosheh. The name of the man who brought us God's law. Read Mosheh as two Hebrew words."

Dov, contented with the game, said, "Hebrew word games. Like when I was a kid."

"We begin. The first word is *Mi.*"

"Which means 'from.' "

"The second is *SeH.*"

"Meaning 'the lamb.' " Dov concluded. "*Mosheh.* Meaning 'from the lamb.' "

"Very good. And now, what is the Hebrew word we use to speak of God's name?"

"*HaSHeM.* Which means 'The Name.' " An answer every Torah schoolboy knew.

"What is *MoSHeH* spelled backward?"

"*HSHM.* Hashem. The Name."

"Well spoken."

"I see the wonder of it. But not the meaning."

"It is as simple as this: Moses was sent *from the lamb* to proclaim *The Name* of the One God to the world. Moses and Torah point the way. *MaShiYah* means the anointed one. Read backward, the name tells us what the Messiah will achieve—*HaY,* 'there will then live,' *SheM,* the name of the Almighty."

"The Name of the Almighty will live in him." Dov cleared his throat. "Here? On earth?"

"In Jerusalem. A hundred yards from where we are. Where Abraham offered his son, Isaac, to the Lord. Because of Abraham's faith, God promised to bless the world through the descendants of Abraham and Isaac."

Dov blinked, unseeing, as the thunder of explosions echoed from the corridors of the Jewish Quarter. He winced with the pain of memory. With a shudder he begged, "Don't stop. Keep talking, Moshe. The Messiah. The lamb of God. The world blessed . . . A Torah school story. What has that to do with my soul?"

"It is everything. Mercy!"

"Abraham's faith made him righteous." Dov sighed. "I have such weak faith. Where is the blessing God promised?"

"Abraham offering his son is half the story. In return God gave His only Son, the Messiah, the Lamb, as the final sacrifice for our sins. For my failings and yours. For Israel first and then for all the world. The blessing of mercy. Of forgiveness. Think of it!"

"Where do you get this?"

"It is written in the prophets that Messiah will come to save His beloved Israel. Isaiah 52:13 through 53:12 describes His suffering for our sake. Psalm 22 speaks of the exact details of His death. At Passover we Jews remember the Lamb who was sacrificed to save us. Exodus 12: The blood of the lamb was placed on the doorposts of every Hebrew household. The angel of death passed over each house where the blood identified the faith of God's chosen people. Then they were delivered from bondage. Passover is a clear picture of the Messiah, descendent of Abraham, son of David, lamb of God, who died to take away the sins of the world. Think of it!"

"All my life I studied the Bible. But never heard this."

"Many deny it. Distort it. Fear it. Ridicule it. Rearrange the facts to suit themselves. But Messiah was a descendant of Abraham like us. Circumcised. Dedicated as a baby in the Great Temple. He taught the people in the temple courts about God's love and mercy for them! Then, during Passover, he was killed, like the Passover lamb, even though he was without guilt."

"So, like millions of Jews, he's dead. Where's the hope in that?"

"Here is the good news! Messiah rose again from the dead after three days in the tomb. He says everyone who calls on Him will one day live again."

"A myth."

"He appeared to five hundred people. He is alive! He blessed Israel and then ascended into heaven from the Mount of Olives."

"Where King Abdullah's cannons blast us."

As if to emphasize his point the bellow of artillery sounded in the distance.

"Soon Messiah will return to that spot. And then there will be peace in Jerusalem and all the world. Zechariah 14:9 says, 'The LORD will be king over the whole earth. On that day there will be one LORD, and his name the only name.'"

"What is Messiah's name?"

"The Hebrew word for 'Savior.'"

"*Yeshua? Yeshua!* So simple. The name we have been taught to hate. Savior. I wish He would come now. Save us. Stop the cannons, eh? Peace for the world. For Jerusalem! And for my heart."

"Until He returns, God sent His Spirit to write one word on the hearts of all who believe. It embodies the whole message of Torah."

"What's the word?"

"*Chesed.* Mercy. You are forgiven. God provided His Son, as the lamb. The sacrifice. His mercy doesn't leave anyone out. There is no sin so extreme that God will not forgive except the sin of rejecting him."

"But . . . how can I have this mercy? If I can't believe . . . everything? I don't believe everything. I have been taught to fear this message."

"Ask God's Spirit to come live in your heart. To forgive you. To teach you truth."

"How will I know?"

"That's a prayer God always answers."

"How will I know he heard me?"

"Lay your doubt at His feet and say, 'Lamb of God, you take away the sins of the world, have mercy on me. Messiah of Israel, Lamb of God, I believe, but help my unbelief."

Dov whispered, "There's guilt on my soul . . . I've lived with it. But I don't want to die with it! Lord, Messiah of Israel, Lamb of God, I believe. *Chesed!* Mercy! Please help me . . . Help my unbelief."

"*Shalom,*" Moshe replied. "There's peace in God's mercy for our Jewish souls. Even though our lives and world are torn apart."

Silence.

Dov sighed. "I'll know soon enough what's true, won't I?"

CHAPTER 23

S o this was the yellow brick road, Ellie mused as she strained to see the goat trail that threaded down the face of the canyon on one side and an even steeper trail on the opposite side.

The floor of the chasm simmered in the heat of a fierce sun baking the rocks and boulders.

Ellie, with Madame Rose on her left and Michael Stone on her right, was disheartened at the monumental task ahead of them.

"If Tin Man makes it back here in time," Stone remarked, "you'll see the Jerusalem crew marching down that path like a tribe of ants."

Madame Rose pressed her thin lips together with concern. "It's not the going down that will be hard. But the going back up."

Stone agreed. Each man from the Jerusalem side of the gulf would be required to pick up forty to fifty pounds of supplies at the bottom and hike back to the top. From there it was several miles before the Jerusalem-bound goods could be loaded onto the backs of camels and donkeys for the next leg of the harrowing journey.

"As we speak, four hundred tons of food and ammunition is on its way here from the ships arriving at Jaffa and Tel Aviv," Stone explained. "We can get it this far by truck and then camels. Then your people will have to carry it down the path from this side. Down to the bottom of the canyon. They'll meet up with the Jerusalem porters, transfer the cargo, and then come back up here for another load. Two trips a night I figure. Can they manage?"

"They will manage," Rose promised.

"You need a real road," Ellie said glumly. "Freight trucks. Hundreds of them."

Stone replied, "The road. Yes. I've got an engineer from Seventh Corps on the way up from Tel Aviv. A Scot. Name of Tweedle. He was with Samuel Orde on the Burma Road. Tweedle will know how to do it."

Madame Rose asked the question that had been weighing on Ellie's mind. "What about the Arabs?"

"If they catch wind of what we're doing down here, it'll be a massacre." Stone was honest, but not comforting.

"Where are they?" Ellie scanned the range of mountains toward the north.

"Latrun is about two miles that direction," Stone explained. "We've got our soldiers guarding the ridge between us and them. The two villages we took over are being fortified. If it comes to a fight we'll hold them long enough for your civilians to take cover. After that . . ."

■ ■ ■ ■

Arab Legion mayor Francis Burr strode along the parapet of Latrun's police fort. Beside him was Major Athani.

"We are not being withdrawn," Burr said, slapping his swagger stick against his palm. "The regiments are to remain here. High Command agrees that, despite the drubbing we gave them, the Jews will try again to open the pass."

Both men stared across the ashes of the wheat fields. Stripped and blackened bodies dotted the terrain. There were so many corpses that neither burial parties nor scavenging crows had yet reached them all.

"I did not fully believe they would be that foolish," Burr continued, "until I realized the desperate conditions in Jewish Jerusalem. They say there is no food and not much water."

Sunlight glinted on a glass bottle lying near a dead man. The plain had been littered with them after the battle, but the Arab villagers had plundered most, along with everything else.

"Desperate," Burr repeated. Then returning to business he said, "The Arab villages south of those hills." Burr indicated the far side of the valley. "Beit Susin and Beit Jiz have been abandoned."

"Why?" Athani inquired.

"The usual superstitious native nonsense," Burr began, eyeing the junior officer before continuing. "Muddle of contradictory statements, really," he amended. "A plane attacked them, something fell out of the sky on them, a horde of evil spirits came to them by night. Doesn't matter. If a handful of Jews got up there with mortars they could make our use of the road a bit dicey. Take one company. Once you're in, leave half of it to hold there and double-time it back."

"At once," Athani replied, saluting.

■ ■ ■ ■

There was a noise from the street outside the candleshop.

Moshe awoke with a start. He did not know when he had dozed off and so did not know how much time had passed.

Was Dov breathing?

Moshe touched Dov's face. Alive, thank God!

What was happening outside? Had a Haganah counterattack caused panic among the Arabs?

The sound of running swelled into a torrent, accompanied by loud, excited talk. A large crowd poured through the streets of Jerusalem.

Creeping upstairs Moshe peered out through tiny slits in the metal screen.

A mass of Arabs charged past the candlemaker's shop, but not east in the direction of the Mount of Olives as if escaping a Jewish assault. They were heading west, toward the Christian Quarter.

Abdullah's visit!

The throng raced to find vantage points from which to view the proceedings.

"Dov," Moshe said, returning to rouse his companion. "Wake up."

It was as if their conversation during the hours of night had sapped the last of Dov's waning strength. Moshe could not wake him, got nothing more than moans in response to his urging.

Carrying Dov up to the shop, Moshe placed him on the floor behind the counter, then readied himself for a brief survey outside. If he was right and the way was clear back to the tunnel, he would get Dov and make a run for it.

The street was packed from side to side with spectators. Moshe slipped under the grill.

He turned toward the Wailing Wall. The tunnel! Home!

An even bigger wave of onlookers swelled the lane.

Moshe could not move eastward. Caught in the press he was swept along with the mob. He was carried toward the Church of the Holy Sepulchre.

The human pipeline was bordered by vigilant Legionnaires.

Uniformed Legion troops had weapons, but none were visible in the hands of anyone else. The ordinary soldiers had been ordered to lay down their rifles during the visit of Abdullah to prevent assassination by opposing Muslim factions.

A chance to make a break! This single thought charged Moshe with fresh energy.

Moshe hoped he could jog aside when the route intersected Damascus Road.

No chance.

At that corner another multitude flowed southward from the Arab neighborhood of Musrara, outside the Old City wall.

The conjunction of yesterday's news from Latrun and the appearance of an apparently victorious Abdullah gave Jerusalem's Muslim populace cause for celebration.

Jews lay rotting in the sun!

Long live King Abdullah!

On every hand he heard the same sentiments expressed: surely the Jews must be ready to give up. They must realize their foolish attempt to create a Zionist state will end in disaster if they do not surrender.

The river of excited Muslims carried Moshe beyond the Greek Orthodox Convent and the Chapel of Abraham. The church commemorated the place where the Lord's provision of a ram in a thicket spared the life of Abraham's son, Isaac. Isaac, the son of God's promise, the patriarch of the Jewish people!

Would the tiny remnant of Isaac's descendants be driven from Jerusalem by the descendants of Abraham's other son, Ishmael?

The plaza in front of the entrance to the Church of the Holy Sepulchre was already packed to capacity by the time Moshe was jammed up against it.

The church was not a single building but a hillock of chapels and sanctuaries that grew like barnacles around the shrine. A half-dozen bickering sects crowded into its cavernous interior. It was, Moshe thought, a monument to the dissension within the Christian church rather than a memorial to the one who died to reconcile the hearts of men to a loving God.

And as Moshe watched, these princes of the fractured church bowed low to the Muslim Hashemite king of Jordan, Abdullah.

Moshe could see over the crowd. On a platform at the top of the entry the diminutive Jordanian king was greeted by Coptic priests, Syrian priests, brown-robed Franciscans, and black-gowned Orthodox and Armenians.

How they despised one another! But there were smiles all around.

Beside the king loomed a bulky, bearded figure Moshe recognized as an official of the Greek Orthodox community. The much-larger man appeared to offer a suggestion to Abdullah, who nodded and faced the crowd.

In expectation a hush generated nearest the steps expanded outward in rings of silence.

The king addressed the throng. "On this, the second anniversary of our coronation, we come to the Holy City with a message of peace."

A shell from the Mount of Olives whistled overhead and exploded with a crash in the Jewish-held New City. Peace might be Abdullah's theme, but conquest was his will. His intention was to annex the entirety of Palestine to the kingdom of Jordan. In all of history a nation of Palestine had never existed. King Abdullah, with the help of his allies, would make certain there would be no Israel and no independent state of Palestine!

Palestine and Jordan would be one Hashemite kingdom, in spite of the decree of the United Nations.

And the people in the crowd were overjoyed to hear it. As long as there were no Jews in the united kingdom of Jordan, they welcomed unity under the leadership of the Jordanian king.

And those who had other ideas? Who favored the Mufti? Farouk of Egypt perhaps? Syria? They had given up their weapons for the time being. They, like the clerics, smiled and cheered at the words of King Abdullah.

This was the opportunity Moshe had been waiting for.

Backing away from the square, he edged toward a brick wall.

Continuing his oration after quiet was restored, Abdullah said, "I will go to the Noble Sanctuary upon the holy mount to pray for peace for all my subjects."

The crump of an Arab mortar round carrying over the wall and into the Jewish Quarter punctuated this sentence with irony.

Walking backward, his side pressed tight against the bricks, Moshe forced onlookers to move. To give him room to pass.

"But first," the king announced, "I have come here to pay my respects at the tomb of the Nazarene prophet."

Never mind that the tomb is empty, Moshe thought as he moved to escape the crush of the mob.

Moshe knew the reason the Golden Gate on the eastern wall of the Dome of the Rock had been sealed. The followers of Islam feared this Nazarene prophet would one day enter Jerusalem through the Eastern Gate as Messiah and king of a Jewish Israel! Throughout the famous

Muslim mosque that replaced the Jewish temple stern warnings against following Jesus were written in the mosaic tiles that decorated the arches and the dome itself.

And still these leaders smiled and nodded at the king of Jordan's words. *Peace! Peace! When there is no peace!*

It was a historic contradiction, and of all the crowd only Moshe seemed able to grasp it.

Moshe missed the rest of Abdullah's speech.

Now, while everyone's attention was focused on the Christian Quarter. . . .

Now, before Abdullah moved to the Haram and the streets below it would be doubly patrolled. . . .

Now was the chance to get home!

■ ■ ■ ■

A hornet crawled on the granite surface near Jacob's right hand. When he idly flicked his fingers at it, the insect darted away.

Since Lavie was dead, Jacob was appointed captain of Aleph Company. The company was really the survivors of Aleph and Beth combined into one understrength unit, plus a handful of recruits.

Sixty battered, shell-shocked survivors of Latrun and eleven untried, frightened refugees, all relying on him to keep them alive.

Jacob's seventy-two were to hold a stretch of stony ridge a quarter-mile in front of the villages of Beit Susin and Beit Jiz. Susin was to the east and Jiz to the west, a mile and a half apart. Further up the heights toward Jerusalem the defense was taken over by hardened Palmachniks of the Har-el Brigade.

Too far away to call for help.

As Colonel Stone instructed, Jacob formed squads of five to eight troopers each.

Some of his units patrolled the goat paths and the road connecting the two villages. They were a roaming reserve, to be committed where needed. Their main duty was to intercept Arab scouts that slipped past the front line.

The other squads *were* the front line, gathered at what Stone called "ambush points," to repel Arab patrols.

"We can't let them retake the villages," Stone said. "Worse, they must get no hint we are working on a road. If they do, their artillery will hammer us. Good-bye, road. Good-bye, Jerusalem."

So they must drive the Arabs back; make them keep their distance; but without letting them know what a vital secret was being protected.

"Wait until you cannot miss," Stone warned. "Don't shoot until it's absolutely necessary and then wait for point-blank range."

As if staying alive was not enough.

It was almost too much to comprehend.

Leading in the single way he knew, Jacob located a forward, exposed position. At the point where an Arab probe was likely, he placed his own squad. Leon, Jerome, and Rudolf were joined by Meena, a sandy-haired nineteen-year-old Polish Jew, who said she was a medic.

She also knew how to shoot.

The spur of rocks formed an arrowhead aimed at Latrun. The three-hundred-yard slope dropped into a wadi. A range of low hills five hundred yards away screened the wadi from the Valley of Ayalon. In the distance, over the hills, Jacob could see the heights of Latrun two miles away.

Flying in an unhurried sinuous curve, a hornet drifted away toward the brown haze remaining from the previous day's battle.

■ ■ ■ ■

Things were bad upstairs at the Hurva. People were arguing loudly about whether they should give up. The shrill voices of hysterical women drifted down into the room where Alfie and Rabbi Lebowitz sat beside the tunnel.

"Ten minutes," the old rabbi, Shlomo Lebowitz, said irritably to Alfie. "I will put a stop to this and return in ten minutes."

Alfie peered doubtfully at the hole in the wall where a path wound off into the blackness. "I can't watch over it alone," Alfie said. "What if they come?"

"If it is Moshe and Dov, greet them, and tell them I'll be back in ten minutes." The rabbi rose from his desk and winced as he tried to straighten his back.

"But if it's the others?"

The old man pointed at the plunger. "Push that. They'll go away." He hobbled stiffly toward the stair, leaving Alfie alone and not at all comfortable with so important a task.

Alfie wiped his nose with the back of his hand and stared at the jagged entrance to the tunnel. He sat down on an upturned barrel. Ten minutes. Was that a long time? The old man had just left and it already felt like he had been gone a long time.

The strident voices upstairs paused, began again, then softened. Someone began to weep. They were hot and miserable. Their children were hungry. They did not have enough to drink. Everyone smelled bad because they could not wash.

How could the rabbi deal with this?

The thick beard on Alfie's chin itched. He would have liked to take a bath. If there was water.

Angry at the way everything was going, Alfie said loudly, "Little Abe is watering your roses with his own ration, you know! He's just three and you're . . . old. Things are falling apart. Everyone is hungry! Thirsty! Where are you?"

Silence. Behind him Alfie noticed a cool breeze. Since there was no cool breeze in Jerusalem and especially not in the sub-basement of the Hurva, he knew he was not alone. He did not turn around. He felt peaceful inside. It did not matter anymore if the rabbi came back or Arabs charged out of the hole. Alfie was content. He dropped to his knees and covered his face. He waited for the gardener to speak.

At last he heard it, very small and faint.

"I will lay waste to the mountains and hills and dry up all their vegetation."

"But, sir, the wind. Sucking the life out of everything. They're all so thirsty."

"I will turn back their enemies in shame."

"Can I watch?" Alfie was pleased at the sound of this message.

"I must go now."

"Where?"

"To the sea."

"Take me with you." Alfie always asked to go, and the answer was always the same.

"I'm not finished with you yet."

"Can't I go, too?" Alfie asked. "I would like the sea. Water."

"You must stay here. I will lead the others by ways they have not known."

"But what about the people here? They are dying."

"The course is set. Carry Abraham on your shoulders and in your arms. Hold back the darkness not by your own power, but by my name."

"I don't understand. Will you leave me here alone? Will you be back? What will I do?"

"When the hour comes, my light will lead you."

Alfie sensed the touch of a hand on his shoulder. He was no longer afraid. He was very tired. The voice and the cool wind receded until Alfie knew he was alone in the tiny room again. He turned to see the place where the gardener had been. A stack of scrolls was heaped up on a table. Well, that was a perfect place for Him to be.

Ten minutes must have passed because the rabbi came down the steps. He seemed very grim.

The rabbi asked Alfie, "An uneventful vigil, eh? I see the Mufti did not pop out of the hole."

Alfie stuck out his lower lip. "No. Not the Mufti."

CHAPTER 24

It was the crows that gave the first warning.

A flock of the black birds swooped and darted above the low knobby hill a little north of Jacob's position. Ever since sunup they rode the thermal currents in lazy spirals. The only noise they made was intermittent squabbling.

Then that abruptly changed.

The entire flight broke into a noisy cawing. Their wings clawed at the air in a quest for altitude.

Jacob had just enough time to call, "Get back!" when the advance scouts of the Arab Legion patrol appeared where the black birds had been.

The Jewish squad's ambush position on the ridge included a row of boulders behind which three of the squad crouched. A giant rock, cleft in the center into two upthrust pillars, provided higher lookout posts for Jacob and Leon. The two men lay on their bellies, only their eyes exposed.

The Arab scouts, six of them in staggered line, advanced cautiously. When they did not draw any fire their gaze turned instantly up to the heights looming ahead.

"Keep down!" Jacob hissed. He flattened himself lower, knowing the Arabs were watching for any movement on the ridge.

Two of the Legionnaires conferred, then one trotted back. Waving his arm, he summoned the rest of the Legion force.

Now to see what they were up against, Jacob thought. Six scouts meant how many more? Twenty? Thirty? How many could the five of them hold off? How long would it take to get the rest of the company up there? At least they held the high ground this time.

So much for keeping their presence a secret. Not even one full day had passed since Latrun.

Behind the first rank of Arabs came another twenty and then a further twenty.

From both flanks around the base of the hill appeared more.

At least a hundred Legionnaires.

"Jerome," Jacob called to the young man barricaded below on the left. "When I give you the word, scoot out backward. Get to Beit Susin, and bring up everyone you can find. Send runners out to the roaming parties."

The Legionnaires approached the gully separating the two hills. The Arab officers allowed their men to bunch up. Plainly they did not expect any resistance.

Three hundred yards away.

The slope below Jacob was shaley and steep. Here and there clumps of thornbrush grew and stunted trees. About three-quarters of the way up the incline was the smooth, silver trunk of a long dead oak. Almost the size of the boulder on which Jacob lay, it must have been an impressive sight in life.

The first wave of Legionnaires crossed the dry wash. Immediately they had to scramble for footing on the slick surface of the steep shale. Jacob heard an Arab officer yell at them to keep together, not try to scout for an easier route around the slope. He said they'd get lost in the wadis and wind up in the nightclubs of Cairo.

This got a laugh from the Legionnaires.

How long could Jacob wait to give the order to fire? Should he send Jerome at once, or would that give away their location?

As the slope got steeper the Arabs struggled to stay upright. One slipped and made a grab for a nearby bush to steady himself. He spouted a stream of curses when he got a handful of thorns.

"I can pick off their leader from here," Meena suggested softly when the Legionnaires were two hundred yards away.

"Wait!" Jacob tersely returned.

How long? How far should he let them come?

One hundred fifty yards.

A depression in the slope forced the Arab soldiers closer together. Compacted, the group appeared even larger.

Would someone panic and shoot?

Rudolf was breathing like a freight train, every muscle tensed. He wiped his spectacles, then wiped them again, putting his fingers all over the lenses as he did so.

One hundred yards.

There were too many of them! It was too late to stop them!

Still, Jacob did not give the order to fire. Jerome studied him questioningly. So did Leon.

Forty or so of the Arab soldiers reached the bench where the fallen tree lay. The remainder of their fellows were below, between there and the stream bed.

Seventy-five yards.

Why didn't Jacob have a machine gun? Why not a mortar?

The Legion officer, puffing from the climb, reached the level spot.

Reversing his rifle, he set the butt of the weapon on the trunk of the oak and leaned on it.

The rifle plunged through decayed wood into a hollow interior. Embarrassed, he jerked it out.

A dark spray, like a fountain of smoke, emerged from the hole.

Like a malicious whirlpool, the cloud curled around the Legionnaires.

Hornets! Thousands of hornets.

One moment the Arab soldiers were grinning slyly at their leader's gaffe. The next, every man was slapping himself, waving his hands in front of his face, trying to protect the back of his neck, and his cheeks, and his ears, all at the same time.

The ones nearest the geyser of stinging insects broke first, plunging down the slope. Knocking their fellows out of the way, they slid on the gravel, or tumbled awkwardly.

The maddened wasps moved on to the next rank and the next.

And the dead tree continued to gush hornets.

A valiant few, including the Legion commander, tried to rally at the bottom of the slope.

It was not far enough.

The hornets pursued them.

Clawing at his eyes, the Arab leader waved his men back toward Ayalon, back toward Latrun.

Jacob choked, discovered he had been holding his breath.

"Well done," Leon applauded. "You must have nerves of steel."

"I am sorry Lain was not here to see this," Jerome put in. "If hornets had fought for Joshua, it would have been in the Bible." The boy shook his head. "I wish Lain could have see this."

■ ■ ■ ■

No one could explain how the bereaved father of Lain managed to arrive with the road crew.

But he was there, waving his one arm, wild-eyed in his grief. Wearing the long black coat of a Hasid and a wilted broad-brimmed hat even in the withering heat, he was, Ellie thought, mad as a hatter.

"Where is Lain? Have you seen him? My only son. His name is Lain," he asked.

Tears streamed endlessly down his cheeks to dampen his grizzled beard. As work crews were given assignments the Madman wrung his hands and examined picks and shovels, hand carts and wheelbarrows.

He was, it seemed, one among the hundreds who mourned openly over the death of a child. For this reason, Madame Rose, along with a committee of refugees and Sholem, whose grief was also fresh, discussed the situation. It was decided that the Madman should not be taken away. After all, his sacrifice was as great as anyone's in Israel.

A last son killed trying to save Jerusalem.

The Madman was given a water bucket and a ladle. He was made chief of the water boys who passed up and down the line.

He crooned the passage from the second chapter of Jeremiah as he walked: "My people have committed two sins: They have forsaken Me, the spring of living water, and have dug their own cisterns, broken cisterns that cannot hold water!"

"Yes," agreed one who gulped the water. "It is true. We are thirsty. Very thirsty."

Three times Michael Stone suggested the Madman was bad for morale and should be carted off and locked up. But in this matter the commander of the road-building front was overruled by the people.

"Leave him be," was the sad response from Sholem. "He mourns for all Israel."

■ ■ ■ ■

It was the first time in days that the house-to-house fighting halted long enough for Ehud to come to the chamber where Grandfather sat vigil with Alfie and Rachel. Yehudit, her face a mask of strain and grief, followed him.

A chill coursed through Rachel as she saw Ehud. He was haggard, almost unrecognizable beneath a layer of dust and the dried blood of fallen comrades.

He had no words to spare for greeting. He barked his message as though he was commanding men on the barricades.

"Something is happening in the Arab Quarter," he said, avoiding Rachel's eyes. "We can hear them cheering. Roaring. I think they are massing for assault." He wiped his face with his hands as though he was trying to scrub off the effects of horror and sleeplessness. "I'll give it to you straight. Moshe and Dov aren't coming back."

"He says we have to blow the tunnel!" Yehudit cried, running to Rachel.

"Wednesday! It's three days!" Ehud bellowed. "Enough! It's hopeless. *Nu!*"

Rachel looked to Grandfather, hoping he could reverse Ehud's decision. The old man sat frozen, his hand on the open scroll. "Wait until sunset," he asked.

Ehud, excited, responded, "Sunset! They could be crawling over us by sunset. Look! The Hurva may be our last stronghold. To leave a path open to enemy territory is suicide! We can't wait."

Yehudit sobbed on Rachel's shoulder. The sealing of the passage finally meant accepting that Moshe and Dov were lost.

Rachel closed her eyes to hold back tears. Had they come so far for everything to end like this?

"One hour more," Reb Lebowitz said. "We will say Kaddish for the dead before we seal their tomb."

Ehud shifted uncomfortably at this pronouncement. He could not refuse such a request. "The enemy has gathered. On the other side of these walls. If they attack before your last *Omaine,* that is it! The tunnel is going! One hour. Pray quickly. That may be our last hour!"

■ ■ ■ ■

Despite the fact the Egyptians had captured Ramat Rachel, south of Jerusalem, they had not held it. Repeat counterattacks had time and again recovered the village for Israel. Studying daily maps of the settlement drawn with successive lines of who possessed what was like watching a tennis match.

Eventually the Egyptians lost enough men to also lose their enthusiasm for renewing the assault.

Besides, they reasoned, it was enough to hold half the Negev . . . keeping it out of Abdullah's hands while his Legion expended money, arms, and troops in a so-far fruitless attempt to conquer Jerusalem.

Let him exhaust his resources; then the Egyptians would swoop in and take it all.

Jerusalem remained the rock on which ambitions foundered.

King Abdullah stood before the marble sarcophagus in the hexagonal Chapel of the Holy Sepulchre. To his left was the emissary of the Greek Orthodox Patriarch; to his right was General John Glubb. Behind the three principals were ranks of churchmen.

The light of forty-three lamps shown on the smiling face of Jordan's monarch. Soon he expected his kingdom to encompass this place. A gesture of mercy would not go amiss in front of this audience.

Turning to Glubb, but speaking in a voice loud enough to be heard by all, Abdullah said, "At such a time, and in such a holy place, my general, it is our pleasure to propose a means to spare lives. We want you to convey a message to the rebels within the Jewish-held sector. Tell them resistance must cease and they must surrender unconditionally, but we are pleased to grant them until tomorrow to comply. In pledge of our good will, we will temporarily suspend hostilities."

"Magnificent!" praised the Orthodox prelate. "An offer that shows the quality of your Majesty's compassion."

"Thank you," Abdullah said. "You will pardon me if I have private words with my commander."

Withdrawing ten paces until Abdullah and Glubb were between two of the eighteen pillars that supported the dome of the rotunda, the king asked, "About the cannon of which you spoke?"

"By tomorrow, Majesty," Glubb confirmed. "It will be in position to bring the Jewish Quarter down around their ears."

■ ■ ■ ■

The roaring of Abdullah's adoring audience erupted into the chant, "*Allah Ahkbar!* Abdullah! *Allah Ahkbar!* Abdullah!"

The lane ahead of Moshe was clear, empty. He sprinted toward the candlemaker's shop, covering the ground in several minutes.

Slipping beneath the grid he called for Dov, praying he was alive and conscious.

"Moshe?" Dov's voice was weak but coherent.

"Come on!" Moshe urged, not taking time to explain. "We're getting out of here! Going home!"

Moshe maneuvered him out of the shop and into the street.

Dov's legs would barely support him. He stopped every fifty paces. Each breath came in ragged gasps as if every inhalation was a stab wound.

When he tried to open his eyes, he cried aloud in pain. Dov's face was furrowed with the agony in his head. His features appeared to be collapsing inward.

Slinging Dov's left arm across his shoulders, Moshe half carried, half dragged him. They stumbled along toward the Western Wall.

Moshe whispered encouragement to his friend: "Nearly there. Good. Seven more steps and then you can rest again. Stop here. You are doing fine."

An alarm clock in Moshe's mind was ticking steadily toward chiming. Soon the rally in front of the Church would break up, sending the soldiers back to their positions.

The turn into the last crooked passage brought Moshe a sigh of relief. The street was deserted. No one would challenge their entry into Reb Lebowitz's humble dwelling, or observe them entering the secret underground route.

"We have made it," he said. Pressing his left side against the portal, Moshe forced it open while supporting Dov. He towed the barely conscious Dov over the threshold.

The rabbi's house had been converted into an ammunition depot. Floor to ceiling was piled with British crates of war-surplus grenades, mortar shells, ammunition, and rifles.

Moshe carried Dov through the deadly maze to the cellar stairs. They descended the steep stairs. The cellar floor was also packed with ammunition crates.

Such a cache would be enough for the defenders of the Jewish Quarter to hold out indefinitely.

Moshe scanned the treasure with frustration.

■ ■ ■ ■

Something was up. The explosions interspersed with gunfire from the Arab Quarter had stopped. Yacov could hear Arab soldiers cheering from over the rooftops.

Mendel asked, "You think they won?"

Leon snapped the thong of his slingshot. "Won what?"

Mendel shrugged. "The war."

Yacov rammed him with his elbow. "If it was over, someone would tell us."

Mendel asked, "Why should anyone tell us? We're in a cage here. God could smack us with his shoe and *pffft!* No more Jews. We have no more bullets. Nearly everybody is hurt. There are not even any more pigeons to shoot."

Yacov said to Mendel, "At least no more Jewish pigeons."

Leo Krepske pointed toward the very top of the dome of the Church of the Holy Sepulchre. Bells began to ring. A flight of pigeons spiraled upward. "There are plenty of Christian pigeons."

The flock flew to a minaret and landed.

Yacov added, "And they've gone to roost with Muslim pigeons, eh?"

Mendel found a stone and shot it over the wall into what was now Arab territory. "Meanwhile, we're back to eating matzo and monkey fat."

CHAPTER 25

It was a ride unlike any Daoud had experienced. Whatever weariness he had felt before vanished into a pleasurable terror.

The Tin Man took the corner of Gaza and St. George streets almost on two wheels. Racing toward Haganah High Command, he made no attempt to slow until they neared it.

He fought to control the skidding Humber. The bald tires had no grip on the pavement and the brakes no effect at all.

Another speeding auto appeared, approaching from the right. As David jerked the steering wheel, the Humber bumped over a heap of paving stones. Both front fenders flapped loosely from the car's body like the wings of a particularly clumsy bird trying to get airborne.

Narrowly avoiding a collision as the oncoming vehicle screeched to a halt, the Humber ended up crossways in the road, its nose resting against a wrought-iron railing.

The driver of the other car ran up. "Are you all right?" he inquired.

It was Major Luke Thomas.

"Major," David said, as a cloud of steam boiled out of the Humber's engine compartment. "Am I glad to see you."

"Tin Man?" Luke Thomas questioned. "I thought you were in Tel Aviv."

Daoud sat with his arms folded across his chest. He liked the crazy American, but the newcomer was the same Englishman who had locked him up with the farting Druze.

"No, listen," Tin Man said. "I, that is, we, just got here."

"You flew in," Thomas said, nodding.

"No, drove," Tin Man corrected. "Walked and drove . . . from Hulda . . . from Tel Aviv . . . I don't even know how to say it . . . from below Bab el Wad!"

"You came up the pass? You made it through?"

"No. Around it! An old Roman road. A path really. Listen: there is a way around Latrun. Daoud showed me."

"Around Latrun?" Thomas peered more closely and finally recognized Daoud. "But this is the boy who was with the nuns." Thomas shook his head in confusion.

"I don't know about any nuns," Tin Man said. "Let's start over." The flyer quickly told Luke Thomas the story of the trail. "So while Colonel Stone is organizing a relief caravan," he concluded, "he sent me here to scout this end and to organize a column of trucks, jeeps, donkeys, I dunno . . . two hundred guys? To go down the path from Jerusalem. Meet in the middle. But we gotta get men. Trucks. Camels. Whatever. And we gotta get them now! We can resupply Jerusalem. We can do it!"

■ ■ ■ ■

Moshe's fingers fumbled with the catch of the tunnel's concealing panel. Why did it not move? Was he pressing the wrong stone? Just when every second was precious, could he have mistaken the mark? Any minute the guards would be returning.

Wavering, nearly toppling, Dov stood behind him.

Moshe pushed hard and was rewarded with a sharp click.

Shoving the cover aside produced an incredibly loud scraping noise in the confined space. A wash of dank air flooded into the room. The tunnel to the Hurva was still open!

Now, how to alert those at the other end that they were back? What ironic tragedy it would be if the passage blew up in their faces!

Guiding Dov ahead of him, Moshe levered the panel closed behind them.

Four paces forward in the pitch-black passage he shouted, "*Shalom! Shalom!* Help us!"

Blasting the tunnel leading to the Hurva once they were back would safeguard the Jewish Quarter from attack.

There remained the other passageway that led to the cavern beneath the Dome of the Rock. That door opened on the opposite wall of Reb Lebowitz's cellar.

What about the treasure of the ages, the ancient, sacred library, that Moshe had pledged his life to guard?

Could Moshe take the chance the Muslims would not find it?

"Dov!" Moshe said urgently. "You need to go on alone. There is something I've got to do here."

Panting, Dov said, "Home. The thought of it . . . I can walk."

"Good! Put your hand here, on the wall. Feel your way forward. Count fifty paces and then call out as loudly as you can. Go quickly! I'll follow."

Moshe gazed apprehensively down the shaft as Dov groped his way through the blackness toward the Hurva. Long moments passed. Moshe's shoulders ached. He straightened and glanced around the tiny space. There, concealed behind a panel in the walls, was the rabbi's tunnel, which wound away beneath the Dome of the Rock to emerge in the library of the Great Temple.

In the room above the enemy had made a nest. What would happen when the sentries returned and found the blocked passageway that led back to the Hurva? They would know that Jewish saboteurs had entered Arab territory and made their escape through this house. Suppose they examined the cellar for other passageways?

What if they found the opening to the other tunnel?

There was one correct route to the treasure. Every branch off the main path plummeted away into certain death. This fact would put off the discovery for a time, but not forever. The vault of manuscripts that had remained hidden for over two thousand years would be known. Unless . . .

For an instant Moshe imagined slipping away beneath Jerusalem to stand guard over the sacred parchments, perhaps to seal himself up within the chamber. Was it for this purpose that Reb Lebowitz had revealed the secret? For Moshe to die saving it from destruction? But what about the defense of the Jewish Quarter? To leave his command in such a desperate hour would be tantamount to desertion. There had to be another way.

Moshe raised his eyes to the low-domed roof of the cellar and considered his options. He would use the cache of explosives to blow up the house and seal off the route to the precious hoard of manuscripts. One day perhaps the Western Wall and Old City would once again be in Jewish hands.

Until then the tortuous path beneath the Haram would remain locked away safe beneath a pile of rubble.

Moshe climbed the steps. No one was there, but he heard the sound of voices outside in the street.

English words stenciled on the exteriors of crates identified grenades and bandoleers of rifle bullets. Moshe tore open the boxes and eagerly draped himself with bullets and stuffed his pockets with grenades.

Then he caught sight of the true treasure:

CAUTION! HIGH EXPLOSIVES!

Three identical boxes of explosives were stacked in stairsteps. He pried open a box and snapped up an armload of dynamite.

How long did he have before the Legion soldiers returned? Five mintues? Ten? He would need at least that long.

Set the charge and light the fuse. Beat a path back to the Hurva. So simple! His heart was pounding a tattoo as he raced down the steps and began to assemble the explosives.

And then: footsteps sounded above him!

He froze. Fear tasted like iron in his mouth.

Voices. "He will do well, this king."

"I wondered for a time if he could do as well as his father. But today is proof."

Praying, Moshe placed the bombs around the four corners of the cellar. The detonation would collapse the house, hiding the pathways of both tunnels forever!

"After Abdullah leaves, we will finish off the Jewish Quarter. Al-Malik says we will blow through the Hurva. A crate or two of this should . . ." Then the conversation shifted to women.

Moshe held his breath as he unwound four strands of primacord and slipped into the tunnel. Kneeling, he struck a match and touched flame to fuse. It flared and hissed and began its march to the four corners.

Pausing long enough to gaze upward where two guards laughed, Moshe turned and sprinted down the tunnel toward home—the Hurva!

■ ■ ■ ■

The hour had passed.

Grandfather intoned, "Return to Jerusalem, Your city, in compassion, and dwell in its midst, as You promised You would . . ."

Rachel glanced up sharply as Ehud clattered down the stair.

So it was over. She had put the dreams of a lifetime in the hope Moshe would come back to her. He was not coming.

Yehudit wept silently. Alfie patted her awkwardly with his big hand.

Grandfather finished, ". . . rebuild it soon in our day into an eternal structure, and quickly establish David's throne within it. Blessed are You, Adonai, who rebuilds Jerusalem."

Ehud cleared his throat loudly to interrupt. "He will have a lot of rebuilding to do after what the Arab Legion has done." He lowered his voice. "Moshe told me not to wait. Told me to blow the passage. I waited. Now I have no choice." Unceremoniously he strode toward the detonator box. Lifting it, he placed it on the table next to Grandfather's notes and an open scroll. Wires snaked from the connectors into the tunnel.

Yehudit's sobbing increased in volume. Rachel fought back tears. She gazed at the box and then at Grandfather who continued his prayers.

"I'm sorry," Ehud said as Yehudit threw herself into Rachel's embrace.

He lifted the handle, hesitated slightly, then shoved it down hard. The surge of power was audible.

But no explosion followed.

Ehud cursed, lifted the handle again, and shoved it down. The whirring of energy was followed by silence.

Ashen, he stared at the thing. "Have you disconnected the wires?" he shouted.

Each person in the space glanced at the other in puzzlement. No one had touched the fearsome object.

Ehud sighed. "My God. It's disconnected somehow." He peered into the tunnel.

Alfie stepped forward. "I'll go. If there's a break, I'll find it."

Ehud nodded curtly and handed him a candle. "Hurry it up. The charge is set fifty yards down the hole. So, go already!"

"Sure." Alfie lit the candle and, ducking his head, entered the passage.

Hot wax dripped on Alfie's fingers as he passed through one subterranean wall into a second chamber. He waited to listen as a sound from far up the line reached his ears. What was it? A voice?

And in the distance did he catch a glimmer of light?

What was it? Hadn't he been told he would know what he was to do when he saw the light?

He forgot the original reason he had entered the passage. Something broken. Something he had to fix. What was it?

Stooping, he examined the broken gravel at his feet. The red ribbon of electric cord snaked away in either direction. That was it! He was supposed to check to see where the break was.

He scratched his head and moved on. The flickering candle threw a yellowish pool of light around him.

Once again he heard a sound. A voice. He saw a gleam from the far end of the passage.

Had the Arabs found it?

He stopped to listen. A weak voice cried, *"Shalom!"*

Alfie nodded. *Shalom* was a good word. It meant "peace."

"Shalom!" he called back. "Who's there?"

Then the voice shouted, "It's me! It's Dov! I'm blind! Help me find the way!"

■ ■ ■ ■

Pockets stuffed with grenades, bandoleers of bullets weighing him down, Moshe burst from the tunnel into the Hurva basement.

Dov was collapsed on the floor. Yehudit hovered over him, calling his name and stroking his face. Alfie and the old rabbi stood behind Rachel, who rushed forward to fall into Moshe's arms. She kissed his face again and again and called out his name through tears of relief and joy. "You're alive! Thank God! Oh, Moshe! I thought I'd never see you again."

He pressed his lips against hers and held her tightly to him.

Ehud, chagrined, held the detonator box aloft for an instant, then threw it hard against the wall. There followed an enormous explosion from somewhere up the shaft. A blast of dusty debris billowed from the entrance.

Moshe's gaze fixed on Rebbe Lebowitz. The old man knew everything without being told. The house beside the Western Wall, the secret entrance to the ancient passage had been destroyed.

"I'm sorry," Moshe said.

The old man bowed his head. "So. We will remember. *Nu.*"

Moshe kissed Rachel, who clung to him. "We must get Dov to the hospital. How many wounded?" he demanded of Ehud.

"Every defender but thirty-six," Ehud informed him. "And there's something happening in the Arab Quarter. I think they are massing for another offensive."

Moshe shrugged out of the encumbering ammunition. "King Abdullah is in the Old City. They've all gone to see him. To pray at the Haram. Does the radio work?"

"Sometimes." Yehudit cradled Dov.

"If we can get a message to the Palmach in the New City, on Mount Zion, they can attack! Hit Zion Gate at once! We might have a chance!

Do you hear me? The Muslim army has turned its back on us. They're praying with Abdullah at the Dome of the Rock. There's a handful of enemy troops around our perimeter. They've left their positions. We can hit them from behind! Take back Zion Gate! Open the corridor!"

■ ■ ■ ■

From high on the ridge Jacob saw Colonel Stone waving at him. The colonel was near the abandoned Arab settlement of Beit Susin. With Stone was the square-shouldered form of a heavyset woman.

Calling to Jerome, his partner on the sweep of the hillside, Jacob pointed to the village. He saw Jerome look, look again, and then, to Jacob's surprise, bolt down the hill toward the pair of figures.

Jacob joined the group as Jerome hugged the woman around the neck. She wept tears of joy. "I didn't know, you see," she said to Stone. "I had no way to be sure if . . . after yesterday, you know . . ."

Stone introduced Jacob to Madame Rose. "You two should know each other," he explained. "Kalner here is in charge of the defense of this sector of the road. Madame Rose Smith is the organizer of the porters."

Jacob retold the account of hornets turning back the Arab Legion probe. "A miracle," he said.

"God has no shortage of them." Madame Rose mussed Jerome's hair. "Dunkirk. D-Day. The . . . the Alamo."

Stone laughed amiably. "I thought it was crazy to think we could save Jerusalem . . . emotionally right, I thought, but crazy from a military standpoint. But strategically Jerusalem's an Alamo. You're American, you know what that means," he added, nodding to Madame Rose, who bobbed her broad, spadelike chin.

Even though he was not American, Jacob comprehended the meaning of the phrase. By keeping the Arab Legion bogged down, the battle for Old City Jerusalem prevented King Abdullah from deploying his forces elsewhere, perhaps crushing the Israeli defense of Tel Aviv.

"Sam Houston," Madame Rose summarized, "used the time the Alamo garrison gave him to get ready to defeat Mexico's general Santa Anna. The Alamo was lost, but Texas was saved."

Jacob asked, "What happened to the defenders of this Alamo?"

Jerome spoke up. "The Alamo . . . they all died, yes? A heroic bedtime story. *Oui?*"

That was not an agreeable comparison, Jacob thought. Lori was in Jerusalem.

"Not this time," Stone replied to Jacob's unspoken query. "That's why this road is so crucial. Supplies for Jerusalem. Jerusalem may save Israel; we're going to save Jerusalem."

■ ■ ■ ■

The ammunition Moshe brought into the Jewish Quarter was distributed among the defenders who manned the perimeters. Moshe, his presence evidence of a miracle, went from post to post, encouraging his men.

"Get ready! The Palmach will begin the assault on Zion Gate any minute! This time they'll break through! This time we'll hold the corridor!"

Daniel Caan, armed with twenty rounds of ammunition, waved to the three men who remained in the sandbagged nest on the roof opposite the courtyard.

Spirits were high for the first time in days. Hope like a fire burned inside the hearts of everyone.

Lori, expecting the clash of arms to begin at any second, gathered Abe and took refuge far back in the corner of the portico.

The child caught at Daniel's determined smile. "Danny is happy. Are we going home, Lori?"

"Soon," she said, embracing Abe. "Soldiers are coming to save us. Coming soon!"

"Marching? Playing music?"

He was remembering the British soldiers, she knew. Remembering how every day of his young life the pipers of the Highland Light Infantry marched through the Old City streets to remind the inhabitants who was boss.

She replied, "Maybe they will play music. But it will be a new song for us. A song about Israel."

"Will they bring Alfie something to eat?" he asked. "And me? An orange?"

"Yes! Yes, Abe!" she exulted. "And maybe real bread. Butter. An egg."

"Water?"

"Milk! They'll bring you milk to drink."

"But the roses need water."

"Yes. Yes, they do. The soldiers will bring water for the roses," she told him.

"I'll be glad when they come."

She could not remember when she had been so happy. How long

had it been since she had dared to hope? "Me too." She allowed herself to think that she and Jacob might be reunited . . . if he yet lived.

Abe said solemnly, "I will run out to meet them. They will pick me up on their shoulders and dance."

She brushed her lips over his forehead. "Yes. Yes, Abe. We will dance when they come. But for now we must stay here. Can't run out. We'll stay right here until they say it is safe to come out. Yes?"

The boy nodded once and snuggled against her. "Can I listen to your heart for a while?"

Her eyes overflowed with tears as she stroked his cheek. "My heart beats for you, Abe. Listen as long as you like."

CHAPTER 26

The keening of the Madman could be heard above the clink of picks against rock. "Have you seen my son? Lain is his name. They will not let me see his body."

Engineer Tweedle stood on the lip of the ravine, examining the limestone and shaking his head. "Canna be done," he said in a thick Scottish accent.

"I don't want your opinion. I want to know how it can be done."

Ellie heard exasperation in Michael Stone's muttered reply.

"D'ya see this material here?" Tweedle explained, kicking a chunk of white rock over the rim and watching its plunge. "Limestone. Barely six inches of soil to top it. I wouldna promise to build a road down this slope in less'n six months, except what I really mean t'say is that I wouldna try to build a road here a'tall."

Stone corrected, "Don't tell me how tough it is. I can see that. Tell me how to get the job done."

"Madness to even attempt it," Tweedle retorted.

Behind him the Madman set the bucket on the ground, then pounded a ladle against it. "His body must be washed. They won't let me see him."

Irritated by the bizarre commotion, Tweedle barked, "Take dynamite. Heavy equipment. And," he added, jerking his thumb over his shoulder toward Latrun, "no interruptions from hostiles."

"I don't want a highway," Stone pointed out. "Just enough of a track for jeeps and camels. Later we'll fix it to take deuce-and-a-half trucks. But not at first."

Ellie recognized Sholem, who was leveling a stretch of trail nearby. The Russian cut an overhanging bank with a minimum of effort and efficiently filled a rut. He accepted a cup of water from the Madman, then turned to the trio on the canyon's rim. "Excuse me," he said to Colonel Stone. "But a bulldozer I think is what is needed."

Tweedle laughed. "On this incline? When the surface soil lets go, whoever's drivin'll go arse over teacup into the ravine, and no mistake about that."

Sholem examined the switchback trail and clucked his tongue. "I'm sorry," he said. "I should not have interrupted."

Ellie was glad when Stone reached out. "Hold on a minute. Why do you think it can be done?"

"Because when I was operating farm equipment in Russia, I saw what bulldozers could do."

Tweedle was not impressed. "Pushin' manure is different than this," he said.

"I know," Sholem agreed. "But the first cuts for the Dnepr dam were steeper than here. We succeeded."

Tweedle whistled. "You worked on the Dnepr?"

"Yes," Sholem said. "At Zaporozhye. 1932."

"Is that good?" Ellie could not help blurting. "Special?"

Tweedle replied for the modest Sholem. "A dam high enough to raise the river level a hundred and thirty feet? Special doesn't even begin."

The Madman passed on through the ranks of workers, sighing as he went. "My son! Who will purify the dead?"

■ ■ ■ ■

As Alfie and Yehudit carried Dov toward Misgav Ladakh, an odd lull in the rifle and mortar fire occurred.

Then a shrill whistle and a whine was succeeded by a loudspeaker announcement.

"Moshe," Yacov said to his brother-in-law, "they sent me to fetch you. They say you need to hear this."

On the rooftop of the Hurva, Moshe and Rachel heard nothing but the sighing of the wind and then . . .

Broadcast over a bullhorn and echoing down corridors of stone, it was impossible to say if the announcement was really spoken by General Glubb of the Arab Legion or not. It claimed to be him, and the high-pitched nasal voice could very well belong to the pudgy Brit.

"Attention! Attention!" the broadcast said, repeating its earlier announcement. "I say again, you have until tomorrow morning to lay down your arms and surrender. We have cannon inside the Old City walls. Further resistance is futile and will have deadly consequences. We give you tonight to consider. Tomorrow morning your blood will be on your own heads if you choose to reject this offer."

Rabbi Akiva puffed his way to the ring of sandbags surrounding the dome. "Sachar," he said, "did you hear? You must arrange the surrender. This will be our last chance."

"I will consider every option," Moshe said.

"But . . ."

"I said I will consider it."

On the way back to his office Moshe said to Rachel, "It is propaganda, you know, to split our resolve and make us lose heart."

Rachel looked around at the weary, troubled faces she saw everywhere. "It's working," she said.

■ ■ ■ ■

Dov was small and light. Like a feather, Alfie said, as he carried Dov to the hospital at Misgav Ladakh.

Yehudit came along. She talked and talked the whole way because Dov could not see her and would not know she was there unless her heard her voice.

Again and again Dov said, "Yehudit. Beautiful Yehudit. My beautiful Yehudit."

Alfie had always thought she was not beautiful until he saw her with Dov. With her hat she shaded his face and eyes from the sun as they walked.

Her plain face was beautiful with loving him. Pale skin was flushed with excitement. Dull brown hair fell in wisps across her forehead.

"I never stopped believing," she said. "I always knew you would come back!"

Alfie knew this was untrue. For three days she had wept and wrung her hands and said she did not want to be a widow. But what did it matter? It made Dov smile and reach his hand out into the air to find her hand.

"I knew I would see you again," Dov replied.

Of course, being blind, Dov did not see her. And when they went down the stone steps into the underground synagogue, he could not see the misery of the hundreds of soldiers and civilians crammed into that gloomy and airless place. Of course he could smell it. He could hear the hum of misery among them.

He asked Yehudit, "Has it gone so wrong then?"

She answered, "My father wants to end it. Give up."

"How many of our soldiers wounded?"

"All but thirty-six."

Dov rested his head on Alfie's chest in sorrow. He muttered one word, "Warsaw."

Yehudit said, "If we give up, if we lose the Old City, then what has it all been for?"

Dov, being blind, answered, "For the glory that is unseen."

Yehudit brushed his matted hair. "I'll find Dr. Baruch." She picked her way cautiously over the patients.

Alfie said to him, "Stretch out your hand, Dov." Alfie kissed Dov on the brow. "The glory is there. Not unseen. I can see them. Twice as many here, shining, singing, stooping to whisper to the dying. There are more of them with us than there are us."

Alfie wondered how he could let Dov know he shouldn't be afraid of darkness. There was so much light all around them.

"You are a different fellow, Alfie Halder. Somehow you see what isn't there," Dov said quietly. "And since I am blind, when you talk . . . my heart sees what you see."

"Well." Alfie was pleased. "Then you can't be afraid."

"No."

Alfie whispered, "Look there! Look with your heart. Ah! Hello! There beside you. You are not alone. You see him?"

Dr. Baruch covered the face of a dead man with a sheet and then glanced up as Yehudit called to him. Weary. Helpless. What could he do? The medicine was gone. There was not even cognac from Akiva's cellar to clean the wounds. Too many wounds.

Baruch motioned for Alfie to carry Dov to where the dead man was.

"*Shalom*, Dov." Baruch peered into Dov's eyes. "There is not much I can do. This is the best shelter we have for the wounded. That's it. Nothing to be done unless we can get you out of the Old City. Yehudit says the Haganah will try and break through again from Mount Zion."

Yehudit nodded. "They're coming. Moshe sent the message on the radio. They'll break through to us. We'll get everyone out of here tonight."

Baruch motioned toward the shrouded body. "Until then . . . we'll have a mattress for you anyway." He instructed Alfie to put Dov down and then carry the dead man out back to await burial with the others.

■ ■ ■ ■

Palmach commander Nachasch broke into David Shaltiel's office without knocking. "Shaltiel," he growled without preamble. "Radio message from the Old City. Sachar is back. He's alive. Abdullah is in Jerusalem and the Legionnaires and Moquades have flocked to see him."

"A hoax," Shaltiel suggested.

"It's true! I checked with my own eyes! Zion Gate had ten guards. Now I count two! Give me men and mortars, and we'll be inside again in two hours."

"In broad daylight? You must be crazy," Shaltiel retorted. "Weren't you the man who told me, 'No more attacks. I won't see more of my boys killed'?"

"This is different," Nachasch argued, moving forward so only the breadth of a fist separated the two men. "We have been handed a real chance to save the Old City. But I must have more men and more shells. And then even more men and ammunition so that this time . . . this time," he repeated forcefully, "we can hold on to the corridor."

"I don't have either to give you," Shaltiel said wearily. "Luke Thomas has a wild scheme to open an alternate route to the coast. He already took every man I could spare. If it works, maybe then we'll have what we need to break through."

"By then," Nachasch said, "we'll be in time to bury the Old City Jews."

■ ■ ■ ■

The battery of the Jewish Quarter wireless radio was weak, nearly gone. Rachel and Yehudit manned it, listening intently as the reply from David Shaltiel, the New City commander, came through.

Grandfather stood framed in the doorway of the radio room. "So," Grandfather said exultantly. "Now they will do something!"

Shaltiel's tone was hopeful. "Help is coming . . . tonight . . . men, mortars . . . Hold on . . . fully prepared . . . You'll need to hang on . . . until . . ."

Tonight?" Rachel whispered. "But tell him we need them to attack immediately! Tell him the Legion has practically abandoned Zion Gate! They can't wait until tonight! King Abdullah will be gone and . . . Tell him they can take it!"

Yehudit pressed the transmission button and relayed the urgency of the situation. The radio cracked erratically and then went dead.

■ ■ ■ ■

The procession following Sholem down into the ravine included Tweedle, Michael Stone, Ellie, and the Arab Druze, Bashir.

Ellie found herself braced back on her heels and trying not to notice how far it was to the bottom. Four hundred tons of supplies would have to be levered down this slope. It seemed treacherous, impossible.

Neither the loose gravel nor the drop-off bothered Sholem.

Leading the way, he said, "There is where we can take the path further out and make the corner more gentle." The Russian pointed out a natural level place obscured by brush. "Let me mark it."

Trampling down the thick weeds until he reached the location selected, Sholem hammered in a tall iron bar.

"Just like that? On this grade? You can do it by sight?" Tweedle said dubiously.

Using piles of rocks and torn bits of cloth tied to tree branches, Sholem surveyed an improved route down to the canyon's floor. "I need people with picks and shovels to prepare the way down to the first corner," he said. "After that, I manage. The remaining question is where to get the bulldozer."

Stone slapped Sholem on the back. "Already on the way," he replied.

■ ■ ■ ■

"How is Dov?" Lori asked Yehudit as the young woman brought her ration of matzo and sat down beside her.

Yehudit replied, "He is . . . alive. Dr. Baruch says maybe if he gets proper care he will recover." She hugged her knees and gazed up into the starlit sky above Jerusalem. "My father spoke to me about it. Surrendering, you know. Says if we surrender then everyone will be taken care of." She shuddered. "I don't know."

Lori was silent for a long time. She cradled the sleeping Abe, stroking his forehead lightly with her fingers. "I know. I think about it. It's the Legion now. Not the Mufti. But what happens to . . . all this? Would they ever let you come back? I mean, would the Muslims let Jews come back into the Old City?"

"Moshe and Ehud say no. Dov hasn't talked about it. But I know what he thinks. Does Daniel talk about it? Surrender, I mean."

Lori glanced to where the sixteen-year-old was sleeping. "No. I think he'd rather die."

Yehudit sighed. "King Abdullah must still be around. It's calm. Even with a few thousand of his men around us, it's quiet."

"No birds. No crickets. After all the gunfire I hear the stillness louder than explosions," Lori said.

"Even the devil sleeps sometimes," Yehudit commented. "I never get used to the silence, you know. I understand the booming. Things blowing up. But the silence. I imagine they're creeping up on us. I'm going to pass out a load of matzo to the boys and walk away and *blam!* I'll be killed and raped. Hopefully in that order."

"I'm sure that the minute King Abdullah wakens from his beauty sleep and leaves Jerusalem they'll start up again."

"Yes. Sure. Tomorrow will not be so peaceful. At least we'll know what to expect." She gave Lori's hand a squeeze. "Well then, *shalom,* my friend."

"Greet Dov for me," Lori called after her as Yehudit sprinted through the darkness.

Thirty seconds passed. Lori listened to her retreating footsteps, and then a single shot rang out. Somewhere above them, beyond the perimeter! The report resounded in corridors of stone like a hundred shots. A woman's anguished cry followed.

"Help me! Oh, God! I'm . . . hurt! I'm hurt!"

It was Yehudit.

CHAPTER 27

From his rounds, Moshe returned to the military headquarters at the complex of the Sephardic synagogues.

It was here he had grown to manhood.

His grandfather had been *Harishon Le'Zion,* the First in Zion, the Sephardic chief rabbi of Jerusalem. Moshe's father had been a rabbi here. Moshe's brother, Eli, was expected to follow in his footsteps.

Eli had been killed in the Arab uprisings of the thirties.

Moshe, the last hope of the family to continue generations of tradition, had already left the Old City for Hebrew University and Oxford in England. When he finally returned, he had hoped to preserve a way of life.

That hope was rapidly vanishing.

He sensed the presence of his father and grandfather as he descended the staircase leading below street level to the courtyard of the Sephardic compound.

A sense of foreboding haunted him. For the first time he doubted if he could save the Jewish Old City and the heritage of his fathers. He had failed to preserve the passage that led to the concealed chamber beneath the Temple Mount. The secret Rachel's grandfather had passed on to him merely days before lay hidden beneath a mound of rubble.

The Sephardim were adept at hiding from their enemies, Moshe thought, as he studied the modest exteriors of the synagogues. Built low into the ground, each structure resembled an ordinary house on the outside. This kept them from being noticed. It also made them safer.

Misgav Ladakh Hospital was now on the outer edge of the Quarter. If it came under fire, Moshe had already decided that the wounded would be evacuated to this jumble of buildings.

He hoped it would not come to that.

The large Stambuli Synagogue had an entrance that led down a long flight of stairs. Here, Moshe remembered, was a storage place for worn-out sacred texts.

When the chamber became full, the holy writings could not simply be discarded. Two score sacks of scrolls were collected and carried by procession for burial in the Jewish cemetery. One of Moshe's earliest memories was of that event.

It had been a year of peace for Jerusalem. Muslims and Christians joined in the joyful parade. At the head was Moshe's grandfather. In front of him was a Turkish diplomat dressed in silks and carrying a pistol and a sword. Candles were lit. Rose water was sprinkled from the rooftops. The shofar had blown again and again.

Moshe wondered what his grandfather would think, to see Moshe as head of a defense of those same streets. The grandchildren of those Muslims who had danced in the Jewish procession through the streets of Jerusalem wanted to destroy their Jewish neighbors.

Surely Moshe's grandfather would have wished Moshe dead at birth if he had seen this dreadful hour. The Jewish Quarter was slipping irrevocably away.

Moshe knew he was a failure of the first magnitude.

Moshe entered his father's synagogue, Eliyahu Hanavi, where Elijah had come to join a minyan in prayer. The candle beside Elijah's chair burned. This used to be the study hall of one of the larger synagogues. Tonight it was empty.

Moshe peered into an anteroom. A handful of aged Sephardim slept along the walls. The distant sound of praying drifted into the space.

The rabbis were praying Elijah would come, that the Messiah would follow on his heels and save Jerusalem.

Moshe prayed the same prayer. But with the failure of Shaltiel to send help, therefore turning the tide, Moshe had almost stopped believing.

What could he do? Ehud, returned to the watch with his men, had left a list of resources on the table beside Elijah's chair. Moshe sat down wearily and began to comb through the papers. Each note for three days recorded progressive disaster.

On Monday the last water in the main Hurva Synagogue cistern had gone dry.

On Tuesday the secondary cistern had been opened, to reveal that it had cracked and the precious water had seeped away. That left only the water supply here at the Sephardic complex.

Perhaps tomorrow Moshe would have to move all the civilians into the Sephardic houses of prayer.

And for defense?

What resources, besides the stolen ammunition he had brought, were left?

Enough for a day? Maybe two?

He would send another message to Shaltiel in the New City. There could be no more waiting. "Elijah," he whispered. "This is the time."

■ ■ ■ ■

The blood from Yehudit's side dripped like a partly open tap as Alfie rushed her to the hospital. He held his hand over the hole to stop the blood, but still it flowed.

Bursting in, Alfie shouted for Dr. Baruch. In the half-light, heads raised to see what the commotion was about.

It had been so still tonight. One shot fired. Now this!

Baruch emerged from the room where surgeries took place. Draped in a spattered smock, Baruch resembled a butcher who had been a whole day at the slaughter.

"It's Yehudit!" Alfie shouted. Never mind that people were trying to sleep.

Dov sat up and called her name.

At the sound of Dov's voice she stirred in Alfie's arms. She was alive!

"She's bleeding to death," Alfie cried as he stumbled toward the doctor.

Baruch flew into action. Taking her from Alfie, he stripped off the blood-saturated blouse to reveal a fingertip-sized hole beneath her rib cage.

■ ■ ■ ■

Since emerging from the tunnel, it seemed to Moshe that his thoughts never had time to form coherent pictures. Bent over a map, he reviewed the Old City's defensive posture one more time, as though he might spot an unexploited resource, a hidden miracle.

The surviving inhabitants of the district were jammed into an area one-fourth the size of the original from twelve days earlier. The Great Hurva was the northern bastion and the Beit Rothschild apartment block the southern. The Haganah defenders held the western line along the Street of the Jews.

It was the eastern front that was most vigorously attacked. The entire enclave was merely a rectangle barely a thousand feet from north to south and half that in width.

A few acres.

Moshe had conducted archaeological digs on bigger sites.

It was a wonder the Arabs were not attacking from the Armenian Quarter to the west and from the north. If there was a coordinated Arab squeeze of the Jewish district from three sides, it would fall at once. Only the piecemeal nature of the assaults allowed the Israelis to move the paltry reserves they possessed to meet each new threat.

Moshe and Dov had risked everything to destroy the Arab cannon that threatened Notre Dame. Perhaps that action had saved the New City.

What was being done to repay the debt?

When would another Palmach breakthrough come?

When Moshe glanced up again from his map, Rachel stood beside him. He did not know how long she had waited for him to notice her.

"A group of rabbis to see you," she said.

"Is Akiva with them?" Moshe asked. He did not think he was up to facing that annoying man.

"No," she said.

The group of four men Rachel ushered into Moshe's cubicle commanded the respect due to age. Between them they had seen three and a half centuries of living. The youngest was a spry eighty-year-old, the eldest one year short of a hundred.

The bearded, earlocked contingent swayed as one, as if they stood on the deck of a ship. No one spoke.

"Yes?" Moshe inquired.

There was no response, apart from shuffling of arthritic feet and rattling of husky throats.

"Learned sirs, how can I help you?"

The junior member of the group shuffled forward. "It is written . . . ," he said.

"Yes?"

A pair of right hands, one liver-spotted and shaking, the other displaying translucent skin and blue veins, prodded the man from behind. "It is written," he repeated, "that the needless sacrifice of life is abhorred by the Eternal, blessed be He."

"Go on," Moshe said.

Thus encouraged, the tottering rabbi launched into a prepared address. "To needlessly cast away one's own life is suicide, a grave sin. To needlessly cast away the lives of others is akin to murder." The elderly scholar proceeded to instruct Moshe in the precepts of Jewish moral law. Women and children were being killed; more were being endangered by the continued fighting.

The rest of the deputation bobbed their agreement.

"And what is it you want?" Moshe asked when the recitation slowed.

Accompanied by much blinking as though the translation from principle to actual demand was difficult to express, the spokesman said, "Why not arrange a truce so that noncombatants may leave the Quarter?"

Moshe knew that such a proposal had already been rejected by the Arabs. The counterdemand required a total capitulation. To make such a request again was merely to indicate the increasing weakness and division within the Jewish district.

"What is your response?" the rabbi prodded.

"Do you know Dov Joseph, the administrator of civilian affairs in the New City?"

Yes, the rabbis concurred, they recognized the name of the capable Canadian Jew, Dov Joseph.

"Well, then," Moshe continued, "when Dov Joseph was asked a similar question about a partial surrender in Mea Shearim, he replied, 'You must do what you think is right, and I will do the same.'"

The rabbis considered this, and then the eldest asked in a quavering voice, "And did Dov Joseph indicate what he would do?"

"Certainly," Moshe replied. "He said anyone showing a white flag would be shot."

Mumbling and bowing, the quartet of learned men backed out of Moshe's presence.

"You don't mean it," Rachel challenged as soon as the rabbis were out of earshot. "You would never give the order to shoot one of them for surrendering!"

"No," Moshe replied wearily. "But it is important *they* believe it. If they see any wavering in me they will report it to Akiva, and then my leadership here is finished. Remember, the longer we hang on, the better for the rest of Jerusalem, the better for Israel. Even if for one more day."

THURSDAY

May 27, 1948

"Do not think that I have come to abolish the Law or the Prophets; I have come not to abolish them but to fulfill them. I tell you the truth, until heaven and earth disappear, not the smallest letter, not the least stroke of a pen, will by any means disappear from the Law until everything is accomplished."

Matthew 5:17–18

"Remember these things, O Jacob, for you are my servant, O Israel. I have made you, you are my servant; O Israel I will not forget you. I have swept away your offenses like a cloud, your sins like the morning mist.

Return to me, for I have redeemed you!"

Isaiah 44:21–22

CHAPTER 28

The opportunities of Wednesday had passed unexploited.

No help was coming for the Jewish Quarter from Zion.

The soldiers of the Arab Legion resumed their places rank upon rank along the ring of the Old City Wall.

The disappointment among the remaining Jewish defenders was palpable. Everyone knew that King Abdullah would soon be gone. When it was light on Thursday the hammering would begin again.

The walking wounded who manned the barricades hoped lightning would not strike them twice. Those who were whole wondered where they would be this time Friday.

Dead maybe. It was a difficult thought to imagine. The world going on without you. They all thought of it. Stars shining somewhere. People sitting down to supper. Reading the paper. And you not being there.

They each wondered how the story would end.

Moshe made the rounds of every position. He said what he could to encourage them. But the broken promises of the New City Command had a more devastating effect on morale than a cannon fired point-blank.

No one in the Jewish Quarter welcomed this uneasy silence. As Zionist pioneer Jabotsinky had written, *Quietude is like mire. . . .*

■ ■ ■ ■

Back in Eliyahu Hanavi Moshe heard the footfall on the stair. Rebbe Lebowitz emerged from the shadowed alcove and raised a hand to greet him.

They had not spoken since Moshe's return. How Moshe dreaded this moment.

The old man shuffled toward him. He had aged ten years in the last week. His eyes were pained. Was it from the ache in his bones or the tearing of his heart?

He sat down opposite Moshe and said in Hebrew, "In falsehood hope grows cold."

"I'm sorry," Moshe answered quietly. "I have ... let everyone down."

Grandfather gazed up at the cupola. "When I was a young man the Ashkenazim and the Sephardim studied together in this hall. I studied with your father. He was a fine man."

"I disappointed him. When I left this place, he said my name was *sheker*, 'falsehood,' from that hour."

"And so you changed your name to Sachar, one who seeks the dawn. One letter changes the meaning of everything. Your father often called himself *Sachar*."

"He would not acknowledge me after I left."

"He loved you."

"Things did not turn out the way he wanted for me. Or my brother."

"Your grandfather ... First in Zion. Chief rabbi of the Sephardim. A true scholar. He knew much."

"I remember him. I was afraid of him."

"A man of wisdom, your grandfather. I remember the day he was made chief rabbi. The firman was read. The Turkish diplomat poured coffee at his feet in honor of the occasion. It was a stirring day."

"He would hate me, I think."

The old rabbi was silent. "Did I ever tell you the order of things?"

"The order?"

"It is right I tell you. Here in the place where I, an Ashkenazi, studied Torah with your Sephardi father." He was smiling.

"You were good friends."

"Yes. It is good you married my granddaughter. A perfect match. Rachel married to Moshe Sekhel. A good name I always thought."

"I would like my good name back."

"A letter changed here and there more or less separates understanding from falsehood ... seeking truth or running from it. Cling to what is written in God's Word. Leave nothing out and ... here is the tricky part ... add nothing to it. Then you will walk the path to understanding."

Moshe surveyed the small auditorium. "I never knew how much I missed this place."

"Yes. I will miss it too. But I was speaking of the order. Of things. And of your name."

"My name."

"Sekhel. The wisest of men, King Solomon taught us, *Sekhel tov yiten hen.*"

"Good understanding giveth grace," Moshe repeated.

Grandfather stroked his beard. "*Sekhel.* Understanding. And *Mosheh?* From the lamb. And *Mosheh* is *Hashem* the other way round. The Name. So. You are well named: *Seek the dawn of understanding in the name of the Lamb.*"

"It has only recently meant anything to me."

"To seek. It is a good thing. He who seeks understanding finds it, yes? But one cannot be afraid to ask the questions. Cannot be afraid to knock on the door."

"Sure." Moshe followed the old man's eyes as his gaze shifted to the polished walnut ark where the Torah scroll was kept.

Rebbe Lebowitz said, "And now the order of the guardians. You may ask yourself, Moshe, how did Rachel's grandfather choose to tell me the mystery buried in Jerusalem's heart?"

"I wondered. Yes. I supposed it was because of Rachel . . ."

"I wish for you to ponder this mystery." Grandfather stood and hobbled to Elijah's chair. He placed his hand on the back of it. "Nine men prayed in this place. Not enough for a minyan. And there came among us one more. The prophet Elijah, they say. He was here to pray. And then he was not here." The old man pivoted toward the ark. "Come beside me, Moshe Sekhel."

Without understanding why, Moshe knew a rush of excitement as he went to stand beside the old rabbi. Grandfather took his hand and guided it along the branch of an almond tree carved above the door.

The old man queried, "How many blossoms on the branch of the almond tree?"

Moshe counted. "Twenty-two."

"The number of letters in the Hebrew alphabet." The old man's eyes gleamed with excitement.

"Everything means something," Moshe quoted. "What does it mean?"

"You must ask the right questions. *Nu!*" Grandfather said. "What word in Hebrew sounds like almond tree?"

"The word *watching,*" Moshe replied without hesitation.

"As we read in the first chapter of Jeremiah. The Eternal is watching over the doors of Israel to see that His Word is fulfilled. You will find the almond branch many places in Torah and the prophets. And . . . even here. In your father's synagogue." He guided Moshe's hand along the branch to the seventh blossom. "Not now. Not yet," he intoned. "But if things come to an end for us here you must remember. Turn it seven times to the right."

"Another way in!"

The old rabbi held up his index finger. "There is one way. One door. Torah is the beginning. The house where Torah and truth are honored will seek and find the name of the lamb. Remember what a tiny step it is from understanding to falsehood."

Moshe swallowed hard. "I haven't lost the way then?"

"It was always here. It will always be here. It is Jerusalem's heart."

Suddenly the light above Elijah's chair seemed brighter. Each petal on every carved flower took on new importance. Symbols drawn from the pages of the five books of Moses all held deeper significance: the ark that held the Word. The writing of the Ten Commandments.

On the wall above the lectern was a painting of the seven-branched menorah. It was covered in the blossoms of an almond tree. Moshe had never noticed the details before. What other meanings were buried deep within the words written in the Scriptures? Each thing pointed to one truth. Each minute description was a cistern flowing with living water!

If any of you thirst . . .

"Where is Rachel?" Moshe asked. "I need to see her."

"I thought you might. She is waiting on the stair of the women's gallery. I have told her . . . much," Rebbe Lebowitz warned. "Told her you might be gone for a time. But I cannot tell her everything. You must not tell her, Moshe. It would be a danger to her and to your daughter, and to your unborn child."

Moshe agreed. "Tonight I want simply to be with her."

The old man touched him lightly on the shoulder, urging him to go to her.

■ ■ ■ ■

The waning moon bathed the Old City in crimson light. Within the ramparts of the wall, spires, minarets, and cupolas rose and congealed in the glow of the moon.

The end was near for them. Lori knew that. Unless someone broke through from the outside there was no hope for the Old City.

Abe slept, his head on Lori's lap, while Daniel Caan stared at the sky with the kind of awe of a child watching fireworks. Had he given up hope? Surrendered his life to the certainty of death? Did he, too, drink in the color and the eerie silence with the thought that this was the last? The very last night of his life on earth?

Lori ran her fingers through Abe's hair. She thought about the reasons she wanted to live. Living had everything to do with the faces of those she loved here on this earth. Jacob. This child . . . Abe.

And then she remembered all the faces of those who had loved her and had gone before. Would they be there to welcome her when she came? Would they greet her by name and smile and say, "You've made it safely!"?

She thought of Jerusalem, buried in the evil trap of the age-old battle. And she thought of the world, self-absorbed and trivial, far beyond Jerusalem.

Out there, Jerusalem was an item in the newspapers. People walked across the park. Took their children to the playground. Went to the movies on Saturday night or stayed home and listened to the radio if they wanted. Played music on phonographs. Read books. Switched lamps on and off. Slept in beds. The sun came up and people went off to work, not even wondering if they would be alive at the end of a day to come home again. They ate big meals without wondering if they would eat again. Farmers gave corn to cattle and milk to feed pigs. Out there, people drifted, dreaming that life would go on forever, taking it for granted. They worried about a million trivial things. They obsessed over paying bills and their kids doing well in school and what someone said or did not say and what it means. And they could not imagine this hour, this place, these people . . . Jerusalem!

Problems were Life: little puzzles to be worked out, games to enjoy, challenges to have victory over. *Thank God for the small problems!* And what were those things when weighed in the true balance of living or dying?

What would Lori say to Jacob if she had the opportunity? How much of life's tiny expressions of love could be packed into how little a space? And what unthinking harsh words and squandered heartbeats could be reclaimed?

Time was precious, life too valuable to be wasted. And not because of unachieved accomplishments, but for the fleeting opportunities to love and be loved.

What would Lori give to lift Abe out of the path of destruction? To feed him? Bathe him? Read him stories? To play in a garden and not wonder if they would be blown to pieces when they walked to the market?

A shooting star, too reminiscent of a streaking shell, brought Lori back to Jerusalem. She gazed down at Abe. He slept untroubled by the nearness, the certain approach of death.

Every other thought of the world outside drained away. At that instant there was no city but Jerusalem. No people but this battered remnant of God's chosen. *This child!* No sky but the one above her. No light but the blood-red glow of Jerusalem's conflagration.

■ ■ ■ ■

The nighttime scene in the Judean hills had a fanciful, ghostly quality about it. As Jacob and Leon patrolled the slopes between the two villages, they were above the road builders and could view their efforts.

The scene was illuminated by torches, both electric and kerosene-soaked rags tied to tree branches. The lights formed a glowing, segmented worm snaking its way up from the western wadi to Beit Jiz and vanishing into the twisted canyon to the east, beyond Beit Susin.

The figures moving along the trail were apparitions whose shadows swelled larger near each globe of light and shrunk again beyond it.

Not much talking reached Jacob's ears. Instead the air was saturated with a continuous low clicking, like a million beetles or a flock of birds cracking snail shells.

Elderly men picked at the ground with shovels, knives, fence rails, or bits of iron bed frame. Women gathered fragments of stone into aprons or canvas satchels. Boys toted rocks bigger than they could reasonably lift, each striving to outdo the other.

Projecting knobs in the path were scraped away, ruts and holes filled.

The high sides of the route were painstakingly shaved, the low shoulders built up. The path perceptibly widened from trace to trail to roadway.

Chip, click, chip, click.

"This is what I came to Israel to find," Leon said quietly.

Jacob waited.

"Jews working together to build something that exists nowhere else in the world," Leon explained. "This is our last hope."

"You never said what brought you to Palestine," Jacob said. Of those Jacob had grown close to in Aleph Company, Leon's was the story he had never heard.

The two men found a boulder on which to sit. Back to back, they faced away from the lights of the builders and concentrated on watching the moonlit hillside for any movement that might be an Arab scout.

"I was a craftsman before the war," Leon said. "A furniture maker. Good quality. Musical instruments, too. The mandolin I made myself the first year my wife, Nora, and I were married. When the Nazis came, they had me make chairs for them. Soon they forced us out of our apartment and moved every Jew into a ghetto. I gave the special mandolin to the Polish porter of our apartment block to keep for me.

"Later, the Nazis did not want furniture anymore; they wanted slaves. They separated me from my wife and our three children . . . three little girls. When we were torn apart my wife said to me, 'Afterward, come and find us.'"

There was a long wait in which the sounds of the shovels could be heard and then, "So I went to Buchenwald. After liberation I went home to look for my family. No trace. Then I met my wife's aunt. She told me she saw my wife and children in Auschwitz . . . on their way to the crematorium."

Leon's voice was matter-of-fact, emotionless, as if he had long before expended every trace of sentiment. "I went back three times to our apartment block, searching for . . . I don't know what. Ghosts? Memories? The woman living in our old home was Polish. She asked me what I was doing, told me to go away, I wasn't wanted. Said I would cause trouble; Jews always cause trouble. That there would have been no war except for Jews. She said, 'The bad thing about Hitler was that he did not kill all of you.' The old porter was still alive, still working there. So I picked up the mandolin . . . it's all that's left of my life in Poland . . . and came here."

To the purposeful stir of the laborers was added a new harshness. A metallic clanking sound and the rumble of an engine echoed up from the wadi to the west.

Jumping to his feet, Jacob checked his rifle.

Was it a tank? Had the Arabs outflanked the secret road somehow and were coming with tanks?

What could they do against tanks? There weren't any bazookas here, not even any Molotov cocktails.

Incredibly, cheering erupted from down below, from out of sight around the curve of a hill.

The clanking sound increased and into the first bend of firelight rumbled a bulldozer. Clinging to its steel flanks were another eleven men to work on the highway. Towed behind it were two supply trucks.

■ ■ ■ ■

Hugging her knees and straining to hear the indistinct words of Moshe and Grandfather, Rachel waited on the stair to the women's gallery.

What was it the old man was saying? *Hashem, Hashem, Kiddush Hashem . . . for the Sanctification of the Name.* Were they all to die then? Was the Quarter to be sacrificed for Israel?

She could not make out Moshe's reply, just the weariness of his tone.

The rafters of the halls echoed with a low murmuring, like a song drifting across a lake on a summer's day. She could not understand the lyrics or see the singer, but the voice was there.

Grandfather had told her Moshe might have to be gone a long time. Would he be taken prisoner? Was he going into hiding? The riddle of Grandfather's words frightened her.

An hour passed before the two men finished talking. Grandfather said, *"Shalom,"* and went away.

Seconds later Moshe stood in the shadows at the foot of the stairs. He looked up at her but did not come to sit beside her. It was as though he was savoring the sight of her. Memorizing the vision. Counting each breath and storing it up to take out at a future date.

At last she spoke. "Grandfather says you may need to go away."

"Things are bad."

"What is to become of us?"

"The Arab Legion is in control. English officers. Not butchers. If it comes to it, I am certain women and children won't be harmed."

"No, I mean us. What is to become of us, Moshe? You. Me. Our babies."

He climbed and sat on the step at her feet. With a sigh he laid his head in her lap and stroked her leg. "I will always love you," he said tenderly.

"You loved me into wanting to live again. Grandfather says . . . there is something . . . more important than either of us. It may take you from me."

"Don't think about it. Not now. Rachel, Rachel!" He raised up until his face was level with hers. Kissing her mouth tentatively at first, he squeezed her against him. Hungry for her, he scooped her up. She put her arms around his neck as he carried her to the loft.

They were hidden in the darkness behind the lattice of the chamber. The floor was carpeted with pillows. He laid her on the cushions, then stretched out beside her. She felt the warmth of his breath on her brow. Stroking her cheek, he next traced the line of her slender neck with his finger.

"There has never been anyone for me but you, Rachel," he whispered, kissing her throat. "Tell me . . . tell me . . . what you want."

"Touch me." She guided his hand to the slight swell of her stomach. "I carry you in me. You. And me. Our child. Just there."

His mouth covered hers again, harder, more insistent, igniting a fire that uncoiled inside her, then coursed through her body. She kissed him back, holding him tightly. Wanting more. Needing everything. Drawing him to her. Wanting him to hold her like this forever, yet knowing tonight might be their last night.

CHAPTER 29

The bulldozer Stone located to expand his Roman road was a monster. Merely the top of the treads on the D-9 Cat were as tall as Sholem's head. When he climbed up to the operator's seat, he was ten feet off the ground.

It was close to four in the morning when he revved up the diesel and set the blade for its first pass. But the crew Sholem was personally directing had already been laboring for hours to get ready for the machine's arrival.

As Ellie leaned on her shovel handle and tried not to think about her blistered palms, Sholem worked foot pedals and levers with a fine economy of motion. Despite the severe angle of the cliff face, he appeared able to mesh the 'dozer with the contours of the earth. A mist of lime dusted the ravine, coating everyone nearby.

Ellie marveled at Sholem's skill. Without ever discarding his calm, deliberate action, Sholem managed to make more happen than she would have thought possible in the time.

The bulldozer cut, widened, leveled, and compacted. By dawn Sholem transformed the route into a manageable jeep trail.

Michael Stone walked down it with Ellie. "Great," he yelled up to Sholem. "Got to shut it down, though. Too risky in daylight. Can't take a chance the Arabs catch on."

"Not yet," Sholem argued. "There is a bad place back near the closest village. I can fix it in no time at all."

"Make it snappy," Ellie heard Stone say.

■ ■ ■ ■

Three hours remained until the final ultimatum would have to be answered.

From where they lay behind the lattice of the gallery, Moshe dreamed he heard the cries of the wounded resounding from the hospital.

He kissed Rachel lightly. She stirred in his arms.

"What time is it?" she asked.

"We have work to do," he replied.

"You have decided, then." She sat up slowly.

"Yes."

"You have decided to fight them? Even knowing what they can do to Misgav Ladakh? Even though you know their cannon could destroy the Hurva?"

"If we can hold. One more day. Hang on until Jerusalem is resupplied . . ."

"Do you believe help is coming?"

"I don't know. But if it was . . . if somehow what Shaltiel radioed was true. If help was on the way. And if I then did not fight for this place to the last man and the last bullet, what would I be?"

"Alive."

"You too, eh?"

"No," she said sadly. "Not me too. But you asked what would happen if we surrender, and I told you. I know about that kind of surrender. Maybe it is better to die. *Kiddush Hashem,* my grandfather says. For the Sanctification of the Name." She stood up, then reached down to touch his brow. "Do what you must. But the people in the Hurva . . . Moshe? All those people."

"If it comes to it, we must evacuate them," he said. "But not yet." His head ached. "The Arabs will know we have rejected their ultimatum if they see we're moving civilians to the Sephardic compound."

"And if you and the defenders cannot hold the Hurva?" she asked.

"We'll pull back here. It's like a bunker, eh? Our last stand."

■ ■ ■ ■

One by one the lights that guided the road builders through the long night were extinguished. The increasing brilliance of Thursday's dawn brought repeated exclamations of wonder at what had been accomplished.

In the night Ellie had barely been able to see the area on which she worked. Her focus had been one rut, one pile of rocks to be moved, never more than a few yards in extent.

But the sunrise pooled the efforts, joining the individual puny labors into an accomplishment.

What had been barely recognizable as a trail was revealed to be a road. Not a wide, smooth road, but nevertheless something that claimed a destination, a purpose.

With two millennia of overburden removed, portions of the Roman road reappeared: a handful of exposed mile markers bearing chiseled Roman numerals and flagstone-surfaced stretches extended a confirmation, an accolade.

It felt impressive.

Madame Rose accepted a cup of water from the Madman. Ellie could see the woman speaking kindly to him, but he did not respond.

Ellie paused in her digging to wipe her forehead. The day was scarcely begun, and it was already unpleasantly hot. From where she labored in a gully she could see Sholem maneuvering the bulldozer to take yet another bite of hillside. Black exhaust, chalky lime grit, and red dust ballooned up from his efforts.

On a rise in the other direction, a trio of men struggled with a donkey. Loaded with additional shovels for the work crew, the animal had arrived at a patch of grass that looked interesting, and it refused to go any further.

It resisted the efforts of the three humans, despite the fact that two tugged at a lead rope while the third switched it from behind with a stick.

■ ■ ■ ■

East of Latrun, on the higher outcropping known as Gun Hill, Major Burr inspected the Arab Legion artillery battery. He tried not to look at Major Athani's face, though Athani was at his side. The Arab officer's eyes were swollen almost shut, and his lips pouted grotesquely. The welts left by the hornet stings on the sides of Athani's neck had so puffed up the skin that his head appeared to rest on a solid column of flesh growing out of his chest.

Burr know the damage inflicted by the hornets was serious. Three of the worst stung of the troopers were not expected to live and ten more were in hospital. Athani was putting up a brave front to participate in this inspection at all.

Burr had offered to send someone else in command of another company to occupy Beit Susin and Beit Jiz, but Athani begged to be allowed to carry out his assignment. Burr then scheduled the second expedition for after the visit to Gun Hill.

"There is no rush about seizing Beit Susin," the artillery captain maintained. "From here we can drop shells on the village. The Jews could not hold it under our barrage."

Athani turned toward the direction indicated. Squinting, because he could not do otherwise, he said, "I cannot really make it out, but there seems to be dust in the air over there."

Grabbing a pair of binoculars from a startled lieutenant, Burr studied the range of hills that concealed Beit Susin. "There *is* something there," he agreed. "Located between the two villages. Something more than returning villagers or wandering goats to stir up that much dust. Captain," he ordered the artillery officer, "lay down a barrage . . . four rounds per gun. Aim for the road connecting the two towns; we'll try to spare them if we can." Then to Athani he said, "Major, I'm sorry to reverse what I said earlier, but I will lead this force myself. I leave you in command here. Fourth Regiment is to move out in fifteen minutes."

■ ■ ■ ■

After Jacob reported what had happened to the Legion patrol and the wasps, other members of Aleph Company came to the rock fort to see what many were calling "the Hornet's Nest Defenses."

The notoriety gave Jerome Jardin opportunities for elaborately retelling the tale, but as Rudolf pointed out, "There was just one hornet's nest, and it's gone. What happens the next time?"

This observation reduced Jerome's desire to brag, but it was Leon the musician who had the last word on the subject. "The Lord will send the hornet to drive out your enemies," he said across the cleft of the rock when he and Jerome were on guard duty.

This comment caught Jerome off guard. "What is this?" he asked.

"You said you were sorry Lain was not here to see our little miracle. You wondered what he would have said." Leon shrugged. "In Torah, I think . . . there's something there anyway . . . about God chasing the enemy with hornets. I don't know. Lain would have known the verse."

Jerome smiled quizzically. "You Jews. All crazy."

"On a bad day it helps to be a little crazy," Leon replied.

Jacob, standing beside the rock and surveying what he could see of Latrun through field glasses, listened with interest. Yes. They were all nuts. Why else would they be here?

Through the binoculars Jacob saw a bright flash. Then another followed and another.

■ ■ ■ ■

With the first shell burst Ellie shrank to the ground and crouched there. She was not wounded, but the force of the concussion was the same as being hit in the chest by someone's fist.

She put her hands over her ears as another shattering roar erupted and then another.

The noise was so deafening that it blocked every other sound. Ellie felt herself screaming, but could not hear her own cries. She saw others doing the same, but could not catch a single word.

The laborers huddled or lay flat, hugging boulders and tree trunks as if trying to make the earth stop shuddering.

It was like watching an old silent film. Not only was the experience without sound, all expressions were distorted, all movement exaggerated.

In one instant the men and the donkey were a frozen tableau. In the next four lives were tossed upward in a fountain of blood and dirt, as if the earth underneath feet and hooves had exploded upward. On the spot where they had been was a smoking crater.

Ellie saw the Madman. He was walking upright across the hillside, carrying the water bucket, oblivious to the danger.

Putting down the pail, he banged on its side with the ladle. "Water!" he mouthed. He shook the dipper at workers, angry that they had stopped digging. In the rolling thunder of the barrage, his harangue was more terrifying because it was expressed solely in his eyes, his facial contortions, his gestures.

Another blast, this one above and behind Ellie, threw gravel, like a bucket of spent shotgun pellets, at her back.

Madame Rose waved at the Madman. She pointed up at the sky, then made a signal for him to get down.

The Madman shook his ladle toward Latrun.

A jet of smoke burst from the bulldozer. Ellie was astonished to see Sholem continued to operate it. He had not jumped off the exposed perch and run for shelter. Instead, Sholem's concern was for protecting the equipment, moving it out of danger.

To Ellie's amazement, he gunned the 'dozer toward the pit left by a shell's impact.

Only after he had driven the machine into the crater did he leap from the seat and take cover behind its steel flank.

Ellie's attention shifted back toward the Madman.

He was further up the slope, trudging in the direction of Latrun and furiously brandishing the dipper. "Come here," his mouthed words demanded. "You killers of my boy. Come here."

Ellie was knocked backward by another explosion. When she looked again, the Madman had vanished without a trace.

■ ■ ■ ■

Jacob's squad scattered, throwing themselves to the ground for cover. Jacob buried his face in the dirt. Once begun, the artillery assault was a rolling barrage that almost eliminated thinking.

The five troopers at the Hornet's Nest hugged the ground.

The earth rumbled as multiple impacts shook the mountain.

Aleph's duty was to protect the road builders.

How could they protect anyone against this?

How much did the Arabs know? Was this a random shelling or a deliberate, zeroed-in blasting of the road?

Was the mission to construct the secret road already finished?

There was a pause in the shelling. A time to separate the real detonations from imagined shell bursts caused by jangling nerves, and ringing ears from real explosions.

Would it start again?

■ ■ ■ ■

Ellie carefully peered around.

Beyond where the Madman had been, across the top of the rocky range that separated the new road from the Valley of Ayalon, a pillar of dust swept down from the east. Thicker, darker, and many times higher than the billowed smoke of Sholem's bulldozer, it resembled the Madman's ladle, expanded to colossal size.

■ ■ ■ ■

Jacob lifted his chin from the earth. Without raising his body, he peered over the lip of the ravine.

The first Arab Legionnaires had crossed the foothills and were descending into the wadi below the ridge.

This time it was not a hundred of them.

It was hundreds.

"Rudolf," Jacob called, "run to Beit Susin! Hurry! Alert all units and send word to Colonel Stone: major Arab force headed this way. Move all roaming patrols onto line. No shooting! Remind them, no shooting!"

How impossible would that be to achieve this time?

It would take more than hornets to stop . . . Jacob stole another glance . . . a thousand enemy soldiers.

No more hornets!

Was there a promise to cover this?

Oh God, send help!

■ ■ ■ ■

Major Burr moved the Arab Legion's Fourth Regiment like a surgeon's knife. With terse, explicit orders, he wielded a thousand men.

The last shells of the preliminary barrage had fallen, precisely on schedule.

It would take the troopers fifteen minutes to climb the ridge where they would then be above the road and the Arab villages. Whatever opposition they met would be disoriented by the shelling and surprised that the Legionnaires appeared in such numbers.

Overwhelming numbers.

Whatever the Jews were doing, whatever they were planning out of sight of Latrun, it would soon be over.

Burr calculated that even if the Jews occupied Beit Jiz and Beit Susin, they would have neither the men nor the weaponry to oppose him for long.

He had seen how they fought at Latrun: with courage but without leadership; with rifles but without massed firepower.

Besides, there was no way to move even so much as trucks or armored vehicles up or down from the Arab villages. Whatever arrived there came by donkey . . . or on the backs of humans.

He was grateful for the swirl of dust that had alerted him to a potential buildup.

Nip it in the bud; that was the proper way to deal with any threat.

A gust of wind sighed against his cheek. It was cool. No Khamseen, this.

Burr's quietly spoken orders were barked down the chain of command, through the throats of twenty other English officers. Companies moved, flowed, and arrayed themselves on the lip of the creek bed.

The strength of the breeze increased, fluttering the tails of keffiyehs.

Giving the orders to advance, Burr set men in motion across a half-mile front.

The major watched them obey. He was proud of what he and the other British commanders had built in Jordan: a crushing, irresistible force. As fine a weapon for its size did not exist anywhere else in the world. Burr reflected that he was still building, still creating. After this war his Arab subordinates . . . if they paid attention . . . would be better educated, better able to take command.

At the moment, though, most of the responsibility lay on the British leadership.

No British officer would have been so befuddled by hornets!

The wadi was wider and higher at the eastern end than at the west. Funnel shaped.

Dust sifted down from the heights, turning the sun from yellow to orange to red.

Burr blinked his eyes against the grit.

The Legionnaires crossed the gully now, moved up the slope.

The Jews were as good as finished in Jerusalem. Elsewhere too, Burr believed. He would argue strenuously for a push toward Tel Aviv.

Two weeks? A quick . . . if messy . . . little war.

CHAPTER 30

Rudolf was back from delivering the alarm to Beit Susin, but the news with which he returned was not encouraging. The shelling had disrupted communications along the Haganah line of defense. Apart from the two direct hits, no one had been killed, but fifteen among the sentries and road workers were wounded.

He had been able to round up twenty-five armed soldiers out of the rest of Aleph. These were taking their assigned places along the crest, filling in the gaps between ambush points.

It appeared Jacob would have sixty-one troopers with whom to oppose a thousand Legionnaires.

Even the wind was against them again, Jacob thought. Dust, drifting down the wadi, obscured the movements of the Arabs. It was already unthinkable that so few Jewish soldiers could resist so many Legionnaires.

And if the dust got worse, they would never have clear shots.

Looking right and left at his line, he knew Meena and Leon could be relied on as snipers.

The others were as likely to squeeze the trigger first and then check to see if they had hit anything.

The dirty brown column of dust mounted skyward. Jacob could not see through it, could no longer make out the hills on the other side.

Forget seventy-five yards. If the curtain of the sandstorm was that impenetrable, he would never see the Legionnaires until they stepped onto the plateau beside him!

The force of the wind increased, and with it the howl of the storm.

Jacob would never hear the Arabs' approach.

A wave of airborne earth, like a plowed field tipped upright, closed in on the slopes below Jacob's position.

The full energy of the wind struck Fourth Regiment.

Besides the fine grit, handfuls of heavier sand grains stung Burr's cheeks.

A moving pillar of tawny dust exploded out of the head of the wadi, blotting out the light.

A rank of men Burr knew to be ten paces ahead of him vanished in the cloud.

Coughing, unable to see, Burr sensed himself being pushed sideways down the canyon.

He bumped into another Legionnaire. Just the man's eyes showed above the keffiyeh wrapped around his face to protect mouth and nose. The eyes, dust-clogged and red-rimmed, widened with apprehension.

He was struggling to breathe!

Burr experienced it, too. It was like swimming underwater. The air was suddenly too thick to take into his lungs.

A wave of soldiers tumbled backward off the slope, sliding down the shale and being tossed into the gully by the force of the wind.

Burr put his hand up to his forehead. His palm was wet and reddened with blood. His skin was being scoured by the rasp of the dust storm.

"Get back," Burr screamed, grabbing another trooper by the shoulder.

The Arab, alarmed, whirled around with horror. He discharged his rifle into the air, then threw it aside and doubled over, searching for a space of air that was breathable.

A wave of firing broke out in the ranks.

Up and down the wadi, men heard shots, thought they were being fired on, and shot back blindly.

■ ■ ■ ■

The air of the hillside was obscured with a drifting cloud of sulfurous smoke, chalky residue thrown up from the bomb craters and brown dust settling out of the storm pillar that passed just to the north.

Ellie's ears rang. She unfolded from her crouch, discovering she was trembling.

What would happen next? Would the shelling start again?

Or would the sequel be an attack by Arab troops?

She was disoriented. Turning in place she located the Arab villages as landmarks, then stared off toward the west.

At the extreme limit of her vision, she glimpsed a scene like an illustration from her childhood copy of *Arabian Nights:* the silhouette of a caravan advancing over the furthest hill, winding up from Tel Aviv. Ambling toward her were camels. Following these she made out donkeys and a line of jeeps.

Every beast of burden, animal or mechanical, was loaded to capacity with canvas-wrapped supplies.

The relief convoy arrived on the heels of the shelling.

What if they had been ten minutes further up the road?

Ellie pivoted toward the ravine.

A flaw in the wind parted the hanging curtain of dust. Through the rent Ellie caught a glimpse of figures moving about on the Jerusalem side.

Arab Legionnaires closing in?

The veil of airborne debris shut down again, blocking the vision.

Whom should she tell? Whom was there to alert?

Other members of the road crew were raising their heads.

Madame Rose, one of the first to recover her senses after the shelling, was going from worker to worker, seeing to the wounded and comforting the frightened.

Ellie joined her. By shouting she could tell her throat was actually producing sounds. "I saw something," she bellowed, pointing toward the east. "Men coming toward us."

"And so did I," Madame Rose concurred. "The Jerusalem contingent, here to pick up their supplies."

■ ■ ■ ■

Even when the pillar of dust passed, the slope below Jacob's position remained obscured.

How close would the Arab column be? When the dust settled, how many of them would be right on top of him?

Tensing for the imminent battle, Jacob raised his rifle.

Swinging the weapon's muzzle from left to right, Jacob saw Meena doing the same.

They might not stand any chance against such overwhelming force, but they would not give up easily.

The gritty fog rolled back from the brink, gradually revealing more of the incline.

No Arabs on the top hundred yards. That was lucky. Maybe there was time to bring up reinforcements.

The fallen oak reappeared, sanded to a brilliant whiteness by the scouring storm.

But no Arab soldiers.

When he could see the course of the stream bed at the bottom, Jacob fully realized what the tempest had accomplished.

There, where Jacob had seen Legionnaires numbering in the hundreds advancing for the attack . . . there, where he expected to see them regrouping . . . were a dozen motionless bodies, a score of discarded weapons, and no living Arab troopers.

They had retreated back across the foothills toward Latrun.

"Captain?" a voice called from behind.

Jacob whirled around.

It was Arnie Fetterman, another member of Aleph Company, together with fifteen others. "We got here quick as we could after Rudolf's message," he said. "So where's the Arab army?"

Explaining when there was no real explanation possible, Jacob pointed to the dead Legionnaires as his supporting evidence.

"We were headed up this direction anyway," Fetterman said. "Colonel Stone wants us to relieve you. Your squad's to be flankers protecting the convoy to Jerusalem."

As Jacob and the others rose, dusted themselves off, and prepared for the revised assignment, Fetterman added, "Lucky for you the Arabs turned back when they did."

"Yeah," Jacob agreed. "Lucky."

■ ■ ■ ■

Moshe made his way through the wards and hallways of Misgav Ladakh Hospital. Besides Dov and Yehudit, over a hundred and fifty wounded sheltered there. Walking down the corridors with Dr. Baruch, Moshe paused to encourage and comfort. "Yes," he said repeatedly, "I'm sure the Palmach will try again tonight. Rescue is coming. Just hang on."

Hope was the only prescription remaining.

Sometimes he had to shout because of the crash of Arab shells pressing in on the Jewish Quarter on the east.

After parting from the doctor, Moshe went up to the rooftop sandbag nest.

"Something is going on over there," one of the trio of Haganah defenders said, pointing toward the Porat Yosef school.

The brick seminary building guarded the easternmost flank of the

Jewish Quarter. It was the lone strong point remaining between the Arabs and the hospital.

Something was being maneuvered into a position behind the low wall bordering the front of the school.

A chill gripped Moshe. "Those are Arabs," he said. "They have captured Porat Yosef." He froze, considering what this development might mean.

His next observation galvanized him into action. "It's a cannon! Almost point-blank range. Get everyone off the roof. You three take shelter down one floor. Spread the word. Walking wounded to evacuate to the Sephardic complex. Send back stretcher bearers. We have to move everyone out at once!"

■ ■ ■ ■

Eighteen Arab Legionnaires had been killed.

Another forty-three had been wounded before the bellowing British officers made their charges cease firing.

The Arab Legion Fourth Regiment stumbled back to Latrun. It was not an orderly retreat. It was not executed with precision. They straggled and limped, their raw, scraped faces showing bewilderment and shame.

"We fired on a dust storm," Burr reported to Major Athani. "Our artillery zeroed in on a cloud of dirt. That's all there was to it. Nothing more there any of the time."

Athani handed him a message from General Glubb at the Legion's central command. "There is increasing pressure on the British government to stop shipping munitions to us. Therefore you are directed to be sparing with your ammunition, most particularly artillery shells. Do not expend shells unless attacked or you have direct observation of enemy movements."

■ ■ ■ ■

Misgav Ladakh received the full attention of the Arab Legion's cannon. From a hundred yards away, the six-pounder lobbed shells over the shattered remnant of Porat Yosef School. As an Arab artillery spotter on the Temple Mount corrected the aim, the obvious strong point of the brick hospital was systematically battered.

Inside the infirmary was confusion. As each blast struck the roof, people on the floors below threw themselves down and covered their heads. Streams of wounded men hobbled in two different directions.

The ones at the rear of the hospital crowded toward the exit, and the ones nearest the door pushed and shoved to get further inside.

Dr. Baruch emerged from the operating room to instill order in the chaos. "We are evacuating!" he ordered. "Those who can walk must help carry the others. If you cannot lift the weight of a patient, then take bandages, medicine, anything!"

Another shell interrupted Baruch's words. He concluded by saying, "To the basement of the Sephardic synagogues! Go!"

■ ■ ■ ■

BBC, London, briefly reported on the situation in Palestine.

They named Latrun without explaining either its significance or the magnitude of the disaster that engulfed the Jewish attackers.

What they did do was offer an interview with the Anglican bishop of Jerusalem. He was recorded as saying how difficult life had become for the forty people taking sanctuary in the "little British island of St. George's Cathedral." They had ample provisions and thus far just one stray shell had landed, causing no injuries and no structural damage.

The bishop was "most distressed" because of the ravages done to the priceless stained-glass windows.

St. George's Cathedral, in Arab-held territory, was less than a mile from Misgav Ladakh Hospital in the Old City Jewish Quarter.

Alfie Halder ran into Misgav Ladakh.

A shell hammered the top floor of the hospital. Plaster, knocked from the ceiling three levels below the impact, hit Alfie on the head and splattered across the rows of wounded lying in the corridors.

Frantic cries of "Help me!" echoed up and down the halls.

"Who do I take first?" he asked Dr. Baruch. "Who?"

"Alfie," Baruch said, "take anyone!" Another concussion made the light fixtures swing wildly. A table against the wall receiving the shock was jolted over, spilling twenty or so empty bottles. "Everyone must be moved out."

Alfie bent and scooped up a Palmachnik who had been wounded in the knees by shrapnel.

Starting toward the rear exist with the man lying across his arms, Alfie was stopped by the outstretched hands of a Yeshiva student. The boy, with a bullet wound in the back, could not move his legs.

Tucking the Palmachnik under one arm, Alfie bent toward the student. "Grab me around the neck," Alfie instructed.

Then, toting one wounded man and clung to by another, Alfie shuffled away from Misgav Ladakh.

Another artillery round battered the top floor. Chunks of masonry, scattered by the detonation, fell around Alfie and his charges, but the three passed through the avalanche unharmed.

■ ■ ■ ■

Moshe directed the tide of refugees and the reorganized lines of defense. "The best we can hope is that the hospital will hold long enough to get everybody out," he said. "We can't count on more than that."

To Rachel he instructed, "Direct the stretcher bearers to the basements of the Sephardic compound."

With Ehud he reviewed the outline of the district's defenses. "The Hurva and the Sephardic buildings are all we have left as strong points."

Within minutes the size of the remaining Jewish territory in the Old City had been reduced by a third. The revised area occupied by the survivors of 1,500 residents and 280 defenders from outside was about 20 percent of the original quarter.

Ehud nodded.

Moshe continued, "We have to expect them to hit the Hurva next. Will you go there and take charge?"

"And what supplies can you send?"

Moshe gestured at a pile of rifles. "Have as many of those as you want," he said. "We finally possess more weapons than we do soldiers to fire them."

"*Oy*," Ehud said softly. Then, "Bullets?"

"Whatever is in the clips," Moshe said. "That's all there is."

CHAPTER 31

From the back of an elderly camel which he had named *Gene Autry*, Daoud watched as the porters assembled.

The American soldier, Michael Stone, explained how they would carry supplies across the canyon to the Jerusalem side of the ravine.

"We need able-bodied men and boys to make as many trips to the other side as they can manage," he said. "We have a hundred tons of provisions to move immediately and more to follow. I want a hundred volunteers. With your help we can have it in Jerusalem in a week."

There was a buzz from the crowd. A week? Jerusalem was starving. It could not last two more days.

Daoud saw the large woman with a frog's features heft a sack of flour. Daoud knew this woman with the build of a blacksmith was named for a flower. The incongruity made the boy smile.

Stone put out a hand to stop Madame Rose.

"Stuff and nonsense," Daoud heard her say. "I am as able-bodied as anyone here, and I refuse to be left behind."

The American cowboy's red-haired woman snapped Daoud's picture, then took one of Madame Rose.

"Or I," said the Russian mother called Katerine. She helped each of her boys load sacks onto their shoulders and then accepted one on her own.

Instead of a hundred volunteers, there were four hundred.

"Pay attention, Gene Autry," Daoud said to his mount.

The Druze, Bashir, pushed a handcart loaded with three-inch mortar shells. "Are you also coming, Daoud, son of Baruch?" he asked.

Daoud thought of his friends Yacov and Rabbi Lebowitz. Tomorrow would be the start of the Sabbath. It had been a long time since he had been their Shabbes goy, lighting their candles. Did the Jews in the Old City even have candles to light, he wondered? "Of course," he said to Bashir. "Gene Autry and I will carry some of those shells too."

Bashir smiled. "Better you carry medicine," he said, tying a rolled-up canvas parcel containing bandages and antiseptic behind Daoud's saddle.

Sholem perched atop the bulldozer and saluted the procession as it shuffled forward. "I will remain here to finish the road," he said, waving to his wife and children. "We will be together again soon. Next week in Jerusalem!"

■ ■ ■ ■

The steps leading directly up from the street to the Stambuli Synagogue were steep and awkward. Because of this, the door in the north wall of the Ben Zakkai Synagogue was used to gain entry into the Stambuli's sanctuary instead.

The building was the largest and least symmetrical of the Sephardic sanctuaries. It was square, topped by a dome supported by pillars. Stained-glass windows at the base of the dome filtered in a rainbow of colors that splashed across the arriving patients.

Soon after the shelling of Misgav Ladakh began, a steady stream of wounded evacuees flowed through the entrance. Those able to hobble found corners in which to sit. Stretcher cases, like those carried by Alfie, were lined up shoulder to shoulder across the stone floors beneath the dome.

Rachel supervised a group of volunteer women who saw to it that each patient was placed on cushions or at least carpet, since there were no beds.

Grandfather rounded up men to tote the seriously wounded in folded blankets, while he himself knelt beside those in agony of body or spirit.

Dov Avram and Yehudit, bathed in red light from the windows, lay beside one another beneath the gilded ark on the east wall. He stared, unseeing, at the ceiling, as voices echoed upward into the dome and then slid downward until the air reverberated with ravings of fear, cries, and confusion.

Yehudit turned her face toward him and grasped his hand. "I am here," she said weakly. "Beside you, Dov."

"I am glad for it," he said, giving her fingers a squeeze. "You tell me if I'm missing anything."

Yehudit's eyes were bright with fever. The bullet was lodged in her side. No hope of retrieving it, Baruch said, until she was in a proper medical facility.

Dov asked, "The explosions. What did you see?"

"Smoke. Everyone running. Moshe on the rooftop beside Ehud. The two of them and four others facing the Legion. That's all."

Dov lifted her fingers to his lips. "Yehudit. My beautiful Yehudit."

"What does it mean, Dov?" she pleaded. "Misgav Ladakh gone?"

"It means there is nothing to stop them. Nothing between them and the Hurva. It means they will blow up every wall and every house between the hospital and the Hurva. It means the Hurva is next."

A shadow fell over them both, interrupting the wash of scarlet in which they were immersed.

Yehudit strained to focus her eyes. She gave a moan as she recognized her father. Akiva swayed a bit as he peered down at her, then cast a venomous look at Dov.

"They told me you were wounded." Akiva did not greet her, did not speak her name. "I wanted to see for myself."

Dov frowned. "Who is there?" he asked Yehudit.

"Papa." She stretched her free hand up toward her father.

He stepped back beyond her touch. "Baruch says you are in need of a hospital. Medicine. Doctors. A bed." He jerked his chin downward. "I will do what I can. Surely Moshe Sachar will listen to me."

"Papa . . . ," she begged.

"I . . . have said . . . I will do what I can do, Yehudit." At that he turned on his heel and clambered up the steps.

■ ■ ■ ■

The explosions around every side of the Jewish Quarter did not let up. If the Arab attackers had slackened their efforts on Wednesday in honor of King Abdullah, they were more than making up for it on Thursday.

The cannon inside the Old City walls was wreaking havoc with every shell. Sandbagged Jewish sniper positions on rooftops were no longer tenable. One direct hit meant sandbags, snipers, and rooftop were obliterated.

Even solid stone walls were no defense. Repeated concussions caused bleeding from ears and nose. Flying masonry was as deadly a form of shrapnel as steel splinters. Cannon shells battered holes in brick in under an hour. It was clear the Arabs had no shortage of shells.

The Arabs also appeared to have used Wednesday's lull to bring in more high explosives.

Two more houses on the northeastern perimeter fell in an hour, literally blown sky-high.

Another Legion attack from the Armenian Quarter was barely turned back, at a cost of two more Haganah dead and two more wounded.

Moshe was down to fewer than thirty uninjured defenders. The evacuated wounded from Misgav Ladakh were crammed in alongside the refugees already sheltering in the Sephardic synagogues, but there was no medicine, no anesthetic, barely any bandages.

And this was the moment Rabbi Akiva chose to appear.

"Sachar," Akiva said, "I know you don't care about anyone's life, but this time you have to listen to me. My daughter is seriously wounded. She will die if she does not get proper medical attention at once."

Moshe nodded wearily. He knew about Yehudit's wound.

"My daughter's blood is on you. Her life rests in your hands. No one is coming. There is no rescue. There will be no breakthrough, no reinforcements. It is a fraud. The last hope for any of us is to surrender. Immediately and completely. The killing will stop, and our wounded will be cared for. This I know."

Moshe wanted to ask when Akiva had begun to care again for the daughter he had so thoroughly rejected. He wanted to ask how Akiva could doubt everything told him by the Jews who were dying to defend his home and trust so unquestioningly in the promises of those who were doing the killing.

But he framed neither query.

Instead, he said, "A breakthrough is coming. One more day. That is all. One more day."

"We will all be dead in one more day."

"Reb Akiva," Moshe said, "if we surrender . . . if we leave the Quarter . . . they will never let us back."

"They have promised that . . ."

"Listen to me," Moshe said urgently. "They will never let us back. We will have to fight our way back to the Quarter, to the synagogues, to the Wailing Wall. More Jews will have to die just to regain what we walk away from. Can't you understand that?"

"I do not believe you!"

"Then there is nothing left to say," Moshe concluded. "I believe help will come. We must hold out just one more day."

■ ■ ■ ■

Misgav Ladakh was reduced to a smoldering ruin. The Sephardic synagogues were crammed with wounded and the Hurva stuffed with refugees from every part of the Quarter. The need for rescue was desperate, immediate, undeniable.

The direct cannonfire changed everything about holding out.

Then, amazingly, the shellfire ceased.

What could it mean? Was another respite possible?

Moshe groaned when the squawk and squeal of the loudspeaker reached his ears.

"This is your last warning," said a British-accented voice again claiming to be General Glubb. "We are in position to destroy the Hurva Synagogue."

A collective moan of anguish from the hearers reflected Moshe's own sinking heart.

"We do not wish to demolish the historic house of worship," the message continued. "We want to put an end to further bloodshed. Surrender! Save your lives, your families, your district from certain devastation. Do not be afraid. You will not be harmed. But you must give up unconditionally. This is your last warning. You have until noon to signal your compliance."

Ehud drew Moshe aside. "What do you think?" he asked.

"No!" Moshe retorted, reeling as if he had been struck. "You aren't suggesting we agree? That we hand over the Quarter?"

"For myself, no, never," Ehud confirmed. "But I do not know how much longer the rest of the Quarter will follow us. I don't mean the Haganah boys. They're solid. They will stick, *nu?* But it's bad, Moshe, bad. A threat and then a promise of safe passage. Some of Akiva's crew would embrace the first Legionnaire they met. What do I say to those who are wavering?"

"Tell them," Moshe said firmly, "that rescue will come tonight. Tell them we have only to hold out one more day, and we can spit in Glubb Pasha's eye."

"That is the spirit!" Ehud affirmed. "I, myself, will spit in Abdullah's."

"One more thing," Moshe said. "Tell Rachel and the steadiest of our people to begin evacuating the Hurva and the other outlying posts on that side into the Sephardic compound immediately. And send the old rabbis to see me again. I will let them try to surrender the civilians."

■ ■ ■ ■

Word of the renewed ultimatum spread like a fire through the civilians. The night of merciful peace had been like drinking a glass of cool water from a deep well.

Almost all believed surrender was the best solution.

Second to that was the exodus of the Jewish civilians. Surely the Arab Legion would allow it!

A proposal was drafted by the rabbis of the Sephardic community: women, children, and the wounded would be evacuated immediately through Zion Gate to the New City. The Haganah defenders and any who wanted to stay could stay and settle the matter bullet by bullet.

Lori believed the English officers directing the Arab Legion were men of honor. They would respect the request made by the Sephardic rabbis. Surely they understood that civilians kept under siege for months had been used as hostages by the Arab Irregulars. Women and children were a burden to the defenders. Their safety being of prime concern, each action taken by the Haganah had their safety in mind.

Surely King Abdullah, in residence somewhere in Jerusalem, would concur this was the honorable course.

And so two of the aged rabbis of the Sephardic community tied a white flag to the end of a broomstick. They shuffled forward through the debris of a city where they had spent their lives.

Under the watchful eyes of snipers on both sides of the line they crossed the barricades and followed the same route they used to pray at the Wailing Wall.

Walking through the alleyway fifty yards into Arab-held territory, they were met by a trio of Legion officers. Two Englishmen. One Jordanian.

The proposal was extended.

Within a heartbeat it was rejected by the Legion. Surrender was to be unconditional. All or nothing. If a shell burst on the roof of a Jewish house of prayer and those within were women and children, their deaths would be on the heads of the Jewish defenders.

The old men came back with this irreversible reply.

Valiant men, Moshe called them. They had done what they could to stop a slaughter. But their efforts came to nothing.

■ ■ ■ ■

With news of the failure of the Sephardic rabbis to make a way of escape, gloom settled on the populace.

Daniel stretched out on top of the sandbags. His arms under his head, he stared up at the sky.

"Tomorrow is the end of the world," he pronounced.

"For you, maybe." Lori braced herself against the pillar. "I'm voting for the year . . . 2000. I'd like to live a long time."

"You'll be an old lady. What's the point of living so long? Then you get old and . . . *pfft!* You fade away. Why not die defending the Holy City? Be remembered as a martyr, huh?"

"That's your plan, is it?"

"Maybe."

"Martyrdom." Lori thought about it. "It doesn't suit you, Daniel. Sixteen years old is it? You've got too much living to do to die between now and tomorrow."

He grunted his response. "I have lived enough to know this life is not much worth staying in."

"The Panther," Lori responded melodramatically. "Pacing the bars again, are you?"

"What do you know about it? About anything? You're not even Jewish."

"There's nobody here who hasn't seen too much. Grieved too much. Lost too many. You think you're the only one?"

He lapsed into silence. "I am a coward, see? They killed everyone I knew, and I hid out. My sister. I heard her screaming. And I hid out. If I lived a year to see Israel's anniversary . . . you know. While people danced in the street I would remember Kfar Etzion. I would remember the night my fourteen-year-old sister died. While I hid."

So this was the story. Fresh. Vivid. Horrible. Daniel Caan was trapped beneath the weight of it. Trapped as if a house had fallen on his soul and a fire burned ever closer toward him.

Lori asked, "Where would you be if you had not hidden?"

"Dead," he answered. "But don't try that angle with me. My living while she died does not cheer me up. I wish I was dead."

"I know the feeling," she muttered.

"All right. I told you mine. Now tell me yours."

It was a strange and terrible challenge. Prying into his grief left her no escape. And so, after a while, she told him. About her father dying in Germany. Her escape. The death of her mother and baby in the Blitz. How she went out on rescue during the bombings every night, hoping the sky would fall on her and her aloneness. The reason she came here. Jacob. Jacob, whom she had loved from the time she was seventeen. Jacob, who was out there somewhere, maybe still alive and fighting for Israel. Maybe dead. She didn't know, and the not knowing was the worst torture of all.

She finished. It was a shortened and well-edited version. He had not lived long enough to hear the really juicy bits.

He said simply, "No wonder you are . . . what was it you called me? Everybody's worst pain in the ass? Maybe tomorrow we can both stop worrying about it, eh?"

"Speak for yourself," she snapped. "You haven't ever been alive enough to know what you'd be missing."

"What?"

"You haven't thought enough thoughts to write even one poem."

"You're crazy. Tomorrow, you heard. They're coming for us."

"You'd better pray they miss finding you because you have a lot to make up for."

"What're you talking about?"

"You say you hid out. You wish you had died. Well, you didn't. She did. And the others? Your friends too?"

"What's the point?"

"Life. Just one of all of them survived. It was you. They will forever be what they were. Your friends will never know a woman. Sit by her as she gives birth. Hold the baby boy who would have been theirs. Midnight feedings and the first step. Watching him grow. Hearing him say . . ." She faltered. "Say . . . I love you . . ." She stopped as the memory engulfed her thoughts.

"Will I see such a thing?" Daniel asked.

"Only if you live," she resumed.

"My life is a blank spot."

"You haven't lived long enough for love and pain and joy to write even a short poem about you."

"The Panther."

"A beautiful creature trapped in a cage."

"And how can he get out?"

"Until you love someone else more than yourself . . . you can't get out."

He drew a ragged breath. "I didn't love enough to die for her. For them."

"Not *for* them . . . stupid! You would have died *with* them! Then who would be left to *live on* for them?"

"It would have been easier. . . ."

"To die? Sure. Life is the hardest thing. They're gone. You couldn't have stopped it! It hurts so bad sometimes you think you'll break. But you have to go on for the ones who will never have a chance to grow up . . . that's what I mean. Oh, Daniel! That's where real courage is! Not in dying bravely, but in living bravely. In loving someone . . . Like little

Abe here. You know? He doesn't even know where his brother and sisters are. His mama. Then there we are . . . well. He needs us! And we know how to love him because we each lost someone too." She looked up at the heavens. "They're better off. But we're the ones who have important things God wants us to do. To let the fire of our pain purify us. Like gold. God skims off the scum and examines our hearts and finally sees his own face reflected in us. Do you know what I mean?"

"Maybe. I think so."

"Live awhile. Or die now and be forever ignorant."

Daniel scrutinized her in the dim light. "I don't know if I'm supposed to thank you."

"Yes."

"Well then . . . thank you."

"Live and be well."

■ ■ ■ ■

"Why does the Englishman give the Jews a warning?" Hassan el-Hassan asked his captain, Ahkmed al-Malik. "Why does he give them a time to rest? If we push forward, the Jewish Quarter would be ours in an hour!" Hassan waved a clenched first toward the dome of the Great Hurva, which dominated the skyline of the Old City.

"It is true, what you say," al-Malik agreed, "but Glubb Pasha and Abdullah the Hashemite play at their own game, remember. The British king has told Abdullah not to harm the Jewish holy places or Abdullah will not get as much money from them. Glubb Pasha hopes the Jews will surrender and he can keep Abdullah's promise. Do you see?"

"Games!" Hassan remarked scornfully. "I do not understand war which does not overpower your enemy or letting him get up when he is down. And I do not think the Jews will surrender anyway. Nor do I think the Hurva will be so easy to knock down as the hospital."

Al-Malik drew Hassan over to an oblong, tarp-covered object half-hidden behind a pile of lumber. "That is why I have made a plan of my own," he said. "I paid a visit to the workshop of the dead bomb maker, Dajani." Al-Malik nudged the tarp with the toe of his boot. It gave a metallic ring. "A fifty-five-gallon barrel packed with explosives. When Abdullah's scheme fails, we will be ready."

■ ■ ■ ■

"Moshe says everyone, Lori! Do you hear me? Everyone goes into the Sephardic compound!" Rachel warned.

Lori saw where Abe shoved his index finger one knuckle deep into the soil at the base of the rosebushes. "Ready," he muttered. "Come on, Daniel," he called.

Leaning on the stock of his rifle Daniel hopped from beneath the portico to pour water into the tiny hole. "The roses are looking better, don't you think, Lori?" He flashed a grin.

Lori said, "Better. Yes. It's the wind. It's not so hot."

Rachel stared at them in exasperation. "Everyone is pulling out of the Hurva, Lori. Look! Daniel, look!" She waved toward the machine-gun nest opposite. Three defenders. No machine gun. "Moshe told me to tell you. The Legion will hit that position almost the same time they hit the Hurva! Don't you understand? There's nothing between you and the Arab Legion but them."

Lori nodded. "I have Daniel to protect me."

"What about Abe?" Rachel asked.

Lori said with certainty, "He'd die if we took him down there. He's not afraid out here. We've weathered it before. Nothing has hit us, has it, Daniel?"

"Not even close," Daniel noted. "The tops of those synagogues are like targets. Like throwing pebbles into a bowl if the Legion cannon on the Mount of Olives takes it in their heads to . . ."

Rachel held up her hand to stop him. Rubbing her head, she said, "You're right. No place is safe. No place. It's an illusion to think they wouldn't . . ."

Lori shrugged. "I cleaned up a rail station once after a direct hit. Really, Rachel, we stand a better chance here. Behind the sandbags. I'm not being stubborn. Or foolish. I've seen it both ways. In the open in Regent's Park or under the shelter at Paddington Station. I'll take the park anyday. Daniel agrees."

"Better than having tons of roof come down on us. Okay? Tell Moshe I'm ready if they come," Daniel added.

"Not if. Not if. Be ready." Rachel closed her eyes. She was pale. "Oh, Lori," she said.

"I know." Lori embraced her. "We have done what we could. Even if it was just to sit in the garden and pray. It means something. It does. And . . . sweet friend, I'll see you again. On this side or the other."

"*Shalom.*"

CHAPTER 32

The assault on the Great Hurva commenced with cannonfire from the vicinity of Misgav Ladakh. Without machine-gun ammunition or mortars, Moshe possessed no weapon with which to retaliate. All the handful of defenders could do was stay on the ground floor within the solid walls of the structure and ride out the barrage. With every concussion the dome of the synagogue rang like an alarm bell.

Or a funeral observance, tolling the loss of nearly three thousand years of a Jewish presence in the Holy City.

The Hurva, whose name meant "ruin," was no stranger to attack.

The site had originally been purchased by Ashkenazi Jews in 1680 using money borrowed from Arab lenders. When the buyers could not raise the funds to pay off the debt, the Arabs rioted on the day in 1720 when the Torah reading was from Genesis, "Get thee out . . ."

The building was burned, and for a hundred years the Ashkenazim were forbidden to come to Jerusalem or to visit the synagogue named "Ruin."

The years passed, the rulers changed, and the Ashkenazim reclaimed the property, cleansed and renamed the sanctuary "Comforter of Zion," but the former nickname stuck.

The Haganah soldiers riding out the storm of shells wondered if history was about to be repeated.

"They cannot attack while the shelling continues," Ehud called out. "And they cannot shell when the attack begins. Don't be afraid. We are not finished so easily."

Moshe saw the doubtful expressions on the faces of the soldiers. They had participated with Ehud in the defense of Nissan Bek Synagogue days earlier. It had not survived, and here there were even fewer defenders available.

Dov had been there.

Now Dov lay wounded and blinded and unable to defend even himself.

Moshe was startled when Reb Lebowitz emerged from the basement and approached the bema. Oblivious to the constant pounding, Grandfather stood with his eyes closed, swaying in prayer.

"Reb Lebowitz," Moshe said, hurrying over to the man, "we are about to fight a battle here."

"Of course," the rabbi agreed. "You will fight in your way and I in mine."

The shelling stopped.

"And," Reb Lebowitz noted, "you had best get ready. It seems your part is about to begin."

Moshe, Ehud, and the others climbed to the platform inside the dome. Through the eastern and northern windows, Moshe could see the Arab Legionnaires massing for an attack.

"Here they come!" Ehud shouted, even though Moshe and the twenty soldiers with him could see that for themselves.

■ ■ ■ ■

Rachel and Yacov sprinted into the circle of sandbags at Gal'ed as the first detonation tore into the Hurva.

Breathless, Rachel explained to Lori, "Everyone from the Hurva wanted to stay underground. The Sephardic synagogue. I thought about what you said."

"Regent's Park or Paddington Station?"

"We . . . Yacov and I, want to say here with you. See the sky awhile longer, if it's all right."

Lori hugged her. Abe, oblivious to the opening crash of the attack, grasped the dog Shaul by the collar and drew him down to lie against him.

The incessant boom of explosives marked the Muslim encroachment into the Jewish Quarter. House by house the Jewish perimeter shrank as the Legion sappers blasted a hole into Jerusalem's heart. Now the Jewish defense was room by room as walls crumbled and the flood of enemy soldiers poured through.

For those civilians gathered in the garden of Gal'ed, the crump of dynamite marked time until the end. Two Jewish houses fell each hour.

An enormous concussion sent a plume of plaster into the air.

Abe covered his ears, then buried his face in the ruff of the dog.

Daniel murmured, "Just a few more houses. They'll come to the wall of the Hurva. And that will be that." He glanced at his weapon. What could he do with three bullets?

Abe leaned close to Lori and said, "Don't be afraid. They are making a road. They will come into Jerusalem, see?"

She patted his hand. He did not understand that it was the enemy who carved a path into Jerusalem's heart. "Yes," she said, not wanting to explain.

He cocked his head to one side and smiled. "Can you hear them marching? Can you hear them, Lori?"

She listened. She heard nothing except the frantic shouts of Haganah defenders retreating before the next wave of Legionnaires.

The nest of defenders on the roof above them began to squeeze off shots as the Legion assault on this side of the barricades began.

■ ■ ■ ■

Machine-gun bullets clipped the Hurva's plastered ceiling over Moshe's head. Flinging himself to the side, he thrust the muzzle of his rifle around the frame of the shattered window. Discharging two shots into the front rank of rushing troopers, Moshe ducked low and crossed to the other side of the opening before return fire found him.

The deadly game of tag continued: shoot, duck, pop up again in a different spot.

Only the open court that fronted the Hurva offered any margin for the defenders. The Legionnaires had to cover fifty yards of rubble-strewn space while being shot at from above. The closer they came to the bulk of the sanctuary, the harder it was for them to aim upward.

Six Legionnaires were wounded trying to sprint across and two killed.

■ ■ ■ ■

The Arabs changed strategies.

Leaving one rank of sharpshooters a distance away, the other infantrymen rushed the building. Next to Moshe, one of the Haganah took aim at the Arab leading the charge. But an Arab sniper wounded the Jew in the arm, driving him back.

The new threat led to a change of tactics by the Jewish defenders.

"Ehud," Moshe called, "you and I must pick off their sharpshooters."

In a duel of nerves, Moshe crouched and stayed exposed for longer than was safe in order to get a clear shot. He and Ehud succeeded in dropping three of the enemy before the Arabs withdrew.

Stalemate. But a temporary one.

The artillery barrage resumed.

Moshe and his companions returned to the floor of the Hurva to wait for the Legion's next move.

■ ■ ■ ■

Two of the Hurva's meager band of defenders were seriously wounded. Alfie carried each man to the Sephardic complex. In going down an alley behind the Hurva he was exposed to Legion gunfire, but he made the passage four times in safety.

As he returned, a cannon shell passed through a window of the synagogue's rotunda without exploding, then detonated against the far curve of the dome, under a Palmachnik's feet. The platform splintered with a crack.

The defender flew upward and into the air, his arms outstretched as if executing a perfect dive. He hit the flagstone of the sanctuary, face first.

When Alfie reached the man, Reb Lebowitz was kneeling beside him. "Should I carry him to hospital, too?" Alfie asked.

His lips moving in the prayer for the dying, Grandfather shook his head.

■ ■ ■ ■

An Arab Legionnaire reeled backward, his face streaming blood from a bullet wound in his scalp. Stunned, the man dropped to his knees and let a machine gun fall.

Hassan El-Hassan grabbed it up. Loosing a burst toward the dome, he ducked behind a heap of masonry, then fired another volley.

Gathering himself, he was ready to spring toward the Hurva when al-Malik stopped him.

"Wait," al-Malik said. "If the pride of these Legionnaires makes them run into bullets in broad daylight, let them. Our part will come later."

■ ■ ■ ■

Half the Haganah men were out of action.

The battle raged through the afternoon.

Moshe, swinging his rifle in a quest for snipers, saw the tube of a bazooka appear around the edge of a cupola.

Before he could yell a warning, the rocket flamed from the tube.

It hit the outside wall beside the opening where Ehud was posted. The shrapnel did not penetrate the alcove, but the concussion pushed Ehud backward.

His eyes blinded by plaster dust, he wavered on the edge of the platform. His right foot fumbled for purchase, hanging in midair above a forty-foot plunge. Since he refused to drop his weapon, its weight dragged him backward.

"Catch him!" Alfie yelled.

Who was Alfie speaking to? There was no one close enough to lift Ehud's flailing arms and set his feet back on a secure place.

Then Moshe saw Ehud's shoulders thrust forward suddenly, as if he had been shoved hard from behind.

Ehud's hands swung in a wild arc. The butt of his rifle lit a string of sparks where it scraped against the dome.

Then he was kneeling on the platform, wiping his eyes to clear them of the grit.

The bazooka operator, having reloaded, swung his weapon up to the ready position once more.

Moshe hurriedly took aim.

Ahkmed al-Malik watched as the Arab Legionnaire with the bazooka readied for another shot.

Sunlight glinted off the tube of the weapon. In the center of the gleam a round, black dot appeared.

Al-Malik blinked. That was a bullet hole. It created a dimple in the perfect cylinder of the rocket launcher.

The Legionnaire squeezed the trigger.

The rocket ignited, then exploded in the bazooka, a foot in front of the soldier's face.

As al-Malik ducked, pieces of the weapon speared into the crates and stones all around him.

He heard a thud.

The headless corpse of the Legionnaire landed across a stone block six paces away.

Sunset over Jerusalem layered the rooftops with gold, recast the stones in bronze. Jupiter, a shining beacon, pinned the purple drapes of night above the Mount of Olives.

Inside the Hurva there was no illumination except what flickered in at the western windows.

It was, Moshe thought, a dreadful metaphor. Twilight for the home of God's Chosen, nightfall of Jewish hopes.

He forced himself to relinquish the thought. They were holding on; deliverance *could* come in time.

But holding on to the Hurva existed as the thinnest of prospects. The number of unwounded defenders numbered six.

"How many bullets do you have left?" he asked.

The replies from the dusk inside the dome were not encouraging. Handfuls, at most.

"I see stirring on the far side of the square," Ehud noted. "They are coming again."

■ ■ ■ ■

Ahkmed al-Malik gathered Hassan and two other Jihad Moquades to him.

"It is time for us to end this," he said. "The Legion's cannon and troops have failed. They say they will attack once more, but they have no stomach left for battle. They will fight again tomorrow they say, and tomorrow, they say, they will win, *Insh' Allah.*" Al-Malik raised a palm toward heaven in mocking piety but scowled when he added, "But by tomorrow the Jews on Mount Zion may attack again. Abdullah may have promised the world to spare the synagogue, but what is Abdullah's vow to me?"

Whipping aside the tarp, al-Malik revealed the canister of explosives. It rested on a wooden ladder, to which it was secured with ropes. The screw-in fitting had been removed from its side and from the opening protruded a fuse.

"It will take the four of us to carry this," al-Malik explained. "When the Legionnaires start shooting, we will run to the base of the dome, between those two windows there." He pointed to a dark outlined gash framing the last of the sunset's glow. "Once there I will light the fuse, and we shall see which is stronger . . . my will or Abdullah's."

■ ■ ■ ■

The defenders on the roof opposite Gal'ed fought valiantly, driving off wave after wave of assault. Lori barely could make out their silhouettes against the bursts of light and fire above them and around them.

Daniel shouted, "One of them is hit!"

Rachel threw her arms around Abe protectively as the body of a defender flew backward, tumbling over the parapet and dropping onto the flagstones that bordered the garden.

Lori vaulted the sandbags and rushed to the man. Rolling him over she saw his face had been shot away. She crawled back to the nest on her hands and knees.

A shriek sounded from the rooftop.

Another Haganah defender down! One left!

Daniel cried for Yacov to come to him.

"Help me!" Daniel stood upright, leaning against a pillar.

Yacov scrambled to brace him.

Daniel grasped his rifle. "Help me get up there, kid! Come on!"

Rachel shouted. "Yacov, no!"

The boy, his eyes wide with fright and excitement, waved her away. "Leave me, sister! I have to! Tell Grandfather!" Then he sternly shouted at the dog. "Stay, Shaul! Stay with Abe!"

"Lori!" Daniel instructed as he and Yacov limped across the courtyard. "Get to the Stambuli! Go! Go now! All of you! Run for it!"

Rachel, weeping as she watched her brother vanish into the shadows, refused to budge. "Not yet! Not yet! I have to see! Have to see if they make it!"

The women clung to one another as long moments passed. Four green flares arched into the sky and exploded one after another. They hung there sparkling, beautiful, illuminating the devastation.

Rachel cried out as Yacov, bearing Daniel, emerged onto the rooftop and rolled into the nest beside the lone defender.

Yacov ducked down, huddling beneath the protective rim. Daniel flung away the body of the dead man and settled in beside the one remaining Jewish soldier.

Lori watched as he placed the rifle on the sandbag and, with the relaxed ease of an accomplished marksman, squeezed off one shot and then another.

The defender beside him took a bullet in the head and fell back. Just Yacov and Daniel remained alive.

Daniel ordered, "Get his ammunition! Another bullet!"

The flares faded. Lori heard the voice of Yacov screaming, "Run! They are coming! Hundreds! Run for it!"

Lori grabbed up Abe and took Rachel by the arm as another flare illuminated the scene. Dragging Rachel and Abe from the garden she glanced over her shoulder to see the last battle of Daniel Caan and Yacov Lubetkin.

Daniel shouted above the din. "Yacov! Go on, kid! Get out of here!"

There was no sign of Yacov until an instant later, when he helped Daniel stand. Then, propping him up, the child shouted shrilly, *"Kiddush Hashem! Kiddush Hashem!"*

They were back to back.

Daniel swayed slightly. No more bullets. He grasped his rifle by the barrel like a bat.

"Come on!" he shouted defiantly. "Come on!"

So they came. Hundreds against the teenager and the boy.

And this was Lori's last glimpse of Yacov and Daniel.

Daniel swung the rifle at the heads of three Legionnaires. The attackers fell back from his thrust.

Rachel screamed Yacov's name as fifty Arabs swarmed over the roof. The light died. Daniel and Yacov were swallowed by darkness.

CHAPTER 33

Four hundred tons of supplies from Tel Aviv.

Down one side of the canyon and up the other.

En route to break the siege of Jerusalem, one sack of flour at a time.

Three hikes down the path and back up again. Flour. Beans. Rice. Ellie had not seen David among the Jerusalem corps as Michael Stone had promised. Perhaps he had stayed in Jerusalem, she thought.

It was twilight by the time Ellie made her fourth passage down the switchbacks to the bottom of the gorge.

She spotted David while he was on the path leading down the opposite side. With fifty pounds of flour on her back she could not run to him. She called his name. He looked up, recognizing her voice before he saw her among the long line of porters.

Running to her, he took the sack from her shoulder and sat it on a boulder.

Ellie and David stood at the foot of the cliff. He embraced her. Kissed her face again and again. She began to cry, vaguely aware he was crying too. Weeping and wiping away her tears with his dirty thumb.

"I thought you weren't here," she said at last.

"I wouldn't miss this," he replied, hefting her flour sack. Then, on second thought, he placed the burden back on Ellie's shoulder. "Can you carry it up?" He pointed to the Jerusalem side of the chasm. "I'm not letting you out of my sight. Tonight we sleep together on the same side of the canyon."

"Like hiking Desolation Wilderness. Remember?" She smiled.

"Only no bears. Not even any Legionnaires along this route as far as I can see." He snagged a huge bag of rice and another sack of cornmeal, balancing them one on each shoulder.

"How is it in Jerusalem?"

"If we can make it back with this stuff before morning, Luke

Thomas thinks we'll have a shot at relieving the Old City. The Legion was blasting the hell out of it. We could hear it halfway down the mountain. Those people are taking a beating. If we don't get back soon . . . well . . . I don't know. They've been sort of sacrificial lambs. Abdullah is obsessed with taking the Old City. Gives everybody else room to breathe. So far half a ton of ammo is on the way. Mortar shells. They haven't had mortar shells in days."

He led the way toward the precipitous bank at the base of the mountain. It was much steeper than the Tel Aviv side. Turning he called to her, "Can you make it?"

She replied, "I'll keep myself motivated. Think of what we did the night we climbed Mount Tallac together. Tonight in Jerusalem. King David Hotel."

"That'll keep my morale up."

They were only halfway up the dark cliff face when the voice of Sholem's 'dozer coughed, rattled, then roared to life.

■ ■ ■ ■

Cannon-shells had beaten two of the pendent window openings into a massive hole. Beneath this crater the suspended platform was splintered. A gap of fifteen feet existed in its circumference. The cables by which it hung were nicked and frayed.

Bullets zipped through the fissures, pocking the walls of the synagogue. The far side of the dome had been struck so many times that no plaster remained on a third of the bell above the level of the scaffolding.

It was now too dark to see the attackers except as shapes passing in front of lighter stones.

Moshe and the others fired at muzzle flashes. Reb Lebowitz moved about among the wounded, praying, comforting. Alfie was somewhere between the Hurva and the Stambuli, carrying another injured soldier.

A bigger mass detached itself from the shadows on the far side of the square. As Moshe tracked the movement, forcing himself to wait and not waste even a single shot, he recognized they carried something on a stretcher.

"Ehud," he called out. "Don't shoot where you see those four men together. They are picking up their wounded."

■ ■ ■ ■

The firefight continued. Moshe was amazed to see with what bravery the Arab stretcher bearers carried out their task. They were completely exposed to his aim, halfway across the field, picking their way around the scattered debris, directly under his gun.

One of the carriers stumbled.

The stretcher tipped sideways, banging into the stump of an iron railing amputated by the shelling.

A hollow clang reached his ears over the gunfire.

A bomb!

"Shoot, Ehud! Shoot at the stretcher! They are carrying a bomb!"

■ ■ ■ ■

Al-Malik was furious with frustration. The passage through the terrace in front of the synagogue took twice as long as he envisioned. The explosives were cumbersome even for four men to manage, the route in the darkness full of obstacles.

"Faster, faster," he ordered. Already they had nearly dropped the load when Hassan tripped.

A bullet zipped by al-Malik's face, close enough for him to smell the heat of its passage.

Twenty feet to go. The Hurva loomed ahead. Soon the height of the walls would give the attackers protection.

He heard Hassan cry out. Had the fool slipped again?

The rear of the ladder bounced on the ground, tearing the rung from al-Malik's grip.

Hassan was down, gripping his throat, making a gurgling noise.

Al-Malik kicked Hassan's body away from the ladder. "Pull!" he said to the other two. "Just a few more steps!"

They dragged the barrel to the base of the dome. Bullets splatted against the pavement several feet away from where they crouched, but they were too near now. They could not be touched.

Holding a cigarette lighter in his hand, al-Malik warned the other men to split up and run. They needed to put distance and solid walls between them and this blast.

They ran.

He ignited the fuse.

■ ■ ■ ■

"Everybody down!" Moshe shouted. "Down from the dome. Clear the passageway and get outside! Move!"

Ehud and the others made it safely down.

Moshe started toward the closest set of steps.

Another shot zipped into the darkness, glanced off the stones, and severed a rope supporting the ladder. Moshe's exit fell free of the scaffolding, crashed into the center of the dome.

He turned. The next ladder was on the other side of the gaping chasm.

Running toward it, Moshe hurled himself over the abyss.

He landed heavily on the edge of the drop, then clawed his way back up over the jagged splinters. Running again, he slid down the uprights of the ladder, meeting Reb Lebowitz at the bottom. "Come on," he urged. "We have to hurry!"

■ ■ ■ ■

Al-Malik had kept the center exit route for himself. Sending the other two carriers off first would draw the Jews' fire. He had plenty of time.

He ran away from the Hurva.

A hand grabbed him by the ankle, stopping his progress.

"Help me!" moaned Hassan. "Help me, my brother!"

"Let go!" al-Malik shouted, kicking at the encumbrance. A frenzied glance over his shoulder showed him the fuse was already inside the barrel! "Let go!"

He tore free of Hassan's death grip and sprinted on across the square. Leaping over stone blocks, he wasted no time in getting clear.

Al-Malik vaulted another heap of debris, landing beside the shattered iron fence.

Just then a spike of broken railing pierced his robe. As it caught him in midair he was flung to the ground, the wind knocked out of him.

He must get clear!

Trying to yank the cloth free of its skewer did not work. He tried to shed the robe, shrug it off.

But there was no more time.

Two hundred pounds of explosives erupted with a roar.

■ ■ ■ ■

Grandfather and Moshe were in the passageway, nearly at the Hurva's entrance, when the night and the east wall of the synagogue disintegrated.

Both men were pitched headlong.

Moshe was flung into the alleyway, though to get there the door must have blown open in front of him.

Where was Reb Lebowitz?

Moshe found Grandfather on the steps. Was he alive?

He was still breathing!

"Reb Lebowitz," Moshe said, running his hands over the elderly man. "Are you all right?" Skull felt intact. No blood, no broken bones. Knocked out, then. "Reb Lebowitz?"

Moshe's fingers encountered something that did not belong. Something sharp jutting out from the rabbi's side.

A wooden splinter, the size of a knife blade, protruded from between Grandfather's ribs.

Two figures loomed up in the darkness.

Alfie and Ehud.

"Help me carry him!" Moshe urged. "The Stambuli."

"What about . . . ?" Ehud gestured toward the smoke-filled interior of the Hurva.

Moshe shook his head. "Finished," he said. "Nothing more we can do."

■ ■ ■ ■

It was finished.

Scattered noises filtered through the broken windows of Eliyahu Hanavi Synagogue where Rebbe Lebowitz lay dying beneath the Ark on the east wall.

He fixed his gaze on the almond tree carved into the wood.

Rachel cradled her grandfather's head in her arms. He moved his lips. What was it he was asking?

She bent low to hear him.

"Where is Yacov?" he asked.

Emotion closed her throat. She would not, could not tell him the truth. "All the boys are in the Stambuli. You know . . ."

"Good. That's good." He sighed. "He will be the head of the family now."

She turned away quickly, lest he see her tears and know Yacov was irretrievably lost. Lost like their home. Like the Jewish presence in the Old City of Jerusalem. "I'll tell him."

"Moshe?" The old man blinked at the lamp that burned above Elijah's chair.

"He is . . . with the rabbis," she replied.

"You must . . . Rachel . . ."

"What is it, Grandfather? What are you trying to say?"

"Rachel . . ." He coughed. "You must let him . . ."

"Let him?" She stroked his head and wiped a fleck of blood from his lips.

"*Kiddush Hashem.*"

"Yes. For the Sanctification of the Name. Yes. Everyone has fought bravely. And now . . . we have to get you and the others to medical care. To a hospital. You see? We have to leave."

"You must let Moshe go, Rachel." He clasped her forearm hard.

"We will go out together, Grandfather . . . he's talking to the rabbis, you see?"

"Listen to me, daughter. We . . . will leave. But you must let Moshe . . . he will not go with you."

"Please." His warning sent a chill through her. "Don't say anything more . . . Please. Rest awhile. We'll talk later."

He clumsily patted her hand. "Let him go. *Kiddush Hashem.*"

He closed his eyes and drifted into an uneasy sleep.

Rachel looked across the crowded room. She thought about Yacov and Daniel Caan fighting to the death for *Kiddush Hashem.* What more could she give for the sake of the Name! Her mother. Father. All of her dear brothers, including now, Yacov! Their faces were vivid in her mind.

Grandfather was the last of her family, and he would soon die if he did not have the proper care. Would God expect her to also give up Moshe?

She could not bear to think of it. She would not let him go.

It was pitch black outside. Too quiet. Everyone knew there was nothing left to do but throw stones at the Arab Legion. It was over. They had done all they could do. In the morning the matter would be settled.

FRIDAY

May 28, 1948

"This is what the Lord says—your Redeemer,
    who formed you in the womb:
I am the Lord, who made all things, who alone stretched out the
heavens, who spread out the earth by myself . . .
who carries out the words of his servants
and fulfills the predictions of his messengers,
who says of Jerusalem,
    'It shall be inhabited,'
of the towns of Judah,
    'They shall be rebuilt,'
and of their ruins,
    'I will restore them . . .'
and of the temple,
    'Let its foundations be laid!'"

Isaiah 44:24–28

CHAPTER 34

On the floor of Eliyahu Hanavi, Rachel knelt to one side of her grandfather, Alfie on the other. Moshe and Ehud stood nearby, talking quietly in the gray of pre-dawn.

Since the explosion at the Hurva, the Arab attack on the Jewish Quarter had stalled. The hooting and bellowing of noisy looting and the rattle of gunshots being discharged into the air kept the night from being peaceful.

About midnight someone had applied a torch to the shattered hulk of the Great Ruin. The flames of its conflagration turned night into day, driving even the successful assailants back from the scene.

Later the dome collapsed in on itself, snuffing out the blaze.

All the defenders of the Jewish district were crowded into the Sephardic synagogues; bunkers filled to capacity with frightened refugees, anxious about what the morning would bring.

Reb Lebowitz was awake, alert, and said he felt no pain.

The stump of the wooden shard protruding from his side was swathed in layers of blood-soaked cloth.

Mayor Akiva, backed by a phalanx of drawn-faced rabbis, bustled in to see Moshe.

Akiva was shaking with anger. "Sachar," he hissed, "you have caused all this. This devastation is your fault."

"Tonight," Moshe said. "A radio message says supplies are coming. A rescue tonight . . ."

"Hollow promises!" Akiva exploded. "My daughter lies near death. Others . . ." He glared down at Reb Lebowitz but did not acknowledge him, as if Grandfather had somehow gotten what he deserved. "Others also need doctors," he concluded. "We are going out to negotiate a surrender."

"By the Eternal," Ehud thundered. "You heard Moshe say . . ."

Moshe shook his head and touched Ehud's arm. "Let them try again," he said. "You go with them as my deputy. You speak for me."

With an abrupt about-face, Akiva and his contingent swept out.

After Akiva was out of earshot, Moshe said, "Ehud, we need one more day, but we have no defenses left. Let Akiva negotiate. Stall the Legion. A truce will buy us more time. Tell them we must have until tomorrow to decide."

■ ■ ■ ■

The Iraqi thrust into north central Palestine was halted six miles short of the Mediterranean. Vigorous Israeli counterattacks at Jenin and at Mount Gilboa drove them back. The Iraqi army, fearing it would be cut off between the Jordan River and home, withdrew. They had been promised the assistance of Abdullah's Arab Legion, but it did not come. The Legion was too busy with the Holy City and the road through Bab el Wad.

In the south the Egyptians maintained their hold on the Negev but still awaited the outcome of the Legion's battle for Jerusalem before committing more troops.

Three Israeli supply ships, loaded with arms and ammunition, arrived in Jaffa Harbor.

Jerusalem.

Jerusalem was still the key.

The Muslim call to morning prayer silenced the shells falling on New City Jerusalem and drew a sigh of relief from its Jewish residents. Another night survived, another day of bleak uncertainty ahead, but another day of life just the same.

The inhabitants of the western suburbs scarcely knew what to make of the sounds that replaced the thudding explosions. The reverberating braying and bellowing, singing and cheering, an unexplainable discordant hullabaloo made the citizens peer out their barricaded doors and through their shuttered windows.

Stretching as far as their eyes could see was a caravan, a double file of suffering alleviated and hope renewed.

An Arab boy astride a tall, old, wicked-eyed camel urged his meandering mount with a very American-sounding "Giddyap."

Behind him followed a procession of men leading other pack-saddle-laden camels or donkeys, and men wearing backpacks or carrying sacks. Mixed with these were jeeps, their rear axles nearly dragging on the pavement under the heaped-up loads with which they were burdened.

"Welcome to Jerusalem, Els," David Meyer said, sweeping his arm over the skyline of the Holy City as if offering it to her personally.

Madame Rose was everywhere, up and down the line, urging the footsore, weary porters. "Look!" she said exultantly. "We have arrived. This year in Jerusalem. And we do not come empty-handed."

Faster than the words "Relief column!" could be spoken, the scene was swarming with residents.

Having encountered no ambushes by Arabs, it was all Jacob's squad of Meena and Jerome, Leon and Rudolf could do to keep the Jews from plundering the caravan.

Of everyone present, only Jacob was not smiling and cheering. His journey was not yet over—not until he was reunited with Lori.

■ ■ ■ ■

Lori cradled Abe in her lap. The two perched at the top of the stairs that descended into the Stambuli Synagogue. While she and the child had retreated to the Sephardic compound, she was unwilling to force the boy underground. Though Abe was resting and not struggling against her grasp, Lori continued to rock him, needing the comfort of his closeness for herself. The dog, Shaul, lay at her feet.

Daniel Caan! Yacov! Gone! And for what?

Through the partially open doorway Lori saw Yehudit and Dov lying on the floor beside each other. The one sightless, the other perhaps dying.

For what?

The bulky form of Rabbi Akiva pushed past her, dropped down the steps.

His appearance caused the murmuring to cease.

Ehud stopped near Lori and put his hand on her shoulder.

Akiva stomped to the recumbent form of his daughter. He addressed her without looking at her, speaking loudly despite the quiet expectancy that draped the room.

"Though you have rebelled," he said to Yehudit, "still I have pity for you. I will negotiate a surrender. I will obtain for you medical help. I will save your life. I am going now."

Akiva marched back up. One of his followers passed him a broken broomhandle to which was tied a scrap of white shirt.

Surrender!

The word spread like wildfire to every corner of the sanctuary.

"Akiva is going to arrange a surrender."

"Akiva is surrendering."

"The mayor is surrendering the Quarter!"

"We have surrendered."

Akiva's march toward the Arab Legion lines was accompanied by a rank of black-coated rabbis. But these were closely followed by others, pouring out of underground bunkers, emerging, blinking, into sunlight.

"We are saved! We have surrendered!"

"No! Get back!" Ehud warned. "You don't know what you're saying! Tonight! Rescue will come tonight! Hold on for one more day!"

Lori, standing erect with Abe to keep from being trampled by the mob that rushed upstairs, heard Ehud's despairing cry, "Do not do this!" Then she and the child were carried away by the press of the crowd.

Arms raised, hands outstretched, faces beaming, the residents of the Jewish Quarter flowed toward the Arab Legionnaires barricading the Street of the Jews as if they had been let out of prison and were going to greet their liberators.

As Lori watched, the haggard, dirty, emaciated occupants of the Jewish Quarter produced the last of their reserves of food. Chocolate bars appeared, were broken into pieces, and devoured. Bread, cheese, tins of sardines. A bottle of wine passed from hand to hand. Hoarded cigarettes were tossed into the air and scrambled after like prizes at a parade.

"Shame!" Lori heard Hannah Cohen scold the procession that swirled toward the golden calf of peace and safety. "Shame!"

No one paid any attention to her.

"We're saved! Akiva has saved us!"

Lori saw Rabbi Akiva approach the barricade. On the opposite side waited John Glubb, chief of the forces of King Abdullah of Jordan and Jerusalem.

The two men shook hands.

■ ■ ■ ■

Moshe held his head in his hands as the sound of cheering echoed through the high windows of the synagogue.

He had failed.

"*It is over! Hallelujah!*"

"*Surrender! Surrender!*"

Alfie pronounced quietly, "They won't come back here."

What did he mean?

The civilians would not be held back from flocking out to welcome the Jordanian Army. Who could blame them, Moshe wondered in shame. All his promises and the promises of the Jerusalem High Command had proved false. No one had come to their rescue.

Moshe clasped his hands together on the useless lists, like a schoolboy waiting to be dismissed.

Rachel's anguished face turned toward him. She shook her head from side to side as a new round of rejoicing erupted from the Jewish populace.

My brother is dead, her expression seemed to say. *If this is the end of the Jewish presence in the Old City, why did Yacov die?*

Moshe mouthed, *Forgive me.*

It had all been such a waste!

Yacov dead. Many hundreds killed defying the might of the Muslim nations, and for what?

The cries of Jewish exultation grew even louder. Cheering and weeping for joy as the enemy army swarmed forward almost as liberators. How could it be?

"*We are saved!*"

"*Akiva! Akiva has delivered us!*"

At this, Grandfather opened his eyes and muttered scornfully, "Akiva? *Bupkes!*"

Moshe knew no other word that carried such a bitter taste. It was, he thought, what history would record about his command of the Old City. *Bupkes!* Worthless! Trivial! Insultingly short of expectations!

Who was with him now? Rachel. Rebbe Lebowitz. Alfie, a man too half-witted to go.

They were alone in the close, dark chamber.

Moshe stared at the rosewood of the ancient Ark. His eyes lingered on the seventh blossom of the almond tree.

Grandfather murmured, "All of Israel is saved . . . because they died in this place."

Moshe said to Rachel, "Your grandfather will get proper medical attention."

The old man's lids fluttered open. "Moshe. Why are you still here?" he wheezed.

"They will expect . . . me." Moshe began the explanation. "The surrender!"

Grandfather interrupted. "Go. Go at once. They will raze Elijah's house to the ground. The Stambuli will be a stable!"

Rachel tried to soothe him. "Hush now! It's finished."

"No!" The rabbi attempted to sit up. "Only beginning! Find Jerusalem's crown." Agony knocked him back. He lay panting, extending a trembling finger at Alfie. "Ask! Ask him. *Alef! Lamed vav!*" He choked out the Hebrew letters of Alfie's name. "He is one of the Thirty-six! The Righteous! He knows!"

Troubled by the accusation, Alfie glanced behind him to see who the old rabbi was pointing at.

Moshe stared at Alfie in surprise. "Who . . . What . . . are . . . you?"

"Just Alfie." He smiled. "I traveled a long way."

"Moshe! Take him with you! Go now! Before they come!" Grandfather coughed, blood and foam at his lips.

"No!" Rachel cried. "Don't leave me!"

Moshe rushed to her side and knelt on the floor beside her and Grandfather. He took her hand and bent low over the old man. "How can I go?"

"Stay," Grandfather warned, "and die." Then to Rachel, "The Lord has provided a way . . . of escape for him. Let go of him, daughter! You . . . must . . ."

She threw her head back with a cry of anguish that dissolved into racking sobs. "Every one! All of them!"

She was breaking apart before Moshe's eyes. How could he leave her? "I'll stay then. I'll stay if you say the word."

Alfie stood, towering over the trio. "Moshe? They'll kill you if you stay," he said with a certainty that drew Rachel back from the abyss of grief.

Terror filled her eyes. "He's right! Go! Moshe! Hurry! They're coming for you!"

Moshe grasped her shoulders and gave her a shake. "I will come back to you! Rachel! Listen!"

She was staring at the entrance of the synagogue. A British voice filtered into the hall.

Urgently she whispered, "Moshe! Hurry."

He kissed her and caressed her cheek. Wiping away her tears, he said tenderly, "I will come back for you, Rachel! Rachel! *Baruch Hashem.*"

"*Shalom,*" she replied.

As if someone had murmured the secret in Alfie's ear the big man was already waiting beside the ornately carved Ark. Smiling. Smiling. Alfie was happy, like a child coming home after being away a long time.

Alfie stroked the branch of the almond tree and called to Rachel and the aged rabbi. "He is watching. Guarding you. Tell them all. He is watching over the doors of Israel."

Moshe grasped the seventh blossom on the branch and turned it seven times.

He heard a click. From behind the Ark there came a sound like rushing wind and the sweet fragrance of incense.

The door leading to the secret chamber was open.

With one lingering look, Moshe raised his hand in farewell to Rachel. He scanned the room where so many had prayed for the coming of Israel's Messiah. How long would it be before their prayer was finally answered?

"*Shalom*," Moshe whispered.

Grinning at the ceiling, Alfie heard a song no one else could hear. "I see it. Sure," he said to the air. Then he stepped behind the Ark and vanished.

With one last, long glance at Rachel, Moshe followed Alfie.

The sound of the wind abruptly fell silent.

Moshe was gone, and the door sealed behind him.

CHAPTER 35

The celebration of the Old City residents came to a sudden halt when they heard the terms of their surrender.

Banishment.

Exile from the Jewish Quarter of Jerusalem.

The Haganah defenders and all able-bodied men of military age were culled from the herd of residents.

Ehud Schiff, assuming Moshe had gone into hiding, accepted the designation of Old City Haganah Commander. Akiva was nowhere near to say otherwise. And for all the Arab commanders knew, Moshe Sachar had perished at the Hurva defense. Why else would the Jews have surrendered?

There remained just twenty-two unwounded Jewish soldiers and two hundred and sixty men who could be used to fight on another front if they were allowed to go free. These were penned in a room of the Stambuli Synagogue to await transport to prison in Jordan. Dr. Baruch voluntarily went with them. It was, he told Lori, the one way he could continue to fight.

Everyone else, including over one hundred and fifty wounded, were taken to the open courtyard of Beit Rothschild. These were to be directed to Zion Gate and released into the Jewish New City. More to feed, the Arab leaders surmised. More injured to care for. The added burden would speed the collapse of the Jewish New City.

Lori, Abe on her hip and Shaul the dog at her heels, wandered through the milling crowd of civilians and wounded as they waited to be escorted out of the Old City. She found Rachel with her grandfather beside the stretchers of Dov and Yehudit.

The dog whined and nuzzled the hand of Rebbe Lebowitz.

"Ah. Shaul. Stinking mongrel. So you have survived. Well, where is Yacov, eh?" Rachel's eyes were downcast as Rebbe Lebowitz repeated the question, "Where is Yacov?"

Lori guessed that Rachel had not found the courage to tell him how Yacov and Daniel Caan had been overwhelmed in the final on-slaught.

The old man was insistent. "Here is Shaul. But where has Yacov got off to? It will be Shabbes by the time we are underway. Where is Yacov?"

Yehudit asked Lori, "Wasn't he with you in the garden at Gal'ed?"

Abe blurted, "Where is Daniel? Where Yacov?"

Rachel turned away and went to the pillar, pretending to gaze out over the crowd.

Dov somehow guessed that the two would not be coming back. He said, "Rebbe Lebowitz, there are so many of us here. Don't worry about him."

The old man's brow furrowed in consternation. "The boy does not go anywhere without this stinking beast. Where has Yacov gone? We must . . . must find him."

At that instant Abe pointed and squealed loudly, "There is Daniel! Daniel!"

Lori caught sight of Daniel Caan as he moved through the throng! Was she imagining things? A vision? Wishful fantasy brought on by hunger, thirst, and strain?

The crowd parted for the apparition and then . . .

"Hey, Yacov!" Abe called. "I got your dog!"

It was not a dream! Yacov supported Daniel as they walked.

Yacov's face split with a grin as Rachel ran toward him. He was missing two front teeth. Daniel's features were black and blue from a beating, but the two were very much alive!

Yacov called, "Shaul! Come!"

With a yip, the dog bounded toward his young master. Rachel, weeping with joy, embraced her brother.

Content, Grandfather murmured, "Yacov should not wander off. He could get lost. Lost! We are going to the New City. Strangers in a strange land. It will be Shabbes by the time we get where we are going. Tell Yacov he must stay close to me."

■ ■ ■ ■

Peering through the ears of the camel like a gunsight, Daoud framed the conflagration of the Jewish Quarter. A pall of dense smoke rose where the Hurva had once glistened white in the Jerusalem sunlight. A rumble resounded from the cluster of Sephardic synagogues as Eliyahu Hanavi was demolished.

Daoud said to the camel, "Ah, Gene Autry. We have come too late for my friends in the Jewish Quarter. And my father Baruch. Does he live still, I wonder?"

He glanced around at other members of the caravan. Caught up in the riotous joy of welcoming citizens, they did not yet know what the smoke over the Old City meant.

The cowboy, Tin Man, and his wife, Ellie, were grinning stupidly, shaking hands with Jews who swarmed out to meet them. The frog-faced Madame Rose embraced her French son, Jerome, and slapped Jacob Kalner hard on his back over and over. Of the hundreds who carried the load into the suburbs of Jerusalem, only Daoud saw the glaring evidence of destruction beyond the ancient walls.

And then, Jacob Kalner's grin faded. He halted, gaping toward the orange flames licking the Hurva. Even beneath the beard and days of unwashed face he grew pale. He glanced at the Englishman, Luke Thomas, who had tears running down his cheeks.

"We're too late," Jacob said to Luke Thomas.

The Englishman dipped his strong jaw once in acceptance of the truth. He wiped his tears away with the back of a sunburned hand. "Too late," he said, and his voice caught.

Daoud called to Luke Thomas, "Sir, I must find my father, Baruch! He was doctor to the Jewish Quarter! I must know if he lives!"

Jacob Kalner, shaking, cried out, "Lori! My wife is in that."

Luke Thomas moved his head from side to side. "It was the Legion. Not the Mufti's men who took it. They were fighting the Legion. Surrendered to the Legion. It won't be like the Etzion block!"

By this Daoud knew the Englishman was referring to the massacre of the Jews at Kfar Etzion by the Mufti's forces. Maybe since it was the Legion in the Old City the Jewish civilians were alive. King Abdullah would be happy today, Daoud thought. Old City Jerusalem was a part of the Hashemite kingdom of Jordan. Abdullah was ruler of Muslim Jerusalem. He certainly would never allow the Jews to come back. Of course there would be no stopping the looting and the destruction of every Jewish home and shop in the Quarter. That was a foregone conclusion.

Daoud considered his old friend Yacov and Yacov's old grandfather, Rabbi Lebowitz. Yacov had vowed that he and the other Jewish boys would perish before surrendering. Had they died gloriously? Were their ears dangling from a string at some Jihad Moquade's belt? Was Al-Malik lighting his Turkish cigarettes from the conflagration of Jewish holy places? Smoking and gloating over the bodies of his fallen enemies?

Inexplicably, Daoud grieved. Not only for his Jewish friends but for the loss of a life that had existed for centuries in the shadow of the Western Wall. He wept for the destruction and terror of the past days and for the struggle that would surely come upon the peoples of a divided Jerusalem.

A jeep carrying a Jewish officer roared up to the caravan and squealed to a halt in front of Luke Thomas.

"Nachasch!" Thomas extended his open hands in anguish toward the Old City.

"My God, Luke! Unconditional surrender! My God!" Nachasch cried and embraced him. "At least we still hold the West."

"Survivors?" Jacob pleaded.

Nachasch replied, "Civilians. Women, children. The old ones. The wounded. They've been taken to the Russian compound."

Thomas cleared his throat. "John Glubb is a gentleman."

Jacob raised his chin to indicate the destruction. "Well, he couldn't stop that, could he?"

Thomas added bitterly, "They want to make sure there is nothing for the rabbis to go back for."

Nachasch crossed his arms and inhaled deeply. "Smell that? Torah schools. Scrolls. Synagogues. Jewish homes. Shops. Three thousand years of history up in smoke. This isn't the first time the Jews have been driven out of Jerusalem. Nothing to go back for? We always come back. Always. Jerusalem is the secret of our strength. The battle two hundred Jews fought in the Old City has made a nation. Israel. We'll be back. No matter how long it takes. We'll take it back. I hope I'm alive to see it when it happens."

Jacob's hands were shaking as he waited for Nachasch to finish speaking. "I've got to get to the Russian compound. My wife, you see, she was one of them. In there. I have to know if she made it."

Daoud said, "And my father. Doctor Baruch. And my Mother." He coughed nervously. "Mother Superior." He cast a sideways glance at Luke Thomas. "Indeed Mother will be worried after me."

"Come on, then." Luke helped him down from the camel's back. "Into the jeep."

■ ■ ■ ■

Moments after their arrival in the New City Daniel Caan was whisked off to the hospital.

In the distance, from the grounds of the Russian compound, the fires that consumed the Jewish Quarter appeared alive and vengeful.

Mother Superior, her arms laden with slim white candles taken from the stores of the church, remarked, "Satan thinks he has won? It is finished, is it? *Vox et praeterea nihil.* The boasting of the demons is but clanging brass in the ears of God."

Lori put Abe down. "They came at us, you know. The Muslim mob. They wanted to slit the throat of every Jew. And they would have done it, too. Except the English commanding officer ordered them to stop for the sake of King Abdullah's honor. And when that didn't stop them, he ordered the Legion to fire over their heads to turn them back. Except for that they would have slaughtered us. Every Jew. They'll never let us back in the Old City."

"Us?" Mother Superior questioned.

Lori suddenly realized she had included herself among the pitiful crowd of exiles. "Yes. Yes."

"Suffering has made you . . ."

Lori rubbed her forehead. "My God! Oh, God! What's happened to me? I wish I knew where Jacob was! I would tell him. Tell him all of it . . . Tell him Jerusalem is home. His people, my people."

"And his God your God?" Mother asked.

"I suppose my heart will have it no other way."

Lori took Abe by his hand as she walked with Mother Superior among the Old City refugees. Hundreds sat in stunned stillness in the garden of the Russian compound. Eyes vacant from exhaustion and grief too deep to express, they did not glance toward the flames that leapt up from the holocaust of their ancient Jewish home.

The two women moved instinctively toward rosebushes that climbed a trellis on the wall of St. Trinity Cathedral.

Little Abe cried out joyfully when he saw the bright red blooms, "Look! Our roses are here too!" The child ran to stand before them.

Mother Superior smiled sadly. "Did you manage to save your volume of Rilke?"

Lori fished in the pocket of her trousers, withdrawing the bloodstained book of poetry. She extended it to the ramrod-straight nun. "This and nothing else."

"It is something," Mother replied, thumbing through the pages. "And here. Here it is." She began to read,

> *"Exposed on the cliffs of the heart. Stoneground*
> *under your hands. Even here, though,*
> *something can bloom; on a silent cliff-edge*
> *an unknowing plant blooms, singing, into the air . . ."*

Lori turned away and forced herself to watch the smoke of the conflagration. "Can hope bloom even in this terrible hour?"

Mother closed the book. "Faith. Hope. Love. They bloom and sing even on the edge of the deepest abyss. The wind may rage. Try to tear them out. Blast blossoms. Break branches. But these three things endure. Faith. Hope. Love. The three cardinal virtues we call them. Let them take root, exposed on the cliffs of your heart, and one day these virtues make you a virtuoso. You will be singing with them even in the worst suffering. And with the angels you begin to believe the certainty that there is going to be a happy ending no matter how hard life may be! Meanwhile, one day you will find someone else who needs to hear your story. Someone who needs to know you made it through. And something beautiful will grow where there was only the abyss. Your heart will become like Christ's heart. Loving. You will understand something about His suffering and God's great love for the world."

"I am only beginning to understand."

Mother Superior raised her eyes to look over Lori's shoulder. "*Oui.* Well, someone is looking for you."

Lori whirled around to see Daoud running ahead of Jacob! And Jacob, filthy and battered, stumbling toward her with his hands outstretched like a drowning man grasping for a lifeline!

Was she dreaming? She cried out with joy and burst into tears.

"Lori!" He called her name again and again.

She ran to him, burying her face against him, then inviting his kisses, kissing him back as those in the crowd looked on.

"Jacob." She breathed his name. "Jacob! Jerusalem! Home! I will go where you go . . . my love. My love! My home is in your heart!"

Behind them Mother Superior scolded the boy, "Daoud! Stop gawking. Where have you been?"

"Around," Daoud explained. "Here and there. Searching everywhere for my father, Baruch."

"Baruch has gone away with his valiant Jewish brothers into the prison of King Abdullah."

Daoud hung his head. "Of course. *Insh' Allah.* I should have known he would go where he was needed."

"And now," Mother said, thrusting a sack of candles into Daoud's hands, "you go where you are needed. And when you have finished with this, come back to me. Baruch would have you remain safely in my care until he comes home again from prison."

■ ■ ■ ■

The sun dropped like a giant gold coin into the western horizon beyond Jerusalem. And so began the Shabbat of May 28, 1948. The first Shabbat in the lifetime of Rabbi Shlomo Lebowitz that he had ever spent outside the boundaries of the Old City.

It was to be his last.

The old man clasped the hands of Rachel and Yacov who sat on either side of the narrow cot in the teeming ward of the Russian compound hospital. Each ragged breath was an agony.

"Light. *Shabbes,*" he managed to whisper.

Rachel looked to the high windows. The blue haze of twilight deepened. "We have no *Shabbes* candles, Grandfather," she replied, wishing she could light the candles one last time for him.

"Home."

Yacov, his eyes streaming, shook his head. "No. We can't go home. They'll fix you here, Grandfather. We'll stay here until you are well." The boy shouted, "Where is the doctor? Why don't they hurry? Can't you see my grandfather needs help?"

The old man grimaced at his grandson's frustration. "Yacov . . . Let me go."

"We can't go back," the boy spat. "You know if the English officer had not stopped the mob they would have killed us all! They've burned everything! They'll never let us go home."

"Home." The rabbi lifted his eyes heavenward.

"No! I won't! Grandfather! Don't leave us!"

Grandfather gave Rachel a pleading look. How to comfort the boy? How to tell him death was a welcome friend?

She touched Yacov's cheek with her finger, stilling his outpouring of grief. Her caress told the boy he must have courage. Yacov's shoulders hunched forward in a silent sob. He pressed the palm of the old man's hand to his lips.

From the time they arrived in this place Rachel knew Grandfather could not recover. The physicians, overwhelmed with the flood of injured, had simply put Rabbi Lebowitz to one side. It was what Dr. Baruch had done to the mortally wounded in the Old City.

"Fear not, children," Grandfather murmured. "We will someday . . . come back with Him. Jerusalem is in His heart. He promised us."

"What will we do?" Yacov begged.

"You will . . . wait," Grandfather replied.

"How long?" Yacov kissed his fingers.

"Not long," the old man intoned. "*HaMashiach* . . . will . . . come . . . soon." He gasped. "The light. *Shabbes.* . . . The *Shabbes goy.*"

"I have no candle, Grandfather," Rachel replied. And then a glimmer of radiance entered the room. A scrawny Arab boy walked through the press of people in the ward. He carried a flickering candle in one hand. Pausing at each cluster of grieving Jews, he reached into a canvas pouch and removed a taper. Lighting the wick he passed it on.

"It's Daoud!" Yacov cried, leaping to his feet and running to his old friend. Dragging the Arab boy to Grandfather's bedside he said, "Grandfather! You see! A candle! Daoud, our friend Daoud, Grandfather. See! Our *Shabbes goy!* He is here with us again! Daoud, who used to light the *Shabbes* lamps for us! See! We have light, Grandfather!"

Daoud peered down into the face of Rabbi Lebowitz. "Rebbe Lebowitz! I came looking for my father, Baruch. They tell me he went away with the Jewish prisoners. But at least I have found you here! And Yacov! And Rachel! Look! You are alive! And I have brought you *Shabbes* candles. Like I used to in the old days. See? I will light one for you, and Rachel can say the blessing."

The old man managed a smile. "You? Daoud? Yacov. Always were . . . friends. Boys together, *nu?* Remember the friendship. Now . . . Yacov, you are the man. Take care of Rachel, eh? Do not . . . forget . . . Jerusalem. Our hope. The crown, secret of . . . our strength! *Baruch HaShem!* Now it . . . is finished. Look! There . . . He . . . has not forgotten! Messiah . . . is . . . coming . . . soon." With those final words Grandfather's aged eyes flickered in recognition of someone beyond their vision. An instant later life faded away as Grandfather stepped from himself and followed an unseen path.

Yacov threw himself across the body and cried out, "Don't go! Not yet! Come back, Grandfather!"

"*Shalom.*" Rachel clung to the old man's hand and wept.

"*Salaam,*" Daoud said softly.

A single voice began to sing as light from the candles illuminated the dark corridors. One by one other voices joined in until the song became a strong, unfaltering swell in the vaulted chamber of the ward.

> *Out of blood and fire Judea will fall.*
> *Out of blood and fire it will be reborn!*